Robert Owen Minearo

Sid Arthur

A Spiritual Novel

Gallagher Close Publishing and Communications, LLC

All inquiries should be sent to:
Gallagher Close Publishing and Communications, LLC
214 Stratton Arlington Road, West Wardsboro, Vermont 05360
Printed in the United States of America

www.gallagherclosepublishing.com

ISBN: 978-1-7348283-2-0

2022 First Edition-Paperback

CR

Sid Arthur

A Spiritual Novel

Sid Arthur is my attempt to write a modern version and homage to *Siddhartha*, a novel by Hermann Hesse published in 1921. I first read *Siddhartha* when I was seventeen, and it has remained my most influential book. The process of enlightenment is the purpose of our existence in this reality, and spiritual awareness continues beyond the Buddha or Christ in everyday life.

Siddhartha is a novel written by Hermann Hesse during the existentialist period. The book was published in the United States in 1951. Existentialism is the key to the book's prophetic perception of the human condition. Existentialism is a viewpoint that highlights individual freedom of choice during each person's life. Each person has a personal decision to pursue reason in an illogical world.

Hesse starts the novel with Siddhartha and his childhood friend Govinda leaving the comfort of their home and family to live a traditional spiritual path. They denounce all worldly possessions and become part of an ancient religious sect of wandering beggars called Samanas.

A modern version of an ascetic's journey can be comparable to joining the military, being incarcerated, or becoming a medical student, to name only a few ways that one would relinquish their perceptions for another way of thinking.

Siddhartha and Govinda eventually seek the wisdom of the living Buddha. Hesse creates duality by which Siddhartha, fashioned after Prince Siddhartha, who becomes the Buddha, meets the Buddha in the book. Siddhartha realizes that being part of a religious order is not the way to enlightenment.

The meeting between Buddha and Siddhartha challenges the Buddhist teachings. Buddhism is projected as another religion with devotees following a doctrine created by another person instead one following their inner spiritual compass. This meeting highlights the period of existentialism created by Søren Kierkegaard and expounded upon by Friedrich Nietzsche, which dictates that everyone is free to make choices toward enlightenment.

After the meeting with Buddha, Siddhartha leaves the traditional path toward enlightenment to follow his purest spiritual connection.

Siddhartha's friend Govinda chooses to stay and follow the teachings of the Buddha. Their paths intertwine throughout the book, most notably at the end.

Siddhartha follows a path towards Samsara, indulging in the ego by which he becomes a businessman, a gambler, and a patron of a teacher of intimacy and love. He realizes that enlightenment comes from within. The ending of this novel is poetic in that Siddhartha realizes that he is a spiritual being having a physical experience, and the world is ultimately an illusion.

Sid Arthur has many physical experiences during his life. However, he ultimately follows the same process of enlightenment that Siddhartha followed; he surrenders to his purest spiritual relationship denouncing his ego and obtaining nirvana.

A modern similarity I chose was the new religion of start-up companies and fast-talking grifters. Sid Arthur joins a contemporary con where venture capitalists prey on an unsuspecting public. Venture capitalists invest in a start-up, artificially pump up the stock to cash out big during an initial public offering, and then they do it all over again. Sid Arthur finds that this new religion is not the path he thought it was and decides to leave the discipline.

Sid Arthur comes to the same conclusion as Hesse's Siddhartha at the novel's end, where he finds peace in surrendering to his purest spiritual relationship and denouncing his ego.

A germ of an idea started this project based on a grifter becoming unintentionally enlightened. However, as I wrote the novel, I realized that what I was writing was a modern version of the same process of enlightenment the book *Siddhartha* professed. ❧

ॐ

Sid Arthur

A Spiritual Novel

ॐ

Sid Arthur

ଓଷ

Chapter One

Sid was lying back on his bunk with his hands behind his head when the day guard released Vincent into the cell. Sid was a well-manicured young black man, all of twenty-three. He stood six-two with a slender but muscular frame that showed the years he spent on his father's Alabama farm. Vincent was a sinewy twenty-one-year-old white male with scars on his neck and shoulders from fighting or the result of a hard life herding cattle in Wyoming or both.

The guard marched Vincent into the cell with a push; Vincent turned around sharply and said, "Watch it, dip-shit." The guard glared at Vincent, locked the cell, and walked away with a determination only a Rikers Island guard could muster.

Sid looked up at Vincent and said, "That guard is known to stomp inmates that get on his bad side. The big flashlight he carries around has notches on the handle—each notch is a skull bashing."

Vincent sat down on the other bunk across from Sid in their nine-by-nine holding cell. Vincent wiped the sweat from his face with his shirt sleeve and stroked his long blond dusty hair back behind his ears as he had done a thousand times. He replied, "Hell, it wouldn't be the first time I took a good ass-kicking. Two thousand-pound bulls have stomped me, and my father and older brother like to kick my ass for sport. I could survive a skull bashing from that dip-shit."

Vincent laid back in his bunk and put his dirty shoes on the wool blanket at the foot of the bed. He looked at Sid and asked, "So, are you a hard ass?"

Sid sat up in his bunk and swung his legs off the bed, looking at Vincent. He replied, "Hard enough, but you don't have to worry. They don't put gang bangers in these cells; they only put short-timers. How long you in for?"

Vincent laughed and sat up again, looking at Sid. He responded, "Thirty days, how about you?"

Sid leaned back on the cell wall and responded, "I've got five weeks left on sixty days. So, what did you do?"

Vincent leaned his head sideways, trying to remember why he was in jail. He replied, "I wasn't doing anything. I played three-card monte in Tribeca when this smart-ass New York cop hassled me about a permit; the judge gave me thirty days."

Sid looked at Vincent with distrust. He stated, "No way a judge will give you thirty days in Rikers Island for not having a permit."

Vincent snickered. He replied, "Well, I took a swing at the cop, and he and his partner kicked the shit out of me. That's where I got this gash on my neck; it wasn't the first time I had taken a beating.

"Hell, I'm in this cell because I got into a fight in the general population with a couple of hard asses. They walked up to me and told me they made the rules, and I had to follow them. They wanted my shoes, and I told them where they could stick their rules.

"So, instead of putting me in solitary, they stuck me in here with you because I'm a short-timer, and I think they don't want to deal with me. So, what are you in for?"

"Being black in the wrong place at the wrong time," retorted Sid.

"Sure," responded Vincent.

"I was playing poker in an underground game when the cops raided the place. The white heavyweight businessmen from Wall Street got a pass; I got my ass thrown in here," Sid continued with a shrug.

Vincent replied, "I guess you and I are a couple of hustlers? Isn't there a rule where we aren't supposed to talk about our crimes?"

Sid looked up with a smirk. He answered, "That's prison. This hell hole is a jail, and we are a couple of low-level hustlers."

Vincent asked, "What is the difference between prison and jail?"

Sid countered, "You go to prison after trial. Jail is before trial for folks who are too poor to make bail; we are lucky we just got thrown in here for a short time."

Vincent asked, "You from the south? You have a southern accent."

Sid replied, "Yeh, I'm from a small town in Alabama. You sound like you're from Texas."

"Wyoming, almost every town is small. I couldn't wait to get out of there. If anyone tells you herding cows is fun, they're full of shit," responded Vincent.

"Farming in Alabama's hot July sun isn't a picnic," countered Sid.

"Alabama, that must be hard on a black fellow, never been, but I've seen movies," replied Vincent.

"Being black is hard anywhere, especially a dirt-poor farmer in the south," responded Sid.

Vincent continued, "Before I moved to New York, I never saw a black fellow except on television. We have a lot of Indians around where I grew up, and I had a couple of Indian friends.

"Hell, I went to a school with all twelve grades in a few buildings, so the Indians sat next to us in class. Equal rights, that's Wyoming's motto, we learned in school. Hell, if a man is straight with me, I don't care what the color of his skin is; I'll be straight with him."

"You're a true humanitarian," countered Sid.

"What's a humanitarian," asked Vincent.

"Humanitarian is a white man's word for convincing themselves that they are good to all people of color. If they don't try to marry their daughters or move into their neighborhoods," responded Sid.

"You sure talk fancy for a poor farmer from Alabama," asked Vincent.

"My father's a Southern Baptist deacon and a highly-educated man. He was on his way to obtaining his doctorate before deciding to move back to the family farm and make a go of it.

"We always had a lot of books in the house, and my mother home-schooled us. They met at Howard University in Washington, D.C. It's a mystery how my father convinced my mother to move to Alabama and become a farmer.

"My father told us that being black in D.C. wasn't easier than being black in Alabama. Even with his doctorate, he might end up cleaning toilets for white folk. Being a deacon in Alabama gives him a sense of community he didn't find in the big city. Now that I live in a big city, I'm starting to understand what he meant," snapped Sid.

"Hell, New York City isn't Wyoming. I guess we are a couple of small fish in a big pond. I thought I would come east and find my fortune. I heard the sidewalks are made of gold in New York; all I smell is piss," responded Vincent.

"You say hell a lot," retorted Sid.

"Hell, that is just the way folks talk where I come from," answered Vincent.

"Were you winning?" asked Sid.

"What do you mean?" queried Vincent.

"Were you winning at three-card monte before the cops showed up?" asked Sid.

"Didn't matter; letting the mark win kept them around long enough," responded Vincent.

"Long enough for what?" questioned Sid.

"Long enough for my partner to pick their pockets. The three-card monte game was just a diversion to keep the mark focused on the cups long enough for my partner, Frank, to work his magic," retorted Vincent.

"Where is Frank? Did he get arrested?" questioned Sid.

"No, when the cops showed up, he took off. I met him a couple of days earlier at a squat in Queens. I probably won't see him again because he has the money from all the suckers. Hell, he is probably happy I'm out of the picture.

"He doesn't have to divide any money we stashed in the squat. I guess I shouldn't have taken a swing at the cop?" replied Vincent.

"I guess not," responded Sid.

"Were you winning?" asked Vincent.

"You mean the poker game?" retorted Sid.

"Yeh, were you winning?" asked Vincent.

"Unfortunately, yes, I was fifty thousand up. It took me a month to get invited. I don't think the other players saw me coming. They only let me in because I had the cash to buy in. I know all those crackers figured I would be an easy mark.

"I was working them for six hours, giving them hope at first, then taking their money a little at a time, just slow enough, so they didn't notice.

"I was about six hours away from claiming the pot and getting out of there fast. That's when the cops showed up. I've wondered if one of those assholes called in a favor to pull me out of the game. Someone in that game maybe was paying attention.

"Anyway, the cops busted in, and everyone scrambled. I lost my money in the confusion, and the cops weren't in the mood to let me cash out before they booked me and tossed me in Rikers.

"I'm sure the cops and those crackers are having a good laugh at my expense," retorted Sid.

"As I said, little fish in a big pond," countered Vincent.

"Ah-man, brother," responded Sid.

"So, the good book didn't rub off on you? Your father is a deacon and all?" asked Vincent.

"No, the good book just rubbed me the wrong way. Too many hypocrites, my father being the leader; he was the big fish in a small pond sucking up all the oxygen, booze, and women," retorted Sid.

"I thought you said your father was some kind of genius," asked Vincent.

"Oh, he was smart, alright. He could talk the panties off any of his parishioners. He became the most influential person in his community; even white people wouldn't cross him.

"He used his position as a deacon to run a numbers game and set up all-night poker games. He dealt with white liquor distributors to control the alcohol in the county. He paid off the police, the mayor, and anyone that got in his way.

"If things got too hot, he would hide behind the good book. He was telling his flock that God had ordained him to have the power to do good and control most of the black wealth coming in and out of the county.

"The farm was just a diversion for his true avocation, being a major hustler. He taught me to play poker at six. He wanted me to take over the kingdom he had built up, but I didn't want anything to do with his empire. I broke his heart when I walked out." answered Sid.

"Sons can do that," countered Vincent.

"Sons can do what?" asked Sid.

"Break their father's heart," answered Vincent.

"Did you break your father's heart?" asked Sid.

"Well, if my father had a heart, which I cannot contest, I broke it. He wanted me to take over the small herd of cattle he had been building. My father was a big talker, and we grew up hearing about his dream of having the largest cattle ranch in Wyoming.

"We ended up having a few acres of scrub brush and rock. We saw rich folk from the city come in and buy hundreds of acres of prime cattle country, only to come up a couple of weeks a year and fly fish.

"My father just got old and beat up from caring for other folks' ranches. Before I left, he got a job managing a trail ride for wealthy people; it was a sad sight.

"That's where I got the idea of moving to New York City. I worked with my father on a trail ride and met a Wall Street fellow, and he's the one that told me about New York City gold.

"All I found was cold hard concrete. I guess the gold is in those fancy homes near the park. Hard to get at for a couple of hustlers because the real hustlers live in those palaces," exclaimed Vincent.

"If you steal a little, they put you in jail. If you steal a lot, they make you king," stated Sid.

"That's good. Where did you come up with that?" asked Vincent.

"It's a line from a Bob Dylan song," answered Sid.

"Who?" asked Vincent.

"He was a fellow New York City transplant like us. He wrote songs about living in an unjust society. Justice is blind, especially for poor folk," replied Sid.

"So, is Sid short for something?" asked Vincent.

"Sidney Poitier Arthur, my father was a big fan of the actor Sidney Poitier. He watched the movie *Heat of the Night* many times," responded Sid.

"I remember that movie. Some poor black fellow gets blamed for a murder, and then he must figure out who did the crime, right?" asked Vincent.

"Yep, he was a black man in the wrong place at the wrong time. So, how does a white guy from Wyoming end up with a name like Vincent?" asked Sid.

"Vincenzo Govinda Aiello, my grandfather, came from a small town in Sicily. Somehow, he ended up in Wyoming. My father, Ratzamo, loved the life of a cowboy. When he was fourteen, he left home to work on a ranch for thoroughbred racehorses.

"Story goes, my father would sneak out of the house to walk twenty miles and live in the horse stalls to take care of the horses. My grandfather would find him and bring him home; this happened a few times until my grandfather gave up and left him. It was a tough time for the family, and my grandfather figured my father could care for himself. At least he was getting food for labor."

"You don't look Italian," stated Sid.

"My mother was Welsh, and my other grandfather came from a mining town in Wales. There were many Welsh miners in the area, not many Italians, and no Sicilians. I quickly changed my name from Vincenzo to Vincent after a couple of school ass-kickings," answered Vincent.

"I guess we both were out of place where we grew up. Maybe it is destiny that you and I ended up here," replied Sid.

"I thought you didn't believe in that kind of stuff," asked Vincent.

"I said the good book rubbed me the wrong way. I didn't say that I don't believe in anything. I've seen some crazy stuff and spared more than dammed. I don't know what I believe in yet, but I feel destined to meet you, just a feeling," countered Sid.

"Hell, I usually don't tell my life story to just anyone. I don't know why I told you, but I feel safe enough in this little cell to spill my guts," responded Vincent. He then laid back on his rack and took off his shoes. His socks were dirty and had holes in the toes.

Sid sat up in his bunk, put his feet squarely on the floor, and said, "Look, we will be lined up for dinner soon. If we watch each other's back, we can come out of this place in one piece. The gangsters are always looking for a weakness they can exploit. If you're not a predator in this hell hole, you're prey. I don't want to be either; I want to do my time and get out of here.

"If we get into a fight and hurt someone, we could get more time. So, the trick is to stay low, stay together, and watch out for each other. We're short-timers and a target for gangsters. They know we are leaving soon, so they will try to trick us.

"They will do some small favor for us and then require us to return the favor when we leave, don't fall for it. If someone approaches, you walk. If we stay together, we can survive in this place."

"Sounds good to me. The two gang bangers I fought earlier told me they would wait for a good time to stomp me. I knocked one down, and the other gangster got a shot to the throat he won't forget. Luckily, the guard showed up before anyone else decided to join in. I want to do my thirty days, get back on the streets, and keep my shoes," retorted Vincent.

A siren went off, indicating dinner time. The guards opened all the cells and rousted the inmates into the corridor to line up. The guard that pushed Vincent into the cell earlier was at the head of the line. He was holding his nightstick in both hands, ready for anything, yelling. "Ok, nuts to butts, head forward and keep your hands down at your side. Move into the chow line, get your food, and sit down. You have fifteen minutes to eat and then out into the yard for two hours."

All the inmates lined up behind each other without hesitation and with military precision. They kept their hands to their sides, and all moved towards the prison cafeteria in unison like some southern chain gang tied together with an unseen tether.

Vincent motioned to Sid that the two gang bangers he had fought earlier were in front of them. The guard told Vincent to shut up and keep his head forward.

Sid was right behind Vincent. He whispered over Vincent's shoulder, "Remember, stay together, and we survive. We watch each other's back."

Vincent nodded in agreement. ☙

CB

Chapter Two

Vincent woke up with a horrible jolt; it was 3:33 a.m. The two cellmates made it another week with only a few close calls. Vincent looked up and saw Sid standing in the middle of the cell, talking to someone through the bars.

"Hell, Sid, it's 3:30. Who are you talking to?" asked Vincent, barely awake.

"Caesar Ramirez," responded Sid.

"Caesar Ramirez? Hell, he's dead. A couple of Bloods got him in the shower two days ago," retorted Vincent.

"I know he's dead, but he's standing in the hallway," countered Sid.

Vincent rubbed his head, smoothed his long blond hair behind his ears, and slapped himself to ensure he wasn't still sleeping. He looked out and didn't see anyone standing in the hallway.

Sid sat down on his bunk and laid back against the wall. Sid continued, "He's gone now, but he told me what we need to do."

"You're telling me the recently deceased Caesar Ramirez, the former head gangster, was visiting you?" asked Vincent with a confused look. Then he asked, "Are you nuts?"

"I might be, but he wanted me to convey a message to his lieutenant, Diego," responded Sid.

"What's the message?" asked Vincent.

"Caesar told me that the Bloods didn't kill him. A rival in his gang orchestrated the assassination. Caesar thought it was only fitting that he stopped a war between the Bloods and his gang. The rival is planning to take down Diego. Caesar told me something that only he and Diego would know. We need to figure out a way to get this message to Diego," replied Sid.

"We?" asked Vincent.

"Yes, we, in for a penny in for a pound," exclaimed Sid.

"What does that mean?" asked Vincent.

"It means the only way we stay alive is together, and we could find ourselves in the middle if there is a war between the Bloods and the Mexican Mafia. We only have a couple of weeks left, and I would like to leave here on my feet, not in a casket," countered Sid.

"So, you're telling me you can talk to ghosts?" queried Vincent.

"Yeh, as long as I can remember. Initially, the spirits scared the hell out of me when I was a kid. After a few years, I got used to it. Like anything in life, things are strange, and then they become routine. My experience with the dead has become common—not normal because most folks don't see them.

"There are a lot of ghosts walking these halls. Most keep to themselves, and many don't know they are dead," stated Sid.

"You're joking, right?" asked Vincent.

"No, the dead are around us all the time, but we don't pay attention. You've never had an experience with a phantom?" asked Sid.

Vincent leaned up against the wall on his bunk. He smoothed back his long blond hair behind his ears. He replied, "Yeh, a few weeks after my mom died, I watched the Cowboys kick the Rams' ass in the fourth quarter."

"Cowboys and Rams?" interjected Sid.

"Yeh, the University of Wyoming football team, the Cowboys, against Colorado State, Rams. Anyway, I fell asleep on the couch. I woke up, and my mother was standing over me, and she kissed me on my forehead and then disappeared." recalled Vincent.

"When did your mother die?" asked Sid.

"She died two years ago. The strange thing is she was fifty-eight when she died, but when I saw her spirit, she was much younger, maybe in her thirties." recounted Vincent.

"How did she die?" asked Sid.

"The doctor said she died of heart disease, but my father beating her down is what killed my mom. When she passed, she looked worn out. In Wyoming, life with my father was not easy on a good soul like my mother. Anyway, I don't like to talk about it." said Vincent.

"The dead always reflect how they perceive themselves, good or bad. Your mother probably felt best in her thirties, and it was probably a good time in her life," replied Sid.

"You mean the dead can control how they look?" asked Vincent.

"Yeh, they're spirits, not bodies, just a wisp of energy," responded Sid.

Vincent laid down on his bunk with his eyes wide open. He rolled around and then sat up again, "Now, I'm wide awake with all this talk of ghosts," bellowed Vincent.

"They're not going to hurt you. Spirits want us to resolve things," responded Sid.

"Hell, I have more important things on my mind than ghosts. Like what I'm going to do once I get out of here. What about you? Have you decided what to do when you get out?" asked Vincent.

"A few things, nothing in concrete," replied Sid.

"Hell, I've been thinking a lot about that fellow's song. "If you steal a little, they put you in jail, and if you steal a lot, they make you king," responded Vincent.

"Yeh, Bob Dylan, what about it?" asked Sid.

"Well, I've tried jail, and I don't plan to spend much more time here. So, I liked to be the king of anything. I figured three-card monte in New York ain't the trick, so I need a big con. I don't think New York is the place because all those suits on Wall Street play the big con and take suckers for all they have. I don't believe we could compete, so I figure we would need to leave New York and find a smaller pond," concluded Vincent.

"We?" questioned Sid.

"Yeh, why not we? As you said, destiny found us, and maybe we can find a con that would make us both kings. Anyway, you said you didn't have any plans, and I could go for a smart partner, such as yourself," exclaimed Vincent.

"I'll think about it, but we have more pressing matters. We need to get word to Diego before the place erupts into a gang war. Look, it's almost 5:30, and the guards will roust us out for 6:15 breakfast and two hours in the yard. We need to find a way." replied Sid.

Vincent said, "There are no safe places on Rikers Island, but some are more dangerous than others. Hell, all inmates know these places soon after arriving."

Sid continued, "We need to set up a meeting with Diego to stop a gang war in one of these places. Breakfast is only fifteen minutes, so we don't have enough time in the cafeteria, and there are too many people watching—there are always people watching, for good and evil."

After breakfast, all the inmates moved onto the yard. The yard is the center of the universe, like a United Nations for criminals. Each part of the yard had an invisible line separating one gang from another.

The white supremacists were in the northwest part of the yard, and the Mexican Mafia took up the territory near C block. The Bloods stood in the middle between the two. There were minor gangs like the Vietnamese, Koreans, and the recently arrived Somalians.

There were sections on the yard where non-gang members could hang. Predators were always looking for an opportunity, and prey were those who just wanted to do their time and get out.

Vincent and Sid hung out in these neutral zones but never with weaker prey. Sid could spot fresh meat; his prophecy would soon become a reality for the poor soul. The gangs would always start with a small favor, and then it would end badly.

Sid and Vincent stood near the bathroom entrance looking for a chance to speak with Diego, but he was better guarded than the president because of the hit on Caesar. It would be foolhardy for Sid to try to reach Diego because the last person he would trust is a black man.

"Vincent, you have to reach Diego," exclaimed Sid.

"Me, why me? You're the one talking to ghosts," replied Vincent.

"Look, Diego isn't going to trust a brother, even one from Alabama. He isn't going to trust you either, but he might be off guard enough by you approaching him that he will give you a minute before they stomp you. It might give you a second to pass him this note," countered Sid.

"What's on the note?" asked Vincent.

"It's what Caesar told me to tell Diego. Our only hope is to reach Diego before a gang war," Sid replied.

"Hell, maybe the gang war won't be so bad. The worst that can happen is that we end up in lockdown for the remainder of our sentence," countered Vincent.

"The worst that could happen is getting our throats cut during the chaos. You know the gang members you pissed off still have it in for you, and an all-out war on the yard gives them the chance to take you down." disputed Sid.

"Okay, what's the play?" asked Vincent, accepting their predicament.

"I think the best approach is a full-frontal attack. Just walk up to Diego and hand him the note. If he takes the note, walk back here. He will take the advice in the note, or he will not. We did what was asked of us and after that, whatever happens, happens." continued Sid.

"That easy, huh?" asked Vincent.

"Yes, it should be that easy. If it is not, it won't work," replied Sid.

"What are the directions in the note?" asked Vincent.

"You, Diego, and I parley alone in the bathrooms," answered Sid.

"Just the three of us?" asked Vincent.

"Yes, just the three of us," said Sid.

"Hell, you only live once, right? It might as well be exciting," exclaimed Vincent.

Vincent snapped the note out of Sid's hand and started walking toward the Mexican Mafia's territory. Everyone in the yard began to look intently at Vincent as he crossed one turf after another. Vincent kept thinking about World War II movies. He felt that D Day on the beach in Normandy was like the few hundred feet he had to travel to reach Diego. He could see every glance and stare. No other gang member tried to stop him. He started to feel like destiny was protecting him.

When Vincent reached Diego's territory, two massive Mexican gang members stopped Vincent in his tracks. "Are you loco, white boy?" asked one of the thugs.

"I have an important note for Diego," replied Vincent.

"Let me see it?" asked a gangster.

"It's for Diego's eyes only," replied Vincent with a sense of purpose that gave him strength.

"How about I cut your eyes out, ese?" asked a gangster with a shive in his right hand next to his thigh so the guards could not see it.

"If you cut my eyes out, Diego doesn't get the note and later finds out what's in the note. Anyway, you figure it out," replied Vincent.

The gang members looked at Vincent for a long time, then one of them went over to the benches Diego was sitting on and whispered in his ear. Diego glances at Vincent for a moment, then waves him over.

"You got balls, white boy. Your information better be good. These two want to stomp you," said Diego.

Vincent didn't say a word. He handed the note to Diego, then walked away and didn't look back or at any other gang member. He made it back to Sid, standing up against the outer wall outside the bathrooms.

"You did it," said Sid.

"Yeh, something gave me strength. I think Caesar was along for the ride," exclaimed Vincent.

"Maybe so; let's see what happens now," said Sid.

Diego stood up and walked over to a corner behind the benches. After reading the note, a shocked look came over his face. He glanced at Sid and Vincent, then walked over to the two thugs and whispered in their ears. They walked directly toward Sid and Vincent. The other groups around Sid and Vincent parted like the Red Sea.

"Diego will meet you in the bathroom, alone. You have five minutes, and it better be good, ese?" reported one of the gang members.

Vincent and Sid slowly walked into the bathroom, ensuring no one was hanging out in a stall. When first put into the general population, new prey hid in the stalls, but they soon discover there is only safety in numbers, not hiding where they could be caught alone and vulnerable.

Sid and Vincent knew that meeting Diego in the bathroom could be their demise, but they felt they had no other option. The guards won't help, and going to the warden would put them in even more trouble for being snitches.

Ten minutes passed in the bathroom. Diego moved with caution, learned from years on the street. He walked into the bathroom alone and checked all the stalls before stepping up to Sid and Vincent. He looked at Vincent and asked, "How do you know this information, white boy? Only Caesar and I knew about this. Speak, or I will cut your throat."

Sid interjected in the tense situation, "I'm the one that wrote the note, and I am the one that Caesar contacted."

"What do you mean contacted? When would Caesar meet with your black ass? You're just another target on the Serengeti; feel me," exclaimed Diego.

"How would I know what I wrote in the note if I didn't get it from Caesar?" asked Sid.

"Okay, I'll give you that. What is it that you want?" asked Diego.

"The Bloods did not kill Caesar. Your second in command murdered Caesar, Emilio. Caesar wanted you to know this because Emilio will make a move on you to consolidate power. Caesar didn't want a war. This information is his gift to you, his long-time friend," said Sid.

Diego looked at Sid for a long time studying his eyes. Diego felt he could see a man's soul and intentions in his eyes.

"Why would I believe your black ass over my lieutenant? Maybe you're a spy for the Bloods? Maybe I will kill you right now. I should kill you just knowing the information in the note, and you too, white boy," replied Diego.

"Caesar said you would not take this information at face value, so he told me another bit of information that only you and he would know from childhood," Sid leaned in and whispered something in Diego's ear. Diego reared back when he heard what Sid told him.

"Okay, I believe Caesar talked to you. Why would he tell you and a shit kicker from Texas to stop a war?" replied Diego.

Vincent interjected, "Wyoming."

Diego just stared at Vincent, waiting for an answer from Sid.

"Does it matter how I got the information? You only need to follow up and find out if it is true. Caesar said you, and he played a game when you were young setting traps for the neighborhood cats. He said you need to set a trap for Emilio so that you know who is working with him and who you can trust," stated Sid.

Diego started to walk out of the bathroom and turned around to say, "If this is bull shit, I will come after both of you with full force, feel me?"

"We understand," replied Sid.

Diego walked out of the bathroom into the light with four gang members walking close behind him.

"So, what do we do now?" asked Vincent.

"We wait and watch. We don't tell anyone else what just took place. Any information might find its way back to Emilio, which would not be healthy for us," responded Sid.

After three days, the tension between the Mexican Mafia and the Bloods continued to build. Nothing seemed to be happening. At least, Sid and Vincent could surmise nothing. Diego was hanging out without care, and business seemed to move as usual in the yard.

Diego went for a shower on the fourth day, and his four guards got distracted by a minor scuffle in the yard. Emilio entered the shower room with two other gang members to take down Diego. When Emilio and the two gang members entered the shower room, they walked into a trap. Diego was waiting with his crew. Emilio and his coconspirators didn't make it out alive.

The word of Emilio's death moved fast around Rikers Island,

and the information that Emilio orchestrated Caesar's death made it to the Bloods.

Once this information got out, things started to go back to normal, as routine as can be at Rikers Island.

"Diego wants to see you both in the yard," said a Mexican gangster.

Sid and Vincent walked over to the bench Diego hung out at every day. Diego told the guards surrounding him to move out so he could speak privately with Sid and Vincent.

"So, what do you two want for saving my ass?" asked Diego.

"We just want peace until we get out of here," answered Sid.

"Peace is expensive in Rikers, but I can make it happen. No one will touch you while you are here. Tex, those two you pissed off are history," replied Diego. He then waved off Sid and Vincent and called back his guards.

The other gang members moved away as Sid and Vincent walked across the yard. They could now walk freely with the confidence that no one would hassle them, and no one would take Vincent's shoes. ଔ

☙

Chapter Three

"Hey Sid, I've been looking for you everywhere," said Vincent in a huff.

"You couldn't be looking for me everywhere because I exist in just this space," replied Sid with a smug look.

"Hell, for a low-life hustler in prison, you sure talk good," said Vincent.

"It's jail, not prison, and I talk well, not good," answered Sid.

"Whatever, look, Diego talked to his fancy lawyer in New York, and he has worked it out, so we leave Rikers at the same time. He's been good to his word. I can walk anywhere, and no one will hassle me, even those two gang bangers I fought with when I first came here," exclaimed Vincent.

Sid looked up with a restrained expression and said, "Look, I told you to be careful taking any gift from a gangster, especially one from the king. He is going to want something in return. I asked for us to be left alone, but this might be another favor."

"Hell, I thought you would be happy. How could Diego reach us once we get out of this hole?" asked Vincent.

"Diego may be king here, but he is part of a larger organization. He could easily have us killed if he wanted," refuted Sid.

Vincent leaned back in his chair with a frustrated look and smoothed his long blond hair behind his ears. He said, "Hell, if we are going to be partners, we must ride under the same star."

Sid looked up from reading and replied, "I haven't decided yet."

"About being partners?" asked Vincent.

"Yes," answered Sid.

"Well, you better decide soon because we have five days left," replied Vincent.

"I'm leaning toward the same star," answered Sid.

"Hell, that's good. What are you reading?" queried Vincent.

"I found this old book on physics in the library. It's strange because the content stops with theories in the early nineteen sixties," responded Sid.

"Physics, you mean working out and such?" asked Vincent.

"No, have you heard of Albert Einstein?" questioned Sid.

"Of course, he is that smart fellow who discovered relativity. In high school, we talked about that; I remember e=mc2 but don't remember what it meant," answered Vincent.

"This book is mainly about Max Planck's quantum theory and Albert Einstein's unified field theory. Many facts are old and outdated, but reading this book is fascinating, " Sid replied.

"Why?" questioned Vincent.

Sid put down the book. He continued, "Because it has to do with our situation. Einstein's theory of relativity is apparent in jail; I mean, the nature of this place is doing time.

"Remember when you were in sixth grade, and it was the last day of school before a long summer? I kept looking back at the Gilbert clock on the wall over the door to freedom. Every time that minute hand moved forward, it first moved back two spaces. Elementary school was the first jail that indoctrinated us into a fixed system. Of course, I didn't know it then, but the education system trains good little employees.

"We were doing time in that schoolroom, and we are doing time in this place. After you ran out of the door in sixth grade, summer went by in a flash because you were not aware of time anymore. When you are aware of the time, you are doing time—no matter where you are," exclaimed Sid.

"Sid, you're an intelligent fellow. Why didn't you end up in some fancy job making a bunch of money?" asked Vincent.

"I guess the sins of the father," responded Sid.

"I don't follow," said Vincent.

Sid continued, "I grew up with my father telling me and my siblings, don't be a chump and work for a paycheck. He would say rich people make money by creating, investing, or on the backs of suckers. He told us that we must look for opportunities to make money. If we get a paycheck, we will never build real wealth.

"If you think about it, working for a paycheck is like doing time. I remember my uncle working at the local chicken processing plant. He would always announce how many years he had left before he could retire at any family gathering. He would talk about a vacation to Europe he and his wife would take when he retired. He had a heart attack on the job and died."

"Yeh, my father wanted that ranch in Wyoming but worked for peanuts for a bunch of rich stiffs from the city. My father was not counting downtime; time wore him down.

"If you would have won that pot at the poker game, how much would you have walked away with?" inquired Vincent.

"The pot would have been around one hundred and twenty thousand," stated Sid.

"Hell, that's a lot of money. You almost made it," replied Vincent.

"Yes, but you see, that is just the dilemma. Rich folk don't want a couple of hustlers like us to make it. It starts in school. Have you ever wondered why they don't teach kids about money in elementary school? It's because rich folk wants us to be good employees. They don't want us to challenge them for the kingdom," professed Sid.

"Talk of the kingdom. Have you come up with any ideas on our big con?" asked Vincent.

"Well, I know it can't be in New York City because too many grifters are running the show. It needs to be in an area where a black and white guy could pull something big off. It needs to be big, no more small hustles, and it must be grandiose," declared Sid.

Vincent and Sid were allowed to spend their last few days of incarceration in the day room watching television, another favor offered by Diego. Vincent and Sid were amazed at how much power Diego had at Rikers. So far, Diego hadn't asked for anything or talked with them again. Vincent felt that maybe saving his life was enough, but Sid still had doubts.

Even though they were safe from harm or labor, time went by slowly. Time was especially slow the last few days before they were set free. They spent a lot of time watching daytime soap operas and infomercials. Vincent and Sid were left alone in the day room until late. Even the guard with notches on his nightstick wouldn't mess with them. The guard knew that Diego could easily reach his family.

Vincent sat quietly in a bright red plastic chair that was most likely a hand-me-down from a local high school. He sat back and incessantly smoothed his long blond hair behind his ears.

"I know your poker tell," proclaimed Sid.

"Poker tell?" responded Vincent.

"Yes, your poker tell. A player will show a poker tell when they are nervous about a poker hand or are bluffing. A habit that novice poker players are not aware of but continually engage.

"My father taught me that the best players could quickly spot a poker tell. Good poker players know how to read their opponents. Anyone can learn to play poker, but few can become good observers of human nature. The stiffs I was playing against at the underground game were easy to figure out," stated Sid.

"You said you figured out my poker tell?" inquired Vincent.

"Yes, when nervous, you smooth your long blond hair behind your ears. If you think about it, smoothing your hair behind your ears is an attempt to listen and be more aware of your surroundings," confessed Sid.

"Hell, I've been doing that my whole life. I never thought it meant anything other than my hair is in my face," replied Vincent.

"Supposedly, we primarily communicate with each other with body language. Verbal communication is a small part of what occurs. It takes listening and a strong awareness of what is happening around us to be able to interpret other people's intentions," declared Sid.

Sid and Vincent looked up at the television and watched a Christian tele-minister. He had the Bible in one hand and a cloth to wipe the sweat away in the other.

He recited a passage from the Bible and then walked up to a parishioner and touched their forehead while yelling, "Satan be gone." He would push forcefully on the parishioner; they would fall backward, being caught by the stage crew.

"How about this fellow; can you read him?" asked Vincent.

"He's easy. He is lying with every breath he takes. He's playing the oldest con in the book. Look at those people. They are like a moth to a flame. Religion is for suckers. My father was a deacon and often told me that the best con is the one no one sees coming." exclaimed Sid.

"How about religion?" asked Vincent.

"You mean as our big con?" replied Sid.

"Yeh, you grew up in it and seemed to know a lot about religion," inquired Vincent.

"I've thought about following my father's footsteps, but Christianity is a crowded field, and there are many better hustlers than us already working the system. Plus, I think most people are tired of Christianity and maybe looking for something new," replied Sid.

Vincent continued, "I remember some guru had a cult following in Wyoming as a kid. He had all these followers living on this large ranch the guru bought with the money everyone was handing over. The guru had ten or twenty Rolls-Royces and was having sex with his followers. I don't know what happened to the fellow or his devotees."

"I remember that guy. He got greedy. One of the first rules of a good con is not to get greedy. Scams fall apart once the hustler starts getting comfortable and believing they are invincible.

"There is always a line that a good grifter should never cross. That guru got so greedy that he became over-exposed in the media, and the government started to take notice. They started to dig into his past," answered Sid.

"How would you play it?" asked Vincent.

"I would create something new but aligned with a traditional religious belief. I would target a small town, but not too small. Too small of a town, and people start to question a newcomer. Everyone knows each other's business. That wouldn't be good for us. Remember, the best con is when the marks don't know they were taken," stated Sid.

Vincent and Sid sat back in their chairs and watched the tele-minister do his magic. The minister spoke directly to the camera every fifteen minutes, asking for prayer pledges. He would guarantee Jesus's good graces with each prayer pledge of one hundred dollars or more.

"I can't believe these suckers are falling for this hustler," said Vincent.

"The shit my father got away with hiding behind the good book. My father is one of the most corrupt people I have ever met, but his parishioners would never believe he was just out for himself. They hoped my father could turn things around for them, but most became poorer. By the way, Caesar revisited me last night," interjected Sid.

"You mean Caesar Ramirez's ghost. I thought he was long gone?" asked Vincent.

"No, unfortunately for Caesar, he will be here for a long incarceration," replied Sid.

"How long?" inquired Vincent.

"Who knows, it could be a few hundred years. Caesar's spirit is so corrupt he has a lot to undo," professed Sid.

"Thanks for not waking me up. The last time Caesar visited, I had difficulty going back to sleep, and sleep is the only escape from this place. So, what did he want?" asked Vincent.

"He told me Diego will offer us a deal, and we should accept," replied Sid.

"You told me we should not take any more favors from Diego," countered Vincent.

"Caesar told me the deal would be good for us, and another unforeseen opportunity would arise. Caesar said he had tried to reach Diego, but the possibility of a ghost shut him down. However, Caesar could plant a seed in Diego's mind.

"Caesar told me that Diego was considering murdering us because of the knowledge I obtained. Instead of killing us, he will offer us this deal, and we need to take it," Sid exclaimed.

"What is the deal?" asked Vincent.

"Caesar didn't give me the details. He just told me to take the deal and trust," replied Sid.

"I don't know if I can trust a gangster, even one dead. I guess it's better to move on than be murdered. I figure in this place, no one would miss a couple of low-life hustlers," replied Vincent.

⅓

Good to Caesar's word Diego was waiting alone in the holding cell where prisoners stayed before being released. Sid and Vincent cautiously walked into the cell. The guard prodded them to move faster and then shut the cell door behind them.

Diego was in the corner of the cell in sweatpants and a hoody. He said quietly but firmly, "Sit down and shut up. I have a proposition for you two idiots. I should have stomped both of you for what you know about my business, but I will give you a pass.

"I still haven't figured out how you obtained that piece of information, only Caesar and I knew what happened. If I find out that you told anyone, you're dead. You feel me?"

Sid and Vincent just nodded their heads in agreement.

"Good, so here is the deal. By the way, the deal is not negotiable, and you have no choice. You understand?" declared Diego.

Sid and Vincent just nodded their heads in agreement.

"There is an underground poker game going to take place in Newburgh, New York. A rival gang is organizing the play; Newburgh is a distribution hub for our more profitable business endeavors.

"I heard you are a good poker player. I heard you could read people?" acknowledged Diego while pointing at Sid. Diego continued, "I will cover the twenty-five thousand buy-in, so you have a seat at the table. I have an informant in the gang that will make it happen.

"What I want from you is to win the pot, but more importantly, look for each member's poker tell. Next month our two gangs are having a sit down to carve up Newburgh, and we need to know when their captains are bluffing before that meeting. Our informant will tell you who the leaders are to watch. You feel me?"

"What if I lose?" inquired Sid.

"Don't; you need to stay in the game long enough to figure out their poker tell," replied Diego.

"Hell, Diego, how will we get to Newburgh?" asked Vincent.

"Look, when you arrive in Manhattan, our people will meet you. They will take you to a safe house in Newburgh. All you need to do is sit your ass down and win. You two idiots understand?" asked Diego.

Sid and Vincent just nodded their heads in agreement.

"Good," replied Diego. He stood up, walked to the cell door, and called for the guard. The guard rushed over to open the door. Diego turned to Sid and Vincent and gave them a menacing stare as he walked out the door. His dead cold eyes were saying everything they needed to hear. He then walked out of the cell and their lives.

"Hell, are we going to do this? Newburgh might be a trap?" asked Vincent.

"It's not; Caesar has no reason to lie to us. He's doing time in Rikers, where the only way out is to undo all the evil he created during his life. There is more at stake than just the law with spirits," countered Sid.

"Did you notice that Diego hardly had an accent?" asked Vincent.

"Yes, one of the mysteries Caesar told me was that Diego is not Mexican, he was born in Spain, and his mother and father moved to the United States when he was only two years old. They both were academics and worked for Yale University in New Haven, Connecticut.

"Diego went to Yale and studied economics. He discovered he had a penchant for illegal activities. Diego moved to New York City and joined a gang. He moved up the ladder quickly because of his intelligence and cunning nature. If any of his cronies knew his real past, they would likely kill him," said Sid.

"Hell, I guess he is also a hustler," replied Vincent.

The guard with the notches on the nightstick opened the door to the cell and said, "It's time to go. The van is waiting on you two, so you better hustle, or you will need to stay here another day. Let's go."

"Hell, you don't need to tell me twice," exclaimed Vincent.

The ride out of Rikers seems a lot faster than the ride in. There is a single bridge to the island; each prisoner rides in a van passing over the bridge. On the way in, prisoners watch the island get closer and closer. It's like descending into Dante's inferno. On the way out, prisoners are looking at Manhattan and freedom. ∞

☙

Chapter Four

The Rikers Island van driver pulled into the Port Authority bus terminal, opened the doors, and exclaimed, "It's the end of the line, chumps. Maybe I will see you soon."

The Port Authority in Manhattan is a cesspool of pimps, drug addicts, and crazy people. Vincent went straight to Dunkin Donuts to get a coffee and a couple of Boston cream pie donuts.

Sid passed on the donuts but got a large coffee. He inquired, "I don't understand why someone would work at the Dunkin Donuts in the Port Authority. They could work in any Dunkin Donuts, move to a nice town upstate, make the same amount of money and not have to put up with the insanity of the Port Authority. It doesn't make sense."

Vincent shrugged his shoulders. He replied, "I don't know. Maybe they like being in the middle of the craziness, and maybe they are a little crazy themselves."

Good to Diego's word, two Hispanic gangsters were waiting for Sid and Vincent when they arrived. One of the gangsters was a former bodyguard for Diego at Rikers Island during Sid and Vincent's incarceration. The gangster waved Sid and Vincent over to a light blue Ford minivan. The minivan looked like something a suburban soccer mom would purchase to chauffeur her over-entitled kids and their friends around.

A sign on the bumper indicated that the minivan's owner had a child on the dean's list at a local New Jersey elementary school. Garfield, the cat, was plastered to the rear window, implying that there might have been a baby on board.

"Nice ride," Vincent said with a grin on his face.

The gangsters pushed Vincent and Sid into the back of the minivan. He exclaimed, "Look, white boy, you are just along for the ride. Diego only needs your buddy, so you better shut that smart ass mouth, feel me?"

Vincent thought the gang banger was correct; they only wanted Sid, not him. He could jump out of the van and walk away, but something deep down convinced him to move forward with his newfound friend.

"Vincent, are you thinking about jumping ship?" asked Sid.

"For a moment, but like you said, in for a penny in for a pound," countered Vincent.

After spending time at Rikers Island, the trip to Newburgh seemed surreal to Sid and Vincent. As they moved out of New York City, they passed through crowded boroughs and affluent suburbs full of the wealth they both coveted.

There was a brief respite with nature before they finally reached their destination. Newburgh, New York, is a schizophrenic city split by two gangs and between rich and poor. It's sixty-two miles from Manhattan and sits on the Hudson River. The waterfront has been gussied up by rich folk to give the impression there is some reason to visit the city. Walk a half-block into the town's interior, and you will see neighborhoods in third-world poverty.

Gangsters like Newburgh because it sits on two major highways, one is going east-west and the other north-south. It is a perfect place to transfer drugs, contraband, and even human trafficking throughout the northeast.

The minivan pulled up to a row house along a deserted street late in the evening. The two gangsters got out first and looked around carefully for anyone that might cause them problems. They motioned for Sid and Vincent to follow them into a townhouse blended tightly with other buildings.

"Look, Homey, there is plenty of food in the fridge, cable television, and two bedrooms. The game is tomorrow night, so don't go anywhere. If you do go out, there is a good possibility that you will get jumped, so don't leave until we come for you tomorrow; feel me?" stated one of the gangsters, pointing his finger at Vincent's chest.

Sid and Vincent just nodded their heads.

Both gangsters walked out onto the porch, looked around carefully, returned to the minivan, and sped away down the street.

"I'm starving. How about you?' asked Vincent.

Vincent walked into the kitchen and opened the refrigerator. The fridge was full of packaged burritos, two pizzas, a bucket of fried chicken from KFC, and two cases of beer. Multiple packages of Raman and refried beans were sitting on the counter, and three boxes of Captain Crunch cereal, but no milk.

"Hell, I was hoping for something upscale, but lobster is a lot to expect from a couple of gangsters. Oh well, when in Rome, right?" asked Vincent.

"At least it is better than the food we got at Rikers. This stuff would go for a lot inside," responded Sid.

Vincent grabbed a couple of burritos and tossed them in the microwave. He cracked two beers and handed one to Sid, "My first beer after four weeks of New York City hospitality." Vincent took a long pull on the beer and continued, "This stuff is good; at least our hosts have good taste in suds."

Sid downed his beer in one gulp and exclaimed, "A real scary shit-hole, huh?"

"You mean Newburgh?" inquired Vincent.

"Yeh, this place makes my hometown look like paradise. My brothers and sisters shouldn't live like this; I thought poverty like this only existed in Mississippi," expressed Sid.

"You didn't live in poverty in Georgia?" asked Vincent.

"No, because my father's farm is in Alabama. We were lucky. We had all the pleasantries of life, like an inside toilet, running water, and appliances that make life easy for folk. I told you that my father ran the black end of the county. He might be a hustler, but he always provided for his family," stated Sid.

"Georgia, Alabama, Mississippi, all the same to me, all south of the Mason Dixon line. It sounds like your father wasn't a complete asshole?" asked Vincent.

"Not a complete asshole, but one just the same," stated Sid.

"Let's see what's on the tube," queried Vincent.

"I'm getting tired of watching the television. I saw all the TV I needed during our last week in Rikers. I think I will take a shower or bath, or whatever is available, and go to sleep," declared Sid.

"You're missing out. These burritos are not half bad. The funny thing is, this will be the first night in many weeks we haven't had to share a room while we sleep," proclaimed Vincent.

"Well, that's a good thing. Don't stay up too late. We have a long day tomorrow; we might have to move fast if things go sideways," replied Sid.

"Right," answered Vincent.

The night was calm other than an occasional gunshot and a car screeching its tires in the distance. Sid and Vincent knew they were in a war zone because of their tension.

Sid woke up around 9:00 in the morning. He walked around the townhouse looking for Vincent, but the place was empty. He started to get concerned when Vincent walked through the front door with a brown bag in his hand.

"Where have you been? It would be best if you did not leave the townhouse?" exclaimed Sid.

"Hell, Sid, I had to have milk with my Captain Crunch. I just walked down to the corner bodega. You should have seen this place. The market looked like it was in a third-world country. The shelves were mostly empty, with just a few cans of food and a couple of loaves of bread. Lots of beer, but only a couple of cartons of milk. I hope the milk I bought is still good." confessed Vincent.

"Anyone give you any trouble?" asked Sid.

"No, but I was the only white boy. Everyone looked at me like I was an alien. I don't think they knew what to make of me," replied Vincent.

Sid sat at the small kitchen table and poured Captain Crunch into a clean bowl. Vincent handed Sid the milk, and he cautiously smelled the contents before pouring it over his cereal. Sid continued, "I had a vision last night."

Vincent asked, "You had a dream? Did a ghost visit you?"

"No, I had a vision. It's different from a dream, but it's like having a dream; when you are wide awake," said Sid.

"What happened?" asked Vincent.

"I was lying in bed, and a thought came to me. My inner voice asked if I was ready for what was next, and I replied yes, and then an image of an older white man with silver hair wearing a red bow tie and an expensive suit was across from me at a poker table," recalled Sid.

"You are freaking me out, now you have visions?" inquired Vincent.

"I've had them my whole life. This one was the closest to the reality that I have ever experienced. Most of my past visions were about something of no consequence, like missing a bus. This vision had great meaning, but what I don't know yet." contemplated Sid.

"Maybe this guy is at the poker game tonight, but it seems unlikely that a white guy would sit in on a poker game in a place like Newburgh," responded Vincent.

"Well, it's unlikely that a couple of small-time hustlers would sit in on a high-stakes poker game in Newburgh when they were incarcerated in Rikers Island yesterday," exclaimed Sid.

"I had something strange happen last night," replied Vincent.

"What?" asked Sid.

"I placed all my stuff on the night table beside my bed. I went in for a shower, and a dime was on my nightstand when I came out. I didn't have any change on the nightstand when I went to clean up. The first thing that came to mind was my mother. I felt her presence, and for a brief second, I could smell her favorite perfume, Shalamar," continued Vincent.

"When an angel misses you, they toss a penny down … sometimes to cheer you up, to make a smile out of your frown. So, don't pass by that penny when you're feeling blue; it may be a penny from Heaven that an angel tossed to you," recited Sid.

"What was that?" inquired Vincent.

"My mother would often recite that poem by Charles Mashburn. She used to tell me that when I was in a tight place, my ancestors would always look out for me, but I never thought much of it," replied Sid.

"I found a dime, not a penny. What does that mean?" asked Vincent.

"Maybe your mother is looking out for you, and maybe she is telling you to trust you are where you should be," countered Sid.

A knock on the front door startled Sid and Vincent. Both just stared at the front door, not moving. The knocking just got louder and louder.

"Anyone follow you?" asked Sid.

"No, not that I saw," replied Vincent.

Sid stood up and cautiously walked over to the front door. He looked out a window overlooking the porch and saw a young man standing in front of the door. The young man was black with tattoos, and his pants were hanging below his white underwear. He had bright red sneakers on with untied laces.

Sid slowly opened the door and asked, "What do you want?"

The young man looked around to ensure no one saw him on the

porch and replied, "I'm Jamal, Diego's friend. Let me in before someone spots me."

Sid opened the door wide to let in Jamal, and then he poked his head outside to see if anyone was watching.

"So, you're a friend of Diego's?" asked Vincent.

"Well, let's say more of an acquaintance. He pays well, and I need to earn," exclaimed Jamal.

"What's the play, Jamal?" asked Sid.

Jamal walked over to the kitchen table and pulled out a chair. He spun the chair around and sat on it backward, resting his arms on the chair's back. He asked, "Before we get into it, why don't you offer a brother some suds and maybe a couple of those burritos I see on the counter?"

Vincent walked over, handed Jamal a beer, and put a couple of burritos in the microwave. They all stood staring at each other until the microwave pinged, and Vincent put the two burritos on a plate and handed them to Jamal.

Jamal downed one of the burritos and took a long drink from his beer. He looked at Vincent and said, "Everyone in the neighborhood was talking about the white boy at the market. Not too smart, especially in this neighborhood, because that market is gang territory."

"I needed milk for my Captain Crunch," countered Vincent.

"I feel you. You need some milk on your flakes. Now everyone knows you are here. Good thing the game is tonight. I don't think you would last more than a week," asserted Jamal.

"So, what's the play, Jamal?" asked Sid.

"You talk funny for a brother; where you from?" inquired Jamal.

"I'm from the southern version of Newburgh. Does it matter?" responded Sid.

"I'm curious about who I'm helping. Just making sure," replied Jamal.

"Sure, about what?' asked Vincent.

"Making sure we are on the same page. I want to ensure you are the two who just came out of Rikers before I hand over the goods." Jamal reached into his coat, pulled out a large envelope, and handed it to Sid.

Sid opened the envelope and pulled out a large stack of one hundred dollar bills and three photos. He placed the money and pictures on the table.

"Go ahead, count it. It's all there. The twenty-five thousand buy-in for the poker game," confessed Jamal.

Sid fanned through the bills and said, "I believe you because if the money is not here, we're all dead. You don't look stupid, and I bet you are well paid."

"Yes, well paid, and I don't plan to screw it up or get stomped," replied Jamal.

"So, who is in the photos?" asked Sid.

Jamal fanned out the pictures on the kitchen table and downed another burrito. Vincent handed him another beer. While he was still chewing, he explained. "The middle guy is Tyrone. He is the main banger in Newburgh. Nothing comes in or out without his approval. He's tied to the Bloods in Los Angeles. The brother on the right is Marquis, a local. He is Tyrone's first lieutenant, who manages all the pharmaceuticals moving down the east coast.

"The brother on the left is Derek. He is Tyrone's main enforcer and controls the tail brought in from other countries. He is a man with a reputation for killing for nothing more than a wrong look. You will be playing against all three. As far as I know, there will be four other players. These are the three that you need to keep an eye on. They will be sitting down with Diego's men to carve up Newburgh."

"Who are the other four?" asked Vincent.

Jamal looked at Vincent and said, "Why am I answering the white boy's questions? Aren't you the one who is sitting in at the game?"

"We're partners, and we go together. So, who are the other four players?" requested Sid.

Jamal took a long sip of his beer and replied, "One is a Russian mafia heavyweight from Boston. Tyrone wants to do business with them, so he invited him to the game. The other three are civilians—a professional poker player from Atlantic City. Tyron's brother met him when they did time together in New Jersey.

"The other player is a mystery. He is a white dude with a two-thousand-dollar suit and Rolex. How he got invited to play, no one knows, but I am sure he is friends with Tyrone or someone close to Tyrone. No one plays in this game without Tyron's okay."

"Is Tyron a good poker player?" enquired Sid.

"No, but he is good at cheating, and he usually gets away with it because most won't call him on it. The Russian guy is serious about the game. So, I don't think Tyrone will play as usual," replied Jamal.

"How long do these poker games last?" asked Sid.

"Tyrone plays with his local crew once weekly, but these games are twice yearly. Playing two straight days is not uncommon." asserted Jamal.

"What is the average payout?" asked Vincent.

"Do the math, cracker. Eight players with a twenty-five thousand buy-in, the winner get to walk with two hundred thousand," claimed Jamal.

"Is there anything else you can tell us about the game?" asked Sid.

"If you win, ensure you have an exit strategy; feel me?" declared Jamal.

"I take it Tyrone isn't a good loser," questioned Sid.

"You take it right. Look, I delivered the goods and gave you some knowledge. Now, I need to leave. I'm going to duck out the back of this place. I will be there tonight, so don't even look my way, feel me?" exclaimed Jamal.

Sid and Vincent just nodded their heads.

Jamal got up from the table, walked back through the kitchen to the door leading into a patio, grabbed two packaged burritos, and disappeared through the kitchen door.

"Jamal described the guy in my vision. The guy with the expensive suit," confirmed Sid.

"What does it mean?" asked Vincent.

"I don't know, but I guess it means what it means. A mystery guy," retorted Sid. ❧

ℭℬ

Chapter Five

Diego's thugs showed up in a different vehicle at the townhouse where Sid and Vincent stayed. Vincent thought the van must have belonged to a local serial killer because it was grey with no windows other than the front and plenty of room in the back to dispose of a body without any detection.

Diego's gangsters never discussed where they got their rides; they didn't discuss much of anything with Sid and Vincent. Sid considered his current driver a subordinate, following orders like a good soldier. However, Sid knew the gangster would cut their throats without hesitation. Sid needed an exit strategy after the game, especially if he won the pot.

The trip took longer than Sid and Vincent imagined. They both considered that the game would be in the basement of some house in Newburgh. The van seemed to be heading towards the Newburgh airport, and then the van turned into the rear entrance of a large hotel.

A tall black man with tattoos on his arms and a red cloth covering his hair was standing near the hotel's rear entrance. The van driver pulled close to the door, turned around, looked straight at Sid, and said, "Diego wants a full report after the game. Don't try to skip out. We will be watching, understand, homey?"

Sid and Vincent just nodded their heads.

The gangster continued, "Tyron's man, Leroy, will take you the rest of the way." The two got out of the van, and the gangster drove away. Sid knew that he wouldn't be going far and that Diego's people would be watching.

"Who's the cracker?" asked Leroy.

"He's my partner," replied Sid.

"Tyron told us that a brother, and only a brother from the south, would be sitting in on the game," Leroy recalled.

"Tyron was told wrong," replied Sid.

"He's your responsibility, feel me?" replied Leroy.

Sid just nodded his head.

Vincent thought that whoever designed the hallway carpet was most likely on drugs. The rug was a jumble of strange angles with a color pattern reminiscent of casinos his family visited when he was a kid. The predominant colors were brown, orange, and green; Vincent considered that no sane person would install such a carpet.

"This carpet is making me dizzy," asserted Vincent.

"Shut up," countered Leroy.

Leroy led Sid and Vincent into a conference room on the hotel's top floor with panels dividing the different rooms. Behind one of the divides was a professional poker table.

There was a foldable table on the far side of the room with coffee, sandwiches, and other small finger food. Next to the foldable table, a small movable bar held liquor, beer, and wine with neatly stacked plastic classes. Behind the bar stood a hotel bartender with a black vest, white shirt, and bowtie. His hotel name tag read Rodney.

A group of five black men and three white men stood talking around the bar with cigars. When Sid and Vincent entered the room, they all turned around and intently stared at the new arrivals.

"We have one left to arrive, and we can start," said one of the black men closest to the bar. The man walked over to Sid and said, "I hear you're a player."

"I do okay," countered Sid.

The man shook Sid's hand and replied, "You and your friend can help yourself to the food and booze. Make sure you buy in before the game starts. My name is Tyron, and my brother owns this place, so don't hesitate to make yourself at home.

"I reserved a room for you in the hotel if we need breaks during the game." Tyrone then turned around and rejoined the other men around the bar.

Sid and Vincent helped themselves to the food and coffee. Vincent looked around the room and said, "This isn't what I expected. This room looks like some strange business conference, not an underground poker game."

Sid replied, "I guess Tyron wants to impress his Russian guests. You know, all-American gangster hospitality."

An outer door to the conference room opened, and an older white man in an expensive suit moved through the door with a young blond woman on his arm. He whispered to the younger woman, and then she turned around and disappeared back into the hallway.

"Good, Marty has arrived. We can start the game." Tyron walked over to Marty, shook his hand, and then motioned everyone to take their seat at the poker table.

"He's the one," whispered Sid to Vincent.

"You mean your vision?" asked Vincent.

"Yeh, down to his red bowtie. I feel that he is our ticket out of here after the game," expressed Sid.

All the players took a seat at the table. Anyone extra, including Vincent, had to sit behind a roped-off area. Tyron was not taking any chances.

Most poker players know the game is as strategic as a football, but the game is more about time than knowledge. Professional poker players stretch out their first few play hours to evaluate their opponents. They secure the most valuable parts of poker: knowing their adversary's level of expertise and their poker tell.

A professional will bet modestly with an excellent hand to wear down opponents during the second part of the game. A good poker player will even let a novice win a few hands to give them a sense of confidence and see how they react to a lucky streak.

The final part of the game is where a professional will start turning up the heat with larger bets testing their challengers' resilience. Finally, when they are sure of their rivals' poker tell, they go in for the kill.

Sid learned this when he was young. His father preached that a good poker player would be able to apply his expertise to any grift. A good con takes on a strategy, not unlike poker. Give the mark a sense of confidence, assess the amount of greed, and then go in for the kill.

After two hours of play, everyone knew that most at the table were professionals except for the Russian. He was boastful with too much alcohol in his system. He made terrible decisions on betting, and his poker tell was apparent to all the other players.

The mobster was young, maybe early twenties. His companions behind Vincent were Russian mafia enforcers, almost certainly sent with

Sergei to protect him. Sid guessed that Sergei was the son of the Russian mob boss Tyron was courting. Most high rollers wouldn't put up with his conceit unless Sergei had connections to someone dangerous.

Sid knew that Tyron had to be careful with Sergei if he wanted to do business with his father. Tyron would have to let Sergei win a little to support his ego, but Sid and other players didn't need to hold back on Sergei. They did have to worry about Tyron whacking them if they beat Sergei too hard.

Sid needed to get Sergei out of the game if he was to zero in on the other players' poker tell. Sergei was sucking all the oxygen out of the room, and the other players were irritated. A novice can disrupt the play as easily as a bull in a china shop. All the players started to focus on purging the bad seed.

In the fifth hour, Marty decided to take out Sergei with one swift move. Sergei had been consuming the free drinks in quantity when he secured a full house jack high. In a drunken haze, he decided that this was his big break to rebuild his pot.

Sergei pushed the rest of his chips into the table's center and said in a heavy Russian accent. "I have a full house, Jacks high." A big smile came over his face, from his poker hand, and from the enormous amount of vodka he had consumed.

"Not so fast, Sergei," replied Marty. Marty slowly laid down his hand. He revealed, "Full house, king high."

Everyone at the table froze and looked over at Tyron. Tyron slightly moved his head, assuring that the play was fair and maybe it was time for Sergei to step out of the game.

Sergei didn't seem to get the message. He stood up and angrily walked out of the room with his bodyguards close in tow.

Tyron stood up and said, "That is going to cost me. It's a good time for a break, but let's return in two hours." He then walked out of the room to catch up with Sergei.

Marty and the other players all stood up and stretched out their backs. Tyron's number one enforcer commented, "A long play is always a bitch; feel me?"

Sid just nodded his head. He then walked over to the food table and grabbed a chicken salad sandwich with a coke. One of the rules he learned from his father was never to get intoxicated during a game. Marty followed close behind. Sid could tell that he had something on his mind.

Marty picked up a chicken salad sandwich with a glass of milk. Marty asked, "Sid, where did you learn to play?"

"Boy Scouts," declared Sid.

"Your troop leader must have been a great teacher because you are one of the smoothest players I have ever met," replied Marty.

"Just lucky, I guess," countered Sid.

"Maybe, but most don't see a player like you coming until it's too late. I played people like you but only in the south, smooth," stated Marty.

Sid wanted to get the subject off him and onto Marty. He was particularly interested in Marty and how he would help him and Vincent with an opportunity. "So, are you a professional poker player?" inquired Sid.

"Poker is more of a side hustle; I have my hands in a couple of different endeavors," replied Marty.

Sid could hear a slight New Orleans accent that Marty had tried hard to disguise, but he could not fake it with Sid. His father had many migrant farmers from Louisiana work on his farm, especially in the tobacco barns. Also, Sid's mother grew up in Louisiana, and he spent summers visiting her relatives.

Sid had a keen sense when someone was trying to cover their tracks. He asked straight, "Marty, you from New Orleans?"

"You are good. I've tried to overcome my roots. A southern accent doesn't get much respect here in the north. If the south is still fighting the civil war, so are the Yankees. I guess one southerner can spot another?" stated Marty.

"You want to ask me something?" asked Sid.

"Straight to the point, I like that. Sid, I have one important aptitude, which is spotting talent. I might have a position in my organization for a fellow like you and maybe your friend," retorted Marty.

"What would be your organization, and how would we fit in?" countered Sid.

"Let's say you and your friend would have a front-row seat to the best new show on earth." regaled Marty.

"What show would that be?" asked Sid.

"Where the level of human greed flows like a river," exclaimed Marty.

"That could mean a lot of things," responded Sid.

Marty picked up another sandwich and a coke, and as he headed towards the door, he said, "Let's talk again before the end of the play."

Vincent walked over to Sid. He asked, "What was all that about?"

"Our ride out of here might be playing us, but I'm not sure yet. I guess at this point. We can only trust that my vision was right about this guy," replied Sid.

"You said you have never had such a strong vision," recalled Vincent.

"Yeh, you're right. I have no choice but to trust. Look, Tyron handed me a key to a room in the hotel; I should rest before the next play," said Sid.

"I'm not tired; I'm going down to the bar to see which way the wind blows," said Vincent.

"Call me before the next play just in case I fall asleep. The room number's 333," responded Sid.

"Sure thing," retorted Vincent.

Vincent walked down to the ground floor, following the signs to the lounge. When he entered the bar, both of Tyron's men were at the bar talking with another black man that Vincent didn't recognize. There were two other people at a table in a dark corner; They looked like they were arguing.

The room was a makeshift bar, previously a bedroom in the hotel. Vincent considered the bar not legal; he bet that most of what went on in the hotel was criminal.

He sat down at the far end of the bar and ordered. "Whiskey on the rocks."

Tyron's henchman, Marquis, turned around. He said, "That's a cracker drink."

"Hell, I'm a cracker," replied Vincent.

Marquis laughed. He asked, "Where's your friend?"

"He's in the room resting before he kicks ass," exclaimed Vincent.

Marquis laughed again. He said, "Well, he better have an out if he wins the pot. Tyron doesn't do well losing to a bottom feeder hustler from Rikers."

"I guess you did your homework?" asked Vincent.

"You don't stay alive in this business long if you don't know your opponent. Do you think Tyron would just let any brother in the game? Jamal informed us of his visit to you before the game. There is not much in Newburgh that we don't know about, feel me?" Marquis laughed again and then turned to the other men at the bar.

Vincent had another drink and walked as fast as he could out of the bar to inform Sid of what he had just learned. He banged on the door to room 333, and Sid opened the door with a haze in his eyes.

"What?" asked Sid.

"You fell asleep. The game is on in fifteen, and you better wake up because something else is going on," exclaimed Vincent.

"What's going on?" asked Sid.

"I was at the bar, and Marquis, one of Tyron's gang bangers, slipped some knowledge my way. I think he felt confident that I was a stupid cracker and would not make the connection," exclaimed Vincent.

"What connection?" asked Sid.

"Something went down with Jamal before we arrived. Tyron knows about our little visit with Jamal, but I don't know what he knows. Marquis didn't say that Jamal sold us out or that Tyron knows that you're here on behalf of Diego," replied Vincent.

"Yeh, I figured that Tyron was wise to the whole thing. A man can discern much about another man during a poker game," countered Sid.

"Hell, when were you going to let me in on the info?" asked Vincent.

"Need to know," replied Sid.

"Hell, need to know?" questioned Vincent.

"Look, a lot goes down during a poker game. I must focus on slight differences. I knew Tyron knew something about me from how he bluffs. Marquis and Derek are in the game only to support Tyron. They are his wingmen; it's Tyron and Tyron alone that Diego must do business with, so it's Tyron that I need to understand.

"Marty and I will dump Tyron's men in the next play, and then there will just be five left," said Sid.

"You and Marty talked about the game?" asked Vincent.

"No, but we have an understanding. I feel Marty wants me in the game for as long as possible. He is observing me for a position in his grift; he must know if I can take the heat," countered Sid.

"How do you know all this from playing poker?" inquired Vincent.

"I don't know, I could always read people, and it worked the way I read it most times. There are two important people in this game: Tyron, so we can fulfill our Diego problem. Marty, so we can make it out of here in one piece. We better get back to the game," exclaimed Sid.

The other players were already at the table when Sid and Vincent entered the room. Sergei and his bodyguards were noticeably absent. Tyron looked at the two with a furrowed brow. He said, "When I say two hours, I mean no more than two hours, or you will be out, feel me?"

Sid and Vincent just nodded their heads.

The game went long into the night. At 3:30 in the morning, Marquis, Derek, and the player from Atlantic City were tapped out of the game, leaving Tyron, Marty, Tyron's brother, and Sid.

Sid knew this was the fourth quarter, but he had to stay in the game long enough to pressure Tyron into relaxing so he could have a strong feel for his tell.

Sid didn't care about the money because he knew it would go to Diego if he did win. He and Vincent had two hundred and twenty dollars between them; Sid knew it wouldn't be enough to get out of town fast.

Sid realized it might be in his and Vincent's best interest to fix the game for Marty. This move would indicate that Sid was on board with whatever grift Marty was playing.

This realization gave Sid new motivation. Sid's heart told him that he was on the right path. Whenever he made the right decision, he could always trust his heart. ❧

⍥

Chapter Six

There was little conversation as the gold-colored Cadillac convertible containing Marty, Sid, and Vincent moved gracefully through Troy, New York, driving east on highway seven. The poker game ended a few hours ago, with Marty taking the pot. After fourteen hours of play, it came down to Marty, Sid, and Tyron, and Marty won on a straight flush queen high.

"We good with Diego?" asked Vincent.

"We're good. I told Diego's thugs what he needed to know before the meeting. Or at least enough to help in his negotiations. I left a few things out for respect for Tyron," declared Sid.

"Why do you respect that asshole?" asked Vincent.

"He let us go without killing us. I suspected that Diego had asked Tyron for a favor. Diego wanted the knowledge, but after he got it, we became a liability, which was easily taken care of by our demise. Also, I didn't win the pot. Gangsters take losses hard," asserted Sid.

"How did you find this out? asked Vincent.

"It made sense; it was what I would have done if I was Diego," stated Sid.

Marty looked over at Sid, sitting in the passenger seat. He asked, "When did you decide to move the game in my direction?"

"After our first discussion. I figured that the best play was to let you win. If I won, I would have lost the money to Diego, Tyron would be pissed at me, and I don't carry the same weight with him that you do. I was supposed to stay in the game, and as your wingman, I knew you would make that happen. You needed a buffer between you and Tryon," recalled Sid.

"You're a strategic thinker. That can come in handy," countered Marty.

"I've had to learn to survive. Sometimes the answer isn't always the straightest path," retorted Sid.

"Look, I will offer you and Vincent twenty percent of the pot. How you want to divide it is up to you, but I know that I owe you, and I like to clear my debt," exclaimed Marty.

"That's forty-thousand," responded Vincent.

"We are still not sold on your opportunity. We need to know more about it before joining forces, but I appreciate the gesture," replied Sid.

"How do you have so much weight with Tyron?" inquired Vincent.

Marty looked at Vincent in the back seat through the rearview mirror and hesitated. He calculated how much he wanted to divulge because he hadn't closed the deal with his would be partners.

Marty recalled, "We grew up together in New Orleans. Tyron tries to pull off a gangster from Los Angeles, but his roots are deep in Louisiana."

"Hell, I guess you never know about a guy," interjected Vincent.

"Vincent, what part do you play in this partnership?" queried Marty.

"Comic relief," retorted Vincent.

Marty again looked at Vincent in the back seat through the rearview mirror with a furrowed brow.

Vincent laid back and smoothed his long blond hair behind his ears. He continued, "I guess Sid and I balance each other out. We have each other's back, and that is how we made it through Rikers. You could say that Sid is the brains, and I am the blunt instrument."

"Are you hungry? I know a great diner in Hoosick," interjected Marty. Without a response, Marty abruptly turned off the highway into the parking lot of the Country View Diner.

All three sat down at a booth near the entrance. An old waitress with too much hair spray and perfume took their orders. Even though it was early afternoon, they all ordered a large breakfast with bottomless cups of coffee.

"So, what are you selling, Marty?" asked Vincent.

Marty replied, "I'm selling the new religion. I'm selling hope, relevance, and a way out of banality."

"You sound like one of those tent preachers we had come around from time to time," replied Vincent.

"You're quick. My father was a Christian holiness minister; I spent summers during my youth traveling the country, spreading the good word, and raking in the bucks," admitted Marty.

"So, what is the new religion?" asked Sid.

"Start-ups, venture capitalism, IPO, entrepreneurship—this is the language of the new religion. As I said before, the new religion fuels the same hope the old one embraced. Setting up marks looks the same as my tent revival days," professed Marty.

"How does this new religion work, and how do we fit in?" interjected Sid.

The waitress showed up with all the breakfast dishes on her arm; she was holding three coffee cups and a large pitcher. She placed everything down and then, without a word, moved on to her other tables.

Marty looked around to make sure no one was listening. He continued, "What does the average person in this great country want? I'll tell you. They want respect, and they want to be rich. Did you ever wonder why ordinary working-class people keep voting for the same scumbags? The same lying sack of shit politicians who only look out for the wealthiest?

"I'll tell you that little secret too. The poor keep supporting the rich because every mother's son feels entitled and thinks they will be loaded someday. They don't want to spoil a good thing.

"The system is rigged against the same suckers that buy into the system. The companies and powerful families that run this country knew long ago that the best way to get the uneducated and unaware on board was to speak their language. To support the belief that someone else is keeping them from their God-given right to wealth and prosperity.

"Christian ministers have known this fact for a long time. You don't need to give them riches, but you need to give them hope that someday they will be wealthy and respected.

"How do you think the southern plantation owners got poor white trash to fight for them in the civil war? They sold them on the illusion that the Yankees were trying to take away their way of life. Lower-income whites still live without adequate education and social services and still believe in the rebel bullshit sold to them.

"If the south won the civil war, none of those lower-educated poor white men would have the vote. Only wealthy plantation owners would run the place, as they still do. Sid and I grew up in that world—we know the score."

"This is a big sales job. So, how does all this talk of wealth and respect translate into start-ups?" inquired Sid.

Marty continued," Every so often, a new opportunity takes off, and everyone wants to get a piece of the treasure. The gold rush in 1849, the industrial revolution, all the way up to the dot-com bubble in the nineteen-nineties.

"The truth is that ultimately like the gold rush, with start-ups, the company store, which in this case are venture capitalists, end up making a killing, and most other investors walk away broke.

"This is the basics of how the grift works. I've picked out three small towns across the country on hard times. This choice isn't difficult because many small towns are struggling. The towns must have fewer than 20,000 residents but no less than 10,000.

"Over the last few years, I have been visiting each city. I get involved with their church and community organizations. I throw a little money around. It doesn't take long for people to trust me, and when a town is ready, I take the con to the next level.

"I purchase one of their landmark buildings, a cornerstone of their little dwindling downtown. Facilities in these diminished towns go for a song. They almost give you the structure hoping that something will come of it, or at least you pay the property taxes.

"Many times, the town and state help fund the renovation. The renovation gives the illusion that city power brokers are finally helping their community. The city economic development director has often been sitting on their asses with a large salary, not knowing what to do. I can't count all the economic development directors hired because of family connections. I mean no experience in business, just pure nepotism."

"So, how do we fit into this grift?" questioned Vincent.

Marty continued, "I renovate the building and created a coworking space, an entrepreneurship center. I fit it with a coffee shop, maybe an art space. In a small city, word gets out fast, and they have been hoping for anything that may change the city's fortunes.

"If the town is dying, where does the money come from?" asked Vincent.

Marty continued, "There is always money in any town. When the economy collapsed a few years ago, legal gambling soared to almost five hundred billion. It wasn't high rollers losing that dough; it was mom and pops. It was the average struggling sap sitting day after day at a casino handing over their Social Security checks, with the ever-present hope that they would walk out with a new life on a turn of luck. Even if they do get a little ahead, they feed the machine.

"I learned from my years on the road with my father's tent revival that the hopeful can always scrape together the cash to feed the machine.

"I have been playing the wealthy investor, willing to take a chance on a community. The city power brokers are starting to see me as the town's savior, which will turn their luck around. And they are ripe for the taking. After my initial investment, they worked hard to secure more funding from the good citizens of the city and the state coffers.

"I need a couple of young lions like you two to run this operation. You're good-looking young fellows, strategic thinkers, and cool black guys are a beacon for want-to-be entrepreneurs."

Sid interjected, "We don't know anything about the world of start-ups."

Marty took a long sip of his coffee. He continued, "It doesn't matter; they don't either. You grew up in a deacon's home, and this whole grift is what you grew up with back in Alabama. We are not selling technical information, we are selling hope, and hope pays big dividends.

"The key to this whole thing is to find just one local with a half-good idea. It doesn't need to be an idea that will take off, but it must be good enough for the community to buy in. As soon as the community buys in, it will start to pay off."

"So, what is the payoff?" asked Sid.

Marty resumed, "My initial investment is about four hundred thousand, and the final payout should be around ten million. Ten percent will be divided between you, five hundred thousand each."

"You've done this before?" asked Vincent.

"I've done different variations of the same grift. The last one was a revitalized oil well in Georgia. That one was a low-cost con because all I had to do was buy the dead oil well, load the line with oil, and fly investors down in a private jet. The payout was six million, but I had two equal partners.

"The scam before that was in real estate. Investors thought they bought foreclosed houses and secured twelve percent interest on rentals. All I needed for that scam was an office and phony paperwork, but the final payoff was around four million. I had the same two partners, so each received an equal share."

"Where are your partners now?" questioned Sid.

"They're out. This one is all me, and that's why you get ten percent instead of an equal share. I have been watching and saving for this con for years. If this pays off bigger than I think, I might retire," asserted Marty.

"Don't you worry about taking money from poor people?" asked Vincent.

"As I said, those same suckers are laying down big bucks at the casinos, and I rather take their money than give it to the gaming world. I don't think the casino president is losing any sleep taking money from grandmothers," professed Marty.

"Have you ever had a scam go bad, and the marks come after you?" questioned Sid.

"Once, a long time ago. My father stayed too long in one town because he got involved with the mayor's wife; she was a true believer and good-looking. The most crucial factor is not to take too long and leave before anyone knows they were scammed.

"Each scam will finally collapse, sooner or later. We must get new cash flow to build it to a larger payout. We will be long gone when everything goes south. Most investors will see it as a lousy venture, not a con.

"Once someone buys into the scam, it is almost impossible to convince them that they were scammed. People want to believe; they will stand by their decision even if there is a mountain of evidence."

The old waitress stopped by the table and asked if there was anything else. The three could tell that they had camped at the table too long. The waitress wanted them to leave so she could turn the table and make more tips.

Marty looked at Sid and Vincent and asked, "I'm ready to move on, but how about you two?" Sid and Vincent knew the question had more to it than just leaving the diner—Marty wanted to see if they were in or out. Sid knew that Marty made decisions fast and was quick on his feet, and he expected his business partners to make decisions just as promptly.

"Hell, in for a penny in for a pound," replied Vincent.

"Yes, I can see it now—you're right. There was a pattern to my father's deceit. He would just lay the foundation, and people who wanted a piece of the treasure would build the structure. I remember people trying to convince my father to take their money because they wanted in on the deal so badly. He would sit back and wait," recalled Sid.

The three got up from the table, and Marty left a hefty one hundred dollar tip. He could see the waitress's reaction as they walked outside the window towards his car.

"That was a big tip," asserted Vincent.

Marty replied, "We camped for two hours, plus that waitress will not forget me. I like this diner and will most likely stop here again. If she isn't working, the story of me laying down a hundred-dollar tip will make the rounds among the other servers.

"Think about human nature. I just won two hundred large playing poker; giving that woman one hundred dollars made almost the same impact on me winning the game. She won't forget me anytime soon, and the next time I'm here, she will treat me like a king.

"I have found during my travels that going a little beyond the ordinary makes a big impression on the average person. That one hundred dollar bill will pay dividends for years to come."

"So, where's our destination?" asked Sid.

Marty replied, "You need to relax and trust. You seem to want to know the whole picture."

"As I said earlier, I had to learn to survive," asserted Sid.

"Rutland is our destination. A town nestled near the green mountains of Vermont, Rutland is perfect for the grift. It has a lot of advantages; it's far from a large city but close enough to access, let's say, talented grifters. It's near New York highway eighty-seven, which runs north to Canada and south to New York." recounted Marty.

"So, what's next?" asked Vincent.

"We find a couple of hotel rooms, where we will divvy up the poker winnings, and then you go shopping. Unfortunately, you will have to spend money on clothes and a lifestyle befitting a couple of high roller entrepreneurs," Marty exclaimed.

"Is that why you are giving us the money?" asked Sid.

"No, I owe you the money. You could take the money, and we go our separate ways. I expect my partners to carry some of their weight. Remember, you both get a big payday and lessons learned at the end of this play.

"Most of the expense will be on my coattails. We could become equal partners in the next one if this works out," professed Marty.

"I guess it was fate that we met," interjected Sid.

"Yes, I knew this would happen the first time I saw you two. I have sought the right partners since I zeroed in on Rutland, and I would have had another long search if you both decided to move on. I guess I walked away with more than just money from the poker game. I do appreciate and recognize my good fortune," stated Marty.

"Sid and I talked about the next big con. I guess you brought it to us on a silver platter," replied Vincent.

Marty looked through his rearview mirror at Vincent with a smile. He said, "You tired? I know a wonderful hotel with a full breakfast in the morning." Marty sped off toward the nearest hotel in Saratoga, New York, without waiting for a response.

Sid considered that working with Marty was going to be a trip. Marty seems to have spent most of his life on the road and knows the route well. ❧

CR

Chapter Seven

The last three weeks in Saratoga had been the most luxurious of Sid and Vincent's young lives. They stayed at the best hotel and ate at the fanciest restaurants; Marty seemed to know everyone wealthy or well-connected in the city.

Sid considered that Marty was showing them what life could be with a substantial amount of money—maybe to motivate them a little more along the path to the grift in Rutland.

The one caveat was that Sid and Vincent had to go to start-up school each morning. Marty knew a tech guru in Saratoga that gave Sid and Vincent a three-week crash course on the world of start-ups.

Marty introduced Steve Kenny as a former true believer. Steve had been an anarchist during the summer of love in the late sixties. He moved from one commune to another, looking for the socialist dream but became disillusioned with the cause.

Many of the hippies of the era ended up in technology or politics. The revolutionaries decided running for office or to make a lot of money was the ultimate screw you to the social elite—especially after the ass-kicking at the 1968 Democratic National Convention in Chicago.

Steve was one of the original innovators of digital gaming. His inventions changed the way young people viewed the world. In the eighties, he became disillusioned again and cashed out to become a venture capitalist.

He tried to find start-ups attempting to change the world for good, but it became more about money than humankind as the years passed. Steve sold his company, moved back home to Saratoga, and started a small entrepreneur think tank.

Sid and Vincent wondered why Steve, a man with a conscience, would work with Marty. They considered that maybe there was more to Marty than met the eye.

Sid split the forty-thousand poker winnings with Vincent and told Vincent they were partners and would get equal shares of any treasure.

Sid and Vincent went shopping downtown Saratoga for clothes and other essentials like the coolest watches, iPhones, and Apple laptops. They both chipped in on a used white Telsa Model Three in excellent condition, thanks to Steve's connections.

Steve let Sid and Vincent off on their last day in Saratoga before moving to Rutland. There was a sense of freedom that they both had never felt. They were in a town they didn't owe anything to, with cash in their pockets.

They roamed the shops, and with their new clothes, haircuts, and manicures, everyone assumed they were wealthy and powerful. They looked like Elon Musk knockoffs. People would automatically move out of their way without knowing why, and the store attendants would climb over each other to serve them.

Marty taught Sid and Vincent to use a critical tool to reveal little; let others make their judgments based on outward appearances. Marty told them that most people create a dialogue in their heads about the person they are chatting with, especially when the person doesn't fill in any information.

The plan was to meet Marty at the Southside Steakhouse in Rutland. Marty left a week earlier to set up Sid and Vincent's arrival in town. He wanted to finish some last-minute business with the coworking space before they opened for business.

The drive to Rutland took Sid and Vincent through backroads in New York State. They drove up U.S. Route Four through tiny towns situated along the shore of Lake George—villages with names that they had never heard of but not unlike where they were both born and raised.

Vincent sat back in his seat while Sid drove. He attempted to smooth his long blond hair behind his ears, but he felt the braided ponytail. Vincent said, "Hell, it will be hard to get used to this new haircut, or doo, as the pretty stylist called it."

Sid looked over and stroked the bristles of his newly grown beard. Sid replied, 'Yes, this beard will take time, but I guess it is all part of the hipster start-up uniform."

Vincent replied, "It's hard to believe these little towns are in the same state New York City dominates. Growing up in Wyoming, I thought the whole east coast was like New York City."

Sid replied, "Yeh, I remember watching French Connection and Fort Apache the Bronx. They don't make big movies about tiny towns that make no difference."

Vincent looked at Sid, gauging where his following comment might land. Vincent inquired, "You know that we don't have to do this; we can move on to something else. We have a car, toys, and more cash than I have ever had in my pocket. We could go out west, to The Golden State."

Sid looked at Vincent with apprehension. He countered, "Remember when you thought New York City had sidewalks made of gold? How much gold do you think is in California?"

"Hell, I guess you are right. I'm a little nervous and don't trust Marty," confessed Vincent.

Sid looked over at Vincent and laughed.

Vincent had not seen Sid laugh much during their tenure, making him more anxious. Vincent asked, "Why are you laughing?"

Sid stopped laughing and exclaimed, "You don't trust Marty? Of course, you don't trust him. He is a grifter, not just a con man but a good one. We satisfy a need he has; that is all there is to it. He would leave us out in the cold in a second if it meant saving his hide."

"Then why are we going along with his grift if he could hang us out to dry?" queried Vincent.

Sid looked over at Vincent, judging if he could disclose information that may create more anxiety.

Vincent had been with Sid long enough to know when something was on his mind. Vincent questioned, "What's on your mind, buddy?"

Sid continued, "I had another vision last night. The vision revealed that Marty was not the end of our journey; he was a steppingstone to something more important. Marty will fade in this play, and our path will take us in another direction."

Vincent looked at Sid with a puzzled look. He inquired, "How do these visions come to you, and why do you trust them?"

Sid professed, "The visions come to me in experiential memory; it is akin to looking back on something that has already happened."

Vincent asked, "What is experiential memory?"

Sid thought about the question, "There is experiential memory, and there is recollection. Recollection is when you recall a phone number or a pin code. Experiential memory is when you remember an event as if you are there again. You are experiencing the moment for a brief second and have all the feelings pushed up from your subconscious.

"It is kind of like what Steve explained to us about computers. There is memory on the computer that is deep in the hard drive, and there is random access memory. Deleting the memory deep in the computer takes a lot, but random access memory deletes quickly.

"I trust my visions because I have no other choice. For a long time, I denied my premonitions and made many mistakes. No matter what direction I started, I always ended up in the same place my visions determined.

"It is like being in a river where the current becomes stronger and stronger. I can hold on to a rock in the stream for only so long until I have faith and let go. I decided long ago to let go and trust where the river would take me instead of fighting.

"We could turn around right now and drive to Los Angeles. I guarantee we would end up exactly where we are now after failure and pain."

Vincent considered what Sid said with a wrinkled brow. He asserted, "I often hear your father the deacon's influence in how you speak. Sometimes you talk like a pastor we had back home. My guess is you didn't get your awareness from your father?"

Sid replied, "No, I got my intuitive nature from my mother. She grew up in a small parish near a swamp in Louisiana. My mother was smart enough to make it to Howard University but kept much of the superstition from the bayou. She was creole, her father was French, and her mother was Haitian.

"I remember my Haitian grandmother vaguely, but I never met my French grandfather. My father's parents worked with us on the farm until I left for New York. They both died around the same time. I guess it's common for one spouse to die, then the other, when they are as close as my grandparents were with each other."

Vincent inquired, "I heard black people in Louisiana practiced voodoo. Is your mother a voodoo princess or something?"

Sid looked over at Vincent with a smile. He refuted, "You watch too many movies. Maybe her kin practiced some voodoo, but she was just a spiritual person.

"She saw the world through a different lens than my father. My father, as you know, wasn't religious; He was in it for the power and money. My mother was a child of the earth.

"My mother taught me some valuable lessons. The most precious was the ability not to feel poor because it costs nothing to learn, be patient, and deny extravagance. These skills have been tested many times during my life, and they have always proved invaluable."

Vincent tried again to smooth his long blond hair over his ears but stopped by his now hipster ponytail. He asked, "Since you have visions, can't you have premonitions about who will win the World Series or what the winning lottery number will be?"

Sid looked over at Vincent with a shrug. He acknowledged, "It doesn't work that way. My intuitions are much more valuable than any material possessions will provide in the long run.

"If you could have everything you ever wanted, what would your life look like?"

Vincent sat back in his chair. He recalled, "Well, if you are talking about everything I wanted in my past, I would be living in Wyoming, married to Lizzy, my high school sweetheart, which would be a living hell.

"She ended up marrying the high school football star and having two children by the time she was twenty. They both live in a crappy trailer on the edge of town, and I hear he likes to take his lack of success out on Lizzy, especially after he gets drunk."

Sid continued, "When God wants to punish us, he gives us what we ask for."

Vincent laughed and replied, "Amen, I will try to trust."

Sid looked at Vincent from the corner of his eye for a long time, and then he continued. "There is more to my awareness than I have told you—I rarely tell anyone what I am about to tell you."

Vincent sat back in his chair and said, "I can take it."

Sid continued, "When I was five years old, I drowned in a lake during summer vacation from school."

"You mean you almost drowned, don't you?" interjected Vincent.

Sid continued, "No, I drowned. I was playing on the water's edge in a small lagoon. I wandered too far from shore and stepped over a ledge into a deep part of the lagoon. I didn't know how to swim, so I started sinking to the lagoon's bottom.

"I knew I was drowning; I began to convulse in the water and grasp for the surface. After a short period, I gave up and just sat on the bottom of the lagoon.

"As my lifeless body sat on the bottom, I felt scared and sad that I would not see my family again. My life didn't pass before my eyes, but what passed through my heart was a feeling of loss, the loss of the people I loved the most.

"In an instant, a warm, loving light descended on me. The light was so pure that I felt comforted by its presence. I started to rise towards the light, and then a voice spoke. With perfect clarity, I heard a voice tell me, 'Sid, everything will be fine. Nothing matters anymore.' I knew at that moment that nothing mattered.

"The problems and worries of the world had faded. I felt at peace; peace was so pure that I felt one with my soul.

"I felt a vibration in the light that communicated with me on an infinite level. The communication was beyond words but with absolute being.

"My spirit rose above the surface of the lake. I looked back on the world and saw a thin vale of black and white. The world wasn't a multi-colored place anymore but an illusion. I saw the world as an experience in an infinite moment that never happened.

"I looked down at the lake I had drowned in and saw people running towards where I had been. I couldn't identify specific people, but I understood that my drowning was causing the commotion.

"The next thing I remember was looking up as people looked down at me. At this moment, I knew that I was back in the world.

"My mother had waded out in the lagoon and miraculously pulled me ashore. As my mother held me in her arms and tried to comfort me, darkness overcame me. This brief experience would drive the rest of my life."

Vincent sat back and looked at Sid for a long time, not knowing what to say. He replied, "Sid, it seems you have some gifts beyond my understanding. I don't comprehend why someone so smart and gifted would lead a life of a grifter."

Sid continued, "When I died in that lake, I was at peace. I went through many dark times when I returned to this world. I have had daemons nipping at my heels, and I've tried hard to have an everyday life.

"Every time I got hired at a job, I would be happy at first, but soon despair would set in that I could not overcome—I would leave without knowing my next step.

"You see, Vincent, this gift can also be a curse. I have no choice but to go along with what I am supposed to do because the emptiness will come back in force if I don't. I need to trust my heart, even if my heart is taking me down a blind path."

Vincent asked, "How do you know the difference between what your heart is telling you and your desire?"

Sid smiled and answered, "That's easy. When I follow my heart, I have peace once again. When I follow my desire, all hell breaks loose."

Vincent looked out the window for a long. He replied, "I've been a hell-raiser for a long time; maybe I need to hear what my heart is saying."

Sid responded, "Yeh, just ask yourself, do I trust my ego or heart?"

Vincent shook his head and replied, "I guess my heart, but my ego right now is asking how we will deal with Marty."

Sid continued, "When it comes to Marty, we must always be a few steps ahead. We need to know what he may or may not do for us. We need to be patient enough to trust that everything will work out and be careful not to buy into the extravagance of having so much money.

"Marty will have power over us if we get too comfortable with an indulgent lifestyle. Marty has often used this simple technique with his marks, and we don't want to become one of his chumps."

Vincent replied, "I'm glad I met you, Sid. You are becoming the best friend I have ever had. I know you are looking out for us; that is a real treasure in this world."

Sid drove over the Vermont state line on U.S. Route Four. Sid and Vincent felt something as they moved into Vermont. They felt lighter energy, the sky seemed bluer, the land seemed greener, and the road ahead seemed to have more opportunity.

On the way to Rutland, they passed through beautiful farmland with green mountains in the background. Behind them, in the far distance, they could see the Adirondack Mountains lining the edge of upstate New York.

Sid asserted, "This is some beautiful land. My grandfather would see this as a farmer's paradise, even though I've heard that Vermont can have some harsh winters."

Vincent countered, "I don't know about farmland, but this would be perfect for grazing cattle. The funny thing is that we used to call farmers sodbusters back home; farming interfered with the cattle business. I never thought a sodbuster would be my best friend."

Sid replied, "Former sodbuster. I'm not thinking about farming; I'm just voicing an observation."

In the distance, the two started to see buildings and a small town formed on the horizon. They came to the intersection of U.S. Route Four and Vermont State Route Seven. Their new GPS informed them they were only a few miles from their destination. Sid knew this was his last chance to turn around before the next part of his path started.

Sid and Vincent arrived at the Southside Steakhouse early in the evening. They parked next to Marty's Cadillac. They both speculated how long he had been waiting. They both knew Marty didn't waste time, and he most likely spent the afternoon schmoozing people he knew and laying the groundwork for the grift.

Sid turned and looked at Vincent with purpose in his eyes. He asked, "This is it. If we walk into that restaurant, we must see this thing through. There is no going back after our first appearance. Are you ready to move forward?"

Vincent answered, "Hell, in for a penny in for a pound." ❧

☙

Chapter Eight

It was 2:33 in the morning, and Sid was wide awake in his new loft apartment. He could still taste the filet mignon and single malt scotch on his breath. He, Vincent, and Marty spent the evening with the Rutland Mayor, the Economic Development Director, and the Chamber of Commerce Executive Director.

Good to Marty's word, Rutland's power brokers didn't once ask anything about Sid or Vincent. They talked late into the evening about their hopes and dreams for Rutland and how impressed they all were with the coworking start-up space. They spoke at length about Rutland's history and the building Marty acquired.

Sid felt they were trying to sell him and Vincent on their city's potential and opportunities. Sid judged that Marty did a fantastic sales job with the higher echelon of Rutland.

Sid got slightly drunk, not only on the expensive scotch and many glasses of excellent red wine but on the adoration he and Vincent were already receiving during their first night in town.

Sid knew he should not get too drunk, but because he and Vincent only had to keep their mouths shut, he felt it didn't matter—Marty's dinner guests did all the talking.

☙

Sid sat in his bed and looked around the large loft he would call home. Sid's apartment and five other large loft apartments were at the top two stories of Marty's renovated building in downtown Rutland.

The building, summarized by the mayor in detail, was a marque building constructed in 1825 during what was known as the quiet years in Rutland after the revolutionary war. The building was owned by a merchant who did business with the Rutland marble quarries.

Over the years, the building changed from a hotel and pub in the late eighteen hundreds to a general store in the early nineteen-thirties. Rutland started to fall on hard times during the nineteen-eighties, and the building was left empty until Marty found purpose in the structure.

The renovation took place over the last three years. Marty's silver tongue got the town and state financially vested in the plan to renovate the building as a start-up center. They poured three million into the project.

Sid got out of bed, put on his slippers, and walked around his living space. He examined his loft with an alcohol haze clouding his mind.

The loft was large, with three rooms separated by exposed brick walls. The floors were beautiful wide boards made of wood Sid didn't recognize. The room had at least ten-foot ceilings that old tin tiles covered.

The bedroom had a queen-size bed with two armoires with mirrors on the doors. There was no carpet or rug on the wood floors, and a night table with a single lamp stood next to the bed. Sid deemed that buying rugs would be one of his first purchases. He opened one of the armoires to find extra sheets, blankets, and pillows.

The living room was the most significant space in the apartment. Artfully arranged couches and chairs rested in the middle of the room with a modern glass coffee table. To the side was a beautiful old roll-top desk. The desk was useless in the computer age but pleasant to look at, nonetheless.

Sid could envision parties and gatherings in his loft. He hadn't seen his office in the coworking space, so he wasn't sure if he would have to work out of his apartment.

The bathroom had shiny new white appliances and plumbing. The kitchen was open and attached to the end of the living room. There was a chrome refrigerator, gas stove, and microwave. Sid looked through the cupboards to find utensils, dishes, and nothing else. Sid's kitchen was designed for a busy entrepreneur who eats out.

The loft seemed beautifully renovated, but as Sid walked around the apartment, he saw signs that his living space was a façade. He and his father did a considerable amount of renovation work back in

Alabama, and he could spot overlooked detail. Sid could see that the contractor painted over nails and screws. Whoever renovated this space did it in a hurry.

Sid walked to the floor-to-ceiling windows that overlooked downtown Rutland. The town had many beautiful old buildings from the city's glory days. He could feel a low energy that permeated the city. This town had been down on its luck for a long time and needed something or someone to bring it back into the light.

Sid had a moment of guilt about the grift he, Vincent, and Marty were planning to bring down on the city. Sid felt like a vulture about to pick his prey clean.

Sid had lived in towns on hard luck and always pondered what makes a city rich and full of opportunity and what makes a town fall short. There seemed to be no rhyme or reason for the destiny of any place.

Sid thought he heard a knock on his door, but he didn't know if it was a knock or if he imagined one. Sid heard the knock again, but this time it was louder. He checked his watch and saw that it was 3:33 a.m.

He walked over to the door without hesitation opening it wide. Standing in the doorway was a young woman, maybe in her mid-twenties. She had red hair and bright blue eyes. She was wearing SpongeBob SquarePants pajama bottoms and a blue hoodie with RISD written across the front. She wore fluffy bunny slippers on her feet.

Sid looked at her for a long time. He was wondering if she was an hallucination. He was still feeling the effects of the alcohol and didn't trust his mind.

The young woman stood in the doorway for a moment, looking Sid up and down. She said, "I'm sorry, I heard you walking around the loft for the last hour. I am your next-door neighbor."

Sid came out of his stupor. He asked, "Sorry, did I wake you?"

The young woman continued, "No, I was awake. Maybe we could have coffee?"

Sid replied, "Yes, that would be nice, but I just moved in, and I haven't had a chance to shop for food, supplies, or coffee."

The young woman continued, "Yeh, I figured. I have coffee in my apartment, but I don't usually let a strange man, whose name I don't know, into my apartment early in the morning."

Sid smiled and replied, "I'm Sid, Sid Arthur."

The young woman smirked, "I'm Joleen Ward. Now that we are

best buddies, you want a cup of good coffee?"

The two walked across the hallway into Joleen's loft. Sid looked around and noticed that her apartment had the same layout as his, but she had scattered boxes, furniture, clothes, and equipment. Art was on the walls, and large oriental carpets covered the wide plank wooded floors. The loft displayed a women's touch, and it was comfortable. The apartment appeared lived in even though she looked to be still unpacking.

Sid asked, "How long have you lived here?"

Joleen walked into the kitchen and poured water into an electric glass kettle. Beautiful blue lights came on around the base when she pushed a button. She replied, "I've been here for around a month. Marty had the contractor finish the six loft apartments before finishing the coworking space.

Sid asked, "So, why are you up so late?"

Joleen replied, "I haven't been able to sleep well yet in this building. I feel a presence watching me. Do you believe in ghosts?"

Sid shrugged his shoulders. He asked, "Do you work for Marty?"

Joleen furrowed her brow and replied, "I thought you would have already known who Marty hired. Marty hired me to run the marketing and design department to promote the coworking space."

The water in the kettle started to boil, and then the device turned itself off. Joleen ground some coffee beans and poured them into a beautiful French glass press with water. The two sat at a small kitchen table near one of the massive windows overlooking the building's rear alley.

Sid commented, "This is good coffee; I rarely have time to drink coffee from a French press."

Joleen replied, "Yeh, it's a local coffee company named Gallagher Close Farm Coffee Roasters out of southern Vermont."

Sid continued, "I take it from your hoodie that you went to Rhode Island School of Design. Is that where Marty found you?"

Joleen continued, "No, RISD was where I went to school. I was working in New York at WeWork when a friend told me about the job in Rutland. I was getting tired of New York, and the company CEO was starting to believe his press.

"I was hired when WeWork had only thirty employees. It was almost a cult, and we all felt we would change the world. It was exciting to get such a great job right out of college, but what the CEO preyed on was young idealists like me who would work unbelievably long hours for little pay and benefits."

Sid asked, "Were you the director of design at WeWork?"

Joleen poured herself another cup of coffee. She replied, "No, I was just one of five graphic designers. The CEO had some college friends of his directing the department. We never knew his background, and he kept his past close to his chest.

"By the way, sorry, I lied to you earlier. I already knew your name. Marty talked about you and Vincent in a meeting on Monday; he painted quite a picture of you two. He told everyone that you and Vincent will be the saviors of Rutland."

Sid exclaimed, "I knew Marty already informed you about Vincent and me, but I guess I just went along with the ruse. However, I wouldn't try to convince anyone that Vincent and I would be Rutland's saviors. We are here to build a successful company."

Joleen continued, "Yeh, I find that Marty can be theatrical, almost preachy."

Sid asked, "You have a slight southern accent. Where did you grow up?"

Joleen replied, "A little town in southwest Virginia called Staunton. The city is not far from Charlottesville. There was one traffic light when I grew up. When I got accepted to RISD, I thought I had won the lottery; I couldn't wait to get out of there. I missed the small-town life in New York, and I guess it's how I ended up in another small town."

Sid interjected, "I've been to Charlottesville. It's great."

Joleen said, "I'm sorry I'm doing all the talking. I talk a lot when I get nervous."

Sid replied, "No problem, I like hearing your voice. Your accent is comforting."

Joleen looked at Sid with a furrowed brow. She asked, "Is Marty the real deal, or is he just another sales guy with an overinflated view of his concept? Of course, any answer will not change my view of the project if I keep getting my paycheck."

Sid thought about how much he could disclose to Joleen. He considered that people would be asking questions, and keeping his mouth shut would not always work.

Sid professed, "Marty is a venture capitalist. He's not in it to change the world; he is in it for the money. You should know this better than most from working at WeWork.

"Do you remember when WeWork's IPO rose to forty billion? This little trick is called pumping up the stock. WeWork's venture capitalists painted a picture of a technology company that would only increase in value. Of course, WeWork is not a technology company but a real estate company.

"The purpose of a VC is to pump up the value to get other investors on board. After the initial public offering, the original investors cash out, be they venture capitalists or angel investors."

Joleen scratched the back of her head and poured Sid another cup of coffee. She asked, "So, are you a true believer? Are you just in it for a payday?"

Sid took a long sip of his warm coffee. He answered, "I guess I'm a little of both. It depends on who walks through the door, their idea, and if they are willing to take it all the way."

Joleen asked, "You mean a unicorn?"

Sid responded, "It doesn't have to be a billion-dollar idea. It could be a one hundred million dollar idea, but it can't be the night of the living dead idea."

Joleen questioned, "Night of the living dead?"

Sid realized that the training Steve did was already paying off. Marty was right because Joleen only knew what she learned at WeWork, and he knew more about the world of start-ups than she did, even though she worked at one.

Sid continued, "We would like to have ten innovative ideas walk into the coworking space. Each idea will get the first round of funding between fifty and two hundred thousand. We expect six ideas to do marginally well, with a couple collapsing soon after the first round. We hope one of the ten will take off like a rocket or unicorn. We expect one to linger on without growing or dying—this is called the night of the living dead business."

Joleen asked, "Is it just about money, or are you going to look for something great?"

Sid replied, "It is all about the money with Marty and his investors. Something great will seal the deal with me, but I have Marty and his investors to appease."

Joleen replied, "When I got out of college, I thought being part of the world of start-ups would be something I could tell my grandkids later in life. They would be proud of grandma, who helped find technology to cure cancer, global warming, or whatever came along. I had high hopes."

Sid sat back in his chair and laughed. He replied, "You're not the only one with high hopes. My friend Steve Kenny started as a true believer and was part of the original true believers back in the nineteen-sixties.

"Kenny told me that the problem wasn't with technology; it was with the egos who can't get out of their way. It ended when he got involved with a start-up because the principals could never see beyond their self-interests. The principals would fight him on everything, and finally, the company would collapse."

Joleen replied, "I hope we find a unicorn that will change the world."

Sid looked at his watch and saw it was almost 4:30. He said, "I think I'll go to bed and attempt to get some sleep." Sid stood up from the table and held his hand to shake Joleen's. He continued, "It was nice to meet you; I hope we have a fruitful venture ahead."

Joleen asked, "You never did answer my question. Do you believe in ghosts?"

Sid replied, "The jury's out on ghosts. A building as old as this may have a few spooks roaming the halls. I wouldn't worry too much about something you can't see and most likely doesn't exist."

Joleen stood up and shook Sid's hand. She said, "Yeh, I guess you're right. Nice to meet you as well. Sleep tight."

Sid walked through the front door of Joleen's loft. He could see the spirit that Joleen grumbled about, standing in her living room the whole time. The specter was a man in business clothes from the early nineteenth century. The ghost stared at Sid and Joleen while they had coffee.

Sid knew that the phantom was aware that he could see him. He concluded that the ghost was harmless and that, in time, Joleen would get used to having him around. She would have to if she wanted to live in the building.

Sid had often come across apparitions that hung out and watched the living. He understood that the ghosts were often unaware they were dead, and the specters wondered why these people lived in their homes.

He found that the older the spirit, the more benign they were unless they were angry spirits, then all hell could be let loose. The ghosts that caused the most havoc were poltergeists. When a new owner renovates a building or home, the spirits become pissed off.

Sid pondered, letting Joleen know that he saw a ghost in her apartment but thought better of it after talking with her. He didn't know her well enough to trust the information would not cause a rift between them.

He might see ghosts and find it an everyday event, but he often reminded himself that others perceive the world differently. Joleen would probably be negatively affected by the knowledge of a ghost in her home.

He could feel that the building had a lot of ghosts wandering the halls. Overall, he thought the structure had positive energy, which was encouraging. He felt the path he would walk was much different from the one Marty sold. ∞

CB

Chapter Nine

"Hell, Sid, I banged on your door this morning, and you were gone?" said Vincent, patting Sid on his back. He then sat next to him at the counter.

Sid looked at Vincent with a weary look on his face. He said, "I'm thanking God that it's Sunday. I slept about four hours last night and still have a hangover. How did you find me?"

Vincent replied, "I asked the contractor where the black guy went. He said you asked for a good breakfast, not downtown, and he directed you to Denny's."

Sid asked, "How did you get here without the car?"

Vincent replied, "I borrowed Marty's Cadillac. He was still in bed when I asked for the keys."

Sid asked with a furrowed brow, "You seemed to get wasted last night, but it doesn't show on your face. Do you have a hangover?"

Vincent replied, "Hell, I grew up drinking whiskey by the time I was ten. Last night would not be considered hammered in my hometown; Cowboys are a hard lot."

An old waitress walked up to the counter and asked, "Honey, can I get you a coffee, and what would you like for breakfast?"

Vincent replied, "I would love a cup of coffee, and I'll take the lumberjack breakfast. Hell, we have a big week ahead."

The waitress looked over her glasses at Sid and Vincent. She asked, "Are you the two managing the new coworking space downtown?"

Sid sat up straight and looked startled. He replied, "How do you know we manage the coworking space?"

The waitress laughed. She replied, "Sweetie, this is a small town;

everyone knows." She poured coffee for Sid and Vincent and then returned to the kitchen to place their order.

Sid said, "I guess trying to hide in this town will be impossible. Next time we want privacy, we will probably have to drive to Middlebury."

Vincent, "We don't have to hide. I think we did well last night. We sat there and listened to those honchos chatter."

Sid replied, "I guess hiding as a black man will be difficult in this state. Vermont is the whitest state I have ever inhabited. Yeh, it was a crazy night; I got drunker on their praise than the alcohol."

Vincent replied, "Yeh, they were doing a big sales job. I felt like the president of the United States for a minute."

Sid said, "Sorry, I left for breakfast without you. I figured you would still be in bed."

Vincent replied, "I get up around 5:00 a.m. every morning, drunk or not drunk. I get up early ever since I was seven or eight—most times, we were on our horses by 6:00 a.m."

Sid replied, "Luckily, we don't have to ride horses. We have a car."

The waitress came through the kitchen's double doors with two large plates of food in her arms and holding a pot of coffee. She hastily pushed the coffee cups to the side and set down the plates in front of Sid and Vincent. She refilled both cups with coffee and asked, "Honey, you need to call Marty when you get back; he's looking for you. Is there anything else I can get?"

Sid replied, "No, this should do it."

The waitress walked through the double doors again and disappeared into the kitchen.

Vincent rolled his eyes. He said, "Hell, you're right. It will be hard to be invisible in this town; we must always be on our guard, playing the game."

Sid replied, "I've been thinking about the startup game. I had a long discussion with Joleen; she helped me to see things in a different light."

Vincent asked, "Who's Joleen, and when did you have time to meet with her?"

Sid replied, "Marty hired Joleen as our marketing director. I was up most of the night, and she knocked on my door around 3:30. We had coffee together."

Vincent asked, "Is she cute?"

Sid replied, "Yeh, she's cute, but it wasn't like that, and by the way, we must be careful with any women in this town. Nothing can foul a grift faster than getting involved in the wrong love affair."

Vincent questioned, "Hell, I guess sacrifice is the name of the game. So, what light did Joleen show you?"

Sid professed, "She helped me to see that Dylan song in a different light."

Vincent inquired, "You mean 'If you steal a little, they put you in jail. If you steal a lot, they make you king?'"

Sid replied, "Yeh, but it should be. "If you steal a little, they put you in jail, and if you steal a lot, it makes you respectable."

Vincent asked, "How's that?"

Sid declared, "Joleen told me about her experience working in the design department at WeWork; how the venture capitalists would pump up the company's value by making it look good. They would purposely fund the founder and CEO. So, he could drive a fancy car and have a large house to sell the illusion that the company is highly successful.

"I mean, WeWork was appraised at forty billion. Their nearest competitor, Regus, was valued at three billion, but they had been in the business of workspace rentals for many years. The managers at Regus couldn't even understand why WeWork was priced so high."

Vincent invited, "So, what's the point?"

Sid continued, "Well, so the VCs pump up the stock so high, then it goes public, and they cash out, making themselves rich, and then they do it all over again.

"How is what they are doing different from any grift or what we are doing? Joleen pointed out that Marty is a hustler, maybe no different than any startup CEO or VCs. But she didn't seem to care because that is the nature of business.

"The bigger the grift, the more people respect the process of getting rich. The bigger the con, the more you become normalized in our consumerist culture. Marty figured this out long ago because he seemed comfortable with what we were trying to do. Even the power brokers in this small town are on board because what we are doing is serving their self-interests."

Vincent took a long sip from his coffee. He asked, "So, I see the point, but I don't see the problem, and I see an opportunity."

Sid sat back and looked around the diner. He professed, "I guess you're right. I used to admonish my father for his twisted sense, but I didn't see that the world was not unlike Rikers Island. You're a predator, or you are prey.

"The predators in this world feed off the weak. One thing my father did give his congregation was hope; most were impoverished people just trying to survive.

"Without my father selling the good book for his self-interest, most people in the county would be poor without hope. I guess denial and delusion are a cushion against the reality of poverty."

Vincent replied, "I understand what you are saying. I've been thinking a lot about our work with Marty. I know it is a world away from three-card monte in Manhattan, but it is the same in many ways.

"It's all about distraction and feeding off the greed of most individuals, especially those who come into a city to make it big. I find it strange that you rejected your father's way of life while taking people with your poker skills."

Sid sat up and exclaimed, "That's just it; I earned money with my poker skills. When I sit down at a poker table, everyone at the table knows the score. They all want to cash in big. It does take skill to win at poker, and poker is not a scam. Even the fish at the table know the score."

Vincent asked, "So, what's bothering you?"

Sid rested his weary head on his crossed arms on the counter. He admitted, "I don't know what's bothering me; I thought it might be nice to do something good for people in this town. Maybe this situation will play out in a whole different direction."

Vincent interjected, "I have found in my young life that you never know where you will end up. A few weeks ago, you and I were on Rikers Island, fearing for our lives. Now we are sitting in Vermont managing a coworking space with money in our pockets, beautiful clothes, toys, a car, and the town honchos kissing our asses.

"Who knows where we might be in a few weeks from now? It all depends on who walks through the coworking space's front door with what idea. If it fails, everyone, as you said, knows the score and the risks. If it is successful, we may change the world or make a couple more bucks, who knows."

Sid and Vincent looked at the diner's front door and saw Marty standing in the foyer. Marty looked around and saw Sid and Vincent sitting at the counter's far end. He walked over and sat down next to Sid.

Marty said, "Well, I waited for you to show up, but I didn't want to wait anymore, so I had the contractor drop me off.

"I know it is Sunday, but there is much to review before our employees show up to work on Monday."

Vincent asked, "Have you had breakfast?'

Marty replied, "Yeh, I had a little something at the bakery downtown after you picked up my keys, but I could go for a hamburger. Their food here is rather good for Dennys."

The waitress saw that Marty had sat down and instantly walked over to take his order. "Hey Marty, good to see you back in town. The usual?"

With a big smile, Marty said, "Yeh, the usual, Bettie."

The waitress quickly turned around and entered the kitchen to place Marty's order.

Sid asked, "It seems that you have a reputation in town. Bettie seemed to know all about you and what we are doing."

Marty sat back and chuckled. He said, "Remember the hundred-dollar tip? I gave one to Bettie two years ago, and she has never forgotten it; she treats me like a king."

Vincent asked, "So, what's the play for tomorrow?"

Marty replied, "We meet with all our employees. We have one week left to open our doors, and we need to get everyone on the same page."

Sid replied, "I talked to the contractor this morning. He said they will finish the co-workspace on Monday, but the secondary offices might take a little longer."

Marty shrugged and said, "We will be ready to open our doors in one week; I guarantee it. Joleen told me she had coffee with you early this morning. What did you two discuss?"

Sid sat up and looked at Marty for a long time; he had a sinking feeling that something had gone down. He replied, "The nature of the business, especially her experience at WeWork.

"I was talking to Vincent about my experience with Joleen. I figured if we don't watch it, we may become respectable citizens of Rutland."

Marty looked at Sid with a perplexed expression. He said, "Follow my primary rule and be careful how much you disclose to anyone. This thing can go sideways fast."

Vincent asked, "So, we have a week. What is the big hurry?"

Marty took a sip of his water. He replied, "We have five new tenants for coworking offices showing up tomorrow morning. I wanted to give you a heads-up on who they are and how to play them. They already have rented space on the second floor but want to come in and fix their spaces before we open our doors."

Vincent interjected, "Any potential unicorns?"

Marty stopped talking and gestured to Sid and Vincent to be silent as Bettie walked out of the kitchen with a hamburger, French fries, and coke. She walked up to the counter with a big smile, then placed the dish and coke in front of Marty. She asked, "Anything else I can get you, Sweetie?" She winked at Marty.

Marty smiled and replied, "Maybe a little bit of sugar later, but this should do for now." He winked back at Bettie. They both laughed, and she returned to her other tables.

Vincent looked surprised. He asked, "Damn, you hit that?"

Marty rolled his eyes. He replied, "No, we flirt with each other, but I like women a little younger and firmer."

Sid asked, "Yeh, what happened to the babe you walked with into the poker game? She seemed to disappear."

Marty replied, "Yeh, Brandy is a cocktail waitress in Manhattan, but I only see her when I am in town. Women like Brandy are dangerous, and I advise you to avoid such perils, especially in Vermont."

Sid asked, "So, who are these tenants we will meet tomorrow?"

Marty took a few bites of his French fries and continued, "All four are want-to-be entrepreneurs; a coworking space attracts them like moths to a flame. None of them have good ideas but want to feel important and respected. They are not even close to what we want for investments, but they are important to our plan."

Sid asked, "How's that?"

Marty took a bit of his hamburger. He replied, "They are filler for the business, and if we treat them well, they will be some of our best word-of-mouth advertising.

"The hope is that some intelligent person with a great idea will walk in that door, but we must create a safe and supportive space for that to happen.

"Think of luring a baby deer into a trap—you need to give your prey a sense of trust before pulling the lever."

Vincent asked, "What are their ideas?"

Marty took a bite of his burger, waited a moment, and replied, "It doesn't matter, but so that you know for tomorrow. One designs crappy jewelry, and she is damaged goods, be careful with her. You know the type, purple hair, tattoos, and nose ring; daddy didn't pay enough attention.

"One guy has an idea for a trade newspaper. The whole print world is failing, and this guy thinks he can beat the odds. Rutland already has an established newspaper; his newspaper idea involves recycling; he works at the Rutland town dump.

"All five have full-time jobs. You will hear them lament how they could be the next Bezos if someone would invest in their ideas.

"One is developing another app for Apple. This guy is a dollar short and too late because the whole app industry has been winding down for the last few years. There are more apps than anyone could download in one lifetime, and most are free.

"The other two have crazy ideas. One is a coffee cup for farm equipment, and the other has an idea for a shoe hammer. Neither is an industrial designer or engineer, but they believe in their concepts."

Vincent asked, "You don't seem to have much respect for these folks?"

Marty shook his head. He replied, "Look, these fish are essential for a background effect, but they will suck you dry if you let them. They delude themselves into believing that their idea will make them a millionaire or billionaire.

"We need to listen and support them but be careful they don't pull you in too close. Fish will take up all your time and leave you dry.

"The people we need to be concerned about are the other grifters walking through the door. They're not in our coworking space to build a company. They talk a good game but want the first round of funding, and then they disappear with the money. This con happens more than you might consider.

"There is nothing worse than a cheated grifter. The startup world is full of hustlers trying to become wealthy—this is the nature of the business."

Sid replied, "Yeh, I'm starting to see that everyone is a predator or prey. Before you walked in the door, I told Vincent about Joleen's experience at WeWork."

Marty replied, "That's why I hired her. I know she has no illusions about changing the world with a single idea. Joleen will be a valuable information source for you but be careful what you disclose to her. She is brilliant and capable.

"Joleen will manage all the marketing, design, web development, and social networking. She has one graphic designer working with her, Raymond. She has a great idea for marketing to other hi-tech hot spots in the United States."

Vincent asked, "What is a hi-tech hot spot?"

Marty pushed his plate away with most of this hamburger and fries still not eaten. He continued, "Tech companies started to leave Silicone Valley and New York about five years ago. Around fifty cities are vying for these tech companies and young entrepreneurs. We need to sell them on moving to Vermont, especially to Rutland.

"We need heavy hitters with big ideas, venture capitalists, and angel investors to take a serious look at backing our startups. Remember, the game is don't use your own money; use other people's money.

"Look, I need to discuss the second floor with the contractor. I told him this morning that I will fire him and hire someone else if he doesn't finish by next weekend."

Marty got up and threw down forty dollars. He paid for Sid and Vincent's breakfast with another forty dollars.

Marty waved to Bettie and walked towards the front door. He stopped at almost every table to talk with customers and seemed to know everyone. ◌ଷ

ଔ

Chapter Ten

The coworking space underwent many variations during its first six months; one significant change was a Vermont summer into fall with its brilliant colors.

Sid rarely experienced significant weather changes in the south; it snowed once for fifteen minutes. Vincent grew up in Wyoming; he had not seen the intensity of fall color, mainly living among evergreen trees.

Another apparent change was the energy that ran the operation. Much was up for debate in the early days of managing the company, but the coworking space ran like a well-oiled machine after many months.

Marty hired the right people because everyone who worked at the coworking space hit the ground running. A sixty-hour work week was not uncommon, and human resources, leasing administration, and technology development worked as one collaborative venture.

Marty's eye for talent paid off because Sid was a natural leader who was confident directing the day-to-day operation. He had a charm that attracted his employees and tenants; anyone walking through the door was drawn to him instantly.

Vincent was a loyal and capable second in command; he also had a knack for charming people, primarily females. After only a few weeks, he pulled out his braided ponytail and set free his long blond hair; women instantly noticed.

Joleen managed the most impressive department, marketing, design, and communications. WeWork clipped her wings when she was a lowly graphic designer, but now that she was in charge, she took flight with her talents, and so did the organization.

Joleen implemented a marketing plan to lure hi-tech entrepreneurs and venture capitalists to the coworking space. She created the Vermont Innovator media group. She zeroed in on the fifty high-tech hotspots growing across the nation through social networking, database analysis, publishing, and website development.

Most of the residents at the coworking space were low-level business-people or want-to-be entrepreneurs. Small Vermont associations rented some of the offices, many of them with only one employee.

The coworking space occupants paid the bills, but the group desperately needed at least one heavy hitter to take root in the organization. Marty, Sid, and Vincent hoped ten innovative businesses would hear Joleen's call.

Their best bet was to draw in entrepreneurs from other areas of the U.S.—even competing for talent with Burlington, a sister city to the north of Rutland. Burlington was one of the fifty high-tech hot spots growing entrepreneurial culture.

Marty had to keep the Rutland power brokers happy, and they were starting to complain about their return on investment. He knew that time was ticking down, and he would have to find a unicorn or someone close to it soon or walk away before the scheme collapsed.

Marty sold success to the Rutland elite, and they were expecting a lot in return. Even though he never established the time it may take to build a successful start-up, he knew from experience that people could get impatient, primarily when they invest considerable money.

Marty knew that a successful start-up would draw the money the coworking space would need to continue. Ultimately, if the coworking space failed, there would not be a nest to incubate the next big thing, at least big enough to make everyone wealthy. It was a Catch-22 situation— Sid and Vincent never understood the reference when Marty voiced it.

Sid had an ultra-cool front desk built and positioned in the foyer of the coworking space next to a large room set up as an art gallery. A small coffee shop with bakery goods from a local vendor was on the other side of the lobby. They wired the whole place for sound and internet with a T-Three line.

Sid hired young trendy men and women to work in the front businesses of the coworking space. They all wore black and had a chip on their shoulders; Vincent would often say they were well-balanced because most had a chip on both shoulders.

Sid wanted to depict the space as being ultra-cool. Marty taught him that attracting is much better than chasing. Sid and Marty wanted prospects to see their access to the coworking space as a favor. They wouldn't make it easy for entrepreneurs to inhabit the offices.

After the leaves started to fall and trees started to lie bare, a turn of events took place that could change the group's fortunes. Two men and a woman walked through the door of the coworking space early Monday.

They walked up to the front desk and asked, "Can we talk to the director of the coworking space?"

Sheela, a new receptionist, reluctantly looked up. She looked at them with indifference and picked up the phone. She said, "Sid, three people at the front desk want to talk with you."

Sid replied, "I'll be right out."

Sheela put down the phone and said, "He'll be right out. You can wait in the art gallery if you like. We have great coffee if you are interested in a cup, it's Gallagher Close Farm Coffee Roasters, a local favorite."

All three smiled, and then one replied, "No, we already had coffee at our hotel." They walked into the gallery; Sheela could make out that they were murmuring something. She heard her name several times but didn't know what was said.

They all walked into the gallery and studied each painting carefully. The art exhibit consisted of modern images created by an artist Marty knew from New York. The artist was world-renowned and sold paintings for thousands of dollars.

The visitors expected local yokel paintings with a country fair art exhibit quality. The three visitors were impressed with the characteristic of art in the gallery, which is what Marty wanted.

Marty felt that first impressions were critical, and having extraordinary paintings in the gallery would lend to the aura of the coworking space and help draw in the right entrepreneurs.

Sid walked up to the woman standing closest to the door. He said, "I'm Sid, the director of the coworking space. What can I do for you?"

She turned around and said, "I'm Debra. These are my partners, Peter and Justin. We flew in from Silicon Valley; we received *Vermont Innovator* magazine and thought we might move our start-up to Rutland."

Justin interjected, "I grew up in Vermont and had wished to move back, but I didn't see the opportunities until I read *Vermont Innovator*."

Sid asked, "Let's go into my office and discuss what you're

looking for at our workspace. I would be interested in hearing about your start-up."

Sid didn't show it, but he was excited about the possibility of real entrepreneurs and a real start-up moving into the coworking space. He felt that this might be their big break. He knew he had to play it cool, but inside he was thrilled.

The meeting was short and to the point. Sid walked his new prospects out and bid them a speedy journey back to Silicon Valley. After they walked out of the coworking space's front door, a huge smile came over his face. Sid walked back into his office and dialed Marty's cell number.

Marty's phone rang only for a moment, and then he answered. Sid always found it strange that Marty would pick up when his phone rang, no matter what he was doing. Marty said, "Hey buddy, what's up?'

Sid replied, "I think our unicorn just walked through the door."

Marty paused on the other line, then replied, "I'll be there in about forty-five minutes."

Marty rarely spent any time in the coworking space. He was at a meeting with a bigwig selling most of the time, always selling. He told Sid and Vincent, "I'm an old guy, and if I spend too much time at the coworking space, it might become not so ultra-cool."

When Marty arrived, he walked directly into Sid's office. Sid and Vincent were waiting. They both had a large cup of Gallagher Close Farm Coffee Roasters, Tanzania Peaberry coffee; Vincent preferred it with ten sugars and four creams. Sid always joked with Vincent because he desired his coffee to be black and beautiful.

Marty slumped back into one of the comfortable leather chairs in Sid's office. He asked, "So, what's the story about this unicorn?"

Sid took a sip of his coffee. He replied, "I just had three entrepreneurs from Silicon Valley walk into the coworking space. They received *Vermont Innovator* a few weeks ago and considered moving to Rutland and building their business here."

Marty smiled and replied, "Thank God for Joleen. I knew the minute I hired her that she would be good luck. So, what's their start-up?"

Sid replied, "As far as I can discern, they are developing an algorithm and physical platform to manage the electrical output for the retail market. When people set up solar or wind power for their homes, they become hooked to the grid. The electrical company controls the energy flow from the independent source, and the homeowner has no say in how they use their electricity.

"Solar and wind power creates direct current, but it transfers into alternating current to the grid during the upload. During this transition, energy decreases rapidly. Their software utilizes the lost power for the home—kilowatts add up.

The software and hardware they are developing would give the homeowner more control over the energy flow from their alternate energy source.

Marty asked, "Do they already have funding?"

Sid replied, "Yes, they already had first-round funding from venture capitalists in California."

Marty asked, "So, why do they want to move to Rutland?"

Sid replied, "One crew member, Justin, grew up in Vermont. He received an engineering degree from the University of Vermont. He'd been in San Jose for ten years and wanted to move back to Vermont. They all are tired of the high cost of living in California, and most of their friends have moved out to other high-tech hot spots.

"They were considering Austin or Denver, but those markets are already getting saturated and becoming just as costly as Silicon Valley. They thought of Bali or Singapore because the business environment is excellent. They attended a presentation the Bali government gave and were impressed with their financial and tax support if they took their business offshore.

"They want to be in a place that might be ahead of the curve to grow their start-up. So, they are considering taking a risk on Vermont. I showed them the third floor, and they were impressed with the possibilities."

Marty asked, "How many employees do they have?"

Sid replied, "As far as I could gather, it's the three partners, and they have five others involved with the project. They weren't sure that all five would make the transition to Vermont.

"I sold them on the point that Burlington, New York, and Boston were not too far for them to recruit new talent."

Vincent inquired, "Hell, why don't they just move to Burlington?"

Sid replied, "I asked them, and they told me Burlington seems to be on the other side of the curve. They want their start-up money to go as far as possible."

Marty asked, "Do you know how much is invested in their start-up?"

Sid replied, "No, they were vague about the amount. They did pull out some numbers to impress me, but nothing specific."

Marky asked, "Are their investors okay about them leaving town?"

Sid replied, "I asked, and they said it's not a problem. They could do their start-up almost anywhere in the world with a T-Three line. The VCs are fine with the company moving if they get an ROI."

Marty asked, "What's the name of the company?"

Sid replied, "Sun-Potential."

Marty pulled out a small paper pad and wrote down the name. He said, "I have a couple of contacts out in Silicon Valley; I will have them check them out. Hopefully, these guys are the real deal."

Vincent asked, "Doesn't it matter if investors are already involved in the company?"

Marty replied, "No, they seem just to be starting. They are going to need many more rounds of funding. I was at a meeting with an angel investor when you called. He wants to help build Rutland back into a great city. I have seven angel investors just waiting for the opportunity to back a sure thing. What other potentials do we have working in our space?"

Sid pulled out a sheet with a list of tenants. He said, "We have a couple of local engineers working on software for an accounting system for small-diversified farmers. I talked with them last week, and they are looking for the first round of funding but have not yet been able to secure any interest from investors."

Vincent interjected, "That sounds promising. There are a lot of start-up farms with young people moving out of the city. A few days ago, I had a guy from Boston asking about farmland in Rutland County."

Marty smiled and replied, "That's good we are becoming an information source. What other prospects do we have?"

Sid continued, "I have three software engineers working on a new social networking site. The company's name is Karmakal. I discussed the business with one of the partners, who said that the social networking site is for spiritual-minded individuals. He said something about the Tibetan wheel of life. I didn't quite grasp the concept, and he was vague."

Marty frowned and said, "The accounting software sounds good, but his spiritual networking site sounds too far out. Plus, Facebook owns the social networking world, and it would be hard to crack if they got Karmakal off the ground."

Sid replied, "Actually, I like this one the best of all the start-ups. It seems these guys are doing something good for humanity."

Marty replied, "Doing good can be a positive for marketing the coworking space, but often it doesn't pay the bills or make us wealthy. Keep an eye on Karmakal. What else do you have?"

Sid scanned the list. He replied, "Some engineer is developing an app for employee benefits. A company, college, or organization would purchase the app so their employees would have 24/7 access to their benefits."

Marty replied, "I know the insurance industry is going through significant changes with Obamacare. Like every other industry, mergers and acquisitions decreased the sector to about six corporations managing employee benefits.

"The challenge these guys will have is state insurance regulations. We could expand on our service fees if we could set up a department in the coworking space helping businesses with local, state, and federal regulatory issues."

Sid replied, "I'll look into it."

Marty asked, "What else do we have?"

Sid continued, "The only other prospect worth looking into is one of our newest occupants. Two women are working on a tool for home use. This tool makes things easier for women to do basic renovation work. Women won't have to rely so much on a man for strength. As far as I know, it uses leverage to complete the tasks."

Marty asked, "So, what's the tool do?"

Sid replied, "I don't know because they are vague about the product. Many of our tenants keep their ideas close when I inquire about them. I feel these two women are on to something. Even when I talk about investors, they don't want to discuss their invention.

"Sandy told me they have patented the product, but she also said a patent is only as strong as the lawyers that defend the device."

Marty replied, "When Sun-Potential is a sure thing, start to talk with all the start-ups about investors. Some of these people may see the light when there is money.

"I'll start to talk to our local benefactor about the start-ups. Our progress will get them off my back for a few moments."

Vincent interjected, "Hell, that's four good prospects and a potential unicorn. Maybe it's time to bring in the investors."

Marty slumped back in his chair. He replied, "Not bad, I was hoping for ten, but five potential start-ups is a good beginning. If or when Sun-Potential comes through, we can set up an investor symposium and start to grease the wheels of fortune. We can have the meeting in our art gallery with the usual wine, cheese, etc.

"Talk to Joleen about putting out press releases. I'll give her my angel list, and she can design invitations to the event. Make sure someone follows up with all the angel investors. These people have big egos that need stroking for them to show up. Joleen will know what to do. WeWork used to put these things on all the time."

Vincent interjected, "I was talking with some of the tenants, and they thought it might be helpful for marketing if we came up with a name for the coworking space."

Marty replied, "Yeh, that would be great. Any suggestions?"

Vincent replied, "Plenty of suggestions, only one that I thought would work. How about the Vermont Innovation Incubator?"

Marty replied, "I like it. It sounds professional." ❧

သ

Chapter Eleven

The moon was full the night of the Vermont Innovation Incubator investors' summit; the importance of this night weighed on everyone's mind. Sid, Vincent, and Marty prepared for any questions potential investors might have about the five companies on the block.

The summit started at 1:00 p.m. with the Governor of Vermont as the keynote speaker. He had invested a few million dollars of taxpayer money into the coworking space and needed to see it become a success; his political career depended on the outcome.

Each company had a fifty-minute window to sell to potential investors. The highlight of the conference was Sun-Potential.

Marty sat at the round table discussion with the three engineers that were the founders. He assisted them in making their case and translated the complex technical information into a format the average investor would understand. Marty was a master at taking something complicated and making it comprehensible for the average person.

The conference started to heat up at 7:00 p.m. with an open bar. Marty, Sid, Vincent, and the staff mingled with the northeast financial power brokers. Many local Vermont angel investors and businesspeople were interested in where their tax dollars went.

Want-to-be entrepreneurs from local colleges and universities attended for knowledge, free food, and alcohol.

Around 9:30, Sid, Vincent, and most staff slipped out of the summit. Marty took notice; he always noticed everything, especially what Sid and Vincent were doing.

❧

"What are you drinking?" asked Marty as he sat at the bar next to Sid.

Sid looked surprised that Marty found him so late at night but not surprised at the same time. Sid held up his beer and replied, "Magic Hat #9." Sid questioned, "So, how did you find me so fast? I thought Strang-Fellows was a locals' bar?"

The bartender watched Marty settle in and then walked over. He stood in front of Sid and Marty, cleaning a shot glass. He asked, "The usual, Marty?"

Marty nodded his head. He replied, "Yeh, Billy, with a chaser." He then turned back to Sid and responded. "I've been patronizing Strang-Fellows Pub since I first came to Rutland five years ago; I do most of my best sales work at bars. Most people see financial ventures differently when they have a few drinks. I'm not a proponent of the three-martini lunch, but a few drinks are not a bad idea after dinner.

"If you want to be anonymous, your best bet is Killington Ski Resort. Most locals don't hang out there because it is so expensive. Most of the barflies at Killington are white-collar from Boston.

If you want to hang out with financial movers and shakers, you might try Bar-802 at Stratton Mountain Ski Resort. Bluebloods from Greenwich, Connecticut, own most of the condos. Stratton Mountain Ski Resort has more hedge fund managers per square foot than any other resort on the East Coast. Speaking of financial ventures, I noticed you left the investors' forum early?"

Sid professed, "Yeh, the northeast financial elite depleted me after eight hours. I couldn't take another conversation about how cool they are and how I should be happy to know them."

Marty countered, "It can be exhausting. Their egos take a lot of stroking. So, where is your shadow?"

Sid took a long sip from his beer. He recalled, "I think Vincent got lucky. He spent the evening chatting up a young woman from Castleton University. I overheard her say that she was an English major with a minor in music. She seemed to mesmerize Vincent; he seemed enchanted with all the young women buzzing around him."

Marty grinned, "Yeh, Vincent has a way with women. His long blond hair and chiseled Montana good looks go a long way with the female species."

Sid interjected, "Vincent is from Wyoming."

Marty laughed. He replied, "It doesn't matter; the cowboy thing is working for him. I've noticed women light up when you are around; Joleen watched your every move tonight."

Sid professed, "My father told us, 'Never stick your quill in the company ink.'"

Marty disputed, "I remember you telling me that your father used to stick his quill in many of his congregation?"

Sid took a long sip of his beer. He retorted, "Well, my father wasn't one to take his advice."

Marty admitted, "It's good advice. Nothing can take down a venture faster than a bad love affair."

Sid took another pull from his beer and motioned to the bartender for another. He said, "I thought you would still be wheeling and dealing. You looked on fire tonight. You had all those venture capitalists and angel investors pumped up; I thought you could take on the English Army."

Marty laughed. He answered, "You did well, my friend. You played the room like a real pro. I must hand it to myself to spot talent; I knew you would be a big asset when I sat at the poker table."

Sid looked at Marty from the corner of his eyes. He never knew when Marty was being authentic or just blowing smoke. He questioned, "So, how did we do tonight? Did you close the deals? What is our end looking like?"

Marty took his shot of whiskey and dropped it into his beer. He took a long pull on his drink. He admitted, "Most deals were closed before we even opened the doors to the investors' conference."

Sid looked confused. He inquired, "What do you mean?"

Marty sat back in his bar chair and waved over to the bartender. Billy walked over and asked, "What can I do for you?"

Marty replied, "Billy, we'll take another, and how about you choose three of your best appetizers." Billy served Marty and Sid another drink and then walked back into the kitchen to place Marty's order.

Sid knew Marty liked to pause before telling him the news that may or may not upset him. Sid asked again, "So, what's the deal?"

Marty stated, "After our initial meeting in your office, I had a colleague contact each of the potential five ventures to secure twenty-five percent ownership through my limited liability company in Boston."

Sid grimaced, "You did this without telling Vincent or me?"

Marty took a sip of his drink. He confessed, "Yes, I did it without you knowing. If you did know, you would be under a lot of pressure, maybe too nervous. I needed you at your best."

Sid asked, "How much did it take to secure twenty-five percent?"

Marty replied, "I secured twenty-five percent of the three local entrepreneurs for $150,000 each. Sun-Potential took $750,000. I secured twenty-five percent of Karmakal for you; it cost me $125,000.

Sid looked surprised. He queried, "You secured ownership for me in Karmakal; why?"

Marty replied, "I'm not hot on the idea, but you are. I see it as hedging my bet. If you have ownership in one of the ventures, you will hang around longer. I see you and Vincent as one of my best investments, and I always take care of my assets. Since the investors' fair was a big success, you will be able to pay me back with your end."

"Did each company get a cash infusion from investors at the conference?" inquired Sid.

Marty replied, "Yes, we increased our initial investments by 67% with the new capital."

Sid asked, "You did this before the investors' fair?"

Marty professed, "Yes, I've built relationships with eight angel investors and a venture capitalist firm. I wasn't about to let other investors come in during the fair and scoop up these companies without giving my primary investors the first opportunity. Every good business has a tiered system; that is just good enterprise.

"The investors and I met before the conference; we decided to create the Vermont Innovation Consortium. All the investments went into this financial consortium, so the consortium owns fifty-one percent of each project, except Karmakal."

"Except Karmakal?" asked Sid.

"Yeh buddy, Karmakal is all yours. I wanted to give you total control to see what you could do with the company. If you need more cash, we can work that out."

Sid asked, "Why fifty-one percent of the other companies?"

Marty took a long sip of his drink. He replied, "So, we can fire the founders if they don't perform. It's common to replace the originators with more experienced management—the average founder lasts eighteen months after a venture capitalist's first round of funding."

Sid declared, "That's cold."

Marty replied, "It's a cold world."

Sid asked, "Why did you secure twenty-five percent ownership through your Boston LLC?"

Marty continued, "Conflict of interest. I didn't want anyone to get wise about what I was doing, and I didn't want my primary investors to feel like I was going behind their backs, which is what I did."

Sid inquired, "So, what now?"

Marty replied, "We were lucky the way things turned out. I was ready to pursue the same publicity plan with local entrepreneurs, but all the ventures seemed solid.

"Sun-Potential is a gift from heaven. I don't know if you are my lucky charm, Vincent, or both, but you have brought together a dream deal. An arrangement beyond my wildest imagination, and I can envision a lot.

"I originally thought we could walk away with ten million, but we will be there sooner than I imagined. We could take Sun-Potential to an initial public offering—I think Sun-Potential could be our unicorn."

Sid asked, "We never talked about one of the companies going public. How long do you think that would take?"

Marty conferred, "I think Sun-Potential could go public in twenty-eight months. A more significant possibility is that an energy company would want to buy Sun-Potential. A lot of traditional energy companies are trailing behind the technology curve.

"Companies have been fighting against the green tide for years. With solar, wind, and thermal energy advancement, they will have to embrace the new world or be left behind. Sun-Potential is one of the best ideas in that sector."

Sid inquired, "How much would Sun-Potential be worth to an energy company?"

Marty smiled and took a long pull on his drink. He replied, "I think three hundred million."

Sid exclaimed, "Three hundred million?"

Mart sat back in his chair and smiled. He continued, "The company's potential makes the ten-million look like chump change."

Billy walked out of the kitchen with hot food plates, napkins, and utensils. He cleared an area between Sid and Marty and placed everything down. He asked, "You ready for another round?"

Sid and Marty just nodded their heads.

Sid asked, "So, what's next?"

Marty smiled and replied, "We have Joleen go on a media spree. With press releases, national marketing, and social networking, we want everyone to know what is going on in Rutland. I have friends at CNBC; they will start the buzz about the Vermont Innovation Incubator.

"We will start to hype the companies, especially Sun-Potential. The publicity will attract new entrepreneurs and investors to the coworking space. Remember what I told you; it is always better to attract than chase."

Sid slumped back in his chair. He looked out the window for a long time, gazing at the moving lights in the darkness of the cityscape.

Marty looked at Sid with a furrowed brow. He asked, "So, what's the problem? We are on fire, buddy, and you look like you're going to a funeral. Isn't this what you wanted?"

Sid professed, "Yeh, I should be happy, but I still feel empty. It isn't the success of the coworking space; it's something that has plagued me my whole life. I have been looking for something that will scratch an itch that I can't reach.

"When I was a child, I thought there was more to this world than I could see. I used to consider that the world was just a mirage. I admonished my father for being a con man, but now I see that all business is a little fantasy."

Marty interjected, "Have you ever heard of the term 'Fake it till you make it?'"

Sid replied, "Yeh, my father used that phrase."

Marty continued, "All business is a bit of fairy magic—nothing would get done if people only invested in solid companies. Most small businesses in the United States are one or two months away from insolvency.

"I worked with a company in New Jersey that had an outstanding loan with the Mafia. Most small business owners will do anything to stay in business, lie, cheat, or steal.

"Like you, I grew up farming in Louisiana when we weren't on the road preaching the Good Book and pulling in prayer donations.

"To grow anything, you must pile manure on soil and load a pile of shit on the foundation to grow any business. As much as there is bullshit in business, there is also a little magic."

Sid looked out the window again at the lights of Rutland. He replied, "Yeh, I guess you are right. You talked of Vincent and me being a lucky charm, but I don't think it's luck. When I first drove over the border of Vermont, I felt something that I have not felt since I was a child. I felt a field of energy flowing through the mountains of Vermont. The closer I came to Rutland, the stronger the energy vibrated.

"When I was a child, my mother used to talk about the field of energy where she grew up in a Louisiana bayou. She used to say to me, child, if you sit quietly in the still of the night down in the bayou, you can hear the field of energy sing a most beautiful song."

"I never knew what she meant until I was twelve, and we traveled down to her family's home deep in the swamp. She held my hand, and we stood on the edge of a great marsh late at night. When the stars came out, I heard a vibration in the water that started to sing a beautiful song. My mother's people called it the song of the universe; I think spiritual people call it 'Ohm.'

"I've heard that same field of energy vibrate through the mountains around Rutland. I think magic happens often and is happening now in this little town on the edge of a great forest. I feel that this energy brought us together to create something that may change the world."

Marty responded, "I don't know if I'm here to change the world. Most of the world that I have experienced is dark and cold. I've always had the mind to care for myself, and it may be a stretch for me to help others."

Sid replied, "I don't think someone has to help others actively to benefit others."

Marty looked at Sid sideways. He asked, "Your mother was Creole?"

Sid took a sip of his beer. He revealed, "Yeh, her mother was Haitian, and her father was French. She grew up in a parish in dire poverty on the edge of a swamp. She worked hard to get out of that situation. She attended Howard University in Washington, D.C. She rose above her position, but I think that magic, that field of energy in the swamp, still permeated her soul.

"My father and mother are a lot like the business we are in, a little bit of grift and a little bit of fairy dust. I couldn't wait to get away from my family, but I see I'm right back where I started."

Marty replied, "Field of energy, huh? I remember hearing about

Muscle Shoals in Alabama when I was a kid in the nineteen-sixties and seventies. Fame is a small-town recording studio on the edge of the Tennessee River. The company produced one hit after another. The building was no bigger than a double-car garage, but the music from that studio changed how I saw the world.

"People would talk about the energy emanating from that area; it was like the music was born out of the mud from the delta. My friends and I were part of a generation listening to blues, soul, and rock and roll. The sound didn't go over well with my parents, who were from another time and feared the new music.

"For a moment, Muscle Shoals had the field of energy. You're right: maybe we are amidst a field of energy. Whatever it is, it is going to change our lives. We shouldn't second guess it; we should go for the ride.

"I grew up in Louisiana, I'm not Creole, but I have a little Voodoo in my bones. Anyone growing up in the bayou has a little Voodoo in their bones."

Sid smiled. He replied, "Yeh, maybe a little bit of gumbo too."

Marty sat back in his chair. He grabbed a potato skin from the appetizer plate. He said, "I told all three principals at Karmakal that you own twenty-five percent of the company. They all like you and are interested in what you could bring to the table. I think they are looking for a leader. All three are engineers, but none know where to take the business. Maybe you can help?"

Sid replied, "So, you want me to run the coworking space, help build our investments, and run Karmakal? When am I going to sleep?"

Marty laughed and took a long pull on his beer. He replied, "You're a young man, Sid. I have total faith that you can work magic."

ભ

Chapter Twelve

Sid's visions always started the same. He felt a sense of being extended outside of himself, watching himself, not part of his body. Then a haze began to form in his mind. When the fog clears, a picture of future events starts to take focus. Each vision is symbolically not unlike a dream, but he is wide awake when he experiences the epiphany. Each time he has an image, it becomes a premonition of a significant turn of events in his life.

His most crucial vision was just before he left his small family farm in Alabama and set out on his life's journey. In that vision, he remembered being able to fly. When he awakened, he knew he had foresight during the epiphany.

In his vision, he flew over the lake in which he drowned. He was able to control his flight. He had similar waking dreams before, but this one was different because a net covered the lake, and animated characters were chasing him. He didn't know if the beings were trying to harm him, but he sensed a sinister objective.

In past visions, he would always get caught in the net and die, but the last time he had this vision, he could break through the net and reach the lake. He felt the cool water of the lake flow over his body.

Sid wanted to leave the farm, but his father would convince him that his place was as his heir apparent. The vision helped Sid break away from his father's power over him.

Sid considered that the vision he was experiencing now was more important than the one he had when he left home. The image only lasted a moment, but it seemed it went on for a time without end.

Sid's vision began in a long dark tunnel. In the distance, he could see a single point of light. Sid felt himself running down the tunnel. He heard his steady breathing and felt the sweat on his brow. With every step, Sid felt pain and despair. His body ached, and his mind was on fire, but he continued to run into the night.

Sid ran through the emptiness that was civilization and saw people in their cars looking out at him. Their faces were blank with apathy. They were close enough to see his pain but distant enough not to feel it. They rushed by on their way to nowhere and were always in a hurry to do nothing.

Sid continued to run through the dark tunnel that seemed to go on forever. He kept getting a glimpse of a light in the far future of his run. He saw the sunrise for a second, which gave him hope with every step he took.

Sid's pain slowly turned into pleasure, and his body felt a sense of freedom that only came with the passing of time and space.

There is a point when Sid's pain and pleasure are one, and at that point, he finds his true self. The union of pain and pleasure makes him feel alive, waking him up from the world's dreams and setting him free.

Sid's body and spirit became one as he entered the second leg of his run. It was still dark all around him, with a glimmer of light in the sky. Soon, there will be a sunrise—a rising that he felt would give renewed hope to the world.

Sid's pain was gone now, and all he could feel was the beating of his heart and the steady movement of his breath.

He ran along a beautiful beach on a distant blue planet traveling through an endless galaxy. The stars and moon are above him, and the glimmer of sand is below. In the sand, he saw the many faces that had come before. The faces beckoned to him for salvation from their self-imposed prison.

Sid reached down to make right what was perfect already. He held the sand tightly in his hands only to have it flow through his fingers to rejoin the whole, and then he ran on into the night.

He left the beach and into his third and final leg. The miles pass below his feet as years in his life. The last stretch is a long, empty road leading home again. It's a second before dawn, and there's stillness in the air that could only be experienced just before sunrise.

The miles have taught him many lessons. The most important lesson he has learned is balance. He ran into the night, where the sky meets the earth and pain meets pleasure.

Sid saw the brilliant light from his home, and a single figure patiently waited to embrace him. He increased his stride until his heart wanted to explode, and his feet were aching with the pain of desire. Sid started to weep with the long and lonely miles behind him. It had been so many lonely miles that he never thought he would be home again.

The moment he was home, he realized that he had never left, and the dream of the world passed before him, standing perfectly still. The long and lonely miles passed through his heart only to heal him, and with a gentle touch, Sid's spirit assured him that he was truly home again.

The vision lasted a moment, but the message was profound. Sid realized that the home he sought was not his family farm in Alabama but a place that he touched for a moment when he died in the lake. He seeks a connection, a path that will show him his divine purpose; he feels that Karmakal is the beginning of that purpose.

"Sid, wake up, buddy," exclaimed Vincent.

Sid is startled back into the world by Vincent. He looked around as if he had been gone for many days. He looked at Vincent glazed and said, "I had one of the most profound visions. I ran down a long tunnel in a city next to an ocean that I have never visited."

Vincent sat in the chair in Sid's office, smoothed his long blond hair behind his ears, and inquired, "What did your vision tell you?"

Sid sat up in his office chair behind his desk. He replied, "My vision told me I would have a significant perception shift; I will soon see the world in a new light."

Vincent looked at Sid for a long time. He asked, "How do these visions come to you?"

Sid thought about the question for a long time and replied, "Do you ever hear that voice in your heart telling you what to do?"

Vincent laughed and replied, "You mean the one that tells me to do stupid things?"

Sid chuckled and replied, "No, the other one. The one that tells you not to do stupid things, but you do them anyway. Then you pay the price?"

Vincent laughed again and replied, "Hell, you mean the good angel. That one doesn't get through too often; I'm prone to do stupid things."

Sid took a long sip of his coffee. He replied, "Well, I think I met my spiritual self in the vision. I have heard a faint voice try to direct me my whole life. Of course, I fight the suggestions more times than I take them.

"When I died in that lake, I heard a voice so pure and full of love tell me everything would be okay. I think I met that spirit in my vision, and I think the spirit is an important part of my soul. Does that sound crazy?"

Vincent sat back in his chair and put his boots on Sid's desk. He replied, "I think we are way past crazy. Once, you were talking with a ghost at Rikers."

Sid continued, "I was hoping our paths would merge when I met Marty. He is the Buddha of the grift, and I thought I would be his loyal devotee. I knew down in my heart that Marty was only a steppingstone. My ego wanted to stay and play the game with Marty, but deep in my heart, the spiritual voice told me otherwise."

Vincent sat up in the chair. He asked, "You're not leaving?"

Sid continued, "No, not physically, but I know now that my path will eventually lead me away from here, or at least away from Marty."

Vincent furrowed his brow. He said, "I don't know, buddy, we have a good thing here. I don't know if I will continue down another road with you. As my mother used to say, one in hand is better than two in the bush. If we walk away from this success, life may start to be hard again."

Sid continued, "Look, I'm not leaving tomorrow. I am saying that a perception shift will occur. In other words, I will see the world in another way."

Vincent furrowed his brow again. He replied, "Sometimes, buddy, I have difficulty understanding you. I came in to talk about what was moving through the grapevine. I heard you have part ownership of Karmakal—I thought we were partners. Why didn't you discuss this with me first?"

Sid sat back in his chair. He replied, "We are partners. Marty bought twenty-five percent of Karmakal, so I would have a reason to stick around. I just found out about it after the investors' fair. He told me he bought a significant percentage of each business, including our unicorn. He plans to take Sun-Potential to an IPO."

Vincent asked, "So, fifty-fifty on Karmakal?"

Sid smiled and replied, "Yes, fifty-fifty. I didn't put down any cash. Marty didn't think the idea would go anywhere, but my inner voice had told me otherwise. I think Karmakal has a lot of promise, not just for money, but for growth and awareness."

Vincent smiled. He replied, "Money will do, but I'm open to awareness if only to keep up with your visions. Do you know what Karmakal is about?"

Sid continued, "I know that Karmakal is a social networking site for spiritually-minded people."

Vincent asked, "Hell, I thought you were not going to sell religion?"

Sid continued, "I said spiritual, not religion. My mother used to quote Vine Deloria JR. 'Religion is for those who fear going to hell, but spirituality is for those who have already been there.'"

Vincent laughed. He replied, "I guess you could call me spiritual because I have already been to multi-levels of hell."

Sid laughed. He replied, "Amen, brother. I don't know the details of Karmakal, but the three founders want to have a meeting, but away from the office and Rutland.

"They want to take a day and hike up Camels Hump Mountain near Richmond, Vermont. They told me they are excited that you and I will be part of their start-up. They will go over the specifics once we reach the top. They told me it takes about two hours to hike up the mountain."

Vincent furrowed his brow. He replied, "Hell, sounds a little strange, what I am saying. I'm friends with the vision guy who talks to ghosts. In for a penny in for a pound, right?"

Sid looked out his window for a long time because he was thinking about something that had plagued him for his entire life.

Vince asked, "So, what else is on your mind? I can always tell when something heavy is about to occur; maybe I have some intuition."

Sid sighed and asked, "Have you ever considered what the world is? Have you ever wondered why we are here?"

Vincent asked, "You mean Rutland?"

Sid continued, "No, I mean the world. Ever since I was a kid, I felt the world was a mirage. When I was a child, I used to go into my closet and pretend that there was a door leading to another reality or multiple realities."

Vincent replied, "Hell, I think everyone thinks about the meaning of their life every so often, but I don't believe that most ponder the question as much as you do. This coworking experience is the first time

I have not had to scratch out a living or be wary of trouble right around the corner. So, I haven't had the luxury of contemplating the world.

"I think fellows like us are not used to being well-fed and well-kept. When you have too much leisure time, your minds wander."

Sid sat up in his chair. He replied, "You're right. Now is the first time I have had a stable life; I'm not concerned about food, shelter, or safety. These thoughts have been in the back of my mind. Now that we are emperors of our universe, ideas have time to flow over my subconscious."

Sid stood up and walked over to the window, looking out on downtown Rutland. He continued, "When I was seventeen, I underwent a major perception shift."

Vincent asked, "I don't understand. What do you mean by perception shift?"

Sid continued, "I went through a hard time when I was seventeen. I started to have an overwhelming feeling that the world was not real. I tried to find comfort with my father, but he wasn't any help.

"My mother told me that I was going through a heart awakening. She said that deeply spiritual people connect with their spiritual selves when they turn from a child into an adult. This heart awakening can be painful; sometimes, it's more than someone can handle. In Christianity, the transformation is called the 'Dark Night of the Soul.'

"She gave me the book *The Dark Night of the Soul* by Thomas Moore. The book talks a lot about perception. Supposedly, as we journey through this world, we build our perceptions that each one of us is only separate by our perceptions, but our hearts are all connected.

"The world outside us reflects how we see ourselves; the world is a hologram reflecting how we perceive ourselves.

"If you see that the world is a hard and ugly place, you may feel that you are a hard and ugly person. If you feel that everyone you meet is lying to you, you may feel that you are a person who deceives others, especially yourself. If you feel that the world is a beautiful place, you may feel that you are a beautiful person."

Vincent asked, "How can we be connected but separate simultaneously."

Sid continued, "That's a paradox."

Vincent asked, "What is a paradox?"

Sid laughed and leaned back in his chair. He continued, "What you asked about is a paradox; a paradox doesn't make any sense but is true.

You asked how we can be connected and separate at the same time.

"Supposedly, there are two realities. Do you remember when I was reading that old physics book at Rikers?"

Vincent thought and replied, "Yeh, the one with Einstein's theory and the other guy's theory; I don't remember his name."

Sid replied, "Yeh, Albert Einstein's unified field theory and Max Plank's quantum mechanics theory. The unified field theory is that physical and virtual fields combine to make up the physical world we see outside, and the physical world we see is one field of energy.

"In simple terms, Plank's quantum mechanics theory dictates that the world reacts differently at sub-atomic levels. Where Einstein considered one unified field, Plank thought there were multi-universes. We can be in many places at the same time."

Vincent rolled his eyes. He asked, "I have no idea what you just said."

Sid thought and continued, "You see, both Einstein's theory and Plank's theory work out mathematically, but they do not work out with the other's concept.

"So, it is a paradox because both theories are true, but not with each other. This paradox indicates that all living things are connected and separate at the same time.

"The spiritual part of both concepts of connection and separation has not been mathematically interpreted; in my opinion, it will never be construed, at least in this reality.

"I know deep in my heart that we are both connected and separate, I just haven't figured out how this is true, but I know that it is; you see a paradox."

Vincent started to laugh hard. He replied, "I don't know why I find that so funny, but I can't stop laughing."

Sid laughed, too; he replied, "My mother used to tell me that we laugh whenever someone speaks the truth."

Vincent composed himself. He replied, "Hell, I still don't know why we would be connected and separate simultaneously, but since you don't know either, I guess it comforts me."

Sid sat back in his chair. He replied, "Amen, brother." ଔ

ભ

Chapter Thirteen

Sid was wide awake, resting in bed at 3:30 in the morning next to Joleen. She was asleep; he was looking tenderly at the contour of her face and connecting her freckles in his mind. They decided to keep their love affair secret, even though they felt most of the crew knew.

The ghost in Joleen's apartment wasn't present during their love-making. Sid thought that maybe the spirit possessed decency even though he was dead. Sid had a brief conversation with the specter while waiting for Joleen to get ready to go out one evening. Sid gleaned that the ghost was the manager of the hotel in 1880. The love of his life had been a no-show at the wedding, and he committed suicide.

Joleen wasn't Sid's first dalliance. His first liaison was when he was seventeen. He and his mother stayed with his uncle Eduard in New Orleans during a rare respite from the farm. There was a break when the crops were planted and harvested each summer. His mother and father would often go in different directions during this time. She would always want to visit friends and family in Louisiana. Sid's father would usually disappear into seedy doings, away from his flock.

The heat and humidity in New Orleans that summer was hotter than usual. Most sit on porches and drink sweet tea when things get that sticky. Sid would stay close to his mother on previous trips to New Orleans, but this year was different. He was becoming a man and was restless and wanted to explore the city.

A chance encounter with his uncle started him on the road to Kamala. His uncle was not unlike his father. Pious during the day and divergent during the night. During visits in years past, his uncle was always a beacon of honesty to young Sid, but this year his uncle seemed a little bit different, or maybe Sid just saw him in a much different light.

Sid's uncle was a powerful politician in New Orleans. He had a large home near the French Quarter on Lake Shore Drive. Sid always wanted to stay with his uncle. Most other relatives lived in less desirable accommodations, some too close to a swamp and too close to alligators and other undesirable sleeping companions.

His uncle was busy with his business for most visits and was only superficially interested in his sister's son. Like his sister, he was Creole but more French than Haitian. A good-looking man with sinewy muscles. He had a clear ebony complexion but, at the same time, had French characteristics. The mix worked in his favor; it gave him a captivating glow. When he walked into a room, he commanded attention. He used his bigger-than-life presence to build his business and long political career.

He never married, so Sid thought maybe he didn't like children. Sid knew he liked women because he always had different companions when they visited.

One Saturday night, Sid, his uncle, his mother, and his aunt Babette were sitting on the large porch surrounding his uncle's home. It was too hot to sit inside, so all four sat on chairs looking out on Lake Pontchartrain. His uncle would usually be out on the town most evenings at a political event or visiting New Orleans's juke joints.

Near midnight Sid's mother and aunt went to bed, leaving Sid and his uncle alone on the porch. Sid was rocking back and forth on the porch swing, his uncle sitting in a folding chair sipping Sazerac. Sid found it a little awkward because, for many years, he would visit his uncle, but they never had conversations.

Sid's uncle took a long sip of his drink and asked, "So, how much nuckie do you get up there on the farm in Alabama?"

The question made Sid blush because he had no sexual experience beyond heated kissing and touching, and Sid was still unsure what to do, how to do it, and when to do it. He replied, "I guess you could call me an eager pupil without much experience."

His uncle laughed. He replied, "Well, young nephew, New Orleans can cure that ailment, and I know just the medicine. Her name is Kamala."

Kamala was a New Orleans courtesan who was friends with Sid's uncle, as far as anyone can be close with a prostitute. Kamala was friends with the most powerful and wealthiest men in New Orleans. She was young, beautiful, and ran her own business. She would say that men were only good for bringing her money and gifts, not controlling her, which many tried to do, including Sid's uncle.

Sid's uncle was good to his word the following weekend. He told his sister that it was time for Sid to see some of the nightlife in New Orleans, but he left out Kamala. The drive along New Orleans thoroughfares was exciting. Sid thought it interesting that the streets were bright with all the lights from bars and restaurants but were dark at the same time.

Sid rejected the idea of losing his virginity to a prostitute. He thought his uncle was messing with him about Kamala and that maybe he shouldn't think much about it. Sid didn't know his uncle well enough to gauge if his uncle was bluffing. He grew up not trusting what his father told him most times; in fact, most men in his life were not to be trusted. He knew he could always trust his mother.

Sid's uncle pulled up to a property with a long black iron gate in the front. A fig grove lined a walkway up to a beautiful white two-story house. The same style of black iron gate surrounded the home's top floor. Sid judged this could not be Kamala's home; he expected a different kind of building and not in such a respectable neighborhood.

Sid knew from a young age where the brothel was in his hometown. He and his friends would often hide in the woods to see who came and went from the house, even though his parents warned him that he was never to venture into that part of town.

Sissy's Place, as the locals called the cat house back home, looked to be no more than a double-wide trailer plopped down on a patch of red Alabama dirt on the edge of a farm.

Sid's uncle looked at him and took a long toke from his cigarette. He said, "Go on, boy, she is waiting for you. She will teach you about the finer things in life. I will be back here in one hour to pick you up, and don't keep me waiting, or you will have to walk home."

Sid's uncle left him in front of the black iron gate as he sped off toward the French Quarter. Sid stood in front of that gate for what seemed to him like a long time.

Sid started to hear music that was sweet and familiar. The music drew him up the front walk towards the house because the melody was comforting.

As soon as he stepped onto the front porch, a woman in a traditional housemaid dress opened the front door.

Sid asked, "Kamala?"

The maid laughed. She replied, "The mistress will see you now."

Sid was directed into a garden at the back of the house. The pungent smell of jasmine and blueberry bushes lined the stone walkway. The maid led Sid to a small courtyard in the center of an orchard.

Sitting back on a chaise longue chair was the most beautiful young woman Sid had ever seen. Her skin was silky light chocolate, and her lips were lush like the berries lining her stone walkway. Her figure was delicate but strong at the same time. While looking a Sid, she sat back in a stunning gold dress with delicate embroidery. She had no shoes, which exposed her long slender feet with carefully pedicured toes painted with a rich purple-red color.

Sid stood looking at this vision of grace for a long time. He could tell from his first encounter that this woman reveled in the attention and power she received from her male callers.

A moment passed, and then a vision entered Sid's mind. He had an overwhelming feeling that he had stood in that same spot for many lifetimes, maybe a thousand. He knew he had been here before. He had to decide to either continue down the road with Kamala or turn around and walk away. He knew that heartbreak was possible, but he also knew that he would always make the same decision.

"Boy, do you have a tongue?" inquired the enchantress.

Sid woke up from his admiration and replied, "Yes, ma'am."

Kamala responded, "Good, I'm Kamala."

Sid replied, "I'm Sid."

Kamala professed, "I was worried that you would stand out in the street all night long, so I had my maid play an old New Orleans song that comforts the soul."

Sid replied, "Yes, ma'am."

Kamala stated, "Now that you are standing before me, we need to understand each other and what rules apply to our lovemaking game. First, I am not a whore you will jump on, so you can brag to your friends that you popped your cherry. Do you understand?

Sid replied, "Yes, ma'am."

Kamala declared, "I am under orders by your uncle to turn you into a man. Becoming a man has little to do with screwing and a lot to do with how you treat the women in your life. Being a man has a lot to do with taking on the responsibility of what lovemaking may bring you in the form of a child. Do you understand?"

Sid replied sheepishly, "No, I don't."

"That's why you are here. You are not here to impress me with your lovemaking skills because you have none. Your uncle told me that you are an eager student with little experience. Consider our relationship moving forward as a classroom in life.

"When a man wants to court a woman, he brings thoughtful gifts. He dresses like a man, not a poor farmer from Alabama. He says sweet things and gently kisses and caresses to gain the affection of his beloved. These are some things a good lover needs to know, and I will teach you. Do you understand?" queried Kamala.

Sid stood dumbfounded. He didn't know how to reply. Sid didn't expect anything like what was asked of him. He started to disconnect from his body. He had an overpowering feeling of watching himself interact with Kamala.

Kamala looked at Sid for a long time. She started to smile and then laugh at Sid's awkwardness. Kamala knew she put him off-balanced as she had done to even the most powerful men. Kamala continued, "Let's start with fine clothes and shoes. A manicure and sweet-smelling hair. A thoughtful gift and maybe flowers and chocolates."

Sid had a confused look on his face. He replied, "You mean now?"

Kamala laughed again at the confusion on Sid's face. She replied, "No, the next time you come to see me. Have fine clothes and a thoughtful gift."

Sid replied, "How would I get these things? I have little money."

Kamala replied, "Part of being a man is finding a way. It is the end of your first lesson until you find these things don't come back. Now, you can find your way through the back of the house; I have a gentleman waiting."

Sid walked through Kamala's garden and found his way back to the street. His uncle was waiting in his car.

Sitting in the passenger seat, his uncle said, "What transpired between you and Kamala needs to stay between you and her. I don't need to hear what lessons she has taught you. Remember how you got here because the next time you see her, you will be on your own and need to bring her your own money."

"She wants me to have fine clothes and thoughtful gifts. How do I achieve these things when I have so little money?" questioned Sid.

Sid's uncle Eduard looked at him for a long time. He replied, "I can help you with money. I have an acquaintance that has a business in dire need of employees. While you are at my house, you can earn the money you need to see Kamala."

Sid sat up with a smile because he undoubtedly felt he was in love with Kamala after one visit. He would do what he needed to to be in her presence again. He had a glimmer of hope that he could be brave enough to play the lovemaking game with Kamala.

Eduard's friend was a notorious bookie working for the local Dixie Mafia. Sid worked for his uncle Eduard's friend running numbers before earning enough to buy a new set of clothes, shoes, and a manicure. He walked along Bourbon Street looking for a shop where he may be able to purchase thoughtful gifts and flowers for Kamala.

He had never bought a gift for a woman other than his mother. He asked his boss, Joseph, what would be a thoughtful gift for a woman. Joseph thought it ridiculous for such a young boy to buy a gift for a girl. He didn't know the gift was for Kamala. He did tell Sid that women like an expensive perfume. Sid thought maybe a fragrance at the drugstore with flowers would fill the order. He was instantly turned away by Kamala. He learned his first important lesson—not to settle for less than the best because Kamala was worth much more.

The summer went by much faster than expected for Sid because of the trial and error of courting Kamala. A few weeks before he had to return home to the farm, Sid finally made it to Kamala's bed. From this point on, she taught him the language of making love. Lovemaking had to do a lot with caressing, kissing, and admiring each other.

Kamala would often say carnal knowledge has little to do with lovemaking and more to do with respect.

Sid spent many hours in bed with Kamala talking about life. He found out that she immigrated from Sri Lanka when she was three years old, her father was French, and her mother was native to Sri Lanka.

She grew up poor, and her poverty often seeped through her fine façade in the form of her grammar. It didn't disturb Sid; it made him feel closer when she let down her guard, even for a moment. He knew that Kamala was only a few years older than he was but already a world apart in experience and wisdom.

Sid learned to be a little bit wiser in his lovemaking. He dressed in fine clothes and shoes. Sid brought her thoughtful gifts and flowers. He understood that a man is respectful of women and treats the women in his life as a treasure—this is what Kamala taught Sid.

He visited Kamala once more before returning home to bring in the harvest. He stood in front of Kamala with tears in his eyes. He vowed his never-dying love for her and considered not returning home but staying in New Orleans. He told her that it would break his heart to leave her.

Kamala sat up in the chaise longue chair with a smile. She stood up and walked over to Sid, and caressed his face. She said, "Dear Sid, you have been my most appreciative pupil. You have learned much about lovemaking during our sessions, but you have one more lesson to know before leaving. You need to understand what it feels like to have a broken heart because that is a lesson that will stay with you your whole life.

"This lesson is not a gift to you but to the future women in your life that fall in love with you. Breaking one's heart can be devastating and, at the same time, necessary. Always be cautious of those who fall in love with you too fast. True love takes time, nurturing, and a deep understanding of each other.

"You can't stay with me because I will never see you again. I taught you what you needed to know to be a man among women. Remember always respect is an essential ingredient in any relationship.

"Sid, I, too, have grown fond of you, almost to the point of love. But unlike you, I can't allow myself such luxuries as love, not in my profession. I must always control the situation so that men who are not so kind and respectful of women cannot take advantage of Kamala.

"I know now that I will be an unforgettable memory in your mind. I know you will think of Kamala every time you make love to a woman. Remembering me is part of my fee for teaching such things.

"It is the end of our lessons and the end of our arrangement. Please show yourself out through the garden. I have another gentleman waiting." ⍟

☙

Chapter Fourteen

Spring came to Vermont in the form of mud season. A bleak time in the green mountains that is not totally out of the grip of winter but gives hope to warm days ahead. Mud season reflects a ship caught in the doldrums out at sea, a place in-between activity, where one waits for the winds of change to take them in another direction.

Whenever Sid is in a place where he is at a crossroads in his life, he always thinks of Kamala. Beautiful, wonderful Kamala, a woman young but with immeasurable wisdom. She was right, Sid thought; she will be unforgettable.

Sid and Vincent made it through their first Vermont winter, as did the coworking space. After the fall investors' fair, the start-ups had jet fuel as a cash infusion to take them to the next level. The pressure generated by the financial attention did create one night of the living dead company. The start-up working on an app for employee benefits hit a wall with state insurance regulators, as Marty predicted. They weren't finished, but they were on life support.

Karmakal was the surprise start-up that grew neck and neck over the last six months with Sun Potential. A surprise to all except the principals at Karmakal. In early January, the social networking site went online, receiving a steady flow of subscriptions. By early March, the website had reached a million subscribers. Not enough to take on Facebook, but enough for investors to notice.

Every Monday, the senior management at Karmakal had a breakfast meeting at a local diner in downtown Rutland. Over the six months, the Karmakal crew grew from the original three founders to Sid, Vincent, and three software engineers.

Eric, one of the three founders and the Karmakal idea guy, was born in Sao Paulo, Brazil. His grandfather immigrated from Germany after World War II. Eric's father started in banking but soon found the Brazilian financial industry corruption too much to swallow. He moved with his young family to Santa Cruz, California, during the early seventies.

Eric's parents became hippies who lived in a commune in Boulder Creek. During the seventies, all the collective farms started to fall apart, as did the high ideals that a new world could be created. The demise of the communal life was caused primarily by California biker gangs and hustlers moving in and turning the whole dream into a nightmare.

Eric's older brother was named Sunshine, and his sister was named Willow. Eric always felt lucky that he dodged the name bullet, being the youngest of three, and when his parents started to distrust the whole new order rhetoric. When Eric was five, his family left the commune, and his father started working at a software company in Silicon Valley. In the late seventies, a talented person could get a job in tech with little experience.

Even though Eric's parents did not profess a new world order anymore, they still practiced a new-age lifestyle at home. They talked a lot about the philosophies of Buddhism, Taoism, and Karma as part of their daily vocabulary. The root of Karmakal was Eric's spiritual upbringing.

Vincent asked, "Eric, I heard that the idea for Karmakal started at a gas station?"

Eric stopped eating his breakfast and looked up at Vincent with a smirk. He replied, "Yeh, how did you hear that story?"

Vincent responded, "It's a small crew; people talk late at night. Is it true?"

Eric sat back and took a long sip of his coffee. He replied, "Yeh, I don't like to spread that story because it gives Karmakal a less professional image."

Vincent countered, "I'll keep it between the crew."

Eric stated, "It's a simple story. I filled up my car at a gas station and dropped a toothpick on the ground next to the pump. I instantly bent over and picked up the toothpick, thinking I didn't want any negative karma.

"I started to laugh because I wondered how much negative karma I would receive from a toothpick left on a dirty gas station floor."

Sid laughed. He questioned, "I didn't hear this story. How did you jump from the gas station floor to a social networking site?"

Eric finished his last bite of breakfast. He recalled, "I started to think about how much we use the word karma in modern western society. Most people don't understand what karma is and that there isn't good or bad karma, but it has become as common as websites and the internet.

"Soon after my experience at the gas station, I started to see the word karma everywhere. Companies used karma in their names, and financial institutions made investments based on good karma buys.

"I saw the world of commerce breaking up into two distinct groups. One group is moving down the same old road destroying the earth for profit, and other companies are starting to move down a road to help the planet and maybe save humanity.

"I watched a documentary where a financial institution changed its investment portfolio to only purchase stocks attached to karma-positive companies. I started to see that maybe there was an opportunity."

Vincent questioned, "Did you think you could take on Facebook?"

Eric acknowledged, "The directors at Facebook profess that they are trying to do good in the world. The social networking site started at Harvard to evaluate women students' beauty and sex appeal, which was not a decent start. I knew I could do better.

"It's funny no one has asked me about the history of Karmakal. I find it strange that we are talking about this for the first time. It has been many months we have been working together."

Vincent responded, "The last few months have been long workdays and no time just to discuss the history of Karmakal." Vincent turned his attention to Steve finishing his breakfast. He asked, "When did you come on board, Steve?"

Steve replied, "Eric and I were roommates at MIT. I remember when he came home and started talking about his karma experience, but I just shrugged it off as a strange idea. Eric spoke about his childhood and his parents' new-age lifestyle.

"He would talk about the Buddhist Wheel of Life and always had a Taoist quip for every occasion. I thought it curious how Eric seemed to dislike his parents' lifestyle but still professed it all the time.

"He wouldn't let the idea of karma in modern society go, so I started to notice. Every student at MIT is looking for the next big thing, so I started to believe in Eric's passion."

Sid asked, "How about you, Peter? When did you become a true believer?"

Peter professed, "I came late to the party. I can't say I am a true believer, but I see the financial opportunity in Karmakal. Eric and Steve already came up with the name Karmakal, and I met them in passing at MIT. Luckily, the same Boston tech company hired Eric and me after college.

"We worked crazy long hours. After work, we would hang out at a local diner and discuss our ideas for a start-up. After a few months of working together, Eric started to trust me enough to discuss his idea for Karmakal. Eric and Peter had been working on the core idea for months. I didn't know when Eric slept. He seemed possessed by the idea, so his enthusiasm and dedication sold me."

Sid interjected, "So, where did the Buddhist Wheel of Life idea come from?"

Eric professed, "My parents lived their lives based on the Buddhist Wheel of Life philosophy. It is a visual representation of the spiritual philosophy of the Buddha, but it is primarily Tibetan, even though Buddha lived 2,500 years ago in India. The Buddha professed we are all living in an illusion where we are continually in the process of death and rebirth.

"We can't break free of this reality or reach Nirvana unless we transcend the six levels that make up the possible range of existence within Samsara. Nirvana is self-enlightenment, and Samsara is the illusion of the world.

"At the center of the Wheel of Life is a cock, snake, and pig, representing greed, anger, and ignorance. This dark trio fuels the world we see outside of ourselves. The Buddha preached that we must break this cycle to be free of the illusion; we need to realize the truth."

Sid interjected, "I thought you said karma is not good or bad?"

Eric continued, "I didn't say good or bad karma; I said negative or positive. My parents explained it to me. Karma is a critical concept in most religions and spiritual practices. Karma means action, work, or deed; it also refers to the spiritual principle of cause and effect, where the intent and actions of an individual influence the future of that individual; in the case of the Buddhist Wheel of Life, how that person may be reborn.

"Our actions in the world do not create good or bad karma; our efforts only add to our perception that we are either a physical or spiritual being—we are in the world and of the world, or not of the world."

Vincent questioned, "What does that mean, in the world but not of the world?"

Eric continued, "Understanding the meaning is part of breaking the cycle of death and rebirth. Your perception of this reality gives sense to Samsara or Nirvana. As I stated, Samsara represents the illusion that the world outside you is real. Nirvana symbolizes your connection to higher infinite consciousness and the purest form of your spiritual self.

"We are spiritual beings having a physical experience. The more we embrace the illusion that we are bodies, the more we will be in a dark place.

"There is a monster that surrounds and holds the Buddhist Wheel of Life. My father explained that the beast is a visual representation of our ego. Our ego, who many may reference as Satan, or the Devil, is continually convincing us that we are bodies, not spiritual beings. The ego's primary purpose is to keep us in the cycle of death and rebirth."

Vincent inquired, "Do you truly believe that the world is an illusion?"

Eric stated, "Growing up on the Buddhist Wheel of Life was academic, and I never considered it more than another religion that my parents were embracing. I understood the Wheel of Life intellectually, but it wasn't until I started working at the tech company in Boston that I saw the Wheel of Life reflecting our modern society.

"I moved into a rental home in Wellesley, Massachusetts, with my girlfriend. It wasn't long before I witnessed the Wheel of Life in my day-to-day experiences.

"The six realms that make up the Wheel of Life are the realms of the gods, the demigods, humans, animals, hungry ghosts, and hell denizens. We are reborn into six different realms based on our karma or actions from a previous life.

"If we have negative karma, we will be reborn in a lower realm and reborn into a higher realm if we have positive karma. We must be reborn into the realm of humans to have a chance to transcend the world, break the cycle of death and rebirth, and reach Nirvana."

Sid questioned, "You witnessed the Wheel of Life during your life in Boston?"

Eric continued, "I witnessed all six realms of the Wheel in Boston.

The Boston tech company was precisely like the tech company in the movie Office Space. Most of my coworkers lived a life of ignorant complacency and dullness, and their primary focus was avoiding pain and seeking comfort. The Wheel of Life refers to this as the realm of animals.

"On my first day at the company, the tech manager told me how he was able to do nothing and get away with it. Two other employees took me out to lunch to ensure I wasn't spoiling their good thing by trying to create something of value.

"Many employees were doing their own thing, doing nothing, and spending most of their time finding ways to look busy. I could never understand how anyone could spend their days doing busy work; what a waste."

Vincent asked, "How about hungry ghosts?"

Eric continued, "Every day, on my way to work from the South Train Station, I would walk through the Hungry Ghost world. The Hungry Ghost is a wasted creature with a vast, empty stomach—people addicted to drugs and alcohol who are never sated.

"They chase a desire that whittles away at their soul. They have fallen into a dark and cold place where they can't see the light anymore."

Steve interjected, "Eric, tell them about the gods and demigods. This story always makes sense because I grew up in Greenwich, Connecticut.

Eric took a sip of his coffee. He continued, "My girlfriend and I decided to rent a house in Wellesley. She was a scholar at Wellesley College. I didn't know I was entering a rat's nest of demigods.

"If you took all the overly ambitious and ruthless students from high school and placed them in one location, it would be Wellesley, Massachusetts.

"The realm of the demigods, they are hyper-competitive and paranoid, driven by a desire to beat their competition, and everyone is competitive. Their priority is getting to the top.

"My girlfriend and I went to a neighborhood event where the host introduced us as the renters. After this event, no one would talk to us or invite us to another event.

"Wellesley is a cancer cluster because they spray the lawns with chemicals. Even though their children, friends, and neighbors get cancer, they still need to have perfect laws, which shows the extent to which demigods desire to be perfect.

"Next to Wellesley is Weston, the home of the gods. Like in the

Wheel of Life, Wellesley residents want to obtain a home in Weston. They want to be gods like the inhabitants of Weston. Weston is full of old money.

"The realm of the gods is the highest and is depicted at the top of the Wheel. The domain of the gods sounds like a nice place to live, like Weston, but the realm of the Gods isn't perfect. Those born in the god realm live long and pleasure-filled lives, having wealth and power. Because the gods have such rich lives, they don't recognize the truth of suffering.

"Their power is, in a way, a curse because they are not motivated to seek liberation from the world. Eventually, their lives end and they must face rebirth in another, less powerful realm. The gods are perpetually at war with their neighbors, as the residents of Weston are at war with each other to be the most perfect."

Sid interjected, "You said there were six realms. You only described four."

Eric took the last sip of his coffee. He resumed, "The realm of hell is not depicted or created by an infinite being as the Bible states. Each person's karma makes their hell—being reborn in the realm of hell is up to each person. In other words, we are our own worst enemy. I believe everyone has a moment in the realm of hell.

"The last realm is the human realm. Individuals are most passionate and wise in this realm. Human beings experience many states of mind, and in this realm, they have an opportunity to free themselves from the cycle of death and rebirth.

"I believe that choosing to create Karmakal was a passionate and wise decision. I live in a human realm, and I'm hoping that I learn something of value during my journey."

Vincent asked, "How is all this tied to Karmakal?"

Eric stated, "I felt that the world has fallen into a dark place, so I wanted to create something that may bring light back to people's lives.

"When I first came up with the idea, it was a simple evaluation of human nature. I was allowing participants of Karmakal to evaluate in their hearts what their actions meant.

"Then I realized that making it a game would make it more interesting. If you consider the Buddhist Wheel of Life a game, then each Karmakal participant plays to break the cycle of death and rebirth, and each Karmakal participant plays to reach Nirvana.

"I think it is serendipitous that we are talking about the deeper meaning of Karmakal because we are beyond the core software programming stage and need to evolve the site. We can't move forwards unless everyone is on-board.

"I don't think everyone has to see the world as an illusion, but everyone has to see the bigger picture."

Sid looked over at Vincent. He asked, "So, Vincent, are you on board?"

Vincent sat back in his chair and smoothed his long blond hair behind his ears. He replied, "Sid, my friend, I have seen more miraculous things since I hooked up with you than in my young life. So, in for a penny, in for a pound." ଓ

☙

Chapter Fifteen

Marty rang the bell at the New York Stock Exchange to start trading Sun-Potential's initial public offering (IPO). David, the new CEO of Sun-Potential, thought it appropriate that Marty had the honor since he was the first true believer and the majority shareholder. Marty initially declared that it might take twenty-eight months for Sun-Potential to go public; it took twenty-four.

Much had changed with Sun-Potential and the coworking space over the two years. Only one of the original three founders remained with Sun-Potential. The founding president, Peter, was forced out after fourteen months by the board of directors. He had no experience managing a large company, and the committee felt Sun-Potential had grown beyond his abilities. The split was not amicable. Marty and Peter had a few words that led to an ugly scene. Marty separated his emotions from business; Peter couldn't.

Peter accused Marty of going behind his back and buying up shares of Sun-Potential so he would have total control; Marty didn't deny having hidden motives. Marty created shadow limited liability companies that were buying up Sun-Potential without the board of directors' knowledge. Before Sun-Potential went public, Marty announced his majority investment holding to the board.

Debra, one of the founders, married Peter. They worked long hours thinking they were building something great for the world. They talked about where they wanted to take the company, but both had no idea Marty would blindside them. Debra left with Peter. They both were given a golden parachute with money and shares in Sun-Potential. The tribute didn't soften the emotional pain both felt from the betrayal.

Justin, the last founder, decided to stay with the company. He was the lead engineer and knew the hardware better than anyone. Marty offered him riches to stay. He was the founding member who grew up in Vermont.

Justin always felt that he was along for the ride. Peter and Debra hired him late in the game. They often reminded Justin that he was there because of his technical knowledge. They always kept him at arm's length, but now he would be a senior manager and shareholder.

Peter asked Justin to leave with them, but the offer from Marty was just too good. Justin felt he could bring a lot more to the table even though he knew he had to watch his back; Marty could screw him instantly.

Marty found David at Green Mountain Power Company, a small utility company in Vermont. David started at Green Mountain right after college and worked his way up to president after twenty years. He originated his stint with Green Mountain Power as an electrical engineer, so he knew the grid and its strengths and weaknesses.

Sun-Potential needed to work with the old grid structure. David also headed up cyber security for the company. Hackers worked to access the grid, and Sun-Potential was required to be secure. The Sun-Potential board hired him before they fired Peter.

Vincent sold his shares of Karmakal to Sid just after it reached two million subscribers. He never got a deep understanding of Karmakal. Vincent was always waiting for the social networking site to collapse; he finally decided he wasn't the right man for Karmakal.

Just before Sun-Potential went public, Vincent took over the day-to-day operations of the coworking space. A rift started to form between Sid and Vincent because Vincent began to align his star with Marty. Sid could feel the distance from Vincent growing but was too involved with making Karmakal a success. Sid found allies in Eric and Joleen.

Marty knew Sid was losing interest in the coworking space and spending more time managing Karmakal. When Vincent took over the coworking space, Sid found it a relief to focus all his attention on Karmakal. Marty needed someone at the coworking space's helm to keep up the high energy. Vincent blossomed into a competent leader for the coworking space.

After ringing the New York Stock Exchange bell, Marty noticed Sid and Vincent in the back of a group of Sun-Potential employees. He pressed through the crowd and stood in front of Sid and Vincent. He inquired, "You are both millionaires now, at least on paper. Have you thought about what you are going to do moving forward?"

Sid and Vincent both stood before Marty with a dazed look. Their expressions seemed like Marty was talking in a foreign language, and Sid and Vincent struggled to understand what he was saying.

Vincent countered, "Hell, I figure I will keep doing what I am doing. I plan to send my father a few dollars to buy better land and a decent herd. I discovered my brother and sister had fallen on hard times; they could help our father with the new ranch. The money will be a big surprise."

Sid patted Marty on the shoulder. He replied, "I don't see making any big moves; I'll probably feed some of the money back into Karmakal. We could always use a few more engineers."

Vincent professed, "Yeh, boss, you brought us this far. I figure there is more to come. In for a penny, in for a pound."

Sid was misleading Marty and Vincent. He had planned to move Karmakal out of the coworking space for many months and needed the money he would receive from Sun-Potential's initial public offering to move to Burlington, Vermont.

Sid had been negotiating with a small technology company in Montreal, Canada. The tech company will merge with Karmakal and set up shop in a building in Williston outside Burlington with its twenty computer science engineers. Sid had been stalling until he sold Sun-Potential shares and set the plan in motion.

Before Sun-Potential's IPO, Sid contacted a broker to sell his shares during the IPO; Sid ended up with twelve million plus change. A hefty sum, but he knew money goes fast, so he would have to get another round of funding soon to take Karmakal to the next level if he wanted the social networking site to survive.

Karmakal had twenty-three million subscribers, not even a speck in Facebook's shadow, but advertisers were starting to take notice of the new social networking site and its possibilities.

After the opening bell at the New York Stock Exchange, the party moved to a private room at Sparks Steakhouse. Marty avowed that Sparks was the best steak house in New York City. He claimed that he had many dinners at Sparks with questionable mob-tied associates.

Sid and Vincent didn't know if Marty was blowing smoke or that he did business with mobsters—if either were the truth, it would not surprise them. Sid and Vincent had built up a warm feeling and a sincere affection for Marty. He has kept to his word and hasn't screwed them, at least not severely.

The party started to wind down around nine in the evening, and most of the Sun-Potential crew had already returned to their hotel rooms at the Conrad Hotel in mid-town Manhattan. Marty was always a master of showing his people a good time. When things were good, Marty lived a life of luxury, and with Sun-Potential going public, he could afford to spread the extravagance around.

David and his wife left after nine. They were a little younger than Marty but couldn't keep up with their younger employees. They were leaving early to spend a week on Martha's Vineyard before returning to the office. They had a house on the island and spent many weeks during the summer relaxing. David knew the IPO was just the start of hard work to build the company. He would have investors breathing down his back. He dealt with investors for years at Green Mountain Power but never felt at peace with the pressure.

Vincent left with his new girlfriend, Cindy, and Joleen at ten. Joleen had already agreed to move to Burlington and take on the design and marketing director role for Karmakal. She wasn't a true believer in Karmakal, but she loved Sid and believed in him. Working at WeWork for so many years had popped her bubble about how people could do something good for humankind. She secretly worried that if Karmakal was successful, Sid might fall into the same ego trap as the CEO of WeWork. She hoped Sid was a better man than her former boss.

Marty and Sid sat at the bar alone. Sid wanted to come clean with Marty, and Marty needed to be honest with Sid.

Marty ordered another round of drinks for them. He ordered the Scottish smoked salmon with onions and capers appetizer; this dish was his favorite at Sparks. He would confess that this appetizer and a twenty-year-old single malt Scotch whiskey may be better than sex.

Marty and Sid toasted their success. Marty drank his shot in one gulp. He put his hand on Sid's shoulder and confessed, "Sid, I know your poker tell. I knew it early in the game back at Newburg."

Sid raised his eyebrows. He asked, "So, what's my poker tell?"

Marty laughed and signaled another round to the bartender. He confided, "I can't tell you because then I wouldn't know when you are not telling the truth."

Sid raised his eyebrows. He inquired, "I'm lying about something?"

Marty countered, "I know you plan to take Karmakal north to Burlington. I deal in information, plus I know a few guys in the Montreal underworld doing business with the tech company you are merging with; it's hard to keep secrets."

Sid looked caught in his lie. He questioned, "So?"

Marty took a sip of his Scotch. He stated, "So, you don't have to keep secrets. When I asked about your next move, I figured you would tell me the truth. The truth is, I'm also moving on. If you remember, I was in this until the IPO and the big payout.

"You might consider me like the guy who works to get a politician elected. After the election, I move on to the next politician. I don't want to manage a company or be part of an administration; I like the risk too much."

Sid asked, "What are you moving on to?"

Marty continued, "I have been working on two other small cities in the Midwest. I think one is ripe for a coworking space and maybe another unicorn."

Sid inquired, "What cities?"

Marty responded, "It doesn't matter because you are not coming. I think you've learned all that I can teach you. I need to find another Sid and Vincent for my next venture."

Sid probed, "I remember you saying something about retiring if we landed a unicorn?"

Marty continued, "Yeh, I have been considering retiring for ten years. Can you imagine me walking a golf course or sitting around watching television?"

Sid laughed. He continued, "No, I guess not. I have never seen a person so alive in the center of a group of potential marks."

Marty professed, "You and Vincent were one of the best teams I have come across. Too bad I can't utilize your talents again for my next venture."

Sid asked, "When are you leaving?"

Marty continued, "At the end of next week. I have already informed David of my plans. I think he was relieved that I won't be around to suck up all the oxygen. He is a solid administrator but not a showman, but I think he is what Sun-Potential needs to take it to the next level."

Sid took a sip of his drink. He queried, "You know Vincent has become your devotee? Does he know that you are moving on?"

Marty took another sip of his Scotch. He continued, "No, I haven't told him yet. I was deciding if I should take him with me, but I don't think Vincent would be an asset without you. I think he will be happy staying in Rutland, managing the coworking space, and living with his new girlfriend.

"I didn't dump all my stocks of Sun-Potential during the IPO. I still own twenty-five percent of the company and the smaller companies in the coworking space.

"I will come up with a title for Vincent, maybe vice president; he can keep an eye on my investments. I'll show up in Rutland twice yearly to keep the wheels moving."

Sid inquired, "How will you find replacements for Vincent and me?"

Marty continued, "The poker circuit. The best place to find talented hustlers. Every state has a big poker game each month, so I will spend the next few months finding my next disciples."

Sid laughed. He stated, "So, after the big payout, you planned to dump Vincent and me?"

Marty recanted, "Not dump. At the start of this thing, I told you that a grift has a short shelf life. You and Vincent would have swum or drowned, and we got lucky with Sun-Potential. The whole thing could have gone south, and we could be packing our bags and skipping town right now.

"I know how fickle investors are with their money; you are a hero on *Forbes* magazine, or you are a fraud and receive a mug shot. Anyway, you were planning to move on, and I just wanted you to know that you didn't have to keep it from me.

"Many of my business connections are fellow co-conspirators. I wanted us to part amicable; I never know when we could help each other." Marty reached into his pocket, pulled out an envelope, and handed it to Sid.

Sid opened the envelope, and inside was a check for one million dollars. Sid questioned, "What's this for?"

Marty professed, "I'm starting to become a true believer in Karmakal. The social networking site seems to be growing, and I wanted in on the ground floor. That's to buy five percent of the company. I know the tech company you will merge with has some major clients that will double Karmakal's profile and profits."

Sid laughed, "Maybe this money is to keep a leash on your former follower?"

Marty laughed and patted Sid on the back. He continued, "Maybe, I always want to hedge my bets and keep an eye on my investments. You have been one of my wisest assets."

Marty and Sid got up from the bar and decided to walk back to the hotel together. Marty left his usual one hundred dollar tip. Sid and Marty walked through the vacant streets of Manhattan late at night, and the lights were still burning bright around them.

A warm feeling for Marty started well up in Sid's heart. He said, "Marty, I want you to know that I have learned much from you, more than you may know. It's strange to be walking the streets of New York with you when Vincent and I resided at Rikers Island a few years ago.

"I have learned from you that wealth and power don't make a person whole. I realize that you are not chasing wealth and power but the game itself. I see that wealth and power mean nothing to you.

"I have learned how thin the line is between a grift and how the whole world operates. I have often considered that the world may be just a deception, and I've learned that everything around me is a little bit of fairy dust and magic.

"Unfortunately, this knowledge has deepened the depth of my emptiness. I've learned that I am not on the path with Karmakal to build wealth and power; creating the business is the payment I seek.

"One of the most important things I have learned from you is to forgive my father. I used to disdain my father for his corruption. I've learned he was giving his parishioners a gift of hope; without hope, the machine breaks down, and people have nothing. I've learned a lot from you, Marty." ❦

CB

Chapter Sixteen

The Karmakal offices in Williston, Vermont, were still in poor condition when most staff arrived. The Karmakal headquarters were formerly a home remodeling company that served Chittenden County for fifty years. Home Depot struck the coup de grace for the remodeling business when the company moved to home services utilizing independent contractors.

During the move from Rutland to Burlington, Karmakal reached fifty million subscribers; companies, investors, and governments started to take serious notice of the social networking site.

Digital privacy was becoming an issue that Sid and his senior management team needed to deal with before they created the same unfortunate legacy still plaguing Facebook. To keep Karmakal from being hacked, Sid created a cyber security department headed by Dmitri, a Russian hacker. He picked up and left Russia in a hurry for unknown reasons.

Marty sent Dmitri to Sid with a recommendation to hire and don't ask questions. Sid was surprised and, at the same time, was not that Marty had connections in the dark places of the world. Marty informed Sid that Dmitri would keep Karmakal safe from the people he used to know. Sid attended a cyber security conference in Burlington, where he found out that six criminal organizations in Russia do most of the hacking in the world. The security conference roundtable mentioned Dmitri as a significant player on the dark web.

Sid's office was still in disrepair, with boxes stacked around the room. The mess created a sense of anxiety in Sid. He tended to be overly obsessive, and chaos added to his angst.

Vincent walked into the office with the two lawn chairs they used back in Rutland. He said, "There you go, buddy. These chairs were the last thing on the truck."

Sid stood up and shook Vincent's hand. He replied, "I appreciate helping us move to Burlington. You always have a place with Karmakal."

Vincent replied, "Hell, I appreciate that, but I think our stars are moving in different directions."

Sid asked, "So, where is your star taking you? Are you staying at the coworking space?"

Vincent replied, "No, I decided to move on with Marty. I don't think Rutland will be as entertaining without you. I dislike being a leader; there is too much administrative bullshit.

"New staff members are starting to form camps and stab each other in the back for power. I might be a grifter, but I have some sense of honor. I never thought that the average office could be so ruthless. I feel like I'm back in prison."

Sid replied, "Rikers Island was a jail."

Vincent and Sid laughed. Vincent continued, "Hell, I will miss you. You were the best friend I have ever had, but I don't feel part of Karmakal."

Sid asked, "Where will you go?"

Vincent continued, "Marty had his eye on two small cities in the Midwest. I'm going to one of them to pave the way for Marty to do his magic. He will find another crew to start another coworking space in the other town. I guess I'm going to spread the gospel, according to Marty. I wish you would drop Karmakal and come with us, but I know that is a non-starter. You have never been Marty's disciple."

Sid shook Vincent's hand. He said, "I'm proud of you, Vincenzo Govinda Aiello. You made your decision, and I know it was a hard one. I felt you relied on me too much, but I see you are your own man. I wish you the best."

Vincent looked at Sid. He said, "I hope we meet again someday."

Sid nodded and replied, "I feel that we will."

☘

The first six months at the new Karmakal offices in the Burlington area were a blur. Karmakal was growing so fast that Sid worried they would already outgrow the space. He had to hire ten new engineers and find another cloud computing company to handle Karmakal's expansive data requirements. He had to prepare for the first board of directors' meeting.

Sid considered that Karmakal might be growing beyond his abilities. He remembered the ugly scene with Sun-Potential's founders and didn't want to replicate the event. He considered offering the board to hire a new chief executive officer and step down to become the chief operating officer. The challenge was that there wasn't any company that reflected what Karmakal had become. Managing and building the social networking site would take a particular person.

Eric knocked on Sid's office door. He asked, "Are you ready? The board is all seated, and they have an itinerary they want to focus on."

Sid laughed. He inquired, "Are they going to fire me?"

A concerned look came over Eric's face. He stated, "No, I think they are happy with your performance. The meeting's focus has something to do with the government."

Sid asked, "The Vermont government?"

Eric continued, "No, I think the federal government."

Sid picked up his papers and walked to the conference room. The directors sat at the conference table, sipping Gallagher Close Farm Coffee Roasters' Brew and eating sandwiches from Mirabelle's Bakery.

The board of directors consisted of Vermont business and government power players. A few of the original investors took board positions, and the owner of Vermont Venture Capital held the position of chairman.

Sid walked in with Eric and sat at the head of the table. Sid welcomed the board and walked them through the schedule, including customary financial statements and action items—the usual bland administrative fodder.

The board voted on the different items on the agenda without reservations to expedite the meeting. Sid considered that the board had a plan; he wondered if Eric was wrong about being fired. He felt that maybe he wanted to be forced out. The job was becoming overwhelming.

Sid hesitantly asked, "Is everyone on the board happy with the direction Karmakal is going?"

The board chairman, Peter Shaw, stood up with enthusiasm. He replied, "I think I can speak for everyone on the board in reassuring you that we feel Karmakal is moving in the right direction with the right leader. We know that the fast growth of a company can become daunting, but we are here to support you. If we felt another could do better, we would pursue it, but no one would come close to your dedication and commitment."

Sid had a confused look. He asked, "So, what does the federal government want with Karmakal?"

Peter sat back in his chair. He continued, "Representatives from the Central Intelligence Agency and National Security Agency met with us last weekend; they wanted to propose a joint venture."

Sid stiffened his back. He questioned, "Why didn't they want to meet with me first?"

Peter continued, "They were concerned about your past and that you may reject their proposal outright before the board had a chance to consider their offer."

Sid asked, "My past, you mean Rikers or poor black farmer from Alabama?"

Peter looked around the room at his fellow board members. He continued, "This doesn't have anything to do with that part of your past. They felt that most leaders of companies have strong emotional ties that are hard to overcome. They knew the board would consider their offer without outright rejection. We would like you to take some time to consider their offer."

Sid questioned, "Okay, so what is their offer?"

Peter motioned to Charles Boles, a chief technology engineer at a healthcare company and a senior Karmakal board member. He stated, "I think Charles would be best to describe the government's offer."

Charles Boles was a colonel in the United States Marine Corps. He did tours as an intelligence operative in Iraq and managed the cyber security transition installed by the United States. After he retired, a technology company hired him to be a liaison between the company and the United States Government.

Sid always considered that the healthcare company Charles worked for did more than develop hospital information software. He believed the company was a bit nefarious and did work for foreign regimes. Sid felt the hospital software was a front. He ultimately didn't care—who was he to judge with his Rikers Island and grifter background?

Sid found as he rose in the higher echelons of industry, many of the companies he did business with were either working on the edge of disaster or had less than-honorable men as leaders. He never forgot the mantra, 'If you steal a little, they put you in jail; if you steal a lot, it makes you respectable.'"

Marty recommended Charles Boles. He claimed that if Karmakal ever got big, they would have to deal with governments, and Charles was the man to head off any conflicts.

Charles sipped his Gallagher Close Farm coffee. He replied, "The intelligence community has been watching the growth of Karmakal for some time. The CIA has been aware that China and Russia know the potential Karmakal has for information gathering."

Sid looked surprised and confused by the assertion made by Charles. He asked, "What information?"

Charles continued, "As we are all aware, the now fifty million-plus subscribers to Karmakal make an emotional judgment call on individual actions. Facebook, Twitter, Amazon, and other social networking sites can collect data on purchases and activities done by their subscribers. Still, no other site can collect the emotional data Karmakal compiles.

"The CIA and NSA have proposed to install an intelligence algorithm in the main operating system of Karmakal that would collect data on the subscribers' emotional views on various subjects.

"The agencies would be able to break down the data into states, regions, countries, age groups, gender, and even political views. The government could even offer subjects to test with the subscriber base."

Sid stiffened his back. He asked, "What would their reason be for collecting this data?"

Charles could see that Sid was irritated by the idea of the government controlling Karmakal. Charles continued, "With this data, they could measure and evaluate the emotional reactions of our citizens to financial decisions, political decisions, or even going to war.

"Most government decisions are executed based on polls done by third-party administrators, but they have found that most people who take a position in a survey are lying. The poll taker will sway their view and often vote differently than they professed.

"The government has concluded that there are no reasons someone would lie in a Karmakal poll. The participants are not using their real names, but we know much about them, so we can more accurately assess how people feel about any subject."

Sid asked, "We?"

Charles raised his eyebrows. He continued, "I mean, the government can more accurately assess how people feel about any subject."

Sid questioned, "So, why would we do this, and what is in it for us?"

Charles looked around the room to gauge the expressions of the attendees. Not everyone on the board knew of the government's interest in Karmakal. Charles continued, "The devil we know is better than the devil we don't know."

Sid inquired, "What does that mean?"

Charles continued, "The government suspects other governments attempting to hack Karmakal but have been unsuccessful, primarily due to Dimitri. They feel that it is only a matter of time before a government like North Korea will have a bug in Karmakal.

"The CIA and NSA would put the full security apparatus of the United States government behind Karmakal to stay secure. They feel if a country such as North Korea or Russia knew the emotional makeup of the American public, they might test the strength of, let's say, NATO.

"If they understood the populace of the United States and Europe were not behind defending a sovereign nation such as Ukraine, then it might be the demise of their democracy."

Sid sat up in his chair in shock. He continued, "That is heavy."

Charles continued, "Yeh, who knew that Karmakal would get large enough for governments to be interested in its data."

Sid asked, "This is all good and patriotic, but what is the bottom line? What is in it financially and socially for us?"

Charles continued, "The intelligence community would fix it, so we would receive a one hundred million dollar investment. The government cannot invest directly in Karmakal or add it as a line item in their budget, as it has too much exposure. If the news media got wind of this deal, it most likely would shut down Karmakal because no subscriber would trust the site.

"The intelligence community would have to invest through back channels. I have had extensive experience working on these deals. Most governments operate through back channels, and most would not exist if their citizens knew what their tax dollars were compensating."

Sid laughed, "So, I guess a large underground facility exists under area 51?"

With a stern look, Charles continued, "I'm not able to confirm or deny that assertion."

Sid laughed. He continued, "I was just joking."

Charles continued, "Well, Sid, during my twenty years in service, I have found that the government lacks a sense of humor about intelligence."

Sid asked, "So, how would this deal help us socially or strategically?"

Charles stated, "The government would allow a small group of Karmakal senior management to access the data to grow the social networking site with a level of accuracy that we could only imagine.

"The government would expand our advertiser list to include major corporations. This move would put Karmakal in a position where a larger company or social networking site would buy us out for billions. This move would put us in the big leagues playing with the major world power brokers. As I stated earlier, helping to secure the world for democracy."

Sid shook his head. He replied, "That is some sales job. So, how long do we have to decide on this government prospect? I expect that we won't be able to change our minds once they are embedded?"

Charles continued, "No, once they spend millions on this algorithm and set up the cyber security system, they won't be easy to disengage. To answer your other question, they gave us thirty days to decide.

"I have a lot of experience working in the intelligence community. If we decide not to play ball with the government, they will likely hack our system and keep it a secret. I don't think Dimitri would catch on to a government hack.

"They are motivated not to have another country access this data; they can't afford to let China, Russia, or even allies access this kind of data. Karmakal could change the balance of power. Never have we had such access to the true feelings of human beings."

Sid asked with a furrowed brow, "So, no choice?"

Charles continued, "We always have choices. One would be to move along with governments damaging our technological infrastructure, or we could shut Karmakal down. Even if we shut Karmakal down, the government would have another social networking company start it back up again. Eric, you came along with a great idea, and it is hard to kill a great idea once it takes flight."

Eric had stayed in the background and kept silent the whole time. He liked that Sid took most of the heat. All the board of directors looked over in his direction.

Charles asked, "So, what do you think, Eric?"

Eric took a moment to consider what to say. He replied, "Well, I feel we have lost our way. I was naïve, thinking I could create something that would remind people of a higher purpose. My parents used to warn me that once you present a spiritual concept into this reality, it will become part of the world and become twisted."

Peter asked, "What better purpose could there be than saving the world for democracy?"

Eric continued, "Democracy, governments, war, and intelligence are things of this world, and these things have continued the deception that we can control the outcome of events.

"I attempted with Karmakal to enlighten people about the world beyond the façade and the world that connects us to our purest spiritual connection with the Source."

Peter interjected, "That is all well and good, but a connection to the Source doesn't keep a company like Karmakal operating. We need to make the appropriate allies to continue the growth and security of the site."

Eric continued, "That is where you are wrong. The connection we have with the Source is the real power behind Karmakal. Without my connection with the Source, I would have never come up with this idea—all knowledge comes from the Source."

Peter raised his hand and motioned for silence. "We can go around and around with this subject, but as Charles stated, we have no option. By raising hands, how many voting board members allow the United States government to install an algorithm to collect data on our subscribers?

"Let the meeting minutes show the raised hands, with no opposition other than Eric." ❧

⊗

Chapter Seventeen

It was three minutes to midnight on New Year's Eve when Karmakal reached one hundred million subscribers. It had been seventeen months since Sid moved the social networking site to Burlington. Sid rented out the Burlington Pub and Brewery for the company's New Year's Eve party and to celebrate the milestone.

The restaurant is an established eatery in Burlington. It is not the fanciest or the best food, but it has an ambiance deeply rooted in Burlington's history. Sid always looks for the most authentic experience, not necessarily the most glamorous.

Sid was firmly the CEO of Karmakal and the majority shareholder since he bought out Peter and David. Peter and David were never true believers of Karmakal; they were only in the game for the payday. They both left with enough money to start another venture or fund other ventures. No hard feelings, just business.

Eric was still invested emotionally in Karmakal. He was not in it for money or ego; something else drove him.

Soon after midnight, the festivities started to die down. Most Karmakal employees began to disperse or hook up as young people do. Eric and Sid were the oldest employees at the company. Most of the new crew couldn't rent a car yet; only youth could put in the sixteen-hour days needed to keep up with Karmakal's growth.

After too many beers, Joleen decided this would be an excellent time, to be honest with Sid. She found him sitting alone in a room situated off the main restaurant. She asked, "Is this a good time to talk?"

Sid sat back with a sigh. He asked, "Talk about what?"

Joleen continued, "Look, I'll get to the point. A company in

Charlottesville, Virginia, offered me a boatload of money and benefits to head their marketing and design team."

Sid sat up with a furrowed brow. He asked, "When did this happen?"

Joleen walked over and sat down at the table across from Sid. She continued, "A friend contacted me last weekend, and he recommended me for the position. I would have to start as soon as possible."

Sid stiffened his back, and his professional facade reared its ugly head. Joleen had witnessed Sid's transformation from a loving boyfriend to a hardened jerk. He replied, "Sounds like a great opportunity."

Joleen's shoulders and head slumped down. She replied, "I knew you would do this."

Sid replied, "Do what?"

Joleen continued, "I know you would push me away when cornered."

Sid asked, "Cornered?"

Joleen continued, "I assumed you might take our relationship more seriously once we moved to Burlington."

Sid continued, "I do take our relationship seriously."

Joleen asked, "Then why haven't we discussed marriage?"

Sid started to relax, and the nice guy started to shine through. He continued, "I love you, Joleen. I don't often let people in my heart. I am confused about our relationship, but one thing is clear: you should not marry me. I'm still dealing with daemons, and I don't want to inflict my pain on you."

Joleen professed, "Sid, we all have daemons. It's a little easier if you have someone to share your pain with; this is the nature of relationships."

Sid stated, "I'm not ready to take that step in my life, even with someone I love as much as I love you. If you need to take that position in Virginia, I will understand. Your leaving would break my heart, but I would be happy for you."

Joleen looked at Sid with tears in her eyes. She continued, "I don't want to be here if there isn't any future for us. I never bought into the idea of Karmakal, and I have never been a true believer. I made this move to Burlington because I love you."

Sid inquired, "I know you had other offers. Why now? What changed your mind."

Joleen responded, "I found out about your deal with the government. I could understand your passion for Karmakal, but I can't understand why you allowed our government to spy on its citizens."

Sid confessed, "Yeh, it's been a struggle. I didn't have any choice other than leave, but I felt that maybe I could salvage the whole thing and still do something good for the world. How did you find out?"

Joleen stated, "Small company, people talk. I'm surprised that it took me a year to find out; I'm more surprised you didn't tell me."

Sid admitted, "I wanted to tell you, but I feared what you might have done. I feared you would leave."

Joleen declared, "You should have trusted me. I'm not leaving because of the government spying; I'm leaving because you kept it from me. I lost my innocence with WeWork and saw how power and money could corrupt.

The CEO at WeWork had the best intentions when he started the company, but the ascension changed him. I feel the success of Karmakal has changed you."

Sid continued, "You're right; with all the success and money, I still feel empty, even more so with the isolation it has created. I love you, Joleen, but I can't make any commitments until I find peace in my heart. When will I know your decision?"

Joleen sunk back in her chair. She confirmed, "I'll tell you next week, but I most likely will take the job in Virginia." Joleen and Sid hugged, then she walked out of the room with her head down. Sid didn't say anything more to dissuade her from moving on.

⋐⋑

Eric left the bar with his Magic #9 lager looking for Sid. He found him alone in a private room. Sid was looking out the window with a dire look on his face. Eric asked, "What's the matter, buddy? You look like you saw a ghost."

Sid looked up from his beer with a grim look. He replied, "Joleen and I just had a big fight."

Eric sat down across from Sid. He inquired, "Bad time to fight. Do you mind me asking what it was about?"

Sid smiled; he took a drag from his beer. He replied, "We had the 'Where is our relationship going talk.'"

Eric sat back in his chair, thought for a moment, and replied, "Oh, that talk. I've had that talk. So, are you going to marry her?"

Sid countered, "I thought I would never get married, but I didn't expect to meet someone like Joleen."

Eric asserted, "Well, you have money, Karmakal is growing, and you live in a great place. Why wouldn't you get married?"

Sid replied, "It's not about the world around me. It is about the emptiness I felt my entire life. I can't shake the darkness, no matter how successful I become. I thought it was about my father for a long time, but I have been away too many years from my past to cause my pain. I don't want to drag Joleen into the pit with me."

Eric interjected, "I think God is working on you."

Sid countered, "I don't believe in God."

Eric responded, "Well, God believes in you, but you may not believe in the God your father professed. That God is corrupt and looking out for a payday, usually at the expense of others."

Sid declared, "Funny because that is the God I worshiped for a long time. I thought being a grifter would bring me peace, but it tore me apart."

Eric replied, "Having a near-death experience can cause a lot of emptiness unless you do the work to see the light."

Sid sat up in his chair with a startled look. He asked, "How do you know that story? Wait, Vincent told you?"

Eric laughed, "Yeh, Vincent spilled the beans, but I think he was more concerned about you than just disclosing your secret. He told me when we were both a little drunk one late night."

Sid inquired, "So, what do you know about near-death experiences."

Eric continued, "Plenty; I died in a car crash when I was fourteen. I witnessed the whole process of moving out of my body and seeing a warm light. I was officially dead for twenty minutes when the paramedics brought me back to life."

Sid replied, "My near-death experience happened at a young age."

Eric continued, "Yeh, but I bet we had the same experience when we returned to this world."

Sid asked, "What would that be?"

Eric continued, "Sadness, depression. I wasn't happy to be back here."

Sid replied, "Yeh, that was my experience. Unfortunately, I cannot shake the feeling of emptiness."

Eric continued, "That's because you still believe in the world outside yourself."

Sid asked, "What do you mean by the world outside us? Is there another world?"

Eric continued, "Yes, the world inside of us. The true connection to our purest spiritual selves. When I came back alive, I was angry and felt deep emptiness. I was lucky, though, at least for moments. I had spiritually aware parents who helped me transcend the darkness. I still get depressed whenever I put too much belief in the world. Did you ever turn to God for comfort?"

Sid took a sip of his beer and looked out the window again. He replied, "I did go through a born-again Christian phase when I was a teenager, but it only helped the emptiness for a couple of years. I started to see what the church was selling, and I became bitter, which only brought back the depression."

Eric continued, "My parents used to quote, Vine Deloria Jr., 'Religion is for folks who are scared of going to hell, spirituality is for those who have been there.'"

Sid asked, "I know that quote, what does it mean to you?"

Eric continued, "What I have become aware of during my short young life is that we must find our truth. When I died in that car crash, I did see my whole life pass before my eyes, not in a visual sense but from my heart.

"I should disclose that you are being told all this by someone who has not transcended this world. I still struggle daily with my ego, and I know that the most important relationship is with our purest spiritual connection.

"After my near-death experience, I wanted to know what this world is, this illusion. I read everything I could get my hands on. I read the Bible, the Quran, and every religious and spiritual text I could find. My need to understand was insatiable.

"One of the many books that helped me see the world another way was *The Course in Miracles*; it helped train me to see the world as an illusion. The primary philosophy of *The Course in Miracles* is that 'nothing real can be threatened, and nothing unreal exists; herein lies the peace of God.'"

Sid asked, "What does that mean?"

Eric continued, "I'll tell you how I interpret it, but you must go through the process to understand it in your heart. It means the world we see outside us is an illusion, and all the violence, hate, and anger do not exist in a spiritual reality.

"That we are spiritual beings having a physical experience. I have found that all spiritual text helps us see that the only way we separate from each other is through our perceptions. The spiritual and religious books help us break down our perceptions that are barriers to our connection with our spiritual self. No spiritual or religious text is the end-all. Spirituality and religion have their truth, but each of us needs to find our path."

Sid asked, "How does Karmakal fit into this philosophy?"

Eric continued, "The idea of Karmakal did start at the gas station with Karma points, but my desire to walk a spiritual path started long before. Karmakal represents a daily reminder of the spiritual principles I have embraced, and I get paid for walking the path."

Sid asked, "If you believe creating Karmakal is your divine destiny, why did you stay after the government bullied us into spying on our subscribers?"

Eric replied, "I don't think creating Karmakal is my divine destiny. Karmakal is a tool that helps me develop a language so that I can connect with my true spiritual relationship. It might seem that the government has denigrated our efforts with Karmakal, but one thing that I have come to understand is that everything has a purpose. Maybe we needed the government to intervene, so Karmakal doesn't fall into the hands of true evil. I don't know how this story will play out, but I know that I am still on my divine path and that Karmakal is still in my heart. I feel that we can do great things with Karmakal."

Sid asked, "How do you know you are on your divine path?"

Eric continued, "That's an easy one. I am at peace in my heart when I follow my diving path. If I stray off the path to satisfy my ego, I instantly feel the emptiness fill my heart. I was attracted to the idea of Karmakal, not through my intellect but my heart."

Sid laughed. He replied, "Funny, I said that same thing to Vincent when he asked how I follow my heart."

Eric continued, "The key is listening to our hearts."

Sid replied, "Yeh, I was instantly attracted to Karmakal and still feel good in my heart about the company, with or without government involvement.

"I told Marty I was interested in Karmakal because it had financial opportunities. The truth was I didn't care if we made one dollar. I knew I had to be part of Karmakal, meet you, and meet Joleen."

Eric continued, "I felt an instant kinship with you when I met you. People with near-death experiences can sense others with the same understanding."

Sid asked, "So, I remember reading Plato and the cave. I understand that what we perceive may only be an illusion, but I've understood this concept intellectually but not experientially."

Eric replied, "The best way to understand that the world is an illusion is to experience it firsthand. It is almost three-thirty, a good time to break down perceptions. Do you want to take a walk around Burlington? It's cold but not too cold."

Eric and Sid left the bar and walked onto Church Street downtown Burlington. There was a stillness in the air Sid had never felt before. He felt the world was ready for him to understand the truth. He knew from the moment he walked onto Church Street he would remember this night. He thought that everyone knew the truth except him and that everyone would welcome him home once he understood. Sid had his vision of running in another world flash over his consciousness.

Eric started to speak in a low, deliberate tone. He said, "There is a concept in physics called physical reality. I have translated this theory into a more expansive meaning than the intended purpose. I understand it as our physical reality is the only reality that exists. In this space, your father and mother in Alabama do not exist. Joleen does not exist. Europe, China, and Russia do not exist. The only thing that exists is the space we now occupy. We are spiritual beings creating this space to understand ourselves in a physical reality."

A transformation started to take form in Sid's consciousness. He looked around and started to see the world as a thin layer of an illusion. He not only saw the world as a mirage but also felt it deep in his heart. He was free of the emptiness for the first time in his life.

Eric continued, "As we walk through this reality, we start disconnecting from our physical selves. We start to observe our physical selves from the safety of our spiritual connection; I call this process extended."

The more Sid listened to Eric, the more influential the feeling of disconnecting from his physical being became. He didn't feel the cold of the night; it faded away. The world around Sid started to become black and white, and all the colors seemed to disappear. As they walked down Church Street, a thin veil of imagery encircled the two.

Eric and Sid sat on a bench in the upper part of Church Street.

They stared at each other for a long time. Eric continued, "The truth is that there is nothing outside you, and you are one with all beings."

Sid deeply contemplated what Eric was saying. He considered that if there was no one outside of him, Eric was also an illusion; Eric was part of him. He realized he was talking to himself since no one was outside him.

The moment he understood this concept at a deep level of consciousness, he looked over at Eric, and for a moment, he saw his face in Eric's face.

Then he felt his mind expand to the size of a beach ball and then compress into a single thin layer of perception cloaked in a veil of black and white.

Eric asked, "You see it, don't you? I feel that you have had a much more powerful experience than I have yet to have. I think I felt that something was dormant in you for a long time; I believe it has finally awakened. ∞

ᘓ

Chapter Eighteen

It was five days since the New Year's Eve party at the Burlington pub, and no one had seen Sid. Eric considered his disappearance a reaction to their spiritual experience. Eric was concerned about Sid. He told everyone that Sid was on a business trip. Joleen didn't buy it; she knew that Sid would never leave and not tell her.

Eric decided to check to make sure Sid was okay. Sid lived at Lakeside Village, an apartment complex for young professionals overlooking Lake Champlain. His apartment had all the modern amenities for young lions climbing the tech ladder. Everything in his apartment was automated. Amazon Eco ran his living space. Sid used to joke that the only thing Siri would need to learn was how to cook and raise his children.

At first, Eric knocked on the door of Sid's apartment; he could see from the outside that the lights were all off. Eric took out his wallet and pulled out Sid's extra key; he walked into a dark living room and asked Siri to turn on the lights.

Sid was lying on the couch motionless. Eric was worried that Sid had died. When he got closer, he saw that Sid was breathing, and his eyes were slightly open.

Sid looked up at Eric with a bewildered look on his face. He asked, "What day is it?"

Eric sat down in a chair next to the couch. He replied, "It's Tuesday; you have been missing for five days; what happened?"

Sid sat up and moved his feet squarely on the floor. He replied, "I don't know, but after our experience late at night in Burlington, I felt completely depleted, like nothing I had ever felt before. I think my realization about the world was more than my mind could take."

Eric laughed. He replied, "Yeh, my parents used to tell me about the spirit connection. I've had some profound spiritual experiences, but never as powerful as the one we shared."

Sid rubbed his face stubble. He continued, "I've been lying on this couch for days with little to eat or drink, contemplating our experience. I felt a freedom I had not felt since I died in that lake. I was hoping it would continue, but when I woke up the next morning, I felt like I weighed ten thousand pounds and could barely move. The freedom and peace I felt were gone; only my heavy heart remained. I didn't know how empty my heart was until I had it filled with light."

Eric sat back in the chair and considered what he would say. He interjected, "Sid, I didn't tell you when it happened, but I saw your head expand, and then it collapsed into a single point of light. I thought I was delusional, but now, I know what I saw was real."

Sid replied, "Yeh, I remember the moment it happened. I saw my face in your face, and I knew I was talking to myself." Sid started to laugh hard, and so did Eric.

Eric asked, "So, what now?"

Sid sighed, "I guess I'll go back to work."

Eric asked, "No profound knowledge from the encounter?"

Sid replied, "No profound knowledge. I've been waiting for a sign from the heavens for the last few days, but nothing."

Eric asked, "Nothing?"

Sid continued, "I guess something. A new understanding and a significant perception shift. I had a vision some time ago where I was running on a distant planet and went through three life-changing experiences.

"I think I went through a significant perception shift the other night. I believe that I am on a different level of consciousness. Other than that, I'm not about to wear a white robe and a pair of sandals and start professing that I am the second coming."

Eric laughed. He replied, "I guess a major perception shift is enough. It will take some time to readjust how you see the world, then what you start seeing will become common."

Sid got up, walked to the kitchen sink, and poured himself water. He asked, "What will I start seeing?"

Eric laughed. He replied, "I understand that most of us walk around with our heads in the proverbial sand. Miracles are happening all around us; most are to help us along our path. I am certain that what we think a spiritual path looks like is not what helps us become enlightened. We are already spiritual beings; it is the physical reality that we need to experience to let go of who we might perceive we are."

Sid sat down with his water and a smirk. "Well, you're the spiritual boy. You tell me what I should be doing."

Eric continued, "I grew up with the spiritual stuff, but my understanding is intellectual. I hadn't had any powerful spiritual experiences outside the car accident until I met you, but that seems like a dream."

Sid replied, "I can hear my inner voice much clearer. I know the experience changed me, but deep in my heart, I have a long road to walk before I transcend to the next level of consciousness."

Eric interjected, "When my parents spoke of Jesus or Buddha, they would reference the belief of a true heart."

Sid asked, "What's a true heart?"

Eric continued, "A true heart is a being born every thousand years that helps humanity transcend to a higher level of awareness. A true heart comes at a dark time in the world when humans are moving away from their purest spiritual connection.

"When people are lost in the dark, a true heart connects humanity with the Source."

Sid sat up and rubbed his knees. He said, "My legs have gone to sleep; I don't think a messiah would have physical issues, do you?" Sid then laughed.

Eric continued, "I don't know if you are a true heart, but our experience a few days ago has me becoming a believer. I don't know your purpose, but I hope it is for good."

Sid laughed. He interjected, "This discussion is heavy. I think I finally have an appetite. Let's go to Henry's Diner. I desperately need a hamburger, fries, and a large coke."

Sid and Eric walked over to Church Street, an old cobblestone and brick open-air walking mall that spans four blocks with small businesses, primarily local entrepreneurs. At the top of Church Street is an old church that has been around since 1800.

Sid and Eric were making their way to Henry's Diner on Bank Street. Henry's is an old Burlington establishment serving good home cooking since 1925.

Snowdrifts dotted the mall. Even though it was January, the sun was out in force. The temperature hovered around eighteen degrees.

Sid and Eric didn't say a word during their walk on Church Street; they were both trying to grasp the conversation they had just had. Halfway down the street, they came across a wedding gown shop.

Sid stopped and stared at the gowns in the window. He exclaimed, "Jesus H. Christ, I forgot all about Joleen. I hope she didn't leave?"

Eric interjected, "No, was she supposed to leave?"

Sid and Eric continued their journey towards Henry's Diner. Sid replied, "Just before our walk at night, she told me she had a great job offer in Charlottesville, Virginia. That was part of our 'Where is our relationship going discussion.'"

Eric asked, "So, you got the condition of moving forward together or apart?"

Sid replied, "Yeh, I've been thinking a lot about her over the last five days; I think I might be sane enough to be a good husband and father. I spent a few hours in front of a mirror asking myself about a child in my life; I do that when I have no one else to discuss an issue.

"I remember having a vision many months ago, sitting at a diner with Joleen. We were having breakfast, and we had a blond child with us. I asked his name, and he said, 'I'm Ian.'

"I can't imagine why I had such a powerful spiritual experience, and then I am supposed to get married and settle down in a domestic life."

Eric interjected, "Maybe the Source was scorching the ground so that you could open your heart to life with Joleen. Relationships are a lot about balance and communication. You could learn a lot with a partner like Joleen. Maybe Joleen will be a big part of your transformation?"

Sid and Eric entered Henry's Diner and sat at their usual seats at the counter. Typically packed, only two other people were seated at a booth in the corner, but it was a weekday in the middle of winter. Sid welcomed the lack of customers because he still was recovering from his experience.

A young blond waitress in hippie clothes came over to take their order. Sid and Eric did not remember her, so they figured she was a new employee. "She asked, "Hi Sid and Eric, can I get you the usual?"

Sid sat up in his chair with a stiff back. He asked, "How do you know us?"

The waitress started to laugh. She replied, "I can't remember how many times you have asked me if I am a new employee. I'm Henry's granddaughter, Angie. I have been waiting on the two of you for the last year.

"You always get the same thing. Two eggs over easy with rye toast and bacon. You like your coffee, as you often say, 'black and beautiful.'"

Sid slunk back in his chair. He replied, "I'm so sorry. I guess I'm just a little oblivious to the world around me. Yes, the usual."

Eric interjected, "Yeh, the same for me."

Angie took their order and dutifully went into the back of the diner to place the order.

Sid exclaimed, "I can't believe I didn't see her before."

Eric replied, "This is what I was talking about; one of the effects of having a powerful spiritual experience. You start to see the world in a whole new way. Many people focus on their day-to-day difficulties but don't take the time to look up. Another thing you may start seeing are numbers."

Sid asked, "What do you mean by numbers?"

Eric continued, "The Source is talking to us all the time, but we are not paying attention. Suppose you learn a language like Italian. You first need to understand the structure of the language, and then over time, you will start to think in Italian.

"When you begin to think in Italian, you will comprehend the world through the Italian language.

"The Source speaks to us in an infinite language. It is a language we all know deep in our hearts, but we must remember to communicate with our purest spiritual connection.

"When we first start to evoke the spiritual language, we see indicators outside ourselves. These indicators are guides that come in the form of numbers and experiences.

"If we walk a spiritual path, we will see these numbers. It's hard to explain how they affect us, but you will know you are on the right path when you start to see Universal messengers."

Sid interjected, "I think I know what you are saying. When I woke up the next day after our experience, I saw the number 11:11 on my digital clock, and I felt a sense of peace and connection when I saw the number. Is that what you are talking about?"

Eric retorted, "Yes, exactly what I'm saying. When these numbers show themselves, it is almost as if time stops, and all your attention is on the subject that reflects the number.

"If you see 222, it means that your angels, people who are spirits, are near you and supporting your decisions. If you see 555, you are about to change your life significantly. If you see 333, it is a powerful spiritual number supporting your transformation.

Sid interjected, "Actually, I've seen these numbers most of my life, but I didn't see the experience as anything other than coincidence. I felt a sense of peace when these incidents occurred, but as I have done most of my life, I disregarded their importance."

Angie came out of the kitchen with Sid and Eric's breakfast in her arms. She put down all the plates and filled their coffee cups. She looked at Sid with a slight smirk. She asked, "Okay, what's my name?"

Sid and Eric laughed. Sid replied, "Your name is Angie, and you are Henry's granddaughter."

Angie put down the bill. She replied, "Good, now we can become good friends."

After breakfast, Sid and Eric drove back to the office. Sid was reluctant to walk back into the building after being gone for five days. He knew he had to face Joleen and ask her to marry him. Even though he knew he was doing the right thing, he was still worried.

Everyone looked at Sid as he entered the office. The crew examined Sid as if he was an alien entering the building. Many thought that there was something strange about Sid. Even though they didn't know what it was, they knew there was something different about him.

Sid walked up to the design department on the third floor. He felt he was walking a mile down a narrow path, and the world was far away—he was observing himself.

He came to Joleen's office door, and he knocked before entering. He stood in the doorway, looking at Joleen sitting behind her desk, working on her computer.

Joleen looked over with a frown. She asked, "So, where have you been for the last few days?"

Sid walked into the office and sat on a chair facing Joleen's desk. He replied, "It's hard to say, but mostly thinking about us."

Joleen stopped what she was doing and turned to face Sid. She said, "That could be good or bad. I've been thinking a lot about us as well. I thought that maybe I cornered you on New Year's Eve. I had a lot to drink and was having a little bit of a meltdown. Sid, I don't want you to feel pressured to marry me. That's no way to start a life together."

Sid smiled and replied, "Joleen, I don't feel pressured to marry. I went through a few days of transformation and felt that marrying you would be the best thing I could ever do in my life."

Joleen sat back in her chair and started to cry. She asked, "Sid, are you asking me to marry you?"

Sid got down on his knees. He asked, "Joleen, will you marry me?"

Outside Joleen's office, other crew members congregated around the large window looking into her office. Everyone in the office started to clap when Sid got down on his knees and proposed to Joleen.

With tears in her eyes, Joleen asked, "Are you sure you want to marry me?"

Sid stood up and hugged Joleen. He continued, "Yes, I am sure that I want us to create a life together."

Joleen gave Sid a long kiss and hug. She replied, "Sid, I would love to marry you. What changed your mind?"

Sid laughed. He replied, "I didn't have a change of mind; I had a change of heart. So, why were you having a meltdown on New Year's Eve? Were you going to leave because I didn't tell you about the government involvement with Karmakal?"

Joleen sat down behind her desk. She replied, "Sid, you should sit down. I need to tell you something that has been troubling me.

"No, I wasn't going to leave because you didn't trust me enough to tell me about the CIA bugging Karmakal. I used that because I was afraid to tell you the truth about what was happening."

Sid sat back in the chair. He asked, "What's going on?"

Joleen started to have tears in her eyes again. She professed, "I didn't want you to marry me because you had to, so I planned to keep a secret from you and move on to that job in Charlottesville. It had nothing to do with Karmakal."

Sid sat forward in the chair. He asked, "What secret?"

Joleen replied, "Do you want to marry me? Do you love me enough to commit to a life with me?"

Sid answered, "Yes, Joleen, I love you with all my heart. I hope that I don't disappoint you. I think I can be a good husband and, in time, a good father. So, what secret?"

Joleen took a long breath and exhaled. She exclaimed, "Well, you'll have a chance to be a good father sooner than you thought. I learned that I'm pregnant; we are having a baby." ଔ

ᚼ

Chapter Nineteen

It was 3:33 a.m., and Sid was awake, looking up at the fan in his hotel room, slowly moving around. Sid judged that the fan might be a prop the hotel owners installed to give the few tourists that visited a sense of comfort because the fan did little to cool the room from the sweltering heat.

Sid was lying in bed, contemplating how he ended up in Belize. He couldn't stop thinking about his last encounter with Joleen. He thought about the previous ten years and how the whole Karmakal project ended with its hostile takeover by a giant tech company orchestrated by his board of directors.

The middle of the night was always difficult for Sid because he often obsesses about his life. His memories were so powerful that he felt he relived traumatic experiences repeatedly, especially at night.

In Vermont, he could get up and watch television or do some work to calm his mind, but he had no luxuries in such a remote place. He could only get up and look out the window at the small Belize city of Dangriga. A few lights were shining in homes but no streetlights, businesses closed early, and the few museums and public attractions in town were only open on Saturday.

He looked back on the last ten years. After his wedding to Joleen and the birth of his first child, Sasha, time seemed to accelerate.

At first, he was at peace with his decision to live a life of a husband and father. Over time he forgot the spiritual experience Eric and he had. The idea of the world being an illusion started to fade in his memory.

The years seemed to pass from one into the other with no drama unfolding or feeling of hopelessness. After the birth of his second child, Darrick, things started to change. Deep down in his heart, his inner voice broke through his life's banality.

He began to realize he didn't recognize Karmakal. During the early years of Karmakal he became so immersed in the work that the change in the company started to take hold of him. A transition took place where Karmakal wasn't a small start-up anymore; it had become a large company that took on a life of its own, moving away from Sid's hopes and dreams.

One day, Sid looked up from the daily fires he was putting out, glanced around the office, and started to see employees he didn't know. Many of the original crew had left with big investment money to create ventures.

He didn't remember when Eric left, but he did remember the heartbreak it caused. His leaving caused Sid pain for only a moment because everyone looked to Sid for strength and leadership. Sid always had to show strength, even if he was pretending.

After a few years of marriage, Sid formed a routine he followed with religious fervor. He's in the office by eight, has lunch at his desk, and then home by seven to put his kids to bed and read three children's books. He would often work on the weekends but always at home so he could spend time with his wife and children.

He did remember when the depression and pain returned. It was just after a board of directors meeting three years ago. A large tech company had offered to buy Karmakal for three billion dollars and change. If the sale went through, everyone was in line to become financially set up for life.

The potential takeover of Karmakal woke him up. He had worked so hard to create something that would be good for the world, and it only caused him to offer his blood, sweat, and tears at the altar of capitalism.

Eric left with a sizable amount of money to start-up a spiritual blog, *The Life Energy Report*. Eric asked Sid to go with him; Sid was too mired in Karmakal. He didn't understand why Eric left, but as the pain in his heart increased, he understood what motivated Eric to pursue a more spiritual path.

As the pain increased, he felt alone at work. There wasn't anyone at Karmakal that he could trust with his deepest feelings and thoughts.

Joleen left the company a few years earlier to become the best mother and wife she could be.

Most new employees were ego-filled with only one motivation, to become rich. He could not show any weakness because the company became hyper-competitive, not unlike all big companies. Most of the crew felt they could run Karmakal better than Sid.

Sid never wanted anyone to know about his background in Alabama or his short stay at Rikers Island. If he showed any weakness, the vultures in the office would pick his bones clean.

Joleen loved Sid and cared for him deeply, but she didn't understand why he was suffering when they had everything anyone would want. They had become wealthy and influential in the Burlington community.

Joleen volunteered at different events and orchestrated charity functions to benefit many causes. She gave great dinner parties in the fall and winter and barbeques in the summer. Sid and Joleen became the hottest ticket in town, if you were lucky enough to be invited to one of their gatherings.

They lived in a large house on twenty acres in Charlotte overlooking Lake Champlain. They bought a vacation home in Italy near Florence, and their kids went to the best private schools in Vermont.

They would have long discussions late into the night, and for a moment, Sid would feel a little better knowing how much Joleen loved him. Then the pain would return, a pain in his heart consisting of profound emptiness.

He would tell Joleen that his pain was like lying naked on concrete with cold rain pouring down. The emptiness would always start in his stomach and move to his heart. Then he would fall into darkness with despair where no one could reach him, even Joleen.

In the darkness, he would obsess about killing himself. He would envision taking a pistol to his head and ending his misery. Sometimes he would imagine jumping off a bridge or hanging himself. He would repeatedly ruminate for hours about ending his life in some way that would have the most negligible impact on those closest to him.

Sid's talk of suicide would always frighten Joleen; she would worry that she would come home and he would be dead. She pleaded with Sid to get help, but he felt that his deep emptiness had nothing to do with his mind—he knew it had to do with his heart.

He started to reread the Bible, and when that didn't calm his heart, he would read other spiritual books. He read every transcendent philosophy he could get his hands on; he was hungry for knowledge. His insatiable need for liberation from his pain brought him to a series of spiritual books written by a prophet living in Belize.

Above all books he read, this mystic spoke to him in ways no other author did. He devoured all three books in the series and then read them repeatedly. Each time he read the series, he discovered details that he missed the first time. The voice deep in his heart started to be clear and loud as he read the books. He knew deep in his heart that his path would lead him to this spiritualist in Belize, but he didn't know when he would leave.

A year passed, then another, and the pain returned. He could tell his abilities and desires were waning; all he wanted was to follow his spiritual path to stop the agony in his heart.

He would continually look for signs from the Source of what he should do or where he should go. He looked to numbers appearing to lead him, and every coincidence indicated his need to reconnect to his purest spiritual relationship; numbers like 11.11 or 333 would lead him astray because he was trying too hard to find peace.

The emptiness worsened when the Karmakal board of directors called an emergency meeting. Sid thought his inability to continue a façade was causing the panel to reconsider him as president. Sid finally realized his worst fear at the meeting. The board of directors allowed a massive tech company to buy fifty-one percent of the Karmakal in a takeover bid.

The board notified Sid that the new corporation wanted him out. They didn't want any entrenched management to cause problems with the transition. Any board member or senior management takeover challenge could cause the stock price to tank during the acquisition.

The board of directors wanted the merger to be secret so that the subscribers would accept the new owners of Karmakal. Sid built Karmakal on a spiritual concept of trust, and the new owners did not have a positive reputation.

A private equity firm full of lawyers looking for a payday owned the tech company that bought Karmakal. The data Karmakal could bring to the table would be sold to the highest bidder, no matter the cost to the Karmakal community.

Venture capitalists invest in companies to bring them to the market. Private equity firms break apart companies to clean the bones of any wealth made at any cost.

Sid collected all his personal belongings in a file box and walked out of the building, never to return. The board compensated Sid for his efforts with millions of dollars and stock options, but the loss of Karmakal and the betrayal by the board of directors cut a deep hole in his heart.

The first few weeks were the worst after he left Karmakal. Sid stayed in his study, lying on his couch with the lights off for days. He wouldn't talk to Joleen or his kids.

Sid ruminated about the betrayal received from the board of directors. He thought many of them were his friend, but when money is on the line, all relationships start to fade away.

At first, he became angry to the point of rage. He had been working at a high rate of speed for years, immersing his heart and soul in the growth of Karmakal. He would push down his ethical and moral compass every time the government spied on the subscribers.

He kept deluding himself that it would all work out in the end, but now a private equity firm will sell off Karmakal piece by piece until there won't be anything else worth salvaging.

Then something happened while he was floundering in the dark. He started to hear his inner voice. Never in his life, when he was depressed, did he hear his purest spiritual connection reach out to him. He relaxed, and peace started to flow back into his heart.

He started to be in a place where he might be able to look at the situation with a new sense of clarity. He began to consider that maybe the Source was orchestrating his separation from Karmakal because it was time for Sid to walk a new path.

The thought that maybe leaving the company was an opportunity, not a disaster, started to seep into Sid's consciousness. He began to consider that maybe Karmakal wasn't the end of his search for peace. Maybe Karmakal was just another steppingstone on his long journey home, back to the place where he perished in the lake, the place where he felt absolute peace.

Six months went by after his separation from Karmakal. Even though Sid spent much time with his family, Joleen always sensed that he was far away. She would often ask what was next for him. Joleen knew that Sid wasn't one to stand still for too long. She was hopeful that Sid would want to start another company or become a venture capitalist. Joleen knew Sid had a good heart and would do well to pass his good fortune to others.

Sid thought about leaving for Belize when he left Karmakal, but his love for his family held him. Over the last six months, the desire to go to Belize and meet the spiritualist who wrote the series became overwhelming. He knew he could not start anything in the world until he went on the journey.

At first, he would convince himself that the trip would only be brief and then return to his family in a short period, but deep in his heart, he knew that this would be a much more extended trek, and maybe it would change him in some unforeseen way.

Joleen and Sid returned with the kids from a weekend in Portland, Maine. Joleen noticed that Sid seemed to take a lot of interest in a boutique coffee shop and bakeshop franchise they visited. Joleen was hopeful that Sid would start the same retail shop on Church Street in Burlington.

Joleen sensed that Sid had been moving farther away from her and his family for many months. She was desperate for Sid to start something solid so she didn't have to worry about him leaving, but she knew he had already left long ago.

The conversation to leave for Belize started innocently enough. While unpacking from their trip to Portland, Joleen asked Sid, "That coffee shop was great, and I was surprised how many people lined up to get an expensive cup of coffee and muffin."

Sid stopped unpacking and took a drink of a beer. He replied, "Yeh, the start-up coffee shop brought back good memories of working with new ideas."

Joleen measured Sid to see if he was open to inspiration. She interjected, "Maybe a coffee shop would be good for you to start. You like small businesses and complain that Karmakal became too big and top-heavy with senior management. Sid, you need to do something; you're too young to hang out at home."

Sid sat down on the bed and held Joleen's hand. He professed, "You're right, Joleen; it's time to make a move in one direction or another.

I already know the direction I need to follow, and I need to travel to Belize and meet someone who may be able to give me some answers to calm the emptiness in my heart."

Joleen sat down on the bed next to Sid. She asked, "You mean to go to Belize for a short period?"

Sid patted Joleen's hand. He replied, "I don't know how long I would be gone. I know deep in my heart that it may change me somehow. I know that my path leads to Belize, for now. After that, I don't know where I might be going. I can't deal with this pain anymore. I must go where my heart is taking me."

Tears started to trickle down Joleen's cheeks. "What about us? What about our children?"

Sid's eyes started to well up. He professed, "I love you and my children with all my heart, but I worry I will fall into darkness and never come out if I do not do this."

Joleen wiped the tears from her face. She replied, "I don't know what to say. I tried to help calm your heart, but I'm also tired. I love you, Sid, but I can't swim against the tide anymore. If you need to go, then go."

Sid walked upstairs and looked at his sleeping children for a long time. He kissed both on the forehead; he changed into jeans, a sweatshirt, and sneakers. Sid grabbed a backpack and baseball cap. He looked at Joleen one more time and walked out the door. ❧

☙

Chapter Twenty

The sun was high in the sky, flooding the Caribbean with light that illuminated the clear blue-green water off the shore of Dangriga. Sid spent three weeks waiting for word from Eduardo Francheze, the author of *A True Heart*. The three-book series, starting with *Journey to the City of Light*, that Sid read repeatedly.

Sid spent most of his time walking the small streets of Dangriga. The town looked like Key West in the United States before wealthy people moved in and made it the Disneyland of Caribbean towns.

Dangriga was colorful but rough around the edges, and it had a large population of black people. Sid could walk the streets without anyone bothering him, even in the poorest neighborhoods, because he wore clothes like ordinary Dangriga citizens.

Sid found out that Dangriga is considered the cultural capital of Belize and the heart of Garifuna society. He discovered that the Garifuna people were descendants of enslaved people who escaped from a sinking ship in the early eighteen hundreds.

The food at many restaurants and bodegas in town served dishes inspired by Garifuna cooking. The staple of Belizean cuisine is rice and beans with potato salad. Dangriga is a fishing village with ten thousand citizens, and the heavy fishing trade adds delicious additions to the staple, such as lobster and shrimp.

A small farming community offers a variety of meat products such as beef, chicken, pork, and even wild game.

Sid asked at public offices and markets if anyone could direct him to Eduardo Francheze. The residents kept rebuffing him with, "I don't know."

It seemed to Sid that he may have traveled to Belize for nothing or that the townspeople were unaware of Eduardo's existence. Sid felt deep in his heart that he was in the right place, but he seemed to have to be patient for an answer.

Sid thought a lot about his family back in the states. He wondered how Joleen was doing and what she told their kids about him leaving. He felt an enormous amount of guilt, but at the same time, his heart started to be at peace the instant he arrived in Belize.

Sid didn't understand why the Universe or God would want him to leave his family. He didn't understand why the Source sent him on such a journey, but he felt peace in his heart. So, he didn't want to go back until he met Eduardo.

The desire in his heart to meet Eduardo increased every day he walked the streets. He would go into the government offices and ask if anyone knew Eduardo Francheze. He finally paid a government official to get word to Eduardo about his presence.

It took Sid three weeks because the Dangriga locals protected their most famous author from tourists who saw him as a novelty.

Sid's relentless pursuit persuaded Eduardo of his intent to obtain knowledge. An unknown benefactor delivered a note to Sid's hotel late at night.

Sid held the note he received from Eduardo to be at the Dangriga docks at 9:00 a.m. The message also read, "I would love to meet you, come to my humble home."

j

The water was so clear Sid could see colorful fish swimming around just a few feet from where he stood on the dock. In the distance, he saw a small fishing boat come around a spit jutting out into the Bay of Honduras. A large amount of smoke billowed from the small vessel's smokestack.

The fishing boat took a considerable amount of time to reach the dock. Sid could hear the diesel engine huffing and puffing as it arrived at the pier. A single Hispanic man with grey hair and a bright white beard was steering the boat. He had a t-shirt and shorts on with no shoes. When the vessel reached the dock, the man threw a line to Sid; Sid took the rope and wrapped it around a cleat on the pier.

The man stood up and greeted Sid. Sid asked, "Are you Eduardo?"

The man replied, "No, I'm Miguel; I work for him. I will take you to Eduardo as soon as I get the mail."

The man rushed by Sid and went into town to pick up the mail. Sid sat next to the boat with his feet in the cool water. Over the last three weeks in Belize, he found that most people live at a much slower pace than back in the States.

It seemed to Sid that the locals never had anywhere to go in a hurry but seemed to be a lot happier. The citizens had good food, a simple lifestyle, and sun. Sid heard of a gang problem, especially in Belize City.

It took the small fishing vessel two hours to reach Eduardo's tiny island, Crab Caye. The boat had to navigate around the barrier reef that went on for miles.

Miguel assured Sid that they would sink in seconds if he hit even one of the reefs. They would have a long swim back to land, and the waters were full of sharks. The thought of sinking disturbed Sid enough to consider how trusting he was of a total stranger taking him to a place he didn't know. Ever since he started to feel at peace, he could hear his inner voice loud and clear; his heart told him to trust.

Crab Caye is south of Coco Plum Island Resort, a hot destination for European tourists. Like most South American countries, Belize tries hard to separate poverty and crime from tourist dollars.

Coco Plum Island is one of many private resorts for tourists who don't want to take a chance with the gang problem back on the mainland of Belize.

Miguel pointed to a small dot of white sand on the horizon. He said, "That's Eduardo's home." The closer they came to the island, the more substantial it became.

The island looked like three square miles, surrounded by bright blue-green water, and it had a heavy canopy of palm trees and a dock extending out on the island's south side. The island looked like a Caribbean postcard Sid had seen once at a store in New Orleans.

Sid saw a modest two-story house through the trees as the boat came close to the dock. It looked to be at the dead center of the island. The home didn't look old, and the architecture looked a lot like the style of New England.

The house had white clapboards on the south side, and the north side had grey shingles. Sturdy bright blue shutters adorned each window, reminding Sid that he was in the tropics and hurricanes were common in the part of world.

A man in a beautiful white shirt and shorts stood on the balcony overlooking a small fountain in the front of the house. He waved to Sid as the boat docked.

Miguel lashed down the vessel to the dock as the man walked up to welcome Sid. He looked more Italian than South American and was five foot seven at most, and he seemed small for the giant Sid thought he must be to write such essential knowledge.

The man walked up to Sid. He said, "I'm Eduardo; you must be Sid Arthur?"

Sid shook the man's hand. He replied, "Yes, I appreciate you inviting me to your home."

Eduardo patted Sid on his back. He continued, "Come, I have lunch prepared. I imagine you have a million questions, but let's eat first."

The two walked up to the home. Sid took off his sandals, feeling the warm sand between his toes.

The light dappled through the palm trees on the sand and a cool breeze moved through the island. He looked back at the boat tied to the dock, wondering how long he would stay.

He stopped on the way to the house. He looked around as if he had been standing in that spot for a thousand lifetimes. He had an overwhelming sense of déjà vu. The sensory experience overtook him, and he sat down on the sand.

Eduardo looked down at Sid. He asked, "Did you just have déjà vu?"

Sid looked at Eduardo for a long time and then stood back up. He had a sense that he had known Eduardo for a long time. They had played different parts in different lives, maybe even different genders in many lives.

That each life over a millennium has led to this moment, this exact moment, on this beach in Belize, Sid remembered that he and Eduardo had been friends, lovers, married, and maybe even reviled enemies in a multi-verse of experiences.

Sid had never felt so close to a total stranger as he stood on that beach. He replied, "Yes, I had an overwhelming feeling that we have experienced different lives together and that I had stood on this beach a thousand lifetimes."

Eduardo started to laugh. He replied, "Good, because I felt it too.

When I saw you on the boat, I knew we had experienced many lives together. I knew it when I heard you were in Belize looking for me. I knew you were a soul mate, a person that has played out many human dramas with me. I have found other soul mates. It is always amazing that we see each other like a powerful magnet.

"Here I am on a small island in the Caribbean, and you make your way to me for some unforeseen reason. I bet you didn't know what questions you would ask me once you discovered where I was?"

Sid started walking again towards the house with Eduardo. He replied, "Yes, I never thought about the questions I might ask you; I only needed to find you. I had an overpowering desire to meet you—I never considered why."

Eduardo countered, "I bet you were in a lot of pain for a long time. Maybe you were going through a Dark Night of the Soul. Every soulmate that I come across has gone through a dark time. How do you feel now?"

Sid stopped and thought about the question. He answered, "I feel totally at peace. I started to feel at peace when I got off the plane. I had a friend back in the states, who I asked how he knew when he was on his divine path. He told me that it was easy. He would feel a deep emptiness if he were on the wrong path. When he was on the right path, he felt at peace. He listened to his heart, not unlike the character in your book '*A True Heart*.'"

Sid and Eduardo walked into the house. The home was sparse, with many windows open to the natural environment. The sun's rays cast long shadows on the wooden floors. Eduardo directed Sid to a sun deck with screened windows overlooking a small pond at the back of the house. There were large colorful Koi fish in the pond.

A small table with white linen and polished silver sat beside a large window. Eduardo laid out a feast of rock lobster, oysters, a salad with greens that Sid did not recognize, and a jug of Chianti wine.

Eduardo motioned for Sid to sit, then sat across from Sid. He poured Sid a glass of wine. He said, "I hope you enjoy your stay in my home. I feel that we have a lot to discuss. I don't receive many visitors. So, I like to use the white-linen and good silver."

Sid took a sip of his wine. He asked, "I tried for three weeks to see you. When did you decide to meet me?"

Eduardo replied, "Ever since I wrote the series of books, I have attracted people with something missing. They think I may have the answer to their emptiness. I learned a lot during my time in this world. I may have some insights, but ultimately I wrote the book because I wanted people to understand that the truth is in each of us.

"I didn't want people to search for me for answers to their darkness. I wanted them to find it in their hearts. I didn't want to become some prophet people would follow. I wanted to help others find their divine path. To answer your questions, you were different.

"I didn't hear about you until ten days ago. You paid a public official that contacted me. At first, I thought you might be another tourist looking for answers.

I did a little background check on you and realized you were the real deal. I found out about your involvement in Karmakal, and I had a nagging feeling in my heart that we needed to meet."

Sid interjected, "How did you do a background check on me from such a remote island?"

Eduardo laughed. He replied, "With all the technology in the world, there isn't any remote place. I have a friend in New York that runs a private investigation company; he did a quick background check on you."

Sid interjected, "New York is a long way from Belize."

Eduardo continued, "Maybe in the distance, but New York has an important place in my heart. I wrote the book series twenty years ago when I lived in Brooklyn.

"Years ago, before I wrote the series, I fantasized about being a famous author, but when it happened after the first book came out, I couldn't handle the attention.

"At first, fame was engrossing. I went to the best parties. New York literature bigwigs interviewed me. They told me my writing spoke for a generation. I started to believe in my press but was miserable at the same time. I had the empty pain you most likely had been dealing with before you came to Belize."

Sid interjected, "What made you leave New York?"

Eduardo continued, "Like any Dark Night of the Soul, it starts slow and then increases in pain as you deny your true path. It's like holding onto a rock in a river as it creates more and more force against you. You finally must let go and let God. In my case, I had a moment of great sadness.

Sid interjected, "A moment of great sadness?"

Eduardo cleared his throat and took a drink of wine. He continued, "After the first book was published, I started to have strangers knocking on my door for answers.

I didn't move out of my tiny apartment in Brooklyn, even though I was beginning to make significant royalties on the books; I was easy to find, and many found me.

"At first, I would tell them that they have the answers in their hearts, but then I realized that many could not hear their inner voice. They thought I could translate what was in their hearts for them. For a moment, I thought maybe I could…." Eduardo stopped, and a tear welled up in his eye.

Sid leaned forward. He asked, "Then what?"

Eduardo composed himself. He continued, "Then a beautiful young woman knocked on my door. She had read my books and drove from some small town in Ohio to meet me. She was troubled and in great pain; she was in a dark place. We went out for coffee, and she poured her soul out to me. I was so overwhelmed by her misery that I told her I couldn't help her.

"She was almost insane with rage and anger from her childhood. I told her that she needed to find a safe place and try to heal. I realized that this beautiful young person was so far from her heart in a dark place that it might take many lives for her to start to hear her purest spiritual connection.

"I knew at that moment that I couldn't and shouldn't try to heal the world. I lost the perspective I had gained before writing the books, and I got caught up in my ego and lost the light I once held sacred.

"Then, a tragic event pushed me over the edge. I learned from a friend that the young woman who reached out to me for help committed suicide; she jumped off the George Washington bridge.

"For a long time, I blamed myself for allowing my ego to run wild. I blamed myself for her death.

That's when I moved to this small island. I let go of my need to save the world. I haven't written another word in ten years, but I have wondered what is next. Then you arrived in town, and I knew in my heart that something would come of our meeting.

"So, you see, my good friend, you may have traveled all this way to find your path, but maybe you are here to help me find my path again, or we will walk down another path together?" ❧

 G3

Chapter Twenty One

Sid started to lose track of time. He couldn't remember if he had been on the island for three weeks or three months; time on the island began to take on a unique feel. A solid warm light permeated his being. He started to see energy emanating from everything around him. He began to see the truth of the world.

"You see it, don't you?" Eduardo walked up behind Sid with a smile.

Sid turned around, and he had a tear in his eye. He replied, "Yes, it reminds me of when I touched the Source back in Burlington; the illumination gives me an overwhelming sense of peace."

Eduardo patted Sid on his back. He continued, "I've been waiting for the transition to happen to you, as it happened for me when I first arrived on the island."

Sid asked, "You didn't tell me about your transformation; why?"

Eduardo kneeled and picked up a handful of sand. He showed it to Sid. The sand sparkled like the stars at night. The sand then flowed through Eduardo's fingers back into the beach, into the whole. Eduardo continued, "I couldn't tell you about the energy emanating from this area because I knew you had to see and feel it for yourself. It wasn't anything I could explain; it could only be experienced."

Sid remembered his vision of running on a beach on a distant planet moving through an endless galaxy. He said, "I once had a vision about this moment, and I think I was drawn to this island to learn about life energy."

Eduardo smiled. He continued, "Yes, that is what I discovered. When I first moved to the island, I was in a dark place, not unlike you. I still carried the guilt about the young woman who committed suicide.

At first, I didn't remember how I even knew about the island or Belize, but somehow I ended up here. I remember a friend in New York telling me about the great barrier reef off Belize. When I heard the story about Belize, an overwhelming desire arose in my heart to leave New York and travel to this tiny island in the Caribbean.

"My transition from New York to this island was seamless, almost effortless. When I arrived here, I felt like I had never lived elsewhere. I felt like I had lived here my entire life, or many lives, as you thought when you first came here. Standing in front of my house, I felt I stood in that spot time after time and life after life.

"I thought I was hiding from the world, but what happened over time was I started to see the truth of the world. The thin veil of illusion began to fade, and I saw what was behind the dream.

"When you arrived in Belize, I knew you were here to see the light, and I knew you were not here to meet me. My book series may have become why you left your family and traveled thousands of miles to come to this small island in the middle of a vast ocean, but now you see that the vast ocean is not water but light."

Sid sat down on a bench overlooking the Caribbean. Eduardo sat next to him. Eduardo asked, "It becomes overwhelming. When I first saw the light, I couldn't sleep for days because I was too full of love and hope. I would often laugh at the absurdity of my life and most of my regrets, seeing that they were all part of the drama.

"I was so full of love and hope for the world that I would hear the sound of Ohm echo in my heart and soul."

Sid said, "Yes, it is more than just seeing the light. I feel a strong vibration of energy moving through my body, and I can hear my inner voice almost as clear as I can hear you."

Eduardo continued, "Yes, that is the other transformation. The light opens our hearts, and we can connect to our most precious spiritual relationship."

Sid asked, "Why here? Have you realized why this island generates so much energy?"

Eduardo continued, "I've discovered that it is not just this island. There are many places with heightened energy, such as Vermont. You described enhanced energy when you first moved to Vermont.

"I believe Machu Picchu, in Peru, is such a place; that's why the Incan Empire was built on top of a mountain. The legendary

Shangri-la, Eden, and Paradise have heightened energy; so high is the energy that few can visit or even see these places.

"Unfortunately, I have discovered many dark places with low energy created by hate, greed, and ignorance—these places also exist in our physical plane of consciousness.

"During my travels, I've realized that the world has permanent and temporary energy, and it is an energy that connects us to the Source or the illusion, which the Buddha referred to as Samsara.

"Permanent energy is the underlying energy that connects our hearts to our purest spiritual relationship. Temporary energy is of the world, and it builds up in our hearts as we move through this reality. There is different energy throughout the world, including even the energy of this island and the Belize mainland.

Sid asked, "How did you know permanent and temporary energy?"

Eduardo laughed. He continued, "I would say it was a coincidental encounter I had with a Naval officer at one of the resort bars, but I know there is no such thing as chance; everything has a purpose.

"It seems that when I needed to obtain knowledge, the Source would send the right person at the right time. I just had to open my mind and listen. Listening is one of the most formidable talents I've ever had to acquire.

"The Naval officer I met at the bar was Bryson Marrel. He spent the last twenty years in the United States Navy. During a drug intervention operation with the United States Coast Guard, he remembered the lightness of spirit he felt in this part of the Caribbean.

"We talked about the energy that seemed to permeate the islands. Bryson said that he had thought about why this part of the world had such heightened energy. He didn't have a spiritual bone in his body, so he tried to make sense of the energy based on the scientific knowledge he received during his training at the Naval Academy at Annapolis, Maryland."

Sid interjected, "This is strangely scientific for a spiritual concept."

Eduardo smiled. He continued, "I think science and spirituality can work hand in hand because they are both tenets looking for the truth.

"Bryson explained how electromagnetic energy affects ships, planes, cars, computers, and any other object in motion on the face of the earth. The earth has a steady flow of electromagnetic energy from the North Pole to the South Pole; this energy is on any object, both large and small, on the globe.

"If you could see the electromagnetic energy flow on an apple, it would flow from the top to the bottom just like the earth."

Sid picked up a coconut off the beach and looked at it intently. He said, "I can see the energy flow, starting at the top and moving over the coconut and entering the bottom." He turned the coconut upside down and observed the same effect.

Eduardo took the coconut and looked at it with a smile. He continued, "When Bryson was a navigator, he was concerned about how this energy affected vessels. The Navy publishes charts detailing the frequency of electromagnetic energy on the face of the earth; the frequency of this energy will differ depending on the area, sometimes dramatically.

"Ships take on a permanent signature of energy predominant to the location where they build the ship. The magnetic compass and all electronic equipment use this permanent energy.

"When the ship moves across the face of the earth, it picks up temporary energy, just like dragging your feet on a carpet and shocking your sibling when you were a child.

"This is where it gets interesting. The temporary energy builds up on the ship's hull and will cause problems with the magnetic compass and electronic equipment, and if left unchecked, it will damage the vessel's hull.

"This effect is not unlike how the world's dark places affect spiritual beings, such as you and me. The impact of negative energy in the dark area of the world causes us pain.

"Bryson enlightened me that shipbuilders have developed ways to control the buildup of temporary energy. They install lead bars on the ship's hull. The temporary energy deteriorates the lead instead of the ship."

Sid laughed. He interjected, "Should we be carrying lead bars?"

Eduardo looked at Sid with a furrowed brow. He continued, "The shipbuilders also install degaussing cables along the horizontal ribs of ships. The Navy monitors this energy because of mines. A boat passes through a minefield and creates a hole in the electromagnetic energy field; the mine falls into the hole and blows up the ship.

"Bryson was able to control the amount of electrical current running through the degaussing cables. He would check the charts supplied by the Navy to ascertain the frequency of electromagnetic energy in that part of the world and then set the degaussing current to an equal frequency of energy with the surrounding area.

"The ship's energy would become invisible to the surrounding energy field by creating a false energy signature with the degaussing cables. More critical, the vessel would become invisible to the mine's electromagnetic energy field.

"If the temporary energy builds up more than the ship's degaussing cables can handle, the Navy has built degaussing fields right off the shore of Naval bases.

"The ship passes over the large degaussing fields. The electromagnetic energy of the areas bombards the ship with energy equal to the temporary energy encompassing the vessel. This bombardment cancels out any temporary energy built up over years of operation. The ship is stripped of its temporary energy so that its permanent energy can control the equipment on the vessel.

Sid interjected, "How does electromagnetic energy have to do with spiritual energy?"

Eduardo continued, "Ever since my conversation with Bryson, I've made parallel distinctions between the effects of this energy on ships, plans, and cars with how it would affect human beings and, more importantly, spiritual beings. I've realized that we have permanent energy connected to our purest spiritual relationship.

"As we move through the world, we pick up temporary energy often referred to as our emotional baggage. This temporary energy surrounds our souls and, if gone unchecked, will eat away at our hearts.

"Of course, I don't think the energy that dictates our reality in this illusion is electromagnetic. I've heard that the energy that binds the Universe is called life energy. An energy that is in the world but not of the world. I believe that life energy is the energy that holds together electromagnetic energy.

"Scientists have been referencing dark energy that seems to bind the Universe together. They have determined that the Universe we see is 99.9 percent empty, but they know that something keeps it all together. I believe that dark energy is life energy. Since the world is just an illusion, the dark energy is the energy that exists in an infinite reality."

Sid interjected, "My friend Eric used the term life energy field. He left Karmakal when the company became too large to pursue a digital blog he called *The Life Energy Report.*

"I didn't understand what life energy was before I came to the island, but after seeing the energy flow around me, I think I am starting to understand.

"Eric did explain before he left why he called his blog the *Life Energy Report*, a story his father told him when he was young.

"Eric's father told him a story about a young Cherokee warrior who was about to go on a journey of self-realization into the wilderness, but before he left, his father wanted to impart some wisdom passed down through generations.

"The warrior's father told him there is great darkness in the world made up of fear and doubt. It's in the shadows of the dark woods, in the minds of men, and it waits for you in your dreams. He told his son this darkness will always be at your heels when you are in the wilderness and your heart when you are most tired.

"Balanced with this great darkness is a delicate veil of life energy woven through all things. This veil of life energy is made up of love and hope and balanced with the great darkness because without one; there could not be the other.

"On your journey through the wilderness, there will be a moment when all seems lost, and you will be empty of all things of the world, and at this moment, your greater divine purpose will become clear.

"A simple truth will emerge as it has done for all that take this journey. The simple truth will be that if you can weave even one small strand of good in the great veil of life energy, you will fulfill your life's purpose."

Eduardo interjected, "Yes, I heard that story long ago. I think places with heightened energy are a lot like degaussing fields. As we travel through this world, we are weighed down with temporary energy. Ever since I moved to this island, I don't feel fear and doubt anymore."

Sid interjected, "Yes, I feel a lot like the moment of my death in that lake. I feel totally at peace, but I know deep in my heart that I can't stay here forever, and this place is a temporary respite from my path."

Eduardo replied, "Yes, I know I must leave too. I have been waiting for a sign of what's next, and I feel you are the key to what is next."

Eduardo and Sid walked around the island on a small path near the shore. The more Sid observed the world around him, the more he saw an intense energy flow. His body vibrated with the energy moving through his heart and soul; he heard Ohm deep down."

Sid asked, "Eduardo, you said you discovered the world's truth?"

Eduardo stopped and sat down on a tree stump near the water. He said, "I've realized that we are not physical beings trying to obtain spiritual perfection; we are spiritual beings having a physical experience."

Sid interjected, "How so?"

Eduardo continued, "When I was writing my books, I understood many of the spiritual concepts I wrote about intellectually, but I didn't understand them until I came to this island. I started to connect to an infinite library that taught me spiritual concepts at a much deeper level. I understood the same spiritual concepts at an infinite level. I realized an infinite mantra that spoke to me like Ohm to a monk."

Sid asked, "What mantra?"

Eduardo smiled. He continued, "We are all part of an infinite being having a collective experience in a reality of separation—here lies the truth of the Universe."

Sid sat down and moved his fingers through the sand. He asked, "I understand, but at the same time, I don't understand."

Eduardo smiled. He continued, "Exactly, a duality. First, I understood that there is infinite reality and the reality of separation, the reality we see around us in the world.

"It is essential to understand that the infinite reality is one hundred percent different from the reality of separation; both realities exist paradoxically.

"I have understood that the Infinite Being wanted to know itself. Since the Infinite Being is infinite, it cannot look at itself, so it created an idea of a reality that would be separate from itself so that it could look upon itself.

"The Infinite Being created the reality we now occupy, the world around us, Samsara. The Universe is only an idea, an illusion. The idea that the infinite took only an infinite second. I realized the Universe already happened, and we are only looking back on the residual effect of the concept created by the Infinite Being.

"The Infinite Being looked at itself through the world of separation and understood what it was not. The world of separation is the opposite of the infinite.

"We are here ultimately to know who we are by who we are not. We are all infinite beings having this experience collectively; the only way we are separate is by our perceptions.

"We are one at our core, permanent energy, and it is the temporary energy that creates our perceptions."

Sid and Eduardo started to laugh uncontrollably, and the world around them seemed to shine even brighter—they heard Ohm moving through the waves and trees. ✧

 G3

Chapter Twenty Two

Sid sat silently, meditating in the shade of a mango tree. A cool breeze rose off the Caribbean moving through the island. Eduardo taught Sid how to meditate and pronounce Ohm, the sacred word.

Sid recited Ohm with every breath. He would meditate under the mango tree for hours, transcending the world, leaving pain, fear, and doubt behind. A heightened sense of energy would penetrate his soul— an aura of pure light would envelop his being.

In the early evening, just before sunset, Sid opened his eyes to see a being of light floating a few feet in front of him. The being spoke to Sid, not in words but with pure communication deep in his heart. Sid both heard and saw his purest spiritual connection to the Source.

The being of light took on the shape and reflection of Sid's physical form. Sid's heart was so full of love that he heard the pure sound of the Universe; the sound was deafening but also serene.

The being of light floated in front of Sid for what seemed to Sid like an eternity. The being spoke to Sid, saying, "The world is prepared for a transformation; you can be the conduit."

Instantaneously with a blinding light, Sid was enveloped by a vision. He was now standing in the middle of Church Street, Burlington, on a beautiful spring day. People were out and about, walking around him, and the being of light vanished. Sid's friend Eric was now floating in front of Sid, with the sun behind Eric's back shining through Eric's blond hair.

Sid's memories started to flow over his consciousness during his vision. He not only remembered all the experiences leading up to this moment, but he relived them entirely with all five senses.

Sid remembered the last time he saw Eric before he left Karmakal and how irritable Eric seemed to be that Sid wouldn't go with him to start *The Life Energy Report.*

In Sid's vision, he noticed a black-haired woman crying on his shoulder while he observed Eric floating a few feet in front of him. Sid knew the woman was Eric's wife.

Sid met Eric's wife only a couple of times at dinner parties. The rumor was that Eric and his wife were separated, and she moved back in with her parents near Boston. Sid associated the irritation Eric had with his marital problems.

In Sid's vision, Eric's wife cried on Sid's shoulder and put her arms around him. As she shuddered with sadness, Sid turned to Eric and asked him what was going on, but he said nothing.

Eric floated in front of Sid with a beautiful light silhouetting his body. Eric looked at Sid with his piercing blue eyes, and his blond hair seemed to radiate with brilliance.

Sid asked, "Eric, what's happening?

Eric's shined with tenderness. Eric replied, "Just love each other."

At first, Sid didn't understand. Sid considered that maybe Eric meant he and Eric's wife should love each other, but then he realized like a diamond shot through his forehead.

Eric was attempting to enlighten Sid to love everyone, to be love for everyone. Eric's message to the world was for all human beings to love each other.

Sid's awareness of the situation came into focus. He knew this was not only Eric's message to the world but his last before he passed.

Sid turned and looked at Eric's wife, and then he turned back to Eric to ask another question, but Eric started floating away. Sid asked Eric to wait, but he just faded into the warm light. Sid woke from his vision and looked at his digital wristwatch, which read 9:05 p.m.

Sid was surprised at how many hours had passed during his meditation. He wondered what his vision was trying to tell him and if Eric was okay. Sid walked to his room and immediately fell off to sleep. He slept more soundly than he had in many years, a deep healthy sleep.

Sid woke in the morning with his smartphone ringing. He sat up in bed and looked at his messages. Joleen had sent a text that Eric had died in a car accident last night. He was driving to Boston to see his wife and fell asleep at the wheel.

Another driver witnessed Eric veering off the road, hitting a large maple tree. The police said he died instantly around 9:00 in the evening. Joleen added that maybe it was time for Sid to come home; his children missed him and needed their father.

Surprisingly, Joleen didn't mention her desire to see him or that she needed him. He considered that maybe he had been gone too long for their life together to move forward.

Sid dressed and walked into the kitchen, and Eduardo was already sitting at the table eating breakfast. Eduardo asked, "Something happened last night, right?"

Sid sat down at the table. He asked, "Yes, how did you know?"

Eduardo smiled. He continued, "We are all one, remember. Your stay on the island has heightened your energy; we are now tightly connected. I had a premonition last night; I considered it to do with you."

Sid professed, "I had a vision last night while meditating that my good friend died and wanted to impart an important message of love to the world. When I woke from my vision, it was 9:05 p.m. Joleen sent me a text this morning telling me that Eric died in a car accident last night around the same time."

Eduardo patted Sid on the back. He asked, "How do you feel?"

Sid continued, "I regret my actions the last time we saw each other. He was irritable with me. He asked if I would leave with him to work on his blog, but I couldn't. I was still emotionally invested in Karmakal and was in a lot of pain. I regret how we left our relationship."

Eduardo replied, "Regret is a tool the Source uses to redirect the drama in our lives."

Sid asked, "What do you mean?"

Eduardo continued, "Regret is the stone that lodges in an oyster to create a pearl. Regret is deus ex machina."

Sid interjected, "deus ex machina?"

Eduardo explained, "Deus ex Machina was a term used in ancient Greece and Rome during a theatrical performance when, without warning, a solution to an insolvable situation in the drama would drop from God.

"What I am telling you is that the experiences we regret are an essential tool used by the Source to change the direction of our lives when we don't seem to have the strength to do it ourselves.

"Pain is an excellent motivator for change. Experiences that cause regrets are pebbles that create pearls in our journey through this reality. When we look back on experiences we regret, we look back on transitional moments in our lives.

"If we change how we see these events as a positive push in the right direction, our past will not haunt us.

"I don't believe that Eric was irritated with you, and I feel deep in my heart that Eric loved you and knew he would die. There is a spiritual insight that people know they will pass on to another consciousness before it happens, sometimes many years before it takes place.

"We know the script of our lives because we look back on what has already happened."

Sid interjected, "Yes, you said that the Infinite Being created our world of separation to look upon what the infinite was not, to understand what it is and that it only took an infinite second."

Eduardo smiled. He continued, "Good, you remembered the concept of infinite reality and the world of separation. I have often talked about this concept to other people who don't seem to understand or hear what I am trying to tell them.

"Sid, it is inspiring to have a like soul to discuss such vital theories. For most of my life, I yearned for this kind of relationship."

Sid smiled. He responded, "Funny, I don't feel that you are teaching me anything; it's more like I am remembering what I already know."

Eduardo patted Sid on the hand. He continued, "Yes, that is exactly right. When you hear what I am saying about the Infinite, you already know what I'm telling you.

"I think other people don't understand these concepts because they have cut themselves off to their hearts and the deeper knowledge of the Universe."

Sid asked, "I understand in my heart that the infinite created a separate reality, but it was only a concept. Our entire Universe is the concept of the infinite, and in the infinite reality, it has already happened in an infinite second. We are only looking back on the residual effect of the Source creating the idea of the reality of separation."

Sid and Eduardo started to laugh. Eduardo composed himself and continued, "Yes, we are only looking back on the residual effect of the Source's concept so that we can know the truth, but we must want to know.

"What I have found during my travels through this reality is that most people do not want to know the truth, most talk about knowing the truth as an impossibility.

"I have come to understand that the truth is our birthright. Ultimately, we are all part of the Infinite Being having a collective experience in a reality of separation."

Sid smiled. He interjected, "The Source is experiencing the world of separation through every being in the multi-universe at once.

"It is curious that I know this at the core of my being but finds it odd nonetheless."

Eduardo interjected, "Flannery O'Connor once said, 'You shall know the truth, and the truth shall make you odd.'"

Sid and Eduardo spent many hours walking on islands dotted throughout the Bay of Honduras and often walked through town at all hours of the day and night on the Belize mainland, even though their energy level would briefly decrease.

They would talk for hours about spiritual, religious, and scientific theories and how all disciplines seemed to work together because each field of study at its core was attempting to find the truth of existence.

Sid would meditate for hours, reaching higher and higher levels of energy. Each time he meditated, it would end with a being of light telling him the same thing—the world is ready for a transformation, where he could be the conduit.

For a long time, Sid kept this communication from the being of light a secret from Eduardo. He didn't know why he kept it a secret, but something told him to wait.

He became confused about the knowledge, not knowing if it came from the Source or somewhere else.

Eduardo introduced the concept that since the Infinite Being wanted to know itself, it created dark energy to stand guard over infinite knowledge.

He explained that the dark energy is known as the ego; some see this entity as Satan, Beelzebub, Lucifer, and others know it as the devil. Eduardo told Sid that the ego's only purpose is to convince humankind that they are physical beings, not spiritual beings, and not part of the Source.

For the Source to truly experience physical reality, it would need to forget that it is limitless, and it would need to fall asleep in the world.

The ego's only purpose was to relentlessly convince the infinite being that it is of the world, that it is not an infinite being, a paradox.

Something rang true for Sid when he heard about the ego, and he knew it was time to disclose the being of lights' information.

Sid interjected, "Eduardo, when I meditate, a being of light comes to me and tells me that the world is prepared for a transformation, and I could be the conduit."

Eduardo laughed. He replied, "Yes, I know, I have been seeing it too. I was wondering when you would tell me."

Sid continued, "Something kept me from telling you. I think it was my ego or the darker angels of my nature. My ego kept telling me that I was delusional and that I should keep the information from you."

Eduardo interjected, "Yes, I wondered why you kept it from me; my inner voice told me what to say. How do you feel about being singled out to help the world transform?"

Sid continued, "My ego kept telling me that I was fooling myself that I could help transform the world, and I didn't know what I would do to help the world. It wasn't until you pointed out the dark energy that attempts to convince us that we are not spiritual, but bodies. After all my uncertainty faded away, your comment made perfect sense."

Eduardo professed, "The temporary energy of the world is becoming darker. People have lost their way. People forget their most special relationship is with their purest spiritual connection to the Source. People believe in the illusion and the Universe is winding down. Remember our discussion about Deus ex machina?"

Sid smiled. He replied, "Yes, the God machine. A person or thing sent by God to change the direction of a stalled drama."

Eduardo chuckled. He continued, "Yes, exactly. Maybe the being of light is Deus ex machina. Maybe the two experiences are God-sent, and your time on the island is ending?"

Sid sighed, "Yes, I have been thinking a lot about my next path, but I'm in conflict with the concept that I can help the world. I have learned that the world is an illusion and there is nothing outside myself except an empty void. So, if the world is an illusion, why do I need to help the world? In this scenario, the world doesn't need help."

Eduardo interjected, "Yes, I've been conflicted with the concept of helping a world that is only an illusion. I have come to understand that because we have a collective experience in a reality of separation, we need to heighten the world's energy to benefit all beings and transcend the lower energy of hate, greed, and ignorance.

"Ultimately, since we are all connected, if one heightens the energy of the Universe, all will benefit with a heightened awareness. Remember, this is the premise for my first novel, *A True Heart, Journey to the City of Light*.

"The world doesn't need saving, but people's energy heightened so that collectively we don't fall into total darkness. Since you arrived on the island, you have rapidly moved beyond my understanding of this world. Most concepts I understand are still just theories, and I believe that you must move beyond ideas to a state of knowing, which is a much higher state of being, even beyond the state of belief.

"I knew you were here to learn about energy, and I was here to remind you of what you already knew. I think your friend Eric is a guide to take you where you need to go. I think you need to return to the world. Do you know what you would do when you go home?"

Sid replied, "I know my purpose in coming to this island was to learn about life energy. Over the last few months, I have been sensitive to the flow and ebb of life energy creating the world. I feel that Eric started Something with *The Life Energy Report* that I need to continue."

"I realized that everything in the world is a duality. I know that by taking over *The Life Energy Report*, I will continue to learn about life energy and advance my consciousness. At the same time, I know that this will help others because we are all connected. So, allowing myself to have Universal awareness will help others become more aware.

Eduardo and Sid laughed. Eduardo asked, "Do you plan to reunite with Joleen when you return?"

Sid professed, "Joleen has stood by me through this process. She has tried to keep in touch with me even on a remote island. I don't know how I feel about her or being a husband and father again. I guess I will have to see when I arrive back home. Of course, it also depends on what happened with Joleen during my stay on the island.

"I know that I have changed, and I wonder if I will fall into darkness again once I am back in the world. I know that Vermont has a heightened sense of energy flowing through the green mountains. I've learned much during my time on this island. One of the essential abilities I have obtained is to meditate and recite Ohm.

"Eduardo, you've talked about leaving the island once you know your next path. I've considered that maybe both of our paths lead back to Vermont and *The Life Energy Report*."

Eduardo interjected, "I have one important task I need to do. I need to go to New York City and spend time with a friend I have been avoiding for a long time."

Sid sat down on a bench overlooking the Caribbean. He professed, "I am a little sad that I must leave, and I know if I stayed here too long, I would start to fall back into darkness. As you said, pain is a great motivator for change." ଔ

CB

Chapter Twenty Three

Sid stood looking out the window of the townhouse he lived in before he and Joleen married. It was early June, and Lake Champlain was smooth as glass with no ripples moving over the water.

Sid had been back in Burlington for a month, learning that the thirty-three months he had been gone had changed more than his consciousness.

After two years, Joleen filed for divorce, claiming a cause of abandonment by Sid. Joleen had married another man, David, whom she met through her many volunteer activities.

When Joleen picked up Sid from Burlington airport, his inner voice communicated what had happened with Joleen before they even talked.

When Joleen first picked up Sid, he felt like a stranger was in the car with him. Joleen, once the love of his life, not counting Kamala, now seemed distant. He wondered if he knew who Joleen was—did she know him?

Surprisingly, Sid felt happy that Joleen had moved on with her life. He could still feel love for Joleen, but not like he did before he left. His inner voice told him that this was the best for both and that he had another path to walk.

Sid still felt at peace even though he was off the island. He realized that his tranquility had much to do with following his divine path and understood that the island was not the total cause of his sense of peace. He was determined to follow his inner voice at all costs.

When Joleen picked up Sid from Burlington Airport, she took him to his favorite restaurant. She wanted to disclose everything before he saw his children. Joleen and Sid walked to the back of the restaurant and sat down at a table. Joleen sat across from Sid. She said, "Sid, you look different. You look happy, even at peace."

Sid patted Joleen on the hand. He replied, "Yes, I found what I was looking for in Belize. I'm sorry I put you through so much during our marriage."

Joleen interjected, "I need to tell you something important."

Sid smiled affectionately. He replied, "I already know that you found someone else."

Joleen looked at Sid with a furrowed brow. She asked, "How do you know?"

Sid replied, "My inner voice told me. I can hear it loud and clear."

Joleen shook her head. She replied, "His name is David. I met him at the Burlington Jazz Festival, and we married eight months ago. He is a good man; you would like him."

Sid laughed. He replied, "Maybe; I hope that he makes you happy. Joleen, I don't regret our time together, but I always knew it was temporary. I knew our paths would only come together for a short time and then go in different directions."

Joleen looked confused. She replied, "You seem so different. You don't seem like the same highly wound person—you have changed. You don't seem upset about my marriage to another man or your children having a new person in their life."

Sid replied, "I love you, Joleen, and our children, and that will never change no matter what transpires. The person you once married is long gone, and I have taken his place. It wouldn't be fair if I were upset about you following your path, not after leaving for three years."

Joleen replied, "Sid, I love you too. I'm glad you found your peace. I always worried about you and the darkness that hung over you. I can see now that the darkness is gone, and there is a light in your eyes."

Sid smiled. He replied, "Yes, I learned a lot about the world. When I heard about Eric, I knew it was time to come back."

Joleen interjected, "Yes, that was tragic. I was at his funeral. His wife told me they discussed making their marriage work just before he died. I guess he was driving to Boston to pick her up. So, what will you do now?"

Sid replied, "I'm going to take over Eric's blog, *The Life Energy Report*, and that is where my next path will begin. For now, I'm tired from the flight, and I believe I still own the townhouse overlooking

Lake Champlain. If you could drop me off, I will contact you in the next couple of days to spend some time with our children."

⟨⟨

Sid found that Joleen had dutifully deposited half their wealth into a bank account for Sid when he returned. She sold the house in Charlotte and moved into David's home after the wedding with the children. Joleen liquified most of their possessions but kept the house in Italy.

She didn't want any connection to Sid or her life with him; she thought it would be best for her and her children to start anew.

At the time, Joleen didn't know if Sid would ever return to Burlington or if he did, when that would happen.

David offered the stable life Joleen always wanted. He grew up in Burlington and was successful. Sometimes Joleen felt that her life with David was a bit boring, but then she would remember the drama she went through with Sid.

When Joleen dropped Sid off at his townhouse, she gave him a package that Eric wanted Sid to have. When he opened the box, he found a thumb drive, a key, and a deed to a property in North Burlington. To Sid's surprise, Eric had bought the property and made him co-owner. Eric must have always known that Sid was going to join him. Maybe Eric always knew that he would die and wanted his creation to live on with Sid.

Sid spent a couple of weeks getting reacquainted with his children before he walked into the empty offices of *The Life Energy Report*. Sid wanted to watch the video he found on the thumb drive when he was in the offices so that he could honor his friend.

Eric had Sid's desk from Karmakal moved to a corner office. Sid instantly recognized his old table. He sat down, turned on the computer, inserted the thumb drive, and downloaded the video onto his desktop.

Sid hesitated for a moment before clicking on the video icon. When the video started, Eric was sitting behind Sid's desk. Eric leaned forward and said, "Hey buddy, I guess if you are watching this, I must be dead. Before I get into *The Life Energy Report*, I need to explain a few things.

"I didn't leave Karmakal because it was becoming too corporate. I left because I had a vision that I would die soon, and I figured I had maybe a few years left and wanted to start something I had been thinking about before leaving this plane of consciousness.

"You were a significant part of my vision. I knew deep in my heart that I was going to start something you would bring to the next level. When you left for Belize, I hoped you would return with a better understanding of the energy I have felt my entire life. Once I left Karmakal, I could hear my inner voice with clarity.

"When I was a kid growing up in California, I could tell what kind of person someone was from a mile away just by reading their energy. I would sit on a bench next to a 7-Eleven and test my ability to read people's energy.

"I used to sense ghosts in my room late at night, and it used to freak me out, but what was freakier was that I could feel the spirit's past and family issues through their energy. I started to notice that there was an energy that was creating emotional reactions, then I came across the allegory about life energy.

"When you didn't leave with me to start *The Life Energy Report*, I was confused because it tested my vision of us doing the work together. It's strange to know that I will die soon, and the knowledge gives me a different perspective on each moment I have left.

"I felt I had to control the situation, but when I finally left Karmakal and started *The Life Energy Report*, I felt at peace. I knew everything would fall into place if I only let go and let God.

"I bought the building *The Life Energy Report* offices are in so I could keep it low-key. I didn't want the business to build like Karmakal and get out of control. I picked the North End of Burlington to hide from the city's power brokers.

"Sid, I'm glad you are back and ready to move forward, so let's get to the heart of the business. When I started *The Life Energy Report*, I had a vague understanding of the energy I felt created cause and effect in our world.

"Then I started to make connections to different spiritual philosophies. One meaningful connection I made is to the seven chakras. I began to realize that there is a steady flow of energy from our purest spiritual connection to our physical reality.

"Everything in the Universe, earth, plants, animals, and humankind are connected to the Source by seven points of flowing energy. These points of energy flow back and forth between the physical and spiritual worlds.

"Part of us resides in the world of separation, and part of us exists in the infinite reality. Each point of energy, or chakra, represents a different connection you need to transcend. Most everyone in the world has blocks to prevent a perfect flow between the two realities.

The first energy point in the physical world is at the base of our spine. In the spiritual realm, the energy of the root point will manifest as a perfect red sphere of light.

"Our ego is most potent during the first point with the root chakra. The first chakra is grounded in the physical world and our primal need for safety in a tribe. Also, the root energy point represents our primary ambition and need to succeed. Masculine sexual energy is predominant in the first energy point. The root, or first energy point, will manifest itself by a red stream of light in the Life Energy Field.

"The base root energy point connects us to a tribe, family, country, or kingdom beyond our own needs. We often blindly follow a leader in situations where our lives and moral compass are compromised. Persuasive people know this and blindly use poor souls to follow false doctrine.

"The root energy explains what happens when two armies fight each other on a battlefield. Why does one group of men follow one leader, and another group follows another leader at the cost of their lives?

"The second point of energy is in your lower stomach. Feminine sexuality, energy, creativity, and self-worth are predominant with this energy point. Emotional freedom and sexuality will blossom with this second energy point. The second energy will manifest itself by an orange stream of light in the Life Energy Field.

"This energy point explains why someone in an abusive relationship will stay no matter how bad it becomes. Our need for intimacy connects to this energy point, which becomes more significant than someone's self-interest or belief system.

"The third point is the solar plexus energy point in your upper stomach area. Personal power, anger, and strength are central to this energy point. The third energy will manifest itself by a yellow stream of light in the Life Energy Field.

"It is important to remember that as we transcend from one energy point to another, our ego will have less control over us. The ego's reduced power will diminish after we move beyond the third energy point. The first three energy points are of the physical world, and the last four are transcendent energy points.

"The heart energy is the fourth point. Love, compassion, and spirituality are central to this fourth energy point. The fourth will manifest as a green light stream in the Life Energy Field.

"The throat energy point is the fifth. Communications and innovation are central to this energy point, and healing and transformation are at this point. The fifth energy point will manifest itself by a blue stream of light in the Life Energy Field.

"The third eye, right above your physical eyes in the center of your forehead, is the sixth energy point. Psychic ability, and higher intuition, are central to this energy point. The sixth energy will manifest itself by a purple stream of light in the Life Energy Field.

"The crown energy point is the seventh and final energy. The seventh energy point resides just behind the top of your skull, and spirituality and enlightenment are central to this point. The seventh energy will manifest itself by a white stream of light in the Life Energy Field.

"Each energy point will reflect how you perceive yourself in the physical world. The seven energy points also represent your past lives and how your perceptions have changed each life.

"As I wrote *The Life Energy Report*, I started to see connections to what was going on in the world and the energy I felt moving through my consciousness. I began understanding that most cause and effect are tied to fear and doubt.

"In college physics, I discovered that there is no cold. There are only different degrees of hot in our physical reality, with absolute zero calculated minus 459.67°F.

"As temperature increases from absolute zero, the physical world reacts. I have realized a parallel in the life energy field. The world reacts depending on the amount of fear and doubt, and the stock market on Wall Street is a perfect reflection of this Theory.

"There is no rhyme or reason why the world's financial stability ebbs and flows other than the amount of fear and doubt investors feel. An economic crash happens when there is too much fear and doubt.

"Stability is based on trust and confidence in the structure of the physical world. I wondered then what cases the fear and doubt, and this was when I began understanding how much the life energy field was the central power behind cause and effect.

"I finally understood the *Course in Miracles'* claim that there is no outside love, and the only love that we can feel is when we open our hearts to the truth. We need to trust to feel the connection we have to the Source.

"When someone falls in love, they are not feeling the love of the other person but the love they have in their hearts. They trust the other person enough to let down their guard and open their hearts to their connection to their purest spiritual relationship.

"The ego's purpose is to close our connection to the Source by deceiving us into believing that the world outside will fulfill our needs, not the Source.

"I made a lot of connections during my experience writing *The Life Energy Report.* Even though I wrote it and sent it off into the world for others to contemplate, I knew that, ultimately, the process was helping me to transcend this reality.

"I hope in my next life I remember all the knowledge I gained during my experience on this plane of consciousness.

"The more I wrote *The Life Energy Report*, the more I knew I was close to a significant epiphany. I know that there is a leap in understanding that I haven't been able to make. I know that there is a structure of the Universe that eludes me. When you discover this Universal mechanism, all the puzzle pieces will fall into place.

"Allow your inner voice to guide you to write *The Life Energy Report.* You need to listen to your heart. As you report and connect with these energy points, you will start to release all blocks between your seven energy points. Doing so will change your consciousness.

"I don't know where this endeavor will take you or what ultimate good it will do, but I did know that this was my path, and now it is your path. Sid, I appreciate our friendship and the wisdom you brought to my life."

Sid clicked off the video and sat back in his chair. He looked up and was surprised to see a young man standing in the doorway of his office. Sid asked, "I'm sorry I didn't see you standing there. Can I help you with something?"

The young man walked into the office and sat beside Sid. He replied, "My name is Charles Ellison, and I was Eric's technician on

The *Life Energy Report.* Eric talked a lot about you and said you would take the *Life Energy Report* to the next level.

Sid asked, "What technical work did you do?"

Charles replied, "We were on YouTube and other social networking sites. I took care of all the video, audio, and other technical details. I hope I can continue with you?"

Sid asked, "How did you know I was here?"

Charles replied, "I live in the apartment right above your office. I could hear you playing the video I helped Eric create, and I figured it was you; Eric built you up into the savior of our business."

Sid laughed. He replied, "I have that distinction cast on me a few times. I'm not here to be the savior of anything, but let's see if we can have a little fun and learn a few things."

Charles smiled. He replied, "Sounds like a plan." ⟡

☙

Chapter Twenty Four

It took Sid seventeen months to develop a heightened awareness of life energy and how it determined cause and effect. He and Charles broadcasted *The Life Energy Report* five days a week on the radio, YouTube, and multiple social networking sites.

Sid built a small following of subscribers. He didn't have the success he enjoyed with Karmakal, but he had a solid thirty thousand listening to his broadcast daily. Sid realized that Eric's gift of *The Life Energy Report* was more to increase his understanding of the Universe than to deliver information to his audience.

Sid knew that since everyone is separated by their perceptions, his audience heard his broadcast based on how they identified themselves, not how Sid perceived his reality.

He would often laugh and wonder why he was even attempting to convey something that was uncommunicable.

Each day his sense of life energy flowing through the Universe became more and more acute, but he still felt that a vital understanding was just outside his vision. He knew that the flow of energy didn't move through our bodies. He couldn't quite grasp the concept of a Universal transfer of energy, but he knew he was getting close.

The Life Energy Report helped to keep Sid's energy at a high level of consciousness, but the energy was not as high as when he was on the island. On the island, he primarily focused on his purest spiritual relationship, but now that he was back in Burlington, his ego pulled him in numerous directions.

Sid had a single interest on the island that changed into multi-interests in Burlington, requiring Sid's time and attention. One substantial concern was his growing children. His daughter, Sasha, who was the oldest, turned fifteen. He could see that she was consumed with her ego as her interest focused on expensive horses, clothes, and boys.

He struggled to accept her position in life, being a teenager and just becoming aware of the world, but his protective father's energy would flash red flags that he had a hard time ignoring.

His absence during the three years had created a divide in their relationship. Before he left for the island, Sasha was daddy's little girl, always trying to please Sid. When he returned, Sasha became a devotee of David.

At first, this did not bother Sid because he expected his children to take on a level of comfort with their new father figure, but as time passed, Sid could see that Sasha was going down a path that would cause her pain in the end.

His son, Darrick, had become a stranger during his absence. Sid thought he knew his son, but when he returned to Burlington, his son was gone, and another person he didn't recognize had taken his place.

Both children were part of the elite in Burlington. The millions of dollars Sid had built up during his entrepreneurial experiences played out as an ongoing soap opera of excess.

Sid had a hard time understanding the world of privilege his children were growing up in because he grew up a poor farmer in the South, many miles away from Burlington.

Sid considered that Joleen suppressed her guilt about leaving him by indulging almost every impulse that Sasha or Darrick had. Most of the children at the private school Sasha and Darrick attended had parents that bought their love with materialism because most of the parents were movers and shakers in the community and purposefully absent from their children's lives. Sid considered wealth a double-edged sword—money could heal and tear lives apart.

A whisper started to rise among the Burlington privileged that David was seeing other women and that there was trouble in Joleen's marriage. Joleen began to lean on Sid for emotional support more than he felt was appropriate, considering the situation.

Sid would attempt to comfort Joleen or reach his children with his spiritual awareness, but any wise words or spiritual ideas would fall on deaf ears. Sid would often wonder what good is having this knowledge if no one close to him was interested in hearing what he had to say.

The more Sid tried to help his family cope with their emotional chaos, the more they dragged him down a rabbit hole of despair. He could see his family drowning in their desires and privileged life. He knew that he couldn't save them from themselves, and his family would only pull him down into the depth of their misery.

In one heated exchange with Sasha, she said, "Daddy, no one cares what you have to say." This experience with Sasha was a defining moment for Sid that changed how he needed to help his family. After this exchange with Sasha, he knew listening was the only way to help.

Sid considered that maybe the experience with his daughter was a wake-up call to stop trying to control the situation and just let go, let God.

Sid longed for the days when he could talk with Eric or Eduardo about the mechanism of the Universe. It wasn't until he returned that he genuinely missed their conversations and understood how precious his time with them was.

Sid realized how far he had moved from his family. Not just in miles but all aspects of his being. He grew so far from their understanding of the world that he couldn't reach them; they were too mired in their egos to hear him.

To add to Sid's daily stress, he and Charles were working on a visual presentation of *The Life Energy Report*, which was going nowhere. Sid wanted a visual representation of how the Universe creates life energy.

In the visual presentation, he would start with the traditional understanding of how chakras transmit energy through the different levels of the physical body. However, when they began the production, he would be blocked by the Source.

He could not make sense of energy flowing through the body when the dynamics of the Source are part spiritual reality and part reality of separation. His inner voice kept telling him that the body had nothing to do with the actual Universal mechanism, but he would not listen because of all the distractions and frustration in his life. Sid's life in Burlington weighed on him. His inner voice became muted and confusing.

Charles was getting frustrated working on the visual project with Sid because Charles was never a true believer in *The Life Energy Report*. He answered an ad on Craigs List that Eric had posted for a technical and visual engineer.

Charles's technical interaction with Sid was based solely on being paid and having an apartment. He was happy when Sid returned to take on *The Life Energy Report* so that he could continue his lifestyle in Burlington.

Before Sid returned, Charles considered moving back to Boston. He had an offer at a news station as a director of the station's technical support staff. Charles had built up a life in Burlington and didn't want to walk away from it, but Burlington was a small community with limited opportunities. Charles often reminded Sid that he should have taken the job in Boston. This constant reminder of losing a key employee was wearing on Sid. All the noise in Sid's life was causing too much chaos.

Many creative people were scratching out a meager life in Burlington; Charles didn't want to be one of them. Eric paid Charles the same salary he once received in Boston. Charles became accustomed to the good life—he saw *The Life Energy Report* and Sid as a ticket to that life.

Sid felt alone for the first time in many years. He had people around him, but none he could connect with at the level he did with Eric or Eduardo. Sid once felt comforted by Joleen, but she had none for him because she was in a midlife meltdown and was struggling to save her marriage.

Sid often wondered why he returned to Burlington. The stress started to take its toll. He knew he couldn't fall back into the darkness and could only save himself.

Sid would calm his mind and reconnect with his highest level of awareness with an early morning run along Burlington's jogging path on the shores of Lake Champlain. He would then meditate at Burlington's waterfront park. As Sid became older, he started to find comfort in his daily routine.

Sid's favorite time to run was winter when there was no wind on Lake Champlain. There is a stillness in winter that is magical. It was a time when Sid could concentrate and connect to his purest spiritual relationship.

During his jog one cold winter day, he obsessed with the concept of how energy flowed from the Source to the world of separation. He could not stop contemplating how the Universe worked and the purpose of this reality.

Then he had an epiphany while running along the shore of Lake Champlain. His vision of the Universal mechanism stopped him in his tracks, and he realized he was not a body and visualized the Universe's absolute truth.

In his vision, he pictured an orb of pure white light. This ball of light was the pure essence of the Infinite Being. Surrounding the sphere was the seven layers of energy that reflected the different chakra colors. Closest to the orb was the color magenta which connects every living thing to the Source. Then a layer of purple encompassed the globe, heightening spiritual awareness. Then a layer of blue promotes communications and green heart energy, then on the outer layers consisting of yellow, orange, and tribal red.

On the outside of the orb was an emptiness that was neither black nor color. The color was without light and form. Sid remembered a passage in the Bible, "In the beginning, God created the heaven and the earth. And the earth was without form and void, and darkness was upon the face of the deep. And the Spirit of God moved upon the face of the waters. And God said, let there be light: and there was light."

Sid realized that when the Infinite Being created the concept of the reality of separation, he formed the known Universe based on perception. Every living entity in the multi-universe was the same orb structure.

The center of each orb in the Universe contained the same pure essence of the Infinite Being. Each sphere was separated by perception—the different layers of energy encompassing the infinite.

He knew that each living entity in the multi-verse had a different perception, but each entity had the exact center of the pure essence of the Infinite.

He realized that we are not bodies but only perceive that we are. Our physical form is a construct of perception that each entity in the multi-universe creates based on their feelings about themselves—that each entity creates its physical form, almost like a Universal avatar.

Each layer of perception dictates a different view of each entity's reality. The farther our perception takes us from the Source, the more fear and doubt enter our hearts.

Sid realized that the Source was experiencing everything based on his understanding of the Universal mechanism. The different layers of perception encompassing the center of the orb acted almost like a movie theater projecting a complete reality based on the five senses.

Sid understood the world only projects back to how we see ourselves in the Universe. If we see ourselves as victims, the world will support our belief in our victimhood. If we see ourselves as heroes, the world will support our view.

Sid realized that the one genuine job of our egos is to convince us that we are separate from the Source, and our ego is relentless.

Sid had another major epiphany—the Source created the Universe to know itself. Sid had heard this doctrine many times in his life, but for the first time, he knew it to be true.

That the Infinite Being cannot know itself because it is infinite. So, it made the world of separation experience an opposite reality to the one it inhabited. By looking upon what it wasn't, it realized what it was, the Infinite Being.

Sid understood that each person in the world had the same ultimate purpose. To know who we are by who we are not. We are not separate from each other, and the world is an illusion reflecting how each one of us perceives our reality in the world.

The primary motivation to know who we are is the pain we feel once we come closer to the purest essence of the Infinite. The more we understand that the world is just an empty void, the more we will let go and embrace our purest spiritual relationship.

Ultimately, we are all the Source having a collective experience in a reality of separation. Sid realized that the whole Universe occurred in an infinite second. That the creation of the Universe for the Source to know itself already happened, and we are only looking back on the residual effect.

Now that Sid knew the universal mechanism, he started understanding how life energy dictates cause and effect. The energy transferred from the Source to the world works through the different layers of perception encompassing the Source's purest essence.

Sid sat on the lawn next to the jogging path and leaned against a beech tree. The epiphany he had just experienced propelled him into such a heightened sense of awareness that the world around him started to take on a vibration he had never felt before.

His heart felt heightened, but his body felt depleted. He sat under the beech tree for a long time, looking at the world outside himself. People were going about their daily lives oblivious to how the Universe works, but he had another revelation. He realized that the people outside of himself were part of the reality he created, so they already knew the truth about the world. They were only waiting for Sid to wake up from his dream.

Sid thought about what he would do with such knowledge now that he knew the Universal mechanism. He wanted to run home to Joleen and tell her, but she was long gone from his life, and she would most likely discount the information as flawed or immaterial to her challenges. This knowledge supported the concept that most people are empty vessels looking for meaning outside themselves.

He knew that the awareness that he had just obtained was his and his alone. He couldn't transfer the process by which he acquired the knowledge to someone outside of himself, plus he understood that the need to do so was of the ego, not from his purest spiritual relationship.

Sid laughed again because he obtained the Universal knowledge of why we are here, and he couldn't tell anyone because no one would understand or take him seriously.

He remembered a story he heard in school about Greek mythology, where Cassandra was a Trojan Princess given the voice of God but cursed by the fact that nobody would believe her. He felt very much like Cassandra.

An idea popped into Sid's mind. He couldn't transfer the knowledge he had just obtained directly, but he could work with Charles to create an animated video of the Universal mechanism. He would call it what Eric coined *The Life Energy Field Theory*. He accepted that he was still in the world and needed a visual reminder of his gift.

Sid often had a conflict in his heart about communicating a spiritual idea that dictates that the world is an illusion. The paradox is why to spend energy sharing a belief in an empty void. The answer he received from his purest spiritual relationship was always the same. He needed to continually affirm his conviction because he was still in the world. Allowing the process to take place was his only hope of becoming enlightened.

Saying the word enlightened out loud startled Sid because, up until this moment, he had never considered his objective to become self-aware. He spent the last few years attempting to gain knowledge of the Universe based on overcoming the emptiness he had felt his entire life. Now that he had a strong foundation of insight, he knew his next goal was enlightenment.

Under the beech tree next to the shore of Lake Champlain, Sid realized that his world had changed significantly. He felt like a snake shedding its skin and starting on a different path with new intentions.

He got up, brushed himself off, and started to run back to the office to broadcast *The Life Energy Report*. His understanding was so acute now that he could again hear his inner voice. ∞

ॐ

Chapter Twenty Five

Sid stood in the bathroom of his favorite Burlington restaurant looking in the mirror for a long time. He had just turned fifty. Sid was examining the grey hair that started to grow on his unshaven face.

The party Joleen, his kids, and friends gave him was a surprise, so he didn't shave before showing up at the Burlington Pub and Brewery.

He still had dark black hair on his head and wondered why the grey was showing up first in his beard. Standing in front of the mirror, he started to have flashbacks of his experiences over the years; many awkward moments made him cringe, and he had uncomfortable memories from his childhood.

He had not returned to his home in Alabama since he left at nineteen. He didn't know his father's or mother's fate and wondered if it was time to visit, to reconcile a few things with his family in the South, or if he considered it was too late to go home again.

Someone started to knock on the door of the bathroom. Sid didn't recall how long he had stood in front of the mirror. Birthday parties and other events involving him were always uncomfortable.

As spiritually aware as he had become over the years, he still couldn't shake the memories that haunted him. The knocking on the door became louder, and someone asked, "Hell, Sid, when are you coming out? You can't hide in there forever."

The voice behind the door sounded familiar to Sid, but he could not quite place it. He opened the bathroom door, and standing in front of him was Vincenzo Govinda Aiello. Sid stood shocked for a moment looking at an older man with chiseled features and a small gut.

It took only a moment to recognize Vincent. He still had his piercing blue eyes and long blond hair, a little thinner and lighter but still blond. Vincent smiled and said, "Good to see you again, old buddy."

The two embraced for a long time, and then they started walking back into the restaurant. Sid asked, "How did they find you?"

"Hell, you can find almost anyone on the internet nowadays. Joleen called me a month ago and asked if I would attend your fiftieth. It was good to hear her voice, bringing back good memories. We had some fun, didn't we? Even Rikers was a wild ride."

It was late in the evening, and most of Sid's friends and family had already left. Sid was surprised that the restaurant was empty, and his party had ended while he was in the bathroom. He wondered how long he had been looking in the mirror.

Joleen was still at the bar waiting for Sid. She said, "Well, I'm glad you finally came out of the bathroom.

"I guess next time I will not surprise you; I'll tell you first." Joleen gave Sid and Vincent big hugs and said, "Happy fiftieth; I'll see you at Sasha's graduation.

"Great to see you again, Vincent. I'm going to leave and let you boys catch up." Joleen picked up a few things from the bar and walked out the front of the restaurant.

Sid and Vincent watched as she left the restaurant. Vincent said, "Joleen told me you two got a divorce a few years back, but it seems like you stayed friends."

Sid replied, "Yeh, I think we were always friends; we just went back to what we knew. She went through an ugly divorce with her second husband, David, a couple of years ago. He wanted half her money. She fought hard and won. This place is closing; you want to go get a drink?"

Vincent replied, "In for a penny, in for a pound."

Sid and Vincent walked down College Street to the Hilton Hotel into the bar overlooking Lake Champlain. There were only a couple of people sitting at the bar talking.

Vincent said, "You're becoming old, brother. This place is quieter than a morgue."

Sid replied, "The other bars in town are crammed with college students. We could not think with the noise, much less have a conversation."

Vincent and Sid sat at a table in the corner and ordered a couple of drinks and some appetizers. Vincent asked, "So, who is Sasha, and what is she graduating from?"

Sid sat back and took a long pull from his beer. He replied, "Joleen and I had two children, Sasha and Darrick. Man, has it been that long since we last saw each other?"

Vincent took his whisky, dropped it in his beer, and took a sip. He replied, "It must be fifteen, maybe twenty years. Too much water under the dam, as they say."

Sid asked, "It has to be more than fifteen because Sasha is graduating from high school, and when we last saw each other, Joleen and I weren't married yet."

Vincent replied, "Hell, I missed the wedding. Not much for formal parties, maybe a good thing."

Sid asked, "So, what happened with Marty?"

Vincent replied, "That's a long story."

Sid asked, "Got any place to go?"

Vincent took another sip of his drink and leaned back in the chair. He replied, "Hell, the whole thing went south. Marty and I built the same co-working grift we did in Rutland, but the town in Ohio was just too poor. This time Marty got most of the investment money from locals who didn't have any money."

Sid asked, "What about the startups, any unicorns?"

Vincent replied, "No, just a bunch of losers trying to scrape themselves out of poverty. You should have seen the downtown; it looked like a war zone. I didn't understand what Marty was thinking; I think he felt invincible after the amazing success in Rutland. We should have quit back when we were emperors of the Universe."

Sid asked, "What happened to Marty?"

Vincent leaned close to Sid and spoke in a low voice, "Marty ended up doing three years in Marion. The last time I saw him was ten years ago. He looked me up when he got out; prison aged him twenty years. He didn't have the same polish; he looked ancient. I think he moved back to New Orleans for good, and I haven't heard a word from him since."

Sid asked, "And you?"

Vincent replied, "I was lucky, or maybe my street skills kept me sharp enough to leave town just before the grift was exposed. Like Rutland, it would not have been a con if we succeeded. Steal a little;

they put you in Rikers, screw up a good thing, and hunt you down. I think I have an outstanding warrant in Ohio; I stay away from the state altogether."

Sid interjected, "Well, I appreciate you making an effort."

Vincent continued, "Marty wouldn't have gone to prison if he didn't use all the suckers' money to keep up appearances. He decided not to use any of his own money. When I saw him last, I asked if he would have given half his money to stay out of prison.

"Marty told me medium-security prison is no different than any elder care facility when you are an old man. He was happy to be out and still rich, even though the feds were trying to find his stash to pay back some of the suckers. As far as I know, they never did find his treasure."

Sid interjected, "So, what are you doing now?"

Vincent laughed and took another sip of his drink. He replied, "Hell, I went back home to Wyoming and took over the ranch before my father died. We have fifteen hundred acres of prime cattle country."

Sid interjected, "If I remember right, I thought your sister and brother were going to work the ranch?"

Vincent sighed. He replied, "Yeh, that was my fantasy, that those two would take over the ranch, but I learned that I couldn't save anyone from themselves.

"It became ugly when the money arrived. My family became a pack of hyenas ripping each other apart for a piece of the pie. My father bought the ranch and paid off my brother and sister to stay off his property."

Sid took a long sip of his beer and ordered another. He replied, "Yeh, it's funny how things work out in life. How did you end up with the ranch?"

Vincent replied, "After the grift in Ohio went south, I decided I had enough of digging for gold. I still had considerable money left from the Rutland deal, not as much as I originally had but enough to start again. I showed up just before my father passed and got a big whiff of the mess I caused with too much money thrown at simple folk; I decided to stay and make a go of it. I think my father was finally at peace, knowing his dream would become a reality.

"I guess I owed him that, being the prodigal son. It's funny how you look back on the terrible things we do in life and wonder what we were thinking. I believe wisdom is doing stupid things and finally knowing they were stupid."

Sid interjected, "Ah, man, brother."

Vincent raised his glass. He replied, "Hell yeah, ah man."

Sid asked, "So, any kids, marriage?"

Vincent smirked. He replied, "You remember that high school sweetheart that married the school football hero? I kicked his ass in a bar fight. She divorced him and married me. We have been married for twelve years now. She had two kids with stupid, and I adopted them. We have a nice little family.

"If you would have told me back in Rikers that I would ultimately return home and take over the ranch and marry my highschool sweetheart, I would have told you that you are crazy. Funny how life turns out."

Sid sat back in his chair and laughed. He replied, "Ah, man, brother."

Vincent asked, "So, your son told me to watch out for the preacher. Darrick told me you have become mister spiritual and will try to lay down some heavy wisdom; kids, huh?"

Sid replied, "Yeh, no man is a prophet in his own home."

Vincent laughed. He retorted, "Ain't that the truth."

Sid continued, "I don't know if I'm mister spiritual, but I learned a few truths over the years that have helped me find peace."

Vincent replied, "I remember back in Rikers when you were adamant about the corruption perpetrated through the good book. The number one example of what not to do being your father."

Sid scratched his head and took a long swig of his beer. He replied, "You seem to be speaking more articulately; what's the deal?"

Vincent smirked. He replied, "I've been taking night classes at the local community college in literature, English, and art. I've always wanted to write, so I decided to educate myself. My wife tells me my intellect turns her on; her last husband was dumb as a stump. What truth have you found?"

Sid continued, "It's a long story."

Vincent asked, "Got any place to go?"

Sid sat back in his chair and contemplated his life for a moment. He replied, "I guess my quest for a Universal truth started last I saw you. I was immersed in building Karmakal, but the more successful I became, the more painful life became.

"I felt a growing emptiness in my heart that would not disappear. I could always distract myself enough during my younger years to control the pain. I thought marrying Joleen would help me to find some peace, but nothing seemed to distract me.

"When the Karmakal board of directors fired me, I was devastated, but looking back, they did me a big favor. I would have stayed building Karmakal no matter how painful life became. The more successful I became, the bigger jerk I was. I often took out my misery on Joleen by becoming stone-cold.

Vincent interjected, "I remember meeting your darker side. You could freeze water in the middle of summer."

Sid laughed and shook his head. He continued, "The kids were too small to get the brunt of my despair, but they still experienced the non-stop arguments between Joleen and myself.

"I asked Sasha and Darrick if they remembered what I was like before I left for the Island. Sasha told me that she remembers Joleen and me arguing a lot, but Derrick didn't remember anything other than I took him out for ice cream."

Vincent sat up in his chair with a surprised look. He asked, "Wait a minute, brother; what Island? Joleen never said anything about you living on an island."

Sid thought for a moment. He continued, "Yeh, after being fired from Karmakal, I had a lot of money and too much time on my hands. Even though I left Karmakal, the emptiness in my heart continued to grow.

"I started reading every spiritual writing I could get my hands on. The more knowledge I obtained, the more I pursued it. The spiritual quest did take the edge off the despair, but only for brief moments.

"I came across a book series, *A True Heart*, by Eduardo Francheze. I related to the book series like no other writing. I read the books repeatedly. I think I went through the entire series ten times. Then the desire, almost need, to meet the author took over. I had a professional detective track him down. He lived on an island off the coast of Belize in the Caribbean.

"One night, I knew I had to decide, either stay in Burlington and destroy everything I worked for and my family or leave and take a chance on finding a truth that may or may not give me some peace."

Vincent asked, "So, did you find peace?"

Sid smiled. He replied, "Yes, I found peace on the Island and brought it back to Burlington. I was gone for three years."

Vincent asked, "What brought you peace on the island."

Sid continued, "Eduardo and I spent three years focusing on what was most important. We built a strong relationship with our purest spiritual connection."

Vincent furrowed his brow. He replied, "I think I remember you once discussing your purest spiritual relationship. If my memory is correct, you once met it in a vision."

Sid retorted, "Good memory. Yes, throughout my life, I had glimpses of my spiritual connection, and it wasn't until I spent time on the island did I connect to another level of consciousness."

Vincent asked, "How did you find this level of consciousness?" Vincent then stroked his hair behind his ears.

Sid smiled and took a long sip from his beer. He replied, "I still know your poker tell."

Vincent laughed. He replied, "Hell, stroking my hair behind my ears?"

Sid continued, "Yes, it is your sign that you are tense. I find it interesting that you haven't discounted what I am saying as crazy. The Vincent I knew twenty years ago would play the purest spiritual relationship down, or at least make a joke."

Vincent sat back in his chair. He replied, "Well, I've had a few more experiences since I saw you that make me feel that there is more to the world than meets the eye."

Sid asked, "What experiences?"

Vincent thought for a long time. He replied, "After my father passed, I started to have visitations from spirits. I would wake up in the middle of the night and see my father sitting in the leather chair I had in my bedroom.

"My grandmother would show up occasionally, and I would see my mother. At first, it concerned me that all these dead relatives were sticking around, but over the years, I started to find comfort in their presence. I figured some of you rubbed off on me."

Sid laughed. He asked, "Do you remember Caesar Ramirez in Rikers?"

Vincent replied, "Hell, how could I forget? Caesar saved us and sent us on a journey to find treasure. I wouldn't be in Wyoming sitting on fifteen hundred acres if it weren't for Caesar. I mean, you never know where a path will take you."

Sid raised his glass. He said, "Ah, man, brother; to Caesar. May he finally be released from Rikers?"

Vincent raised his glass. He asked, "Hail Caesar. You know you didn't answer my question."

Sid asked, "What question was that?"

Vincent replied, "How did you achieve a higher level of consciousness."

Sid thought for a long time about how he would answer such an important question. He replied, "Do you want to know?"

Vincent replied, "Hell yes."

Sid replied, "I mean do you really want to know."

A confused look came over Vincent. He reasserted, "Yes, I want to know."

Sid took a long pull from his beer and put the bottle down hard on the bar. He replied, "If you want to know, you are on the right path. The one Universal truth I learned on the island is that each person is separated by their perceptions.

"We are all part of an infinite being having a collective experience in a reality of separation.

"A true spiritual journey reflects people's perception of themselves in the world. A true spiritual journey is personal and is void of religion, science, or any outside influence.

"A true spiritual journey cannot be communicated or shared. Still, the essential beginning of any spiritual journey is the desire to know the truth." ☙

03

Chapter Twenty Six

After four years of broadcasting *The Life Energy Report*, a major transition occurred when Sid published *The Life Energy Field Theory*, a detailed description of the Universal mechanism he envisioned during his most profound epiphany.

Until the book was published, Sid and *The Life Energy Report* had a small following. Sid had a calm, uneventful life in Burlington, but once the book was published, his subscription base rose rapidly to nine million, and his peaceful life started to fade away.

A national broadcasting company took notice of Sid's success and convinced him to expand the broadcast to a larger audience. Sid moved into a new studio in the same building as a news station in Williston, Vermont. The national broadcasting company hired professionals from New York, which instantly started to force out the original staff, including Charles.

During the transitional chaos, Sid didn't notice his initial staff being walked on or forced out. His primary goal was to grow *The Life Energy Report*, and reaching a larger mainstream audience greatly appealed to him.

Sid recognized that Charles did a lot for the broadcast over the years. However, he constantly reminded Sid that he was not a true believer and only did the energy report for a payday, always indicating that his talents were non-replaceable until he was replaced.

Sid convinced himself that the new staff would bring much-needed energy and expertise to the next step in *The Life Energy Report's* progress. He felt that Charles would be better off finding an opportunity that would better suit him. At the end of the transition, Sid had only one original staff member, Sylvia. She was an office assistant to Sid, and he felt comforted by her presence, so she stayed on after everyone left in pursuit of other opportunities.

Sid's relationship with Joleen started to strain while he produced *The Life Energy Report*, especially when their children, Sasha, and Darrick, went to college in other states. Joleen witnessed her peaceful friend slowly replaced with the obsessed Sid she knew before he left for the island.

Joleen would remark to Sid that *The Life Energy Report* was taking him down the same path as Karmakal. His success was attracting the ego world he once denounced when he left his family and went to the island. Sid would assure Joleen that he was aware of the pitfalls of success but felt he would be able to handle the roller coaster ride.

He thought the Universe would move the rest of the pieces on the board if he focused on *The Life Energy Report*. He firmly believed that everything has a purpose, and the Source is one hundred percent behind his desire to grow *The Life Energy Report*; his mantra was "Let go and let God."

Sid still felt alone in his spiritual pursuits, and he could never convince Joleen or his children of his new spiritual insight. Sid had a hard time reconciling that a woman he loved never knew him and he never knew her. He wondered what attracted them to each other or what attracted other people.

He kept his distance from his audience. He started to have a few subscribers call him and profess devotion to him. Lonely women would try to contact him and induce him to meet them.

This unwanted attention concerned Sid. He would tell these people that the answers to the Universe are in each of us, but they would fixate on him.

He could not find a like soul to share the spiritual transformation he was going through. He hoped that Eduardo Francheze would join the effort and work with him on *The Life Energy Report*, but he discovered soon after his return to Burlington that Eduardo had decided to stay in New York City.

His friend he had to see again was a lost love, and they decided to move forward together in Manhattan. Eduardo did find his voice again and started a new series of books based on his time on the island.

He wondered if he should have stayed on the island, but he knew deep in his heart that, at least for now, the broadcast was his path, for good or bad. He realized that each journey he had taken during his life had taught him valuable lessons that brought him to a higher level of consciousness.

The further Sid moved away from his experience on the island, the more he questioned if the energy he felt was real or just in his imagination. He knew working on *The Life Energy Report* was a double-edged sword because he understood that the world outside of himself was an illusion.

Ultimately, he knew in his heart that the broadcast was taking him on a ride that would hopefully help grow his understanding of the Universe and maybe take him to a heightened sense of awareness or even enlightenment.

Sid was in his office late afternoon when Joleen showed up at his door. She had a resolved look, knocked on the door, and entered without being asked. She said, "Sid, I've made a decision that might affect you, so I wanted to talk with you first."

Sid stopped what he was doing and sat up in his chair. He asked, "What decision?"

Joleen sat down in a chair in front of Sid's desk. She continued, "I've decided to move back to Staunton, Virginia. My mother died, and my father is alone and aging. My brother lives in California, estranged from my father. My brother doesn't want anything to do with my family or Staunton.

"I've decided to move back and take care of my father. I feel I owe it to him. I've contacted my friend in Charlottesville about a job. He said they needed a social networking guru for the business, so I took the job.

"I still have plenty of money left, but now that the kids are off to college, I need to return to my career. I loved being a designer, and I never was good at being rich. You can take the woman out of the holler but can't take the holler out of the woman."

Sid replied, "Wow, I never saw this coming. I thought you loved Burlington. What happened?"

Joleen replied, "I think I was playing a role for a long time, but I never felt comfortable. I so wanted to hide that countrywoman away in a vault, but now that I am older, I am starting to appreciate my former life in Staunton.

"You once told me a story about temporary and permanent energy you discovered on the island. I think my temporary Burlington energy wore off, and my permanent small-town Virginia energy retook hold. I miss my people, and I want to go home."

Sid replied, "Funny, I've been thinking a lot about my family farm back in Alabama. I haven't been back since I was nineteen. The young man who left is different from the one sitting at this desk, and I don't think I even recognize myself from that time in my life. It seems like a movie I watched long ago and not a good one."

Joleen continued, "I've been thinking a lot about going home lately, but I've been worried about you. I still love you and want the best for you, but I know it is time to leave. I fear you will be alone in Burlington now that the children are gone."

Sid sat up in his chair with a smile. He replied, "I love you too, Joleen. I have realized that love is infinite—I will always have love in my heart for you.

"Joleen, you've been one of my wisest teachers, a teacher of compassion and kindness. Until I met you, I didn't believe that people could be caring and generous in spirit. So, when do you leave for Staunton?"

Joleen stood up from the chair, walked around the desk, and hugged Sid. She replied, "I'm leaving this weekend. I start my new job in two weeks; before I start, I want to get reacquainted with my father."

Sid gave Joleen a big hug back. He replied, "If there is anything I can do, don't hesitate to ask."

Joleen replied, "I'm having an estate sale company sell most of my furniture and other belongings, but I'm keeping all the memories of our children. The rest I will have put in storage in Virginia until I know what to do. You know how I like to clear out the past to start anew."

Sid replied, "It seems like you thought this out?"

Joleen replied, "As I said, I have been thinking about going home for quite some time."

Sid sat back in his chair and looked at Joleen for a long time. "You know where I will be, at least for the near future; if you need anything, give me a call."

Joleen walked to the office door and turned around. She replied, "I think I will be fine. If you are ever in Virginia, look me up." She then walked out of the building.

Sid stood up and looked out his office window. He watched Joleen get into her car and drive away. An empty feeling filled his heart. He wondered how long he would walk the path he was on right now. He felt another change in his life was not far off; he didn't know what it was.

Days turned into weeks, weeks turned into months, and a whole year passed. All during the year, heavy energy weighed on Sid. He thought a lot about the friends he had in his life and how they came and went. He thought about Vincent, Joleen, Eduardo, Eric, and even Marty, each close to his heart. When they were friends, he thought they would be part of his life forever, but they all left in different directions. Sid felt alone for the first time in a long time, but he didn't feel lonely.

Sid started to contemplate what was his purest spiritual relationship. He had often talked about it with Eduardo but never examined the importance of the relationship.

Sid valued physical relationships throughout his life but acknowledged that he didn't need a physical relationship. He considered physical relationships transitory because he had a solid connection to his purest spiritual relationship.

Sid contemplated that maybe our spiritual relationship was the only meaningful relationship in anyone's life. We hear our inner voice throughout our lives, but people often discount their purest spiritual connection.

Sid considered that most people in our lives lie to us and try to deceive us with ulterior motives. Sid remembered reading James Redfield's *Celestine Prophecy* while devouring many spiritual philosophies.

The *Celestine Prophecy* talked about how control dramas dictate physical relationships. He didn't truly understand what a control drama was until Joleen walked out of his life. He often wondered what attracted people to each other. Then he made the connection with control dramas from the book.

The *Celestine Prophecy* detailed four central control dramas: intimidator, interrogator, victim, and aloof. That the primary purpose of each control drama was to obtain energy, Sid recognized that he was an interrogator and Joleen was aloof.

He would interrogate people with the primary purpose of obtaining energy from others. He would try this tactic back when he was married to Joleen.

She would play aloof to his need for information or understanding, which would drive him crazy, but what she was doing was obtaining energy from him.

Sid realized that his former technical engineer, Charles, was a victim, and his wife was an intimidator. Charles would often play like a wounded bird to obtain energy from Sid, who would go out of his way to try to help, but a victim doesn't want help; what they desire is energy.

Sid's relationships throughout his life started to fall into place when he considered how control dramas work. He understood that control dramas were not unlike temporary and permanent energy.

Control dramas are temporary energy, and our purest spiritual relationship is permanent energy.

Sid considered that the purest spiritual relationship was of the Source, and control dramas are of the ego. The tumblers of the Universe started to align once more in Sid's mind and heart, and he began to understand the dynamics of physical and spiritual relationships.

He recalled having a pure relationship with Eduardo because he never felt that Eduardo wanted anything from him except to understand the Universe and obtain a higher level of consciousness. Their discussion would equally benefit each other, a zero-sum benefit for both.

He looked back on his relationship with Vincent; they also had a zero-sum game, which translated that each helped the other succeed. Sid considered that without Vincent, he would have never gone down the path he did with Marty.

Marty is an intimidator who desperately tries to control others through his charisma. At first, Sid and Vincent were awestruck by Marty, but Marty would wear down everyone's energy over time.

Sid realized, therefore, that Marty always kept moving. Once he sucked his prey clean of energy; he would move on to greener pastures. Sid always knew, even from the start, that Marty only did things for others based on personal motives; there was not one caring bone in Marty's body. When he gave someone something, he would always want more in return.

Sid judged that most people in his life would lie to him for personal gain, but he realized that his purest spiritual relationship would and has never lied to him. He remembered how often he discounted his inner voice for an ego pursuit that would end in disaster or as a bad memory that still haunts him.

Sid realized that he had been following his ego most of his life, even though his inner voice would try to reach him. He appreciated that he doesn't need physical relationships because they are so transitory and illusionary. Still, he now sees that his purest spiritual connection is the most important.

He wished he had known this early in his life so that he could not have wasted so much time trying to attract people who were users or detrimental to his being. He could have moved on a different path if he knew that the most important relationship was with his purest spiritual self.

Then Sid heard a clear message from his inner voice. It communicated that each moment during his life, he was learning lessons that took him to the next level of consciousness.

He heard Eduardo's voice in his heart talking about the lessons of regret. We should value each transitional moment in our lives for the lessons we learned. The Universe is unfolding as it should, and the Source directs us where we need to go.

Sid heard this message clearly and confirmed that the person with the most control is the one who doesn't need control. Sid felt the peace he felt on the island again for a moment. His mind, body, and heart vibrated with the Universal truth that makes up life energy.

A knock on Sid's office door snapped him back into the world. Sid's producer, Seth, was standing in his doorway, looking at Sid with a confused look. He said, "Sid, I've been knocking on your door for a few moments, and you have been somewhere far away."

Sid laughed and sat back in his chair. He replied jokingly, "I've been riding the wave of life energy. So, what can I do for you?"

Seth sat down in the chair next to Sid's desk. He replied, "David Starr's producer called me again this morning asking if you would go on his show."

Sid sat back with a furrowed brow. He replied, "I've watched his show, and he wants to prove that I am a fake or false prophet. He probably hasn't even watched *The Life Energy Report* or read my book."

Seth moved uncomfortably in his chair. He replied with trepidation, "Look, Starr's producer said they would go after you one way or the other. They feel that you are a public figure professing something people are buying. If you don't come on their show and explain yourself, they will explain what you are doing for you."

Sid replied, "That sounds ominous."

Seth replied, "Yes, it could cost us subscribers, but if you go on the show and explain *The Life Energy Report* clearly, it might help us expand our audience."

Sid replied, "He doesn't allow others to explain themselves, and he only listened when his guests bent to his will. The whole concept of *The Life Energy Report* is that we are all separate by our perceptions, and I know I would not be able to change his perception."

Seth looked at Sid for a long time, calculating what he needed to say to get him on the David Starr show. Seth was not a true believer in *The Life Energy Report*, but he was a true believer in ratings and audience size. He replied, "I think the best way to approach this is to speak the truth. You will either win over people or turn them off; it is up to the Source."

Sid knew Seth was using his dialogue to get him to change his mind about attending the David Starr Show. Sid replied, "I guess let go, and let God." ଓ

☙

Chapter Twenty Seven

Sid looked out the window of his penthouse suite on the top floor of the upper east side hotel that the David Starr Show booked for him. He could see a faint outline of Rikers Island City Jail in the distance as the sun rose.

Sid wondered if the David Starr Show reserved this room because they knew about his past incarceration and wanted to create unease before his appearance on the TV show. He thought it ironic that once again, he was in Manhattan, doing time in a room waiting to be released from an obligation.

Sid finally agreed to go on the David Starr Show after much pressure from his producer, but he didn't agree to be passive.

Sid informed the show's producer that he would cover all his traveling expenses.

Sid didn't want to be obligated to the David Starr Show, but when the day came, his producer told him that all traveling costs were taken care of by the show, and he should go along for the ride.

The David Starr Show flew Sid first class from Burlington to New York City. During Sid's stay in Manhattan, they chauffeured him to the upper east side hotel in a limousine and fully covered all expenses, including food.

When the David Starr Show first approached Sid, they thought he would be thrilled about appearing on the show. Sid knew about the confrontational format of the show and did not want to be interviewed by David Starr.

Sid always knew that an explanation is impossible for *The Life Energy Field Theory*. People who watch *The Life Energy Report* or read the *Life*

Energy Field Theory need to perceive the information by hearing their inner voice, not Sid's.

Sid felt that *The Life Energy Report* had been slipping out of his control since the national broadcasting company took over management. He wondered how long before they would replace him. Sid thought Joleen was right because he was walking down the same path as Karmakal. But like every path he walked, he learned lessons that heightened his level of spiritual awareness.

He realized that anytime a spiritual concept is in the physical world, it transcends into a reflection of the ego. He thought about Christ and Buddha. They both preached pure spiritual ideas of love and acceptance, but their teachings became divisionary over the years, primarily because each person had a different perception.

Each person heard the doctrine based on how they perceived themselves in the physical world, not how Christ or Buddha perceived themselves.

Perception is why Sid didn't want to go on a television show. He professed concepts based on his perception of himself, not the audience's understanding of their reality.

When he reported on the life energy field, he was not professing a concept but the cause and effect of energy flowing through the energy field. Sid didn't feel responsible for the audience's perception of what they were interpreting; he just reported the flow of energy.

He thought that people either wanted to listen or not, and it was up to them to judge the presentation.

Sid started to laugh because he realized that the David Starr Show had achieved their objective of creating angst. Sid realized that the position he needed to take on the show was not even to try to explain *The Life Energy Field Theory* because it is impossible. He knew that each person needs to perceive the principle based on their perceptions.

A knock on the door woke Sid out of his deep contemplation. He walked over to the door, looked out of the peephole, and saw Lyle, the David Starr Show producer. Lyle met him at the airport the night before and ensured he checked in and was comfortable. Sid opened the door and said, "Hi Lyle. Is it time already?"

Lyle walked into the room. He replied, "Yes, we are doing an early taping for later tonight, but we can get breakfast and head to Rockefeller Center station."

Sid asked, "If the show is at Rockefeller Center in midtown, why did you book a room in a hotel on the upper east side?"

Lyle shrugged. He replied, "I don't know. Mr. Starr insisted on this hotel. Have you been to New York before?"

Sid laughed. He replied, "Yeh, I visited a few times, once under city government accommodations."

Lyle looked at Sid with furrowed brow, not getting the reference to Rikers Island. He continued, "We can get a late breakfast at Ellen's Cosmic Diner on Broadway, they are famous for their eggs benedict."

Sid replied, "Actually, I wanted time to meditate before the show. I didn't know it was an early taping, and I assumed the show taped late in the evening."

Lyle replied, "Sorry, that's my fault. Mr. Starr likes to tape the show around eleven and prefers to return to his estate in the Hamptons by early afternoon. Mr. Arthur, we must go; time will move fast today."

Sid replied, "My father is Mr. Arthur; you can call me Sid."

Lyle smiled. He replied, "Sid, we need to stay on schedule."

Sid sat in the David Starr Show green room for a long time, waiting for his appearance on the show. He was poked and prodded all morning by hair stylists, makeup professionals, and clothing designers. The staff wanted him to wear a traditional suit instead of the jeans and cardigan over a white T-Shirt he brought from Vermont. Sid figured if he was going to be on television, he should dress like a Vermonter and show the colors.

Sid watched all the action on the stage from the green room's television monitor. Sid wondered why they called the room the green room. He looked it up on his smartphone and found out that the television industry calls it a green room because, most times, a young and inexperienced actor or comic is waiting in the room for their big break. The green room's name is about youth, not the room's color.

Before the show started, a comedian came out to get the audience in a good mood before David Starr came out and performed his monologue. Watching all the action on the stage made Sid a little anxious, so he turned off the monitor and decided to try to meditate. Once Sid turned off the monitor, the green room was silent.

Sid started to do his usual breathing exercise to put him in a state of serenity. After years of meditating, he became still and focused. His abilities to transcend the world became more and more acute after his teachings by Eduardo on the island. He could almost meditate anywhere and reach a level of consciousness that left the world of the ego far behind.

"Sid, wake up, wake up." Sid opened his eyes and saw Lyle standing over him.

Sid replied, "Is it time to go on?"

With a frustrated look, Lyle replied, "Yes, all the other guests have been seated and are waiting for you. Our stage assistant couldn't wake you, so she came and got me."

Sid replied, "I was meditating. I'm ready now."

Sid and Lyle walked to an entrance onto the stage. Lyle motioned the onstage producer that Sid was ready to walk on the Show. The producer notified the control booth, informing David Starr through his hearing device that Sid was standing by to walk on. All this information moved with military precision from one person to another.

David Starr stopped talking with the other guests and announced to the audience, "Our next guest is Sidney Poitier Arthur.

Sid produces and narrates *The Life Energy Report* to nearly ten million subscribers and is our primary guest for the evening. Let's welcome Sid Arthur."

Lyle, holding a clipboard with giant headphones on, pushes Sid onto the stage when the control booth tells him. Lyle said, "Good luck, Sid. Don't let David bully you."

The stage producer directed Sid to sit next to David Starr at a sizeable black semicircle table, standing in front of a fake window that showed New York City in the background.

Sid looked out at the audience, giving him applause. The experience of being on a popular television show was surreal for Sid. He was still calm from his meditation earlier, but he had instantly moved away from his body.

He looked at the world from somewhere else, observing everything but not connected simultaneously, until he sat next to David Starr.

David Starr shook Sid's hand and patted him on the back. He announced, "Our panel tonight is Jake Newell, professor of theoretical physics at Princeton University and author of '*A Physicist's Guide to the Universe.*' Carrol Thompson, professor of psychology at Harvard University, author of '*A Mind's Eye.*' Thomas O'Malley, Archbishop of Boston and author of '*Is God Talking to Us?*'"

Tonight's Show will focus on *The Life Energy Field Theory* and *The Life Energy Report*. Is this another religious scam or the real deal?"

Starr welcomed all his guests and then turned to Sid. He continued, "First, we will take a little trip down memory lane.

"Sid, you were born and raised on a small farm on the outskirts of Butler, Alabama. Your father and mother both attended college at Howard University in Washington, D.C.

"Your father is a Southern Baptist Deacon, and your mother grew up in a bayou in Louisiana."

Starr looked over at Sid to gauge his reaction. Starr continued, "We have transcripts from your high school. You graduated top of your class but did not attend college, and you left home at nineteen or twenty and moved to New York City."

Starr pulled out a piece of paper and again judged Sid's composure. He continued, "We found your court papers that indicated you did some time in Rikers Island for attending an underground poker parlor." Starr looked at Sid for a reply.

Sid thought about his response for a long time. He started to hear his inner voice come through loud and clear. He knew he had to be truthful, or he would be walking a dark path. Sid replied, "If I remember correctly, they sentenced me to sixty days, but I was released early. I don't remember it being a poker parlor, but someone's dank basement."

David Starr looked at Sid with a furrowed brow. He was expecting Sid to attempt to cover up Rikers Island or at least justify his past incarceration, and Sid did neither, which caused anxiety for David Starr.

No late-night television host wants their primary guest to answer questions with a simple sentence or yes and no. Starr thought this could be a long ninety-minute show if he couldn't corner Sid into a confession of guilt.

David Starr sat back in his chair and decided that Rikers Island was not a trigger for Sid, so he needed to move on so that the show doesn't stall. Plus, he was receiving information from the control booth to move on to the religious aspects of *The Life Energy Report*. David pulled out some more papers. He asked, "So, is *The Life Energy Report* a new religion perpetrated on the public or something more nefarious?"

Sid laughed and took a drink of the water he had on the desk. He replied, "*The Life Energy Report* is about perception, so it becomes anything the audience perceives."

Archbishop O'Malley interjected, "Sid, I've listened to your broadcast of *The Life Energy Report*, and I cannot make heads or tails what you are saying. It seems like another new age fad that will come and go."

Sid replied, "Okay."

David Starr interjected, "Sid, I hope you will not obfuscate the questions. I think the public has the right to know what you are broadcasting across America."

Professor Newell interjected, "Sid, I've read *The Life Energy Field Theory*. You claim the world is an illusion and that we are all connected by an Infinite Source but separate by our perceptions.

"Some of these concepts are in line with Plank's Quantum Physics, and others are in line with Einstein's Unified Field Theory, but most are radical ideas not in modern science or any credible research I have studied. Are you expecting us to take your word on such concepts at face value?"

Sid thought for a moment. He replied, "I have no expectations, and I can't have any, because *The Life Energy Field Theory* reflects the understanding that each person in the world is separate by their perceptions.

"As I speak, you are not hearing me based on how I perceive myself in this reality but how you perceive yourself in the world. It is impossible to communicate a concept that supports the world of separation."

Professor Thompson interjected, "So, you are saying that each person in the world perceives the world differently."

Sid nodded. He replied, "Yes, each person creates and perceives their world differently even though we may feel other people share our views. I think the Bible talked about not judging someone until you walk a mile in their shoes.

"In my opinion, it is a simple allegory for the concept that each person is separated by their perceptions and that it is impossible to know what other people are thinking or why they do what they do."

Professor Thompson replied, "My experience with people dictates that ninety-five percent of the people on the planet see the world the same way I see the world."

Sid laughed. He replied, "You have a rather sizeable ego. As a psychologist, you should understand that we hear what we want, and maybe your test subjects tell you what you want to hear."

Professor Newell interjected, "Let's discuss the world of separation.

Your book *The Life Energy Field Theory* states, "We are all part of an infinite being having a collective experience in a reality of separation." Can you expand or even explain what that means."

Sid replied, "Again, I will try to explain the concept, but you will only hear what I am saying based on how you perceive yourself in this reality, not how I perceive myself."

Archbishop O'Malley interjected, "That seems to be a convenient way to dissociate yourself from a doctrine you profess."

Sid laughed. He replied, "Yes, you're right. The belief means that we are spiritual beings having a physical experience, not a physical being trying to obtain a level of spiritual awareness."

Professor Newell asked, "So, how did you obtain this knowledge you profess to be our Universal mechanism?"

Sid continued, "The desire to know this reality always starts with an enormous amount of pain. From an early age, I felt an emptiness permeate my being, and later in my life, the emptiness turned into a deep depression."

Professor Thompson interjected, "You can get relief nowadays with anti-depressants."

Sid ignored Dr. Thompson's assertion. He continued, "The first significant epiphany I had was in my early twenties. I realized that the world is supposed to be like this, then I concluded that depression had a deeper meaning behind the feeling than just pain.

"I realized that depression is like a barrier in a car race. Depression is an indicator of something that I was doing. I understood that depression is a reaction to a spiritual being believing too much in the physical world. The more we trust that the world outside of us will resolve our challenges, the more we will fall into darkness."

David Starr interjected, "We are running out of time. Let's discuss the religious implications of *The Life Energy Report*. Do you consider the broadcast to be a religious doctrine?"

Sid contemplated his answer for only a moment. Once again, he heard his inner voice. He replied, "No, I do not see it as a religious doctrine. I see it as my attempt to translate spiritual information into a world of separation. I have come to realize that any concept brought into a physical ego-controlled world may in time be mistaken as religious."

David Starr, a prominent anti-religious zealot, retorted, "Any idea, how so?"

Sid sat back in his chair and looked around at the audience. He could see that they were all waiting for him to clarify his last statement. Then a powerful notion came to Sid. He replied, "Well, if you think about it, the David Starr Show could be construed as a religion."

All three other guests and David Starr started to laugh. Archbishop O'Malley retorted, "That's ridiculous. How can the David Starr Show be considered a religion? It's just a television show."

Sid sighed and continued, "To consider what I have heard or read in the newspaper. David Starr has a reputation for being a northeast liberal elitist with a defined set of beliefs that he preaches to a large audience weekly. David Starr has a large fan base who are his disciples.

"David has a larger audience than Christ or Buddha had combined while they were alive. His devotees tune in each week in the millions to prostrate themselves before the wisdom that David professes.

"David receives enormous validation from his followers each week. This validation supports his ego, which builds a structure of relevance that the Catholic Church enjoys."

"The David Starr religion is powerful because my producer pressured me to attend his show even though I didn't want to come on the show. He told me David could sink *The Life Energy Report* if I did not bow to his power."

David Starr started to squirm in his chair. He interjected, "For the record, we just coerced you to come on the show so you could explain *The Life Energy Report*. We did not in any form pressure or threatened you, and I see from my producer that is all the time we have.

"I want to thank my guests and especially Sid Arthur. Until next week, keep seeking the truth; maybe you will find the answers." ‿

CB

Chapter Twenty Eight

Sid looked around at the crowd, excitedly watching their child graduate from Wellesley College in Massachusetts. He squirmed in the hard plastic seat provided to family members. He could see Sasha standing in line, waiting to receive her degree in political science.

Sasha had a smile from ear to ear. She was joking and talking with her fellow students. Sasha always seemed to be so serious about everything. It was nice for Sid to see her happy. Sid felt good that he and Joleen could provide their children with a first-class education, something he didn't have an opportunity to pursue.

It crossed Sid's mind that both his children had never met their grandparents or other relatives living in Alabama. Darrick and Sasha grew up in a liberal city in a primarily liberal state, and he didn't want them to see how the South treated people of color.

He considered that if they were ever inclined to visit his hometown, they could do it as adults. Sid judged that maybe things had changed since he left Alabama, but he doubted the South had changed one iota.

Sid knew racism was part of the world of separation: rich and poor, ignorant and intelligent, powerful and weak. Sometimes his inner voice does not break through. However, the outside world always reflects his perception of the truth—we are all part of an infinite being having a collective experience in a reality of separation.

Sid laughed as he often does when confronted with spiritual truth. Joleen looked over at him with a furrowed brow. Sid smiled and then composed himself.

Joleen's father sat on the other side of her, trying not to lock eyes with Sid. He never approved of his daughter's choice of husband—

Sid or David. He accepted Joleen and Sid's friendship because he deeply loved his grandchildren and wanted access.

Sid's father-in-law watched the David Starr Show when he was on, even though he considers Starr a New York liberal elitist. Joleen's father was a devotee of Fox News.

He didn't mention anything to Sid about watching the show or how he considered Sid must be insane to believe all the garbage he spewed during the episode. He was a good Southern Baptist that kept his opinion to himself.

Sitting in the hot sun in that hard chair, Sid thought a lot about what happened after his appearance at the David Starr Show. Over the last few months since the show aired, Sid's life had changed dramatically.

The phone started ringing and didn't stop. The broadcast company had to hire another assistant to field the calls. After the show, Professor Newell asked Sid to participate in a panel on theoretical physics at Princeton University.

Sid thought it strange that Dr. Newell would ask him to contribute. During the David Starr Show, the good doctor attempted to discount Sid's perception of the world.

Sid was a guest on National Public Radio. He did countless interviews on radio, television, and YouTube. After three months of endless discussions asking the same questions, Sid wondered why he continued interviewing.

He realized early on that he had fallen into an ego trap. Eduardo once told Sid that the ego would use anything to divert our attention. The closer we come to the Source, the trickier the ego will work to distract us from the Universal truth.

The Life Energy Report's subscription doubled only a few weeks after the Show. The broadcast company started to book advertisers that Sid didn't know. He wondered if he wanted to continue the broadcast because he felt it had become a circus.

Sid noticed people around him treated him differently. Some of the crew on the broadcast started to call him Mr. Arthur when they used to refer to him as Sid.

People began to look at Sid and whisper to each other when he was walking down Church Street. He stopped going to his favorite restaurant because people would come up to him and ask for an autograph or they would want to talk about their spiritual beliefs.

Sid felt that the attention would calm down after a short period. He knew that people have a short attention span, and another thing would come along to divert the public's interest. Sid didn't like the public attention he received because he became defensive and less receptive.

Joleen nudged Sid in the ribs when Sasha took the stage to receive her diploma. Sid, Joleen, and her father all stood up and clapped.

As they sat down after the ten seconds of excitement, Joleen turned to Sid. She said, "Sid, you seem far away. Please be present for your daughter."

Sid smiled. He replied, "I'm here, but you know how my mind wanders."

Joleen laughed. She replied, "Yes, Mr. Oblivious, I remember. I guess even prophets get distracted."

Sid looked at Joleen with a bewildered look. He asked, "You've never called me a prophet. Where is this coming from?"

Joleen leaned in and whispered in Sid's ear. She said, "My father ranted and raved in the hotel room about how you are a false prophet and shouldn't be on television spewing non-Christian beliefs. My father wonders why I didn't marry a good Christian, not a heathen."

Sid laughed. He asked, "Yes, why didn't you marry a good Christian instead of a heathen?"

Joleen and Sid both laughed, which attracted the ire of Joleen's father. Her father looked over with a scowl, which Joleen knew all so well.

Joleen interjected, "Sasha wants to come to stay with you in Burlington this summer before she goes off to law school."

Sid sat back with a baffled look. He replied, "I would love her to stay with me, but I have to ask, is this her idea?"

Joleen squirmed a little in her chair. She replied, "Yes and no. She has been talking a lot about getting to know you better. You left for the island at a critical time in her life, and when you came back, she felt you were a stranger."

Sid replied, "I can't change the past, but I welcome her company. I don't plan to go anywhere this summer, so we should have some time to catch up." Sid asked again, "So, was it her idea to spend the summer with me?"

Joleen replied, "Kind of; Anthony and I are taking a river cruise trip this summer, starting in Spain and ending in Germany. I didn't want her to be alone in Staunton; this is her last summer before she enters Georgetown Law School."

Sid asked, "I forgot about Anthony, the lawyer. Did he talk her into pursuing a career in law?"

Joleen replied, "He nudged her in the right direction. It is a good solid career. She wants to pursue a profession in politics, mainly consumer advocacy. Her high school trip to Washington D.C. struck a nerve, and Anthony just solidified her path."

Sid interjected, "Whatever the case, I would be ecstatic to spend the summer with Sasha. I hope she feels the same way. It could be a long summer for both of us if things get difficult."

Joleen interjected, "I've had a few difficult times with our children. If things get tough, it is up to you to find a way. You're her father, and I think she needs you right now. The world is getting scary for her as she becomes an adult; she needs to know you have her back."

Sid smiled. He replied, "I will always have her back. So, what about Darrick? Is he going to be alone in Staunton for the summer?"

Joleen replied, "No, he decided to stay at Stanford University and work for the summer. I'm a little concerned he likes California too much. He is graduating next year and may stay in the Bay Area."

Sid interjected, "Well, he is a computer science major, and Silicon Valley is the center of the Universe for the tech industry. I don't think he could grow in his field in Staunton, Virginia."

Joleen smirked. She replied, "I wouldn't expect him to build a career in Staunton. Washington, D.C., or New York City would be a great starting point, plus close enough to home to see him.

"Look, here comes Sasha, be on your best behavior. She is probably a little nervous right now. So, she will ride with you back to Burlington after dinner."

Joleen reserved the banquet room in the back of Smith and Wollensky, the best restaurant in Wellesley. She invited three hundred people who were friends she and Sasha had made in Burlington. Two hundred and fifty crowded into the restaurant's large banquet facility. The other fifty that didn't show up sent letters of congratulations, some with a tidy sum of money to help Sasha in law school.

Sid looked around the room, considering that most of the people he didn't know. He wondered if he even knew three hundred people and how Sasha and Joleen had so many friends. He remembered his marriage to Joleen in Burlington and recalled being a workaholic, only going out to events when Joleen would prod him.

Sasha fluttered into the room like the queen bee buzzing around everyone. Sid could see from her captivating presence that she would make a great lawyer, more a litigator than a consumer advocate.

Sid felt that Sasha grew up around wealthy people and didn't think she would fight for the poor and oppressed. Sid noticed Sasha was wearing his eight hundred dollar Jimmy Choo's birthday gift. He didn't think she couldn't survive in a dismal street lawyer's office. He did know that she would be successful at whatever she pursued.

Sid felt awkward sitting in the corner of the room, not knowing most of the people who attended the affair. They were all friends of Joleen and Sasha. Joleen didn't think to invite any of Sid's work companions.

Sid started to notice different people looking over at him and whispering. He wondered if it was because he was Sasha's father or if they recognized him from the David Starr Show.

He hoped it was because of Sasha. Sid walked over to the bar and ordered a beer. He stood at the end of the bar watching the festivities, proud of Sasha.

A man that Sid didn't recognize walked up and ordered a vodka tonic. He turned to Sid and said, "I saw you on the David Starr Show."

Sid thought to himself, here it comes. He replied, "Yes, it was an interesting experience. So, how do you know Joleen and Sasha?" Sid tried to direct the conversation away from his television appearance.

The man ignored Sid's question. He asked, "So, you believe the world is an illusion?"

Sid sighed, knowing that he would not be able to get out of this conversation unless he ran out of the building, and that was not an option. He replied, "No, I don't believe the world is an illusion; I know the world is only a reflection of our perception." Sid looked around him and saw that a bunch of people started to circle him, intently looking at Sid.

A woman in the crowd of onlookers asked, "How can you know that the world is an empty void and still attend your child's graduation? Is Sasha an illusion? Are all of us an illusion to you?"

Sid sat back on the bar stool. He replied, "Yes, everyone outside of us is only an illusion, but at the same time, we are all connected, and we are all one. I am only talking to myself, as you are only talking to yourself—herein lies the peace of God."

Sid noticed that the string quartet that Joleen hired stopped playing because many guests were standing in line to ask Sid questions. Sid thought that the crowd would ridicule his knowledge. Instead, most were interested in his understanding of the Universe; this surprised Sid.

ଔ

Sasha and Sid spoke little during the three-hour drive from Boston to the border of Vermont. Sid didn't want to press her to talk, and she seemed wiped out from all the festivities.

Once they passed over the Vermont border near Brattleboro, he broke the silence. He asked, "So, when do you start Georgetown Law?"

Sasha looked over with a look of indifference. She replied, "August 15th."

Sid knew Sasha well enough to know that she was upset about something. She did the same crunched facial expression when she was upset as a child. He used to give her belly rubs, but he felt she was too old for belly rubs. So, he had to devise another plan, or this car ride would end up being long and painful.

Sid asked, "So, what's the problem?"

Sasha sat back in her car seat and folded her arms into a tight ball. She replied, "Don't you know?"

Sid furred his brow, trying to make sense of her remark. He replied, "No, I don't, but I would be more than open to hearing what you have to say."

Sasha sighed. She replied, "Daddy, didn't you notice all my friends and their families busy around you? Asking you for your autograph, trying to have a deep discussion right in the middle of my party? This gathering was supposed to be my day, not yours."

Sid took in a big breath. He replied, "Sasha, I'm sorry, but I didn't ask for the attention. I felt uncomfortable, and people perceived me a certain way and considered me public property."

Sasha looked out the window as they passed the first exit to Brattleboro. Sasha knew from experience that they still had two and a half hours before they reached Burlington. She replied, "Daddy, your existence attracts attention, and it always has, even when I was a young child."

Sid looked over at Sasha. He considered what he might say, listening to his inner voice for guidance. He replied, "I sense something else is bothering you as well."

Sasha replied, "That's just it; you sense this, you sense that." Sasha bit her lip. She continued, "Do you know how embarrassing it was for Darrick and me that you went on the David Starr Show and spewed all that spiritual nonsense?"

Sid took a long breath. He continued, "Sasha, I'm sorry you feel that way, but my spiritual beliefs are part of who I am, for good or bad."

Sasha continued, "Daddy, the world is not an illusion." Sasha smacked the dashboard of the car. She continued, "If the world was an illusion, how could I do that? It doesn't make any sense."

Sid smiled. He replied, "Sasha, I understand how my beliefs could cause you pain, and I am sorry for that, but as I said, it is part of who I am."

Sasha started to tear up a little. She replied, "What I dislike the most about your belief system is your piety. You always diffuse the situation with I'm sorry, or I can understand your feelings. Why don't you ever get angry if you are so dedicated to your beliefs?"

Sid thought about a reply for a long time. They drove north on highway ninety-one in silence until they reached White River Junction and turned onto highway eighty-nine straight to Burlington.

Sid said, "I don't get angry because deep down in my heart, I am finally at peace. The peace I feel is from my connection to my purest spiritual relationship. The world outside of myself has less and less sway over my life the older I get. I hope you and Darrick find peace in your life, but I also know it is a solitary journey to discover this connection."

Sasha looked at Sid like he was talking in another language. She replied, "I can't believe that I found out on television in front of my friends that my father did time in prison."

Sid laughed. He replied, "Riker's is a jail; I never did time in prison."

Sasha looked at Sid with contempt. She continued, "Did you even think about me before you decided to go on national television and make a fool of yourself?"

Sid knew that his daughter's ego made her angry, and he knew he couldn't explain his life to her or anyone. He would have to approach Sasha another way if he was to make the time he had with her a positive experience for them both.

Sid drove into his garage below the townhouse he lived in overlooking Lake Champlain after midnight. Sasha had long fallen asleep, and he could see her drooling in her car seat. It was a full moon, and he could see her beautiful face glow in the moonlight.

Sid sat and watched his daughter for a long time, remembering when she was just a little girl with pigtails and knobby knees. He had a moment where he wondered where the time went. He knew in a blink of an eye that she would graduate law school, marry, and have a family of her own.

He sat looking at Sasha, not wanting this opportunity to fly by without a deep appreciation and reverence he had for the moment with his still-young daughter.

He knew that he could never convey what he had learned through his life in any meaningful way. The very nature of his belief system on the idea that our perceptions separate us. Unfortunately, that also includes his son and daughter. ଔ

ԥ

Chapter Twenty Nine

Sid was about to turn fifty-nine and was alone at Snaps Restaurant in Bristol, Vermont. He was treating himself to his favorite breakfast for his birthday, eggs benedict with a side of homemade corn beef hash. Sid moved to Bristol after selling his home in Burlington and rented a house on the outer edges of the tiny Vermont community under an assumed name.

His media appearances' unwanted attention diminished after many years but did not disappear altogether. Sid had to move to Bristol and keep his address and phone number a secret.

People would knock on his door in Burlington at all hours, wanting to meet him or discuss their spiritual beliefs. Sid often had to ask people to leave because they were too damaged, and he could not reach or help them.

Sid started to get death threats from extreme religious groups after he published his second novel on the *Process of Spiritual Enlightenment*. Extremists felt that he was a false prophet, and they would threaten Sid and his family.

The fanatics would post a picture of Sid's home on social networking sites with his address and phone number. Sid became highly concerned when they published Sasha's and Darrick's photos on social networking sites with their addresses.

Living in Burlington came to a head when a fan of *The Life Energy Report* jumped in Sid's car when he stopped at a light during his usual route to work. After this instance, he changed his way to work and decided to move to a smaller community.

Fortunately, Bristol is a remote open-minded community that

embraced Sid. The residents would feign ignorance of Sid's whereabouts if an unknown person asked around town about Sid. Most times, people who were looking for Sid would go away disappointed.

Sid confronted protestors outside *The Life Energy Report* studios in Williston. He would often try to talk with the religious extremists to understand their point of view, but they were not interested in what Sid had to say. Sid felt threatened, so over time would always come to work through the parking garage.

Many of Sid's staff at the studio would get threats because they worked at *The Life Energy Report*. Sid's team turned over so fast that he often forgot the names of the people he needed to rely on and trust.

His friendship with Joleen slowly faded away after she married Anthony, and they moved down to Florida.

Sasha graduated from law school and stayed in Washington, D.C. She was expecting her first baby with her new husband. Darrick was busy in Silicon Valley, working a hundred hours a week on a new start-up. Sid realized that Darrick inherited his father's workaholic behavior.

Sid was alone but not lonely. He considered his purest spiritual relationship the most important one in his life; it was the one that kept him at peace.

It seemed to Sid that most of the other relationships he had during his life caused painful memories. Joleen moving away from him was the most surprising since their relationship was the closest he had during his life.

Sid looked around the restaurant and saw that most of the patrons were locals; this always gave him a sense of comfort. Most would leave Sid alone or say hi on the way to their tables.

A strong premonition overwhelmed Sid as he sat and ate his breakfast. After many spiritual experiences, he could instantly tell the difference between a premonition and a vision.

The initial feeling was similar, but then it would diverge into something different, often an intense sensation. He was surprised at the level of energy surging through his body. A premonition always had a critical message for Sid; his path was about to change significantly.

He knew for a long time that change was coming because his heart was becoming heavy with despair. Sid would always get an imperceptible feeling just before life would take him in a new direction. He knew the motivation to change would come in three significant signs, always in threes.

"Hey Sid, are you alone?" asked a woman looming over Sid. Sally was a local architect that moved to Bristol from Lincoln, Nebraska, fifteen years earlier. She met Sid through a buddy that worked at *The Life Energy Report*, and she had been struggling to secure a deal with Sid to renovate his condo.

He told Sally that he would have her build him a tiny home on a property he was thinking about purchasing if he decided to stay in Bristol permanently. However, deep down in his heart, he knew that Bristol would be another steppingstone to another chapter in his life.

Sid took a sip of his coffee and gestured for her to join him. He replied, "No, just hanging out, thinking about work."

Sally sat across from Sid and gestured to the waiter for a cup of coffee. She rummaged around in her large cloth bag, pulled out a book, and sat *The Course in Miracles* in front of Sid.

She interjected, "I appreciate the reading suggestion, but after a few chapters, I realized this book is way too Christian. I grew up Catholic, so I'm a recovering bible thumper." Sally took a sip of her black coffee. She continued, "Have you made any decisions about the foreclosed farm property you were thinking about purchasing?"

Sid smiled. He interjected, "No, not yet, but you'll be the first to know when I obtain the property. I'm sorry the book didn't reach you. You may try a series by Wayne Dyer, or one of my favorites is *Stand Like Mountain, Flow Like Water* by Brian Seward. You could try reading the *A True Heart Series* by Eduardo Francheze."

Sally emptied her cup of coffee, stood up, and waved to another customer in the restaurant. She said, "Sounds like a plan." Then she walked over to the other table and sat down.

Sid laughed; he knew that Sally wasn't interested in learning the truth; she just feigned interest in getting Sid's architectural business. Sally was an excellent salesperson through and through.

Sid met many people with ulterior motives because of his local fame. They didn't know they were trying to scam a former confidence artist. He could see a con artist coming from a mile away. Sally wasn't a scam artist. She was trying to build her business.

Sid drove to *The Life Energy Report* broadcast studio in Williston, Vermont. He was thinking a lot about how Sally referenced the *Course in Miracles,* and he realized that she had a perception of the book based on herself, not on how he perceived the book.

Sid remembered back home when he joined a teen bible reading group that his father suggested. They would read a section of the *King James Version* of the Bible and then discuss the meaning of the text.

He attended the group every Thursday for a month until the group leader asked him to stop coming because she said his ideas were too radical for the group. She told Sid that he would be better suited to another group. He had many occasions during his younger years when his perception of something rubbed someone the wrong way.

He learned early on not to argue a point about religion. He felt Sally didn't understand what the *Course in Miracles* offered, but he wouldn't argue the point. He needed to respect her perception if she thought the Course was too Christian.

Once again, he questioned why he was attempting to convey something that was uncommunicable. Since our perceptions separate each person, then what point was it to enlighten people about the truth of the Universe? Then he thought that the truth is felt individually, not collectively.

Sid walked into his office and sat behind his desk to prepare for the afternoon broadcast of *The Life Energy Report.* Sid's assistant producer, Terry, knocked on his door. He entered and placed a copy of *The Course of Miracles* on his desk in front of Sid. He said, "Sid, I appreciate your lending me the *Course in Miracles,* but I can't read it because it is contrary to my Christian beliefs.

"I truly tried to read it but found it too secular. I sat down with my pastor at my Southern Baptist Church to discuss his opinion of *The Course In Miracles.* He said a false prophet wrote it, and I should not consider it equal to scripture." Terry turned around and walked out of Sid's office without Sid uttering a word.

Sid had an overwhelming realization that his interaction with the two opposing views of the same book on the same day was not coincidental. Then he remembered his premonition and recognized that his interactions with two opposing views were the first sign indicating a transitional moment in his life from the Source.

Again, he realized that Sally and Terry read the same book based on how they see themselves in this reality, not how Sid views his reality.

This sign from the Source was the first indicator that maybe he was ready to move on in another direction. If he couldn't convey a critical concept to people close to him, how could he communicate a spiritual concept to his audience?

The larger his audience became, the more he realized he could not reach anyone. He was becoming disheartened with the message he broadcasted each day.

He couldn't get over the fact that each person was separated by their perceptions, so everyone listening to the broadcast only heard what they wanted to hear, not necessarily what he was attempting to communicate.

During Sid's Friday broadcast of *The Life Energy Report*, he included the concept of each one of us seeing the world through our perceptions based on how we feel about ourselves in the world.

Deep down in his heart, Sid knew this might be his last broadcast. He ended the broadcast with a heartfelt appreciation to everyone that listened over the years. He said goodbye without saying goodbye to his audience.

Sid's assistant Debra walked into his office. She said, "Paul wants to see you in his office before you go home." Paul was the executive producer of *The Life Energy Report*.

The broadcast went through many producers during Sid's tenure, and each always came with new ideas and changes that grated on Sid's nerves. On the way to Paul's office, Sid wondered what change the executives at the broadcast company wanted now, then Sid remembered his premonition. He considered that maybe this was another sign.

Paul was on the phone when Sid knocked on his door. Paul waved to Sid and motioned for him to sit in front of his desk. Sid sat down in the oversized leather chair slightly lower than Paul's.

Paul was talking on a headset and fidgeting with his hands. There was sweat beading on his forehead even though his office was airconditioned.

Paul hung up the phone and sat back in his sizeable puffy chair. He said, "Sid, I have some bad news. I'm not one to beat around the bush, so I will tell you. Your former company Karmakal bought the licensing rights to the *Life Energy Report* from our broadcasting company.

"I've been calling around to get an answer. I have devised that the board of directors pressured our broadcasting company to drop the project. The broadcast was becoming too metaphysical, and they wanted to go in a different, more wholesome, all-American direction.

The constant presence of the religious protestors outside our studio wasn't helping. The board was taking a lot of flak from our primary investors. The new president of the broadcast company is a devout Christian and doesn't understand *The Life Energy Report*, even though we have exceptional ratings." Paul leaned forward and kept eye contact with Sid to see how he would take the news.

Sid sat silently for a long time, waiting to see if Paul would continue with his verbal purge. Finally, he asked, "So, where does that leave us?"

Paul started to fidget with the red stapler on his desk. He replied, "Out in the cold, buddy."

Sid asked, "I'm sorry; what do you mean, out in the cold?"

Paul finally calmed down. He replied, "The CEO at Karmakal wants to retool *The Life Energy Report*. They have been negotiating this deal for weeks behind our backs with the bigwigs at our broadcasting company. So, you, I, and all the staff here are gone Monday.

The head honchos over at Karmakal don't want entrenched management, and they don't want any conflicts with you. I guess they already have someone in line to take over for you. Sorry, but this is the business." Paul picked up a pencil and started to bang it on the desk.

Sid could see Paul being distraught about losing a good gig after just three months. Paul moved his family to Burlington from Chicago and just bought a new house.

Jobs that pay the same as a national broadcasting company were hard to find in northern Vermont. Paul was going to have a difficult discussion with his wife when he got home.

Sid sat back in the chair and thought, this is sign two, one more to go. On returning to his office, Sid again ran into his assistant Debra. She said, "Sid, I've been meaning to give this to you, but I almost forgot.

It came in the mail this morning. I thought it was just another fan letter, but then I looked at the name." She handed the envelope to Sid. She picked up her belongings and walked towards the front door. She turned around and said, "Have a good weekend, Sid. I'll see you Monday."

Sid looked down at the return address and was surprised to see his mother's name on the envelope. A shudder ran through his body because he had not seen his mother in almost forty years. He walked into his office and opened the envelope.

He held the one-page handwritten letter in his hand for a long time. He instantly recognized his mother's handwriting and could smell her favorite perfume on the paper.

Sid sat back in his chair and read the letter. "Dear son, I saw you on a television show last month talking about your *Life Energy Field Theory*. You have grown into a fine-looking man, and I am proud that you have come so far in life.

"You talked about building a company called Karmakal and traveling to other places. You appear to have gained wisdom along your way, and others on the television show seemed to listen to every word you said with great enthusiasm.

"I felt it was more than a coincidence that I saw you the same day your father died. I was coming home from the hospital after attending to your father before he passed from cancer. I made a pot of coffee and turned on the television to see my son talking with important people."

Sid slumped in his chair. His father was always alive in his mind, but now that he knew he was dead, he felt a sense of guilt that he didn't go home to see his family one last time. He thought about how fast time went by and how many memories he had acquired during life.

Sid continued reading his mother's letter, "Unfortunately, I have more sad news, your brother Simeon died two years ago. He was plowing the north forty, and the tractor rolled over on top of him. The doctor told us that he died instantly and without much pain.

"Your sister lives in Seattle, Washington, with her husband. I don't see her very often. They come home once a year and spend a week on the farm. She has asked me many times to move into their guest house, but I'm an old woman and have lived too long in the same place to change. I will die here and be buried in the family plot on the farm next to your father. Maybe in the afterlife, your father won't stray as much.

"I think of you daily and often wonder why you stayed away from home for so many years. I know that it was a hard life for you here growing up.

"Your father was not a good example for you to follow. Your father was a good man, distracted by his desires. I know he always loved you and missed you terribly. You were always his favorite. You were like two peas in a pod, too alike to stand each other for any amount of time.

"I know you are a busy and important man and probably don't have time for an old woman, but I would love to see you one more time before I pass.

"I would welcome you home with open arms if you could find it in your heart. Love always, your mother." Sid sat back in the chair and thought to himself. My mother's letter is sign three; maybe it is time to go home. ✠

CƷ

Chapter Thirty

Sid and his mother, Esther, named after her Haitian grandmother, sat on a stump for a long time on the riverbanks that ran through the family farm. It was late in the evening, and a full moon shone down on the ripples in the water.

Sid and his mother sat talking for a long time. Sid told his mother about his experience in New York playing poker and his incarceration at Rikers Island.

He spoke about how Caesar's ghost helped him along his spiritual path and how Marty came out of nowhere and saved him and Vincent from certain death at the orders of Diego, a Mexican mafia leader.

He talked in detail about startup companies and the fine line between being a con artist and a respectable businessman in the world of entrepreneurs.

Sid spoke of the intense energy he felt once he passed over the Vermont border and how the mountains of Vermont were lovely, dark, and deep.

Sid spoke of Karmakal and *The Life Energy Report*. He talked extensively about Joleen and his children, Sasha and Darrick. He reminisced about his experience on the island with Eduardo Francheze and how he learned to meditate and come to understand energy and the vibrations of the Universe.

He detailed his Universal mechanism epiphany when he was running and how it changed his perception of the world.

All through the evening, his mother listened with great purpose. Sid couldn't remember anyone in his life that listened to him as closely as his mother did this night. He couldn't remember his mother having such patience when he was a child. It surprised him how gentle and caring his mother had become over the years.

After Sid had depleted himself of stories, he and his mother just sat on the riverbanks listening to the melody of the river; Sid knew it as Ohm.

Ohm's sound became louder until it engulfed Sid's senses. He recalled his vision many years earlier, where he was running on a distant planet through an endless galaxy. He remembered being lost in a city, watching people come and go without an emotional connection to their world.

He recalled running on a crystal white beach, looking down, and seeing all the faces trapped in the sand and how he tried to pick up the sand and free the people from their self-imposed prison, only for the sand to flow through his hands and join the whole once again.

He evoked a memory of turning onto the last leg of his journey. How tired he was, how drained of purpose. He ran down a long road taking him home again, where a single figure was waiting to welcome him home again.

The memory of his vision flashed before his mind in only seconds, but the meaning was clear to Sid. In the vision, he realizes he never left home. He moved through the world, standing still, observing the world from afar, not engaging. He was in the world but not of the world.

Sid understood that the sand in his vision represented his need to enlighten the world. Still, after working on Karmakal and *The Life Energy Report*, he understood that remembering our spiritual connection is an individual journey, and no one, not Buddha or Christ, can pass on spiritual information outside of themselves.

No matter how hard someone tries, we are all separated by our perceptions, and once a spiritual idea comes into the world, it becomes part of the ego, interpreted by each person based on how they feel about themselves.

Knowing this was both disappointing and freeing at the same time. Sid realized that the world was supposed to be like it was. Sid did not need to save the world, which doesn't need to be because, ultimately, the world outside of us is only an illusion.

Sid began to laugh at the epiphany he had sitting on the banks of the river under an oak tree. His mother started to laugh with him as if she understood why Sid was laughing and was part of it in some unforeseen way. Sid valued his connection with his mother and wondered why he couldn't obtain this level of relationship when he was a child, or maybe he did; he didn't remember.

Sid woke with the sun and a rooster crowing in the distance. Even though he only had a few hours of sleep, he felt more rested than in years.

Sid jumped out of bed with renewed purpose. He could smell his mother cooking his favorite childhood breakfast, fresh biscuits with pork gravy, hashbrowns, and fresh eggs sunny side up.

He remembers the smell so vividly he could almost taste the breakfast before he entered the kitchen. The scent seemed to infuse the home as if it had become part of the walls and floors.

He felt like all his senses had heightened now that he was back home on his family farm in Alabama. The sky looked bluer, the river moved with grace, and the soil out in the fields looked deeper and darker than he remembered.

Sid started thinking about what Eduardo discussed when he examined permanent and temporary energy. When a ship is built, it retains permanent energy, and when the boat passes over water throughout the world, it creates temporary energy. He considered his permanent energy was in line with the place of his birth, and his energy was pulsating throughout his body.

When Sid entered the kitchen, he caught a glimpse of his mother's radiance as she stood over the stove near a large window. He noticed a peace emanating from her soul that he didn't notice as a child.

Sid could see an aura around his mother's body that seemed to jet out in all directions. Her smile was the same as the Buddha he had seen in a book many years ago. She appeared to be totally at peace. Sid's mother seemed almost transparent, with the sun shining into the kitchen for a moment.

After breakfast, Sid wandered around the farm and its many buildings. The house, barn, and coops had seen better days, worn down on the edges; many had sagging roofs and missing boards. The fields around the farm had become fallow with time, and all the machinery needed fixing.

Sid could see an old blue Ford pickup turn onto the long road leading up to the house. As it moved along the dirt road, a cloud of dust chased after the truck on its way to the main house.

The truck came to a sudden stop in front of the house. A

middle-aged, tall black man got out, wearing old blue coveralls and a straw hat that hid his eyes.

The man stopped and looked at Sid for a long time. He said, "I don't believe it; that looks like my cousin Sid Artur."

For a moment, Sid looked at the stranger trying to place the face. Then he looked into the man's eyes and saw his younger cousin standing before him. Sid replied, "Samuel, Sam Arthur is that you?" The two men embraced and patted each other on the back.

Samuel asked, "How long has it been twenty, thirty years?"

Sid sighed. He replied, "It's been forty years; where has the time gone?"

Samuel replied, "Well, around here, every day is the same, so who knows where it goes? So, what brought you back home, cousin?"

Sid laughed. He replied, "I guess it was just about time to come home. So, what happened to the farm? It seems like it is on its last leg."

Samuel leaned up against a fence under an oak tree. He replied, "Well, as you know, your father wasn't much of a farmer, and after your brother died under that tractor over there, the farm has been going downhill.

"Luckily, the property has been paid for, so you don't have to worry about a banker taking the farm. I've been trying to help, but I have a farm and don't have much time to tend to this property.

I spend a few hours each week tending to some of the animals still alive on the property. The two horses over yonder are more than ten years old. Your daddy won them in a poker game but never rode them; he just put them in the fields.

"Your sister moved out of the area a few years back. Her husband had no desire to take over an old farm. He was a local hustler that made good with a car dealership. They moved north to Washington State somewhere and haven't been back since.

"A couple of years ago, after your daddy passed, I discussed selling the property with your mother. She hoped you would come home someday and take over the farm.

"I saw you on a television show once, but I didn't understand what you said about energy. I can't imagine, after being on television, you would want to fix up an old farm; you'd have to trade those fancy city duds for country work clothes. So, are you home for good or just passing through?"

Sid sat down on an old stump. He replied, "I don't know."

Samuel looked at Sid with a furrowed brow. He replied, "Whatever you decide to do, I know you've made your mother happy. When she saw you on the television, she knew it was a sign from God that you would come home soon, and here you are."

Sid replied, "And here I am."

Samuel interjected, "If you're home for good, then I can tend to my own business. My number is on the fridge. Don't be a stranger. You should come over and have dinner. My wife, Clara, makes the best friend chicken in the county."

Sid asked, "How many family members are still around."

Samuel thought about it for a moment. He replied, "Not many. Most went north for jobs or a better life, I guess. Not many want to farm anymore, but there is still a few kin around.

"I'm sure they will come by now that their famous relative is in town. Be careful; many are looking for a payday. Be especially careful with your cousin, Eldridge; he owes everyone in the county."

☙

Sid's transition from city slicker to country folk was slow and purposeful. Days passed into weeks, weeks into months, and before Sid knew it, he had been on the farm for more than a year. His mother would sit for hours on the porch watching Sid's coming and going, and she never said much, just more interested in what Sid had to say.

After a hard day's labor Sid and his mother would sit for hours next to the river long into the night, talking about the river's song of life. Sid realized that the river reflected God. The water is everywhere at the same time. The water was at the falls, in the well, and in the ocean, all the same, all the time.

Sid realized his journey reflected the river because when he became fearful, the river would press on him until it created more pressure than he could stand, and he would let go, and the river would take him along his journey.

Sid realized just like the river, his path was predestined only to bring him home again to show him that he didn't need to leave at all, and in fact, he was only observing his life from a spiritual perspective.

Sid found joy in physical labor and fixing up the farm. He needed to leave to free himself from the desires of the world. He had abundance all the time, but as a young man, he needed to travel into dark places to see the light.

He started working on the main house. Sid wanted his mother to see her farm come alive again. Sid could see his mother's aura radiate around her body.

Sid could see people's energy throughout his life, but he had never seen such luminosity in a single human being. Sometimes he felt that he was dreaming about being home because his mother was much different than he remembered, or his mother was always the same; maybe he couldn't see it when he was young and full of ego.

Sid hired a contractor to help him with the property restoration. They slowly transformed the house, barn, and animal shelters into pristine buildings.

They replaced all the shingles, roofing, and siding on the barns. They painted the house a fine silver with white edging, and the barns were painted the most beautiful color of deep red.

He grew up tending farm animals, but over the year he was home again, he started to witness a rhythm to the livestock. Each animal also had an aura that surrounded it, a life force that connected each animal with everything else on the farm.

After remodeling the buildings on the farm, the contractor and his crew left Sid alone. The farm was in a remote rural area, so most of the time, Sid spent his days alone with his mother, always watching from the porch.

Samuel was incorrect when prophesizing that relatives would show up unannounced. Sid rarely went into town. He had most of what he needed on the farm, and nothing in the supermarket could compete with the fresh produce and butchered meat his mother cooked.

Samuel would show up occasionally to see how the farm was progressing and if Sid needed any help. Samuel had invited Sid a dozen times to dinner over a year to experience his wife's southern cooking, but Sid turned down the offer many times, figuring that no one could cook better than his mother. Sid finally relented after Samuel confessed that he was worried Sid was all alone on the farm and maybe needed a little company.

Sid disregarded the comment of being all alone as just his cousin worried about him doing all the farm work by himself without any hired hand. Sid considered his relatives local yocals without a brain when he was young, but his cousin Samuel was kind and gracious. Samuel was not school-smart, but Sid found him brilliant. The farm knowledge Samuel obtained over the years was equal to a doctorate.

Sid laughed while remembering Mark Twain saying, "When I was a boy of 14, my father was so ignorant I could hardly stand the old man around. But when I got to be 21, I was astonished at how much the old man had learned in seven years." Sid considered this relevant to how he saw his family when he was young and now when he was home again as an adult.

Samuel and his wife and two children lived in a simple two-story home on one hundred and forty acres. They mainly grew sugar beets for sale and a variety of produce and livestock for personal consumption.

Sid had more than a hundred relatives dotted all around the southern and northern states, but as far as he knew, Samuel was the only family member that took up farming. Sid knew that you had to love farming because there were other, more accessible opportunities to make money.

Sid, Samuel, and his two boys, Bernard, and Lester, sat on the porch drinking ice-cold beer and lemonade. It was a hot summer night, and the two boys sat on the porch swing, moving back and forth slowly. Samuel said, "Bernard is twelve, and Lester is ten. Clara always wanted a girl, but I fear that will never happen; she just turned forty this year. I hear it is hard for women to give birth after a certain age.

"We had children late because I was in the Navy for ten years and met Clara a couple of years after I got out. Her family used to run a dry cleaning business; both of her parents are long gone.

"We named Bernard after your great-grandfather and Lester after Clara's grandfather. They're good boys, but both are not going to be farmers, and I fear that I will be the last in my family to farm this land. We started farming down here just a few years after the civil war. Back then, building a farm for people of color wasn't easy.

Clara poked her head out the screen door. She said, "Is he lamenting again about our boys not taking over the farm? Our boys are going to college and get decent paying jobs that don't make you smell bad when you come home each night." Clara closed the screen door and walked back into the dining room. She said, "Dinner's ready; wash your hands."

After dinner, Samuel and Sid sat back on the porch, sipping bourbon and ice-cold beer. Samuel casually mentioned, "Your mother was a great cook, but she always liked my Clara's fried chicken. I wish she could be here tonight; I miss her."

Sid sat back and looked at Samuel for a long time. He said, "What do you mean she was a good cook? She still is. She cooks for me every morning before I work the farm and every evening when I come in. She is still a good cook."

Samuel looked at Sid with a furrowed brow. "Sid, I don't know who has been cooking for you, but your mother passed two years ago. She is buried next to your father in the farm's family grave site on the north corner."

Sid's heart rate started to rise, and his face became flush. He thought that if his mother were a ghost, he would know, then what was she? He interjected, "Samuel, I must go. I'll call you next week. Thank Clara for the great dinner." Sid got up, walked swiftly to his car, and sped away toward his family farm.

Sid went into the house and checked all the rooms for his mother. She was nowhere; then, he heard a melodic sound near the river. He ran to the riverbank, and out in the bayou, he could see his mother floating over the water.

Her body was so luminous that he could see right through her. Her aura was translucent and reaching out in all directions. She lit up the marsh like a full moon.

Sid heard his inner voice clearly say, "Your mother is not a ghost but a transcendent being. Son, I will always be with you in love. I waited for you to come home. Now that you are home, I can finally pass into the light."

Then she vanished into the bayou, leaving no trace other than the memory etched on Sid's soul. ☙

☙

Chapter Thirty One

Sid sat on his porch looking out on the farm, forest, and river as it rushed by on its way to a waterfall, estuary, and finally to the ocean. Early spring came to Alabama, and the river that ran through his farm swelled to almost overrun its banks.

Sid thought a lot about his mother, Joleen, and his children, and he laughed when he thought about Marty and Vincent. He was most grateful that he met and was taught valuable lessons by Eric and Eduardo Francheze. Eduardo helped him shift his perception of the world during his dark night of the soul.

Sid remembered all the people that had passed through his life like a river, and just like water, he felt love and compassion flowing through his heart for everyone he met during his life.

Sid thought about how much he admired his mother for having such remarkable listening skills. He believed that enlightened beings must first know how to listen authentically.

Looking back on his life, he never was interested in what others had to say; he always waited for others to stop speaking so he could have a turn talking.

He thought about Mark Twain's quip, "I never learned anything from talking." He considered that the Source had a lot to tell him, and he needed to be quiet and listen to Ohm.

For most of Sid's life, he had been trying to reach people by professing incommunicable knowledge. He concluded that he wasn't trying to convince others; he was attempting to convince himself.

Sid deemed that if the world is just an illusion and we are all separated by our perceptions, we are all just talking to ourselves.

He knew his desire to reach others with his awareness had ended, a finality he could embrace and cherish, but now what?

Sid sat on the porch, pondering his next path and what he needed to learn. He knew he was not close to the enlightenment he witnessed with his mother and realized he needed to learn how to listen. He needed not just to be quiet and let others talk but to genuinely listen to the world.

Then he looked out on the dark rich soil he had cultivated over the last year. Sid bought a new tractor with a rollbar and other farming equipment. The money he acquired over the years from his involvement with startups never meant as much as it did now that he was back on his family farm.

He understood money was another form of energy transferred from one thing to another. That money, his farm, buildings, and equipment all were reflections of abundance, and abundance needs to be shared with others.

Sid thought that maybe the money he earned over the years was given to him by the Source to learn an important lesson from his family farm, to learn how to hear Ohm not just in the river or from people but in every living thing.

Sid looked out on the dark rich soil, and from deep in his heart, he heard, "Plant the seeds of change."

He knew the first step on his next path was to plant crops that he could share with others. He tried to share awareness with others for most of his life because he had such love and compassion in his heart. He knew he could share the earth's abundance and learn how to listen simultaneously.

Sid grew the first crop of cabbages, kale, broccoli, cauliflower, onions, lettuce, and spinach. The produce was green, crunchy, and more delicious than he had ever known.

Sid could see the energy emanating from the fields. He learned how everything is energy. He was starting to learn how to listen to the earth. The earth was not unlike people; it needed to be fed, stroked, loved, and appreciated.

Sid built a farm store on the edge of his property next to a two-lane county road. Travelers moving through the area would stop and buy Sid's produce and tell him about their lives. He would listen intently, never interjecting a story about himself or interrupting.

Sid knew listening to visitors' stories was a lesson the Source was teaching him. In each narrative, he found substance beyond the words to better understand who was telling the story.

Sid found that if he listened long enough, most people confessed to him something they would never tell anyone they knew; he felt privileged each time he heard their secrets.

Over time tales started to spread that an old sage lived on the farm. Local people would stop by to talk to Sid. The farm began to take on a whole different energy.

When Sid first took over the farm, the fields were full of scrub brush, and the house and buildings in decay. Sid remembered that there were no butterflies and few birds. Even animals stayed off the property. The farm appeared dead, reflecting the demise of the family that had loved it for many years.

When Sid sat on the porch and looked at the property, he saw energy everywhere. Sid's love for the land and his life spread to every corner of the farm.

Sid would wake early each morning, thanking the Source for all the abundance in his life. For the first time, he felt at peace with now. Sid didn't speculate what was around the next corner or on worldly success. He just loved and appreciated each moment he had on the farm.

Word of Sid's farm on the southwest corner of Alabama started to spread beyond the borders of the State. People from all over would venture to the area to see the farm and see if the stories about a wise old man were true.

Many travelers would visit the farm and leave disappointed, pondering why anyone would confuse the old black farmer with a guru when he wouldn't say a word but just smiled and nodded.

Many visitors thought that maybe Sid was an old mute. Several visitors felt that people overestimated Sid's abilities and left the farm angry and frustrated for traveling so far and having nothing to show for their effort. Sid's ability to listen started to teach him many things.

He learned that many travelers who came to the farm had preconceptions of the experience they would have on the property before they even arrived. He could spot their energy instantly and knew they were not on his farm to open their minds and hearts but to have him support their perceptions of the world.

Every so often, a few travelers would come open-minded and good-hearted. They would fall in love with the farm and see the energy emanating from the fields.

Sid could spot a pure heart when they stepped into the farm store. Sid would sit for hours listening to their stories of traveling and searching for answers to the Universal question.

Many found Sid and his farm because they fell into a dark night of the soul and were motivated by pain to venture down to Alabama in search of answers.

Sid would never offer spiritual advice as he was weary of doing so because, for so many years, he tried to communicate what he could not. He felt that what the travelers needed most was to be listened to, and listening was what Sid required to learn.

Some of the pure hearts that visited asked to stay for a while and help Sid work the farm. Since he could not reach people by communicating his awareness through speech, he might be able to connect with people through their love of the farm.

One Sunday afternoon, a young traveler from California entered the farm store. He was a tall black man with a slender but muscular build. He had deep-set eyes that were worldly and proud.

He was young, but Sid could see that his soul was old. The young man reminded Sid of his younger years, so much so that Sid reflected on how fast his life passed and how far he was from his youth.

The young man walked around the farm store looking at Sid. He pretended to shop but kept looking over at Sid. An expression of resolution came over his face. He walked over to Sid and said, "My name is Isaiah. I remember seeing you on the David Starr Show years ago."

Sid looked up and just smiled and nodded. He knew Isiah had something important to say, and this young man had come a long way to say what he needed to acknowledge.

Isaiah sat down in a chair near Sid. He continued, "A friend told me about a wise old man on a farm in Alabama. My inner voice told me that it was you, the man I saw on the television show. I knew I had to come to see you and tell you what it meant to me to hear what you had to say on the David Starr Show."

Sid replied, "That was a long time ago and almost a different life than I have now." Sid handed Isaiah a glass of lemonade and motioned for him to follow him to the back of the store.

They sat on wooden rocking chairs on a porch overlooking the farm.

The young man continued, "I feel compelled to tell you my story for some unknown reason. I traveled far from home to tell you this story. I connected with you when I saw you on the show."

Sid smiled because he knew the power of our spiritual connection. Sid felt compelled many times during his life to follow the instructions of his purest spiritual relationship.

Sid knew this young man needed to work out something in his own time and his way. He knew that trying to tell him what he was experiencing would be futile. The best that Sid could do for Isaiah is listen. Sid replied, "Isaiah, I'm here to listen."

Isaiah took a long swig of his drink. He continued, "When I was twelve, I was in a car accident with my parents and younger brother. A drunk driver hit us head-on with a much larger truck, and our car flipped over and into a ditch.

"I don't remember the accident, but I found out what happened later when I woke up in the hospital. I do remember dying, and I remember a violent death. My body broke up so much that my soul snatched me out to somewhere else, somewhere beautiful.

"I remember floating outside my body, watching the car on fire. I saw people come to our aid, pulling my family and me out of the wreckage. I could see my broken body lying on the road bleeding out. Someone was attempting to give me CPR, and he was pressing down on a wound that was spurting blood.

I could see all this floating above my body like watching a movie. I could see my mother, father, and younger brother lying on the pavement. I saw my father come around and attempt to wake my mother and brother, but they were both gone.

My father started to cry as he realized my mother and brother were dead. I could see all this as clear as I can see you now." Isaiah paused and cleared his throat as a tear ran down his face. He put his face in his hands and started to cry.

Sid patted him on the back. He interjected, "I'm listening, Isaiah."

Isaiah looked up and smiled. He continued, "Then a warm yellow light started to engulf me.

I began to look back on my short life and wonder about the purpose of dying so young. I had this thought as I floated above the ground in another state of consciousness.

"I remember feeling the loss of my family and friends. I started to reflect on my life and what it meant to me to be alive, and then a voice came to me. It said, "Isaiah, love never dies; you have a purpose."

"A moment later, the warm yellow light turned into a bright light in a hospital. I woke up and realized I was back in my body, and my body was thinner and healed. I tried to get out of bed, but I was weak.

"I noticed my grandmother asleep in a chair in the corner of the room. I called out to her, and she woke up. She got up, walked over to me, and stroked my face with the back of her hand.

She said, "Child, you have been gone for a long time. It's good that you came back to us."

"I sat up in bed and looked around the room, and I could see the city of San Francisco in the distance outside the window. I asked, 'Where am I? How long have I been here?'"

My grandmother patted me on the shoulder. She replied, "Take it easy, child—one question at a time. You're in a hospital recovering from your accident, and you've been in this bed for eight months in a coma. The doctors weren't sure when or if you would wake up again. Isaiah, you went through an awful time."

Isaiah paused again to reflect on his life. He continued, "When I woke up at the hospital, I had an overwhelming feeling of sadness that I was back in the world. I was happy that my body healed itself, but I remember that the place I journeyed to was heaven.

"After this event in my life, I knew that there was no death and that the place we go after our bodies die is a perfect place. A place I have often wanted to be, but I also know that I can't make that decision about dying, even though I have thought about committing suicide many times. I know I can't kill myself; I would be altogether in another state of consciousness.

"The years after the accident were harrowing. I became angry and bitter about my mother and brother dying in the accident. I started to lash out and get into trouble.

"I would purposely do awful things to punish my father. I spent a year at a reform school for boys, which only increased my anger and resentment at God for taking my family and the guilt I felt because I was not taken.

"Looking back on that time in my life, I see that my father was also hurting. He tried to help me, but he had nothing to give. When the love of his life died in a car accident, he gave up; he turned to the bottle for solace. When I came out of reform school, I went to live with my grandmother.

"Then I turned seventeen and had an awakening that shifted my view of the world. The experience when I was twelve overcame me, and I started to see the world as an illusion and couldn't make sense of why I was saved, and my family destroyed.

"I turned to my grandmother for answers, but she didn't have the awareness to help. My grandmother is a good God-fearing Christian, but her belief system was of no help. I couldn't just be at peace with faith alone.

"I felt I was given a gift and knowledge beyond faith. I know what happens after we die, and I needed to understand how the Universe works and what part I play in the cosmic drama.

"Then I turned on the David Starr Show, and you spoke about the Universal mechanism you came to realize after your major epiphany.

"I instantly had an overwhelming connection with what you were saying. I knew that you were a like soul, and we had the same knowledge. I watched the television show repeatedly. Each time I watched, I got a new understanding of what I was going through.

"I started reading all the books you recommended. I read *The Life Energy Field Theory* you wrote. I read *A True Heart* by Eduardo Francheze. I read all your books and couldn't get enough of the information. I was nourishing my soul with the words.

"Mr. Arthur, I came all this way to thank you and to tell you that you saved me. I don't think I would be alive if I didn't come across your appearance on the David Starr Show.

"After consuming all the information you presented in your books. I know now that there are no accidents, everything is written, and we are just looking back on the past.

"I have found peace with my family's passing, and I know their love will always be with me. I know the next step on my path, which is all we can know."

Isaiah and Sid stood up and hugged each other for a long time. A deep loving smile came over Sid. He realized that maybe he did help others in a way they needed saving, not by forcing his need to be heard. Sid realized he had learned the most from Isaiah in a long time by simply listening.

Isaiah released Sid from the embrace. He walked to the front of the farm store, looked back at Sid for the last time, and then walked through the front door, never seen by Sid again. **ೞ**

ଓ

Chapter Thirty Two

Vincent Govinda Aiello sat in his leather chair, looking into the fire. The ambers burst and sputtered in his fireplace. He tried to smooth his long blond hair behind his ears, but the hair was gone, and just a buzz cut was left. He sat wondering what was left for him to do.

He buried his wife just after his seventieth birthday. His children had long moved away from home—as far as they could go from the responsibility of continuing the family cattle ranching legacy.

Vincent's son was in the Army and stationed in Germany, and his daughter married a man from Thailand when she was traveling abroad and decided to stay. Both didn't make it back for the funeral, and both left, declaring not to come back.

Vincent and a couple of hired hands were the only ones left on the fifteen-hundred-acre cattle ranch he had built over the last thirty years. Ranch help came and went with the seasons. It was a hard life, and only hard people endured.

Vincent knew he would leave the ranch to his foreman Pet who had built the farm with Vincent. His children didn't want anything to do with the property; Vincent still held out hope.

Running a large cattle ranch was the only dream that Vincent's father ever talked about with him or his brother.

Vincent was the owner of one of the last working cattle ranches in Wyoming, fulfilling his father's dream, but he still felt empty; he still was thinking about gold. He still had an unfulfilled desire in his heart.

Vincent sat looking into the fire, wondering where the time went and what good he did in the world. Then he remembered his brief time with Sid Arthur when they both were young and fearless.

He remembered when the world seemed magical because of his friend Sid Arthur. It was one of the most powerful moments in his life.

Vincent saw Sid Arthur on the David Starr Show many years ago. He listened intently to what Sid Arthur was saying. Vincent wondered if Sid was pushing another grift, but deep in his heart knew that Sid was the real deal.

He knew that Sid had become aware of something extraordinary, something wonderful. Over the years, the memory of Sid Arthur and his moment of spiritual insights never left his heart.

Vincent learned three months ago that he had lung and throat cancer from years of smoking. He knew he only had a short time to live; Vincent needed to visit his friend one more time before he passed. Vincent hoped that maybe Sid Arthur had a little comfort for him. Maybe his friend could give him insight before he passed to calm his fear of dying.

He wrote a simple handwritten last will leaving fifty percent of the cattle ranch to his foreman, Pet. He gave twenty-five percent of the property to each child, ensuring they always had a place to come home.

He left the will on his beautiful oak desk under a large smooth stone he found on the shores of Lake Champlain in Vermont. He packed a few things in an old saddle bag. He got into his Ford F-150 and drove off the ranch for the last time.

 ⅓

Sid was planting a cover crop on a small plot of land. It was late fall, and a chill was in the air, promising a cold rainy winter. Most of the trees had already dropped their leaves. The path to the house was covered in gold, red, and yellow. The river stood silent and serene with an autumn drought that covered most of the south.

Sid looked up and observed a stranger walking towards him from the farm store. He was tall, wearing jeans, cowboy boots, a blue cotton shirt, and a cowboy hat. Sid thought the visitor was a curious sight because most southerners don't wear such garb.

The closer the stranger came, the more he seemed familiar. Sid could see a small gut protruding, and his skin looked weathered from working outside. When Sid looked into the eyes of the visitor, he instantly recognized Vincent.

Sid stood up and walked over, and the two men embraced. Sid said, "Vincent Govinda Aiello, it's good to see you, my old friend."

Vincent replied, "Hell, we did get old, didn't we?"

Sid patted Vincent on the back. He replied, "Let's get some sweet tea on the porch." Sid and Vincent walked to the house and sat on chairs next to a small table. A glass pitcher of sweet tea and a few glasses were already waiting. Sid asked, "How did you find me, old friend?"

Vincent said, "There is an internet rumor that a mystic lives on a farm in the southwest part of Alabama. When I read the story, I knew it was you, even though they never mentioned your name or where the farm was. I knew I had to come to see you."

Sid looked at his friend for a long time. He replied, "I feel that there is a finality in that statement. You knew you had to come to see me—before you pass."

Vincent smiled. He replied, "Yes, before I pass."

Sid replied, "I sense something has damaged your ability to communicate."

Vincent laughed and then coughed up blood. He replied, "Hell, I see you are still seeing ghosts. Yes, I have a tumor in my lungs and throat. It's funny that you pinpointed my ability to talk because I have always had difficulty telling my family that I love them."

Sid smiled and patted Vincent's hand. He asked, "Did you find the gold you desired when we were young?"

Vincent grimaced. He replied, "I found gold many times, but often it would turn into lead weighing down my heart."

Sid asked, "How so?"

Vincent continued, "I thought living in New York City would win me gold, but as we both know, there is only hard cement for poor people in Manhattan.

"I felt following the teachings of Marty would bring me gold, but I received heartache and a close call with prison.

"I thought marriage and having children would bring me gold. My family was gold at first, but then, as time passed, they all started to break my heart because I broke their hearts with alcohol, gambling, and other women. I thought, I could have all the gold, but I was wrong and stupid.

"My ranch was gold, but then I realized over the years that I was only working for my father's approval, which I would never receive. He died before I built up the ranch. Even at the farm's pinnacle, my father would still be unhappy and disapprove of my effort.

"The ranch became a burden heavier than lead. The responsibility weighed down my heart and made me impossible to live with because of the emptiness."

Sid radiated a deep loving smile. He replied, "It looks as if you have found some of the gold I found along my path."

Vincent furrowed his brow. He asked, "What gold?"

Sid took a long sip of his sweet tea. He continued, "I have also had many heartbreaks in my life, but what gold I have found that is more precious than any other is wisdom. Unfortunately, wisdom cannot be shared, given away, or sold, and most importantly, wisdom cannot be communicated.

"Knowledge can be communicated, but wisdom cannot. Wisdom is gold that is specific to each soul's journey. Wisdom is the cushion between our misperceptions of the world and our purest spiritual relationship."

Vincent asked, "What is our purest spiritual relationship?"

Sid's radiance increased with every passing moment. Sid replied, "Our purest spiritual relationship is the voice in the night bringing us back into the light, and it is the better angel of our nature and sits on our right shoulder, showing us the truth along our path.

"You have a purest spiritual relationship; we all do. You must listen, which, most of the time, we deny its existence, and listen to the other voice, the voice that takes you on the path to heartbreak.

"Your purest spiritual relationship brought you to Alabama to visit your old friend Sid Arthur."

Vincent smiled. He asked, "Sid Arthur, you say I have a guide in my heart. Looking back on my life, I can see that I was always looking for someone or something to point me in the right direction. Did you not find a religion or principle you could follow during your life?"

Sid Arthur's brilliance became profound as he sat on the porch and talked the truth with his dear old friend. Sid Arthur continued, "I have found that each journey for each being is as individual as a grain of sand on a distant shore, but also each journey is like a river all going in the same direction—taking us back to the whole.

"I have found dogmas to be deceptive because each being will perceive them concerning how they perceive themselves in the world of separation. The nature of the world we all occupy is separateness, and the disconnectedness of this reality's very nature is to deceive us from the truth."

Vincent asked, "What truth, my friend?"

Sid Arthur continued, "The truth is that we are all one being having a collective experience in a reality of separation. That we are spiritual beings having a physical experience."

Vincent contemplated what Sid Arthur had said for a long time. He replied, "I don't understand, and at the same time, I understand. I can see that you have found peace and tranquility.

"Even an old cattle rancher has a moment of clarity, and I can see that you are radiating something ethereal. Is there no comfort that you can offer an old friend?"

Sid Arthur had a radiant smile, and his hands became like beacons of energy. He replied, "Let's go down to the river, and maybe I can help you with the peace you came here to obtain." Both men walked down the river and sat on the same tree stumps Sid, and his mother occupied.

Sid continued, "When I returned to the family farm, my mother was home alone. The farm was falling apart, and the fields had gone fallow. My brother had died on the tractor over there. My sister moved far away and has never returned. My father passed before I returned home."

Sid continued, "My mother and I would sit for hours on this riverbank and watch the river come from the waterfall, move to inlets, and finally travel down to the ocean.

"My mother believed that the river held all the secrets of the Universe. The river spoke to us of God and the sacred Ohm. Sometimes the river would laugh at us because we were foolish to believe we were special and love was outside our hearts.

"My mother learned to listen while observing the river. She listened more intently than any other person I had ever encountered during my many years of traveling. She deeply loved the river and hearing the Source in each person.

"I discovered that my mother was a holy person, she lived on this farm most of her life, but she found the sweet sound of Ohm in the river. She knew more about this world than I did, wandering about the country and searching for answers. When she finally passed on, she became radiant and walked into the forest to become one with her purest spiritual connection.

"Over the years, I have found that Ohm is more than just in the river. The sacred sound of creation is in the fields, trees, sky, and all living things in this reality. I have listened to all these entities and heard the Universal song.

"You came here for comfort from your old friend Sid Arthur before you passed. I can give you no comfort because words will always be misleading, but what I can offer you is the truth in the form of listening.

"Cancer that riddles your body is a reaction to not speaking the truth and listening to the wisdom of your heart. You had opportunities all your life to tell the ones closest to you that you loved them, but you chose not to because of fear and doubt. Now fear and doubt riddle your body.

"The only way to let go of fear and doubt is to truly listen to the Universe and let the vibration of Ohm give you peace and comfort."

First hours, then days, and then weeks passed, with Sid Arthur and Vincent sitting at the river's edge, listening to the water flow on its way everywhere.

At first, Vincent saw no benefit in sitting by a river and listening to the water. His ego worked on him to deceive and distract Vincent from the knowledge he so desperately needed. The understanding that death is not the last door he goes through and that death is only another path along our journey to self-realization.

After a few weeks, his cancer weakened his body. Vincent had no other choice but to sit and finally listen. He found that one of his life's most challenging tasks was to sit and listen genuinely.

He had been a man in motion most of his life, constantly consuming others' energy around him. Cancer that ravaged his body was a double-edged sword. It was the cause of his pain, but at the same time, it stopped him long enough to learn how to listen to the Universe and hear God speaking deep in his heart.

One cold winter day, Vincent heard the song of the Universe in the river and the trees and his body crying out, chastising him for the ill use of such a perfect vessel.

Vincent started to see the many faces in the water who came and went during his life. He could see his children and wife laughing at him for being such a fool and Marty with a crooked smile using him. He could see his father's disappointment in his life and disappointment in Vincent, even at the end of his life. Vincent could see his mother's face radiate grace and compassion.

Vincent realized that spiritual awareness was not due to his listening but his love and admiration of his longtime friend Sid Arthur. He could hear the Universe in every fiber of Sid Arthur's being. Sid Arthur radiated pure love and compassion. The comfort that he traveled so far to feel he received it in the simple presence of Sid Arthur.

Sid Arthur came to the river one day and sat next to Vincent. Sid Arthur knew a transformation would take place with his dear old friend. Cancer continued to consume Vincent's body even though he had found peace and comfort in the presence of Sid Arthur.

Vincent was wrapped in a wool blanket, sitting on the stump next to the rushing river. He looked over at Sid Arthur sitting down next to him. He said, "Today is my last day. Is it not my good friend? I can feel my body finally giving up to the blight that has overtaken me."

Sid Arthur patted Vincent on his hand. He could always tell when it was the end for any soul that visited the farm. He would often talk with visitors about their most secret stories knowing that the person would pass from the world soon.

Many people who visited Sid Arthur were ghosts before they even died and had lived a life with no risk, love, or compassion. They would also come to Sid Arthur for comfort, but all he could ever give them was a gift of listening. He replied, "Yes, this is your last day as Vincent, but it is the first day along another path that will lead you to your purest spiritual relationship."

Vincent smiled a radiant smile. He replied, "I want to thank you, my dear old friend, for preparing me for the next path on my journey. I now know not to fear death. I welcome the end of Vincent, the end of this leg in my journey. I'm glad I am here with you at the end of everything."

Sid Arthur and Vincent sat by the river for a long time, not speaking. Vincent watched the world with more intent than he ever had during his life.

Vincent looked at the cold water dance across the smooth rocks that dotted the riverbed. He watched the beautiful puffy clouds move across a bright blue sky and breathed in the pure air. He saw the wind shudder through the trees, moving dead leaves on the branches. Vincent heard the song of the Universe and then passed away.

Sid Arthur held his friend's diminished body in his arms. He remembered the long blond hair that Vincent always pushed back over his ears.

A shimmer of light flickered in the forest. Sid Arthur caught a momentary glimpse of his good friend Vincent Govinda Aiello standing near his body as it lay on the ground. He could see that Vincent had a serene smile on his face. Sid Arthur smiled back. Vincent then vanished into the deep dark forest. ☙

❧

Chapter Thirty Three

Sid Arthur sat meditating under his favorite fig tree. The fig tree was brought back from his mother's childhood home in Louisiana and planted on the family farm when Sid was a small child.

The giant fig tree sat alone on a knoll overlooking the entire valley and river that ran through Sid's farm. The fig tree bore red succulent fruit that Sid's family savored, especially in the summer heat. The tree's large canopy of leaves created an expansive dark shadow that cooled any tired soul.

Sid would wake up at 5:30 in the morning before the sun rose over the rolling hills to the east of his farm. He would milk the three cows he had left and then head to the fig tree to meditate.

After many years of restoring the farm, meditating under the fig tree became the primary focus of his life. He relied on hired hands to do most of the hard labor on the farm, but he still sat on the porch behind the farm store and listened to travelers tell their stories.

The more profound Sid's meditation became, the more his ego tried to distract him from reaching a deep connection with his purest spiritual relationship.

Sid's ego would continually remind Sid of painful memories in his life, and Sid would relive his uncomfortable experiences during his younger years. He would remember being arrogant and angry with those he loved. He recalled reacting to others without considering the consequences of his actions.

All his harsh memories would flood his mind while meditating. Sid learned long ago on the island that all experiences are part of self-realization. Instead of attempting to block all the terrible memories in his life, Sid would embrace them like jewels that needed to be cherished. He would re-experience each memory and then let them go.

He would not punish himself for anything he did because he understood that the memory of such difficult moments was punishment enough. Sid considered that if there were a hell, it would consist of reliving the same awful memories for eternity.

After a brief period of meditating, the memories would start to dimmish and wither away from his consciousness. Sid knew if he tried to block memories, it would cause more pain and give meaning to his ego. He could visualize each memory flow over his consciousness and disappearing into the fog of eternity.

Each day Sid meditated, his ego attempted to distract him with greater and greater force, but each day Sid would process his memories through his heart and let go let God.

After a short period of meditating, Sid's consciousness would be blank, and he would reach a state of grace where the awareness of the infinite mind started to fill his soul in the form of a single point of warm light.

Sid would focus on this single point of infinite light and free himself from the chains that bound his mortal soul. On this day, he went farther than he had ever traveled before. His heart and soul radiated love and compassion, filling his being to the point where he entered a heightened sense of spiritual connection.

G3

Sid opened his eyes and found himself floating in eternal light. He felt he was still Sid and in a body, but when he observed his limbs, they were beans of light with an outline of a physical form.

The world didn't fade away; it became an infinite point of white light moving in all directions.

A shimmering wall of bright light materialized in front of Sid. The shimmering light took on the form of a mirror, reflecting Sid's physical perception of himself.

He looked at the reflection of his physical being for a long time; then, he heard it speak.

Sid's spiritual reflection said, "Now, there are no physical boundaries between who I am and who you are."

Sid contemplated for a long time what was said. He asked, "Who are you, and who am I in this place? Is this place heaven?"

Sid's spiritual reflection smiled. It replied, "This place is between an infinite possibility and a physical assumption. You and I are one but still separate in this place."

Sid asked, "Who's assumption is this place?"

Sid's spiritual reflection replied, "This place is part of the world of separation that the infinite created, but now is a residual effect."

Sid started to laugh, and his reflection also started to laugh. The level of awareness Sid was experiencing was flowing through him like a bolt of lightning.

He both knew where he was and didn't know at the same time. A part of him was in this place, and another part of him was bound to the physical reality.

Sid asked, "Are you the infinite being? Am I not in an infinite reality?"

Sid's reflection laughed. He replied, "If you have to ask that question, then you know that you are not in the infinite, and we are not the infinite."

Sid replied, "If this is not an infinite reality, then where am I?"

Sid's reflection replied, "You have obtained a higher level of consciousness by letting go of the physical perception of yourself.

You are a spiritual being having a physical experience. When you let go of the perception of your physical experience, you become who you are, a spiritual being. This place is the purest form of a spiritual reality in the world of separation."

Sid replied, "I thought when I reached Nirvana, I would be one with the infinite."

Sid's reflection replied, "There are two realities that exist side by side. There is an infinite, and there is a reality of separation. Both realities exist but are different from each other; it is a paradox because they exist but not with each other.

"The infinite is one hundred percent different than the reality of separation. The reality of separation is one hundred percent different than the infinite. Time and space do not exist in the infinite. The infinite doesn't expand or contract. The infinite has no past, present, or future.

The infinite exists beyond our ability to intellectualize its existence. The closer we come to our spiritual selves in the reality of separation, the more we can feel the presence of the infinite.

"The spiritual reality you exist in is a buffer between the two realities. You have let go of most of your physical perception in this spiritual reality, enough to connect emotionally with the infinite through your heightened awareness."

Sid thought for a long time about what was said. He considered each question carefully as he asked his spiritual self. He didn't know how long he had been in this realm or how many questions he could ask. Sid asked, "Why did the Source create the reality of separation?"

Sid's reflection replied, "I can only communicate why the Source created the reality of separation in a manner that would make sense in this reality, not in the infinite.

"Consequently, the infinite wanted to know itself, but because it is infinite, it cannot look upon itself and know what it is, so it had an idea. The idea was to create a reality that would facilitate the infinite's need to know itself.

"Since the infinite is so powerful, its idea was enough to create a reality that would support the idea. Our multi-universe was designed to support the infinite's idea. Time, space, and history were all created in an infinite second so that the infinite could look upon itself and know what it was by what it is not.

"The world of separation is exactly the opposite of the Source; the infinite is light, and the reality of separation is dark. Our Universe is an empty space that reflects a physical reality but is an illusion.

"Once the infinite looked upon itself, it became infinite once again. Because it is infinite, the world of separation was just an illusion it created that was only an idea."

Sid asked, "What purpose do I have in the cosmic drama?"

Sid's spiritual reflection replied, "You are the light in the canopy of night, and you are the reason the infinite created the Universe."

Sid thought about what was said. He asked, "How so?"

Sid's reflection continued, "The infinite created the reality of separation to experience what it would be like to know itself. Even the idea of knowledge itself was foreign to the consciousness that exists in the infinite.

"At the center of every living thing in the multi-universe exists the infinite. Our perceptions are the only way we are separate from each other.

You and I are still separate because you perceive me to be a purely spiritual being, and I perceive you to be a physical being, but we are both Sid now existing in the same time and space.

"The Source experienced a world of separation through every living thing in the multi-universe.

"Just like the river at your farm, the Source is everywhere simultaneously. The Source is a person who is homeless on the street of a large city.

"The Source is a financially wealthy person in a high-rise building. The Source is the explorer deep in the jungles. The Source is the child abused by parents.

"The Source is the soldier dying on the battlefield. The Source is in the monk obtaining enlightenment. The Source is in all of us, experiencing all moments in each being's existence.

"The Source suffered every physical experience in the reality of separation, and then it knew what it was by what it is not—the infinite is not a physical being.

"The infinite looked upon the reality of separation and knew what it was by what it was not; then, it became infinite again.

"From the big bang to the collapse of the multi-universe was just an infinite second. We are only looking back on the residual effect of the Source's idea of a reality that would be separate from itself."

Sid asked, "Why did you refer to me as the reason that the infinite created the Universe?"

Sid's reflection became more and more solid before his eyes. Sid could see that he now had his arms and legs back. Both he and his reflection were sitting on a small field of bright green grass.

Sid's reflection replied, "You are in a higher level of consciousness in the reality of separation. I am your purest spiritual relationship. You've heard me deep in your consciousness for your entire life. I'm your guide, and I will never lie to you.

"You are the reason that the infinite created the Universe because your only purpose is to know who you are by who you are not. The infinite desired to know who it was, but because it is infinite, the Source cannot be separate from itself.

"The infinite created an idea of a Universe whereby it could look upon itself and know itself by what it was not. You have just risen to higher consciousness and fulfilled that concept. Every moment in the multi-universe, enlightenment occurs with every being.

"A being starts on the lowest level of creation, and through rebirth, the being becomes self-aware and looks upon its physical form to know the truth.

"This being could be a greedy person who destroys those closest to them for perceived personal gain. This person could be reborn a thousand lifetimes reliving the same deceit until a sliver of awareness starts to shine in the darkness of their soul.

"Then, another thousand rebirths could see this person become the Buddha, Christ, or A True Heart that brings the multi-universe to a heightened level of consciousness.

"We are all part of the infinite having a collective experience in a reality of separation. You are the culmination of thousands of rebirths for the Source to become infinite once again.

"You are the path that all living things will follow so that collectively the Source will know itself by what it is not."

Sid considered what he had just heard. He asked, "Then what you are telling me is that I am the Source having the experience of knowing myself."

Sid's reflection replied, "Yes, you are the Source. Every living being in the reality of separation is the Source at our core."

Sid replied, "If I am the Source and I am all-powerful, then how can I not know what I am?"

Sid's reflection continued, "When the Source created the idea of the reality of separation, it made the ego.

"Some also call the ego the devil or Satan. The ego was created to convince the infinite that it is not infinite. The ego distracts, deceives, and misleads all beings in the reality of separation that we are physical beings, not spiritual beings, and the ego is relentless at its job.

"The closer we come to the truth of this reality, the harder our egos work to convince us that we are not infinite. Our ego does this primarily through fear and doubt.

"To become spiritually enlightened, we must let go of our perception that we are physical beings one hundred percent. If filled with fear and doubt, then we cannot transcend the illusion."

"The Source gave this job to the ego because the infinite being knew that to know itself, it would have to lose itself in the reality of separation. If the Source had any knowledge of its infinite self, then the reality of separation would not be able to contain such a powerful being."

Sid thought long and hard about his next question. He knew that to get the correct answer, he would have to ask the right question. He realized that his spiritual self is absolute truth, and truth has no room for ambiguity. Sid asked, "What purpose do I serve as a physical being in my present reality?"

Sid's reflection laughed. It replied, "Good, you understand the context of a spiritual reality. All self-aware beings' primary purpose is to heighten the awareness of the collective.

"Even though you exist in a perceived limited physical environment, your very existence heightens the awareness of each being in the multi-universe.

"Your physical reality is connected to all perceived physical realities. Outside your physical reality is only an empty illusion, and there is no physical reality other than the one you occupy."

Sid asked, "What about all the people in my life? Do they not exist in my physical reality?"

Sid's reflection replied, "Each person that becomes part of our physical perceived reality is also part of the world of separation. They exist in their physical reality and are connected to us through the Source. Your wife, children, friends, and co-workers are all separate from you by their perceptions but one with you through the Source.

"Since everything in your physical reality is perception, then every being was created by you in your physical reality through your perceptions. When you married Joleen, you had a certain perception of this person, but as time passed, you started to perceive her differently.

"Not because she changed but because your perceptions of the world changed, and you perceived everything and everyone around you differently."

"As time went by, you started to see everyone as a total stranger, but what was happening is that you started to see the truth of this reality, and you were transcending the world and letting go of your perception of the physical reality."

Sid asked, "If the infinite is separate from the reality of separation, then where does creation exist?"

Sid's reflection replied, "All history, moments, time, and thoughts exist between the infinite and reality of separation in this spiritual space.

"Creation expands and contracts infinitely because of the idea created by the Source, but creation is very much part of the reality of separation.

"Since the whole multi-universe already happened, we are only looking back on the residual event that took place, but where we are looking is the barrier of creation that holds the two realities together. All memories are held in this spiritual realm to be translated for the infinite being to know itself by what it is not."

Sid asked, "What should I do with this knowledge?"

Sid's reflection replied, "Walking a spiritual path is like breathing air as a physical being. The more you think about breathing, the harder it becomes. You are on your path, and it has taken you to a heightened level of awareness. You need to do nothing but continue."

Sid opened his eyes to see the sun rise over the hills to the east of his farm. He was sitting under the fig tree, and the shadow that covered the ground was gone; only light remained.

Sid sat for a long time, looking out on his farm with love and compassion. He didn't want to move to disturb the peace in his heart. He now knew absolutely what he needed to do; he needed to…

Reference Material

A True Heart, Journey to the City of Light:	Novel by Robert Owen Minearo
Sid Arthur:	Novel by Robert Owen Minearo

Material That Helped Me

Siddhartha:	Novel by Hermann Hesse
Divine Comedy:	Poem by Dante Alighieri
Odyssey:	Poem by Homer
Narcissus and Goldmund:	Novel by Hermann Hesse
Zen and the Art of Motorcycle Maintenance:	Book by Robert M. Pirsig
The Hitchhiker's Guide to the Galaxy:	Series by Douglas Adams
Dark Night of the Soul:	Poem by John of the Cross
Dark Night of the Soul:	Book by Thomas Moore
Anatomy of the Spirit:	Book by Caroline Myss
The Bible:	King James Version
Sacred Contracts:	Book by Caroline Myss
Complete Book Series:	Dr. Wayne Dyer
Stand Like Mountain, Flow Like Water:	Book by Brian Luke Seaward
The Power of Now:	Book by Eckhart Tolle
Conversations with God:	Neale Donald Walsch
The Matrix:	Movie written by Wachowskis
No Such Thing:	Movie written by Hal Hartley
The Four Agreements:	Book by Don Miguel Ruiz
The Alchemist:	Novel by Paulo Coelho
The Secret:	Book by Rhonda Byrne
The Seven Spiritual Laws of Success:	Book by Deepak Chopra
The Celestine Prophecy:	Novel by James Redfield
A Course in Miracles:	Book by Helen Schucman
Tao Te Ching:	Religious Text
The Seat of the Soul:	Book by Gary Zukav
The Prophet:	Book by Kahlil Gibran
Illusions:	Novel by Richard Bach
Johnathan Livingston Seagull:	Novel by Richard Bach
The Last Temptation of Christ:	Novel by Nikos Kazantzakis

Printed in Great Britain
by Amazon